THE COMPLETE NOVELS
OF
MARK TWAIN

THE AMERICAN CLAIMANT

* * *

PUDD'NHEAD WILSON

BY

MARK TWAIN

NELSON DOUBLEDAY, Inc.
GARDEN CITY, NEW YORK

Published by arrangement with
HARPER & ROW, PUBLISHERS, INCORPORATED

TRADE (BY S. L. CLEMENS. MARK TWAIN.) MARK,

[TRADE MARK.]

PRINTED IN THE UNITED STATES OF AMERICA

THE
AMERICAN
CLAIMANT

CONTENTS

EXPLANATORY

THE Colonel Mulberry Sellers here reintroduced to the public is the same person who appeared as *Eschol* Sellers in the first edition of the tale entitled *The Gilded Age*, years ago, and as *Beriah* Sellers in the subsequent editions of the same book, and finally as *Mulberry* Sellers in the drama played afterward by John T. Raymond.

The name was changed from Eschol to Beriah to accommodate an Eschol Sellers who rose up out of the vasty deeps of uncharted space and preferred his request—backed by threat of a libel suit—then went his way appeased, and came no more. In the play Beriah had to be dropped to satisfy another member of the race, and Mulberry was substituted in the hope that the objectors would be tired by that time and let it pass unchallenged. So far it has occupied the field in peace; therefore we chance it again, feeling reasonably safe, this time, under shelter of the statute of limitations.

MARK TWAIN.

HARTFORD, 1891.

THE WEATHER IN THIS BOOK

No WEATHER will be found in this book. This is an attempt to pull a book through without weather. It being the first attempt of the kind in fictitious literature, it may prove a failure, but it seemed worth the while of some dare-devil person to try it, and the author was in just the mood.

Many a reader who wanted to read a tale through was not able to do it because of delays on account of the weather. Nothing breaks up an author's progress like having to stop every few pages to fuss-up the weather. Thus it is plain that persistent intrusions of weather are bad for both reader and author.

Of course weather is necessary to a narrative of human experience. That is conceded. But it ought to be put where it will not be in the way; where it will not interrupt the flow of the narrative. And it ought to be the ablest weather that can be had, not ignorant, poor-quality, amateur weather. Weather is a literary specialty, and no untrained hand can turn out a good article of it. The present author can do only a few trifling ordinary kinds of weather, and he cannot do those very good. So it has seemed wisest to borrow such weather as is necessary for the book from qualified and recognized experts—giving credit, of course. This weather will be found over in the back part of the book, out of the way. *See Appendix.* The reader is requested to turn over and help himself from time to time as he goes along.

1

The Earl of Rossmore *vs.* the American Claimant—Viscount
Berkeley proposes to change places with the Claimant—
The Claimant's letter—Lord Berkeley decides to visit
America

It is a matchless morning in rural England. On a fair hill we see a
majestic pile, the ivied walls and towers of Cholmondeley Castle,
huge relic and witness of the baronial grandeurs of the Middle
Ages. This is one of the seats of the Earl of Rossmore, K.G.,
G.C.B., K.C.M.G., etc., etc., etc., etc., etc., who possesses twenty-
two thousand acres of English land, owns a parish in London
with two thousand houses on its lease-roll, and struggles comfortably along on an income of two hundred thousand pounds
a year. The father and founder of this proud old line was William
the Conqueror his very self; the mother of it was not inventoried
in history by name, she being merely a random episode and in-
consequential, like the tanner's daughter of Falaise.

In a breakfast-room of the castle on this breezy fine morning
there are two persons and the cooling remains of a deserted meal.
One of these persons is the old lord, tall, erect, square-shouldered,
white-haired, stern-browed, a man who shows character in every
feature, attitude, and movement, and carries his seventy years as
easily as most men carry fifty. The other person is his only son
and heir, a dreamy-eyed young fellow, who looks about twenty-
six but is nearer thirty. Candor, kindliness, honesty, sincerity,
simplicity, modesty—it is easy to see that these are cardinal traits
of his character; and so when you have clothed him in the formidable components of his name, you somehow seem to be contemplating a lamb in armor; his name and style being the

Honorable Kirkcudbright Llanover Marjoribanks Sellers Viscount Berkeley of Cholmondeley Castle, Warwickshire. (Pronounced K'koobry Thlanover Marshbanks Sellers Vycount Barkly of Chumly Castle, Warrikshr.) He is standing by a great window, in an attitude suggestive of respectful attention to what his father is saying and equally respectful dissent from the positions and arguments offered. The father walks the floor as he talks, and his talk shows that his temper is away up toward summer heat.

"Soft-spirited as you are, Berkeley, I am quite aware that when you have once made up your mind to do a thing which your ideas of honor and justice require you to do, argument and reason are (for the time being) wasted upon you—yes, and ridicule, persuasion, supplication, and command as well. To my mind—"

"Father, if you will look at it without prejudice, without passion, you must concede that I am not doing a rash thing, a thoughtless, wilful thing, with nothing substantial behind it to justify it. *I* did not create the American claimant to the earldom of Rossmore; I did not hunt for him, did not find him, did not obtrude him upon your notice. He found himself, he injected himself into our lives—"

"And has made mine a purgatory for ten years with his tiresome letters, his wordy reasonings, his acres of tedious evidence—"

"Which you would never read, would never consent to read. Yet in common fairness he was entitled to a hearing. That hearing would either prove he was the rightful earl—in which case our course would be plain—or it would prove that he wasn't—in which case our course would be equally plain. I have read his evidences, my lord. I have conned them well, studied them patiently and thoroughly. The chain seems to be complete, no important link wanting. I believe he is the rightful earl."

"And I a usurper—a nameless pauper, a tramp! Consider what you are saying, sir."

"Father, *if* he is the rightful earl, would you, could you—that fact being established—consent to keep his titles and his properties from him a day, an hour, a minute?"

"You are talking nonsense—nonsense—lurid idiocy! Now listen

to me. I will make a confession—if you wish to call it by that name. I did not read those evidences because I had no occasion to—I was made familiar with them in the time of this claimant's father and of my own father forty years ago. This fellow's predecessors have kept mine more or less familiar with them for close upon a hundred and fifty years. The truth is, the rightful heir did go to America, with the Fairfax heir or about the same time—but disappeared somewhere in the wilds of Virginia, got married, and began to breed savages for the Claimant market; wrote no letters home; was supposed to be dead; his younger brother softly took possession; presently the American did die, and straightway his eldest product put in his claim—by letter—letter still in existence —and died before the uncle in possession found time—or maybe inclination—to answer. The infant son of that eldest product grew up—long interval, you see—and *he* took to writing letters and furnishing evidences. Well, successor after successor has done the same, down to the present idiot. It was a succession of paupers; not one of them was ever able to pay his passage to England or institute suit. The Fairfaxes kept their lordship alive, and so they have never lost it to this day, although they live in Maryland; their friend lost his by his own neglect. You perceive now that the facts in this case bring us to precisely this result: morally the American tramp *is* rightful earl of Rossmore; legally he has no more right than his dog. There now—are you satisfied?"

There was a pause; then the son glanced at the crest carved in the great oaken mantel, and said, with a regretful note in his voice:

"Since the introduction of heraldic symbols, the motto of this house has been *Suum cuique*—to every man his own. By your own intrepidly frank confession, my lord, it is become a sarcasm. If Simon Lathers—"

"Keep that exasperating name to yourself! For ten years it has pestered my eye and tortured my ear; till at last my very footfalls time themselves to the brain-racking rhythm of *Simon Lathers!— Simon Lathers!—Simon Lathers!* And now, to make its presence in my soul eternal, immortal, imperishable, you have resolved to —to—what is it you have resolved to do?"

"To go to Simon Lathers in America and change places with him."

"What? Deliver the reversion of the earldom into his hands?"

"That is my purpose."

"Make this tremendous surrender without even trying the fantastic case in the Lords?"

"Ye-s—" with hesitation and some embarrassment.

"By all that is amazing, I believe you are insane, my son. See here—have you been training with that ass again—that radical, if you prefer the term, though the words are synonymous—Lord Tanzy of Tollmache?"

The son did not reply, and the old lord continued:

"Yes, you confess. That puppy, that shame to his birth and caste, who holds all hereditary lordships and privilege to be usurpation, all nobility a tinsel sham, all aristocratic institutions a fraud, all inequalities in rank a legalized crime and an infamy, and no bread honest bread that a man doesn't earn by his own work—*work*, pah!"—and the old patrician brushed imaginary labor-dirt from his white hands. "You have come to hold just those opinions yourself, I suppose," he added, with a sneer.

A faint flush in the young man's cheek told that the shot had hit and hurt, but he answered with dignity:

"I have. I say it without shame—I feel none. And now my reason for resolving to renounce my heirship without resistance is explained. I wish to retire from what to me is a false existence, a false position, and begin my life over again—begin it right—begin it on the level of mere manhood, unassisted by factitious aids, and succeed or fail by pure merit or the want of it. I will go to America, where all men are equal and all have an equal chance; I will live or die, sink or swim, win or lose as just a man—that alone, and not a single helping gaud or fiction back of it."

"Hear, hear!" The two men looked each other steadily in the eye a moment or two; then the elder one added, musingly, "Ab-so-lutely cra-zy—ab-so-lutely!" After another silence, he said, as one who, long troubled by clouds, detects a ray of sunshine, "Well, there will be one satisfaction—Simon Lathers will come here to enter into his own, and I will drown him in the horse-pond. The poor devil—always so humble in his letters, so pitiful, so deferential; so steeped in reverence for our great line and lofty station; so anxious to placate us, so prayerful for recognition as a relative, a bearer in his veins of our sacred blood—and withal so poor, so needy, so threadbare and pauper-shod as to raiment, so despised, so laughed at for his silly claimantship by the lewd American scum around him—ach, the vulgar, crawling, insufferable tramp! To read one of his cringing, nauseating letters— Well?"

This to a splendid flunky, all in inflamed plush and buttons and knee-breeches as to his trunk, and a glinting white frostwork of ground-glass paste as to his head, who stood with his heels together and the upper half of him bent forward, a salver in his hands.

"The letters, my lord."

My lord took them, and the servant disappeared.

"Among the rest, an American letter. From the tramp, of course. Jove, but here's a change! No brown-paper envelope this time, filched from a shop and carrying the shop's advertisement in the corner. Oh no; a proper enough envelope—with a most ostentatiously broad mourning border—for his cat, perhaps, since he was a bachelor—and fastened with red wax—a batch of it as big as a half-crown—and—and—our crest for a seal!—motto and all. And the ignorant, sprawling hand is gone; he sports a secretary, evidently—a secretary with a most confident swing and flourish to his pen. Oh, indeed, our fortunes are improving over there—our meek tramp has undergone a metamorphosis."

"Read it, my lord, please."

"Yes, this time I will. For the sake of the cat:

14,042 SIXTEENTH STREET,
WASHINGTON, May 2.

My Lord—
It is my painful duty to announce to you that the head of our illustrious house is no more—The Right Honorable, The Most Noble, The Most Puissant Simon Lathers Lord Rossmore having departed this life ("Gone at last—this is unspeakably precious news, my son") at his seat in the environs

of the hamlet of Duffy's Corners in the grand old State of
Arkansas—and his twin brother with him, both being crushed
by a log at a smokehouse raising, owing to carelessness on
the part of all present, referable to over-confidence and gaiety induced by overplus of sour-mash—("Extolled be sour-
mash, whatever that may be, eh, Berkeley?") five days ago,
with no scion of our ancient race present to close his eyes
and inter him with the honors due his historic name and
lofty rank—in fact, he is on the ice yet, him and his brother
—friends took up a collection for it. But I shall take immediate occasion to have their noble remains shipped to you
("Great heavens!") for interment, with due ceremonies and
solemnities, in the family vault or mausoleum of our house.
Meantime I shall put up a pair of hatchments on my house-
front, and you will of course do the same at your several
seats.

I have also to remind you that by this sad disaster I, as
sole heir, inherit and become seized of all the titles, honors,
lands, and goods of our lamented relative, and must of necessity, painful as the duty is, shortly require at the bar of
the Lords restitution of these dignities and properties now
illegally enjoyed by your titular lordship.

With assurance of my distinguished consideration and
warm cousinly regard, I remain

Your titular lordship's
Most obedient servant,
Mulberry Sellers Earl Rossmore.

"Im-mense! Come, this one's interesting. Why, Berkeley, his
breezy impudence is—is—why, it's colossal, it's sublime."

"No, this one doesn't seem to cringe much."

"Cringe—why, he doesn't know the meaning of the word.
Hatchments! To commemorate that sniveling tramp and his fra-
ternal duplicate. And he is going to send me the remains. The
late Claimant was a fool, but plainly this new one's a maniac.
What a name! *Mulberry* Sellers—there's music for you. Simon
Lathers—Mulberry Sellers—Mulberry Sellers—Simon Lathers.
Sounds like machinery working and churning. Simon Lathers,
Mulberry Sel— Are you going?"

"If I have your leave, father."

The old gentleman stood musing some time after his son was gone. This was his thought:

"He is a good boy, and lovable. Let him take his own course—as it would profit nothing to oppose him—make things worse, in fact. My arguments and his aunt's persuasions have failed; let us see what America can do for us. Let us see what equality and hard times can effect for the mental health of a brainsick young British lord. Going to renounce his lordship and be a man! Yas!"

2

Colonel Mulberry Sellers and his art gallery—He receives a visit from Washington Hawkins—Talking over old times—Washington informs the colonel that he is the congressional delegate from Cherokee Strip

COLONEL MULBERRY SELLERS—this was some days before he wrote his letter to Lord Rossmore—was seated in his "library," which was also his "drawing-room," and was also his "picture-gallery," and likewise his "workshop." Sometimes he called it by one of these names, sometimes by another, according to occasion and circumstance. He was constructing what seemed to be some kind of a frail mechanical toy, and was apparently very much interested in his work. He was a white-headed man now, but otherwise he was as young, alert, buoyant, visionary, and enterprising as ever. His loving old wife sat near by, contentedly knitting and thinking, with a cat asleep in her lap. The room was large, light, and had a comfortable look, in fact, a homelike look, though the furniture was of a humble sort and not over-abundant, and the knickknacks and things that go to adorn a living-room not plenty and not costly. But there were natural flowers, and there was an abstract and unclassifiable something about the place which betrayed the presence in the house of somebody with a happy taste and an effective touch.

Even the deadly chromos on the walls were somehow without offense; in fact, they seemed to belong there and to add an attraction to the room—a fascination, anyway; for whoever got his eye on one of them was like to gaze and suffer till he died—you have seen that kind of pictures. Some of these terrors were landscapes, and some libeled the sea, some were ostensible portraits, all were crimes. All the portraits were recognizable as dead Americans of distinction, and yet, through labeling added by a daring hand, they were all doing duty here as "Earls of Rossmore." The newest one had left the works as Andrew Jackson, but was doing its best now as "Simon Lathers Lord Rossmore, Present Earl." On one wall was a cheap old railroad map of Warwickshire. This had been newly labeled "The Rossmore Estates." On the opposite wall was another map, and this was the most imposing decoration of the establishment and the first to catch a stranger's attention, because of its great size. It had once borne simply the title SIBERIA: but now the word "FUTURE" had been written in front of that word. There were other additions in red ink—many cities, with great populations set down, scattered over the vast country at points where neither cities nor populations exist to-day. One of these cities, with population placed at 1,500,000, bore the name "Libertyorloffskoizalinski," and there was a still more populous one, centrally located and marked "Capital," which bore the name "Freedomolovnaivanovich."

The "mansion"—the Colonel's usual name for the house—was a rickety old two-story frame of considerable size, which had been painted, some time or other, but had nearly forgotten it. It was away out in the ragged edge of Washington, and had once been somebody's country place. It had a neglected yard around it, with paling fence that needed straightening up in places, and a gate that would stay shut. By the door-post were several modest tin signs. "Col. Mulberry Sellers, Attorney at Law and Claim Agent," was the principal one. One learned from the others that the Colonel was a Materializer, a Hypnotizer, a Mind-Cure dabbler, and so on. For he was a man who could always find things to do.

A white-headed negro man, with spectacles and damaged white-cotton gloves, appeared in the presence, made a stately obeisance, and announced:

"Marse Washington Hawkins, suh."

"Great Scott! Show him in Dan'l, show him in."

The Colonel and his wife were on their feet in a moment, and the next moment were joyfully wringing the hands of a stoutish, discouraged-looking man whose general aspect suggested that he was fifty years old, but whose hair swore to a hundred.

"Well, well, well, Washington, my boy, it *is* good to look at you again. Sit down, sit down, and make yourself at home. There, now —why, you look perfectly natural; aging a little, just a little, but you'd have known him anywhere, wouldn't you, Polly?"

"Oh yes, Berry, he's *just* like his pa would have looked if he'd lived. Dear, dear, where have you dropped from? Let me see, how long is it since—"

"I should say it's all of fifteen years, Mrs. Sellers."

"Well, well, how time does get away with us. Yes, and oh, the changes that—"

There was a sudden catch of her voice and a trembling of the lip, the men waiting reverently for her to get command of herself and go on; but after a little struggle she turned away, with her apron to her eyes, and softly disappeared.

"Seeing you made her think of the children, poor thing—dear, dear, they're all dead but the youngest. But banish care, it's no time for it now—on with the dance, let joy be unconfined is my motto, whether there's any dance to dance, or any joy to uncon-fine—you'll be the healthier for it every time—every time, Wash-ington—it's my experience, and I've seen a good deal of this world. Come—where have you disappeared to all these years, and are you from there now, or where are you from?"

"I don't quite think you would ever guess, Colonel. Cherokee Strip."

"My land!"

"Sure as you live."

"You can't mean it. Actually *living* out there?"

"Well, yes, if a body may call it that; though it's a pretty strong term for 'dobies and jackass rabbits, boiled beans and slapjacks, depression, withered hopes, poverty in all its varieties—"

"Louise out there?"

"Yes, and the children."

"Out there now?"

"Yes, I couldn't afford to bring them with me."

"Oh, I see; you had to come—claim against the government. Make yourself perfectly easy—I'll take care of that."

"But it isn't a claim against the government."

"No? Want to be postmaster? *That's* all right. Leave it to me. I'll fix it."

"But it isn't postmaster—you're all astray yet."

"Well, good gracious, Washington, why don't you come out and tell me what it is? What do you want to be so reserved and distrustful with an old friend like me for? Don't you reckon I can keep a se—"

"There's no secret about it—you merely don't give me a chance to—"

"Now look here, old friend, I know the human race; and I know that when a man comes to Washington, I don't care if it's from heaven, let alone Cherokee Strip, it's because he *wants* something. And I know that as a rule he's not going to get it; that he'll stay and try for another thing and won't get that; the same luck with the next and the next and the next; and keeps on till he strikes bottom, and is too poor and ashamed to go back, even to Cherokee Strip; and at last his heart breaks and they take up a collection and bury him. There—don't interrupt me, I know what I'm talking about. Happy and prosperous in the Far West, wasn't I? *You* know that. Principal citizen of Hawkeye, looked up to by everybody, kind of an autocrat—actually a kind of an autocrat, Washington. Well, nothing would do but I must go Minister to St. James, the Governor and everybody insisting, you know, and so at last I consented—no getting out of it, *had* to do it, so here I came. *A day too late*, Washington. Think of that—what little things change the world's history—yes, sir, the place had been filled. Well, there I was, you see. I offered to compromise and go to Paris. The President was very sorry and all that, but *that* place, you see, didn't belong to the West, so there I was again. There was no help for it, so I had to stoop a little—we all reach the day some time or other when we've got to do that, Washington, and it's not a bad thing for us, either, take it by and large and all around—I had to stoop a little and offer to take Constantinople. Washington, consider this—for it's perfectly true—within a month I *asked* for China; within another month I *begged* for Japan; one year later I was away down, down, down, supplicating with tears and anguish for the bottom office in the gift of the Government of the United States—Flint-Picker in the cellars of the War Department. And, by George, I didn't get it!"

"Flint-Picker?"

"Yes. Office established in the time of the Revolution, last century. The musket-flints for the military posts were supplied from the capital. They do it yet; for although the flint-arm has gone out and the forts have tumbled down, the decree hasn't been repealed—been overlooked and forgotten, you see—and so the vacancies where old Ticonderoga and others used to stand still get their six quarts of gun-flints a year just the same."

Washington said, musingly, after a pause:

"How strange it seems—to start for Minister to England at twenty thousand a year and fail for Flint-Picker at—"

"Three dollars a week. It's human life, Washington—just an epitome of human ambition, and struggle, and the outcome; you aim for the palace and get drowned in the sewer."

There was another meditative silence. Then Washington said, with earnest compassion in his voice:

"And so, after coming here, against your inclination, to satisfy your sense of patriotic duty and appease a selfish public clamor, you get absolutely nothing for it."

"Nothing?" The Colonel had to get up and stand to get room for his amazement to expand. "*Nothing*, Washington? I ask you this: to be a Perpetual Member and the *only* Perpetual Member

of a Diplomatic Body accredited to the greatest country on earth
—do you call that nothing?"

It was Washington's turn to be amazed. He was stricken dumb;
but the wide-eyed wonder, the reverent admiration expressed in
his face were more eloquent than any words could have been.
The Colonel's wounded spirit was healed, and he resumed his
seat pleased and content. He leaned forward and said, impressively:

"What was due to a man who had become forever conspicuous
by an experience without precedent in the history of the world?
—a man made permanently and diplomatically sacred, so to
speak, by having been connected, temporarily, through solicita-
tion, with every single diplomatic post in the roster of this
government, from Envoy Extraordinary and Minister Plenipo-
tentiary to the Court of St. James, all the way down to Consul
to a guano rock in the Strait of Sunda—salary payable in guano
—which disappeared by volcanic convulsion the day before they
got down to my name in the list of applicants. Certainly something august enough to be answerable to the size of this unique
and memorable experience was my due, and I got it. By the
common voice of this community, by acclamation of the
people, that mighty utterance which brushes aside laws and
legislation, and from whose decrees there is no appeal, I was
named Perpetual Member of the Diplomatic Body representing
the multifarious sovereignties and civilizations of the globe near
the republican court of the United States of America. And they
brought me home with a torchlight procession."

"It is wonderful, Colonel, simply wonderful."

"It's the loftiest official position in the whole earth."

"I should think so—and the most commanding."

"You have named the word. Think of it. I frown, and there is
war; I smile, and contending nations lay down their arms."

"It is awful. The responsibility, I mean."

"It is nothing. Responsibility is no burden to me; I am used
to it; have always been used to it."

"And the work—the work! Do you have to attend all the
sittings?"

"Who, I? Does the Emperor of Russia attend the conclaves of the governors of the provinces? He sits at home and indicates his pleasure."

Washington was silent a moment, then a deep sigh escaped him.

"How proud I was an hour ago; how paltry seems my little promotion now! Colonel, the reason I came to Washington is— I am Congressional Delegate from Cherokee Strip!"

The Colonel sprang to his feet, and broke out, with prodigious enthusiasm:

"Give me your hand, my boy—this is immense news! I congratulate you with all my heart. My prophecies stand confirmed. I always said it was in you. I always said you were born for high distinction and would achieve it. You ask Polly if I didn't."

Washington was dazed by this most unexpected demonstration.

"Why, Colonel, there's nothing *to* it. That little, narrow, desolate, unpeopled, oblong streak of grass and gravel, lost in the remote wastes of the vast continent—why, it's like representing a billiard-table—a discarded one."

"Tut-tut, it's a great, it's a staving preferment, and just opulent with influence here."

"Shucks, Colonel, I haven't even a vote."

"That's nothing; you can make speeches."

"No, I can't. The population's only two hundred—"

"That's all right, that's all right—"

"And they hadn't any right to elect me; we're not even a Territory, there's no Organic Act, the government hasn't any official knowledge of us whatever."

"Never mind about that; I'll fix that. I'll rush the thing through; I'll get you organized in no time."

"*Will* you, Colonel?—it's *too* good of you; but it's just your old sterling self, the same old ever-faithful friend," and the grateful tears welled up in Washington's eyes.

"It's just as good as done, my boy, just as good as done. Shake hands. We'll hitch teams together, you and I, and we'll make things hum!"

3

Mrs. Sellers pronounces the colonel "the same old scheming, generous, good-hearted, moonshiny, hopeful, no-
account failure he always was"—He takes in Dan'l and
Jinny—The colonel originates "Pigs in the Clover"—He offers one of his art treasures to propitiate Suggs—One-
armed Pete, the bank thief

MRS. SELLERS returned now with her composure restored, and
began to ask after Hawkins's wife, and about his children, and
the number of them, and so on, and her examination of the
witness resulted in a circumstantial history of the family's ups
and downs and driftings to and fro in the Far West during the
previous fifteen years. There was a message now from out back,
and Colonel Sellers went out there in answer to it. Hawkins took
this opportunity to ask how the world had been using the
Colonel during the past half-generation.

"Oh, it's been using him just the same; it couldn't change its
way of using him if it wanted to, for he wouldn't let it."

"I can easily believe that, Mrs. Sellers."

"Yes, you see, he doesn't change, himself—not the least little
bit in the world; he's always Mulberry Sellers."

"I can see *that* plain enough."

"Just the same old scheming, generous, good-hearted, moonshiny, hopeful, no-account failure he always was, and still everybody likes him just as well as if he was the shiningest success."

"They always did; and it was natural, because he was so
obliging and accommodating, and had something about him that
made it kind of easy to ask help of him, or favors—you didn't

feel shy, you know, or have that wish-you-didn't-have-to-try feeling that you have with other people."

"It's just so yet; and a body wonders at it, too, because he's been shamefully treated, many times, by people that had used him for a ladder to climb up by, and then kicked him down when they didn't need him any more. For a time you can see he's hurt, his pride's wounded, because he shrinks away from that thing and don't want to talk about it—and so I used to think *now* he's learned something and he'll be more careful hereafter— but laws! in a couple of weeks he's forgotten all about it, and any selfish tramp out of nobody knows where can come and put up a poor mouth and walk right into his heart with his boots on."

"It must try your patience pretty sharply sometimes."

"Oh no, I'm used to it; and I'd rather have him so than the other way. When I call him a failure, I mean to the world he's a failure; he isn't to me. I don't know as I want him different— much different, anyway. I have to scold him some, snarl at him, you might even call it, but I reckon I'd do that just the same if he was different—it's my make. But I'm a good deal less snarly and more contented when he's a failure than I am when he isn't."

"Then he isn't always a failure," said Hawkins, brightening.

"Him? Oh, bless you, no. He makes a strike, as he calls it, from time to time. Then's my time to fret and fuss. For the money just flies—first come first served. Straight off, he loads up the house with cripples and idiots and stray cats and all the different kinds of poor wrecks that other people don't want and he *does*, and then when the poverty comes again I've *got* to clear the most of them out or we'd starve; and that distresses him, and me the same, of course. Here's old Dan'l and old Jinny, that the sher- iff sold South one of the times that we got bankrupted before the war—they came wandering back after the peace, worn out and used up on the cotton plantations, helpless, and not another lick of work left in their old hides for the rest of this earthly pilgrim- age—and we so pinched, *oh,* so pinched for the very crumbs to keep life in us, and he just flung the door wide, and the way he received them you'd have thought they had come straight down from heaven in answer to prayer. I took him one side and said,

'Mulberry, we can't have them—we've nothing for ourselves—we can't feed them.' He looked at me kind of hurt, and said, 'Turn them out?—and they've come to me just as confident and trusting as—as—why, Polly, I must have *bought* that confidence some time or other a long time ago, and given my note, so to speak—you don't get such things as a *gift*—and how am I going to go back on a debt like that? And you see, they're so poor, and old, and friendless, and—' But I was ashamed by that time, and shut him off, and somehow felt a new courage in me, and so I said, softly, 'We'll keep them—the Lord will provide.' He was glad, and started to blurt out one of those over-confident speeches of his, but checked himself in time, and said, humbly, '*I* will, anyway.' It was years and years and years ago. Well, you see those old wrecks are here yet."

"But don't they do your housework?"

"Laws! The idea. They would if they could, poor old things, and perhaps they think they *do* do some of it. But it's a superstition. Dan'l waits on the front door, and sometimes goes on an errand; and sometimes you'll see one or both of them letting on to dust around in here—but that's because there's something they want to hear about and mix their gabble into. And they're always around at meals, for the same reason. But the fact is, we have to keep a young negro girl just to take care of *them*, and a negro woman to do the housework and *help* take care of them."

"Well, they ought to be tolerably happy, I should think."

"It's no name for it. They quarrel together pretty much all the time—'most always about religion, because Dan'l's a Dunker Baptist and Jinny's a shouting Methodist, and Jinny believes in special Providences and Dan'l don't, because he thinks he's a kind of a free-thinker—and they play and sing plantation hymns together, and talk and chatter just eternally and forever, and are sincerely fond of each other and think the world of Mulberry, and he puts up patiently with all their spoiled ways and foolishness, and so—ah, well, they're happy enough, if it comes to that. And I don't mind—I've got used to it. I can get used to anything, with Mulberry to help; and the fact is, I don't much care what happens, so long as he's spared to me."

"Well, here's to him, and hoping he'll make another strike soon."

"And rake in the lame, the halt, and the blind, and turn the house into a hospital again? It's what he would do. I've seen a plenty of that and more. No, Washington, I want his strikes to be mighty moderate ones the rest of the way down the vale."

"Well, then, big strike or little strike, or no strike at all, here's hoping he'll never lack for friends—and I don't reckon he ever will while there's people around who know enough to—"

"Him lack for friends!" and she tilted her head up with a frank pride—"why, Washington, you can't name a man that's anybody that isn't fond of him. I'll tell you privately that I've had Satan's own time to keep them from appointing him to some office or other. They knew he'd no business with an office, just as well as I did, but he's the hardest man to refuse anything to a body you ever saw. Mulberry Sellers with an office! laws goodness, you know what that would be like. Why, they'd come from the ends of the earth to see a circus like that. I'd just as lieves be married to Niagara Falls, and done with it." After a reflective pause she added—having wandered back, in the interval, to the remark that had been her text: "Friends?—oh, indeed, no man ever had more; and *such* friends: Grant, Sherman, Sheridan, Johnston, Longstreet, Lee—many's the time they've sat in that chair you're sitting in—" Hawkins was out of it instantly, and contemplating it with a reverential surprise, and with the awed sense of having trodden shod upon holy ground:

"*They!*" he said.

"Oh, indeed, yes, a many and a many a time."

He continued to gaze at the chair, fascinated, magnetized; and for once in his life that continental stretch of dry prairie which stood for his imagination was afire, and across it was marching a slanting flame-front that joined its wide horizons together and smothered the skies with smoke. He was experiencing what one or another drowsing, geographically ignorant alien experiences every day in the year when he turns a dull and indifferent eye out of the car window and it falls upon a certain station-sign which reads, "Stratford-on-Avon"! Mrs. Sellers went gossiping comfortably along:

"Oh, they like to hear him talk, especially if their load is getting rather heavy on one shoulder and they want to shift it. He's all air, you know—breeze, you may say—and he freshens them up; it's a trip to the country, they say. Many a time he's made General Grant laugh—and that's a tidy job, I can tell you; and as for Sheridan, his eye lights up and he listens to Mulberry Sellers the same as if he was artillery. You see, the charm about Mulberry is, he is so catholic and unprejudiced that he fits in anywhere and everywhere. It makes him powerful good company, and as popular as scandal. You go to the White House when the President's holding a general reception—some time when Mulberry's there. Why, dear me, *you* can't tell which of them it is that's holding that reception."

"Well, he certainly is a remarkable man—and he always was. Is he religious?"

"Clear to his marrow—does more thinking and reading on that subject than any other, except Russia and Siberia; thrashes around over the whole field, too; nothing bigoted about him."

"What is his religion?"

"He—" She stopped, and was lost for a moment or two in thinking; then she said, with simplicity, "I think he was a Mohammedan or something last week."

Washington started down-town now to bring his trunk, for the hospitable Sellerses would listen to no excuses; their house must be his home during the session. The Colonel returned presently and resumed work upon his plaything. It was finished when Washington got back.

"There it is," said the Colonel, "all finished."

"What is it for, Colonel?"

"Oh, it's just a trifle. Toy to amuse the children."

Washington examined it.

"It seems to be a puzzle."

"Yes, that's what it is. I call it Pigs in the Clover. Put them in—see if you can put them in the pen."

After many failures Washington succeeded, and was as pleased as a child.

"It's wonderfully ingenious, Colonel—it's ever so clever. And interesting—why, I could play with it all day. What are you going to do with it?"

"Oh, nothing. Patent it and throw it aside."

"Don't you do anything of the kind. There's money in that thing."

A compassionate look traveled over the Colonel's countenance, and he said:

"Money—yes; pin money; a couple of hundred thousand, perhaps. Not more."

Washington's eyes blazed.

"A couple of hundred thousand dollars! Do you call that pin money?"

The Colonel rose and tiptoed his way across the room, closed a door that was slightly ajar, tiptoed his way to his seat again, and said, under his breath:

"You can keep a secret?"

Washington nodded his affirmative; he was too awed to speak.

"You have heard of materialization—materialization of departed spirits?"

Washington had heard of it.

"And probably didn't believe in it; and quite right, too. The thing as practised by ignorant charlatans is unworthy of attention or respect—where there's a dim light and a dark cabinet, and a parcel of sentimental gulls gathered together, with their faith and their shudders and their tears all ready, and one and the same fatty degeneration of protoplasm and humbug comes out and materializes himself into anybody you want, grandmother, grandchild, brother-in-law, Witch of Endor, John Milton, Siamese Twins, Peter the Great, and all such frantic nonsense—no, that is all foolish and pitiful. But when a man that is competent brings the vast powers of *science* to bear, it's a different matter—a totally different matter, you see. The specter that answers *that* call has come to stay. Do you note the commercial value of that detail?"

"Well, I—the—the truth is, that I don't quite know that I do.

Do you mean that such, being permanent, not transitory, would give more general satisfaction, and so enhance the price of tickets to the show—"

"Show? Folly—listen to me; and get a good grip on your breath, for you are going to need it. Within three days I shall have completed my method, and then—let the world stand aghast, for it shall see marvels. Washington, within three days—ten at the outside—you shall see me call the dead of any century, and they will arise and walk. Walk?—they shall walk forever, and never die again. Walk with all the muscle and spring of their pristine vigor."

"Colonel! Indeed, it does take one's breath away."

"*Now* do you see the money that's in it?"

"I'm—well, I'm—not really sure that I do."

"Great Scott, look here! I shall have a monopoly; they'll all belong to me, won't they? Two thousand policemen in the city of New York. Wages, four dollars a day. I'll replace them with dead ones at half the money."

"Oh, prodigious! I never thought of that. F-o-u-r thousand dollars a day. Now I do begin to see! But will dead policemen answer?"

"Haven't they—up to this time?"

"Well, if you put it that way—"

"Put it any way you want to. Modify it to suit yourself, and my lads shall still be superior. They won't eat, they won't drink—don't need those things; they won't wink for cash at gambling-dens and unlicensed rum-holes; they won't spark the scullery maids; and, moreover, the bands of toughs that ambuscade them on lonely beats and cowardly shoot and knife them will only damage the uniforms, and not live long enough to get more than a momentary satisfaction out of that."

"Why, Colonel, if you can furnish policemen, then of course—"

"Certainly—I can furnish any line of goods that's wanted. Take the army, for instance—now twenty-five thousand men; expense, twenty-two millions a year. I will dig up the Romans, I will resurrect the Greeks, I will furnish the government, for ten millions a year, ten thousand veterans drawn from the victorious legions of all the ages—soldiers that will chase Indians year in and year out on materialized horses, and cost never a cent for rations or repairs. The armies of Europe cost two billions a year now—I will replace them all for a billion. I will dig up the trained statesmen of all ages and all climes, and furnish this country with a Congress that knows enough to come in out of the rain—a thing that's never happened yet since the Declaration of Independence, and never will happen till these practically dead people are replaced with the genuine article. I will restock the thrones of Europe with the best brains and the best morals that all the royal sepulchers of all the centuries can furnish—which isn't promising very much —and I'll divide the wages and the civil list, fair and square, merely taking my half and—"

"Colonel, if the half of this is true, there's millions in it— millions."

"Billions in it—billions; that's what you mean. Why, look here; the thing is so close at hand, so imminent, so absolutely immediate, that if a man were to come to me now and say, Colonel, I am a little short, and if you could lend me a couple of billion dollars for— Come in!"

This in answer to a knock. An energetic-looking man bustled in with a big pocket-book in his hand, took a paper from it and presented it, with the curt remark:

"Seventeenth and last call—you want to out with that three dollars and forty cents this time without fail, Colonel Mulberry Sellers."

The Colonel began to slap this pocket and that one, and feel here and there and everywhere, muttering:

"What *have* I done with that wallet?—let me see—um—not here, not there—oh, I must have left it in the kitchen; I'll just run and—"

"No, you won't—you'll stay right where you are. And you're going to disgorge, too—this time."

Washington innocently offered to go and look. When he was gone the Colonel said:

"The fact is, I've got to throw myself on your indulgence just this once more, Suggs; you see, the remittances I was expecting—"

"Hang the remittances—it's too stale—it won't answer. Come!"

The Colonel glanced about him in despair. Then his face

lighted; he ran to the wall and began to dust off a peculiarly atrocious chromo with his handkerchief. Then he brought it reverently, offered it to the collector, averted his face, and said:

"Take it, but don't let me see it go. It's the sole remaining Rembrandt that—"

"Rembrandt be damned; it's a chromo."

"Oh, don't speak of it so, I beg you. It's the only really great original, the only supreme example, of that mighty school of art which—"

"Art! It's the sickest-looking thing I—"

The Colonel was already bringing another horror and tenderly dusting it.

"Take this one too—the gem of my collection—the only genuine Fra Angelico that—"

"Illuminated liver-pad, that's what it is. Give it here—good day —people will think I've robbed a nigger barber-shop."

As he slammed the door behind him the Colonel shouted, with an anguished accent:

"Do please cover them up—don't let the damp get at them. The delicate tints in the Angelico—"

But the man was gone.

Washington reappeared, and said he had looked everywhere, and so had Mrs. Sellers and the servants, but in vain; and went on to say he wished he could get his eye on a certain man about this time—no need to hunt up that pocket-book then. The Colonel's interest was awake at once.

"What man?"

"One-armed Pete they call him out there—out in the Cherokee country, I mean. Robbed the bank in Tahlequah."

"Do they have banks in Tahlequah?"

"Yes—a bank, anyway. He was suspected of robbing it. Whoever did it got away with more than twenty thousand dollars. They offered a reward of five thousand. I believe I saw that very man on my way east."

"No—is that so?"

"I certainly saw a man on the train the first day I struck the

railroad that answered the description pretty exactly—at least, as
to clothes and a lacking arm."

"Why didn't you get him arrested and claim the reward?"

"I couldn't. I had to get a requisition, of course. But I meant
to stay by him till I got my chance."

"Well?"

"Well, he left the train during the night some time."

"Oh, hang it, that's too bad!"

"Not so very bad, either."

"Why?"

"Because he came down to Baltimore in the very train I was
in, though I didn't know it in time. As we moved out of the station I saw him going toward the iron gate with a satchel in his
hand."

"Good; we'll catch him. Let's lay a plan."

"Send description to the Baltimore police?"

"Why, what are you talking about? No. Do you want them to
get the reward?"

"What shall we do, then?"

The Colonel reflected.

"I'll tell you. Put a personal in the Baltimore *Sun*. Word it like
this:

A. DROP ME A LINE, PETE—

"Hold on. Which arm has he lost?"

"The right."

"Good. Now then:

A. DROP ME A LINE, PETE, EVEN IF YOU HAVE TO
write with your left hand. Address X. Y. Z., General
Post-office, Washington. From YOU KNOW WHO.

There—that 'll fetch him."

"But he *won't* know who—will he?"

"No, but he'll want to know, won't he?"

"Why, certainly—I didn't think of that. What made you think
of it?"

"Knowledge of human curiosity. Strong trait, very strong trait."

"Now I'll go to my room and write it out and inclose a dollar and tell them to print it to the worth of that."

4

A Yankee makes an offer for "Pigs in the Clover"—By the death of a relative Sellers becomes the rightful Earl of Rossmore and consequently the American Claimant— Gwendolen is sent for from school—The remains of the late Claimant and brother to be shipped to England—Hawkins and Sellers nail the hatchments on "Rossmore Towers"

THE DAY wore itself out. After dinner the two friends put in a long and harassing evening trying to decide what to do with the five thousand dollars reward which they were going to get when they should find One-Armed Pete, and catch him, and prove him to be the right person, and extradite him, and ship him to Tahlequah in the Indian Territory. But there were so many dazzling openings for ready cash that they found it impossible to make up their minds and keep them made up. Finally, Mrs. Sellers grew very weary of it all, and said:

"What is the sense in cooking a rabbit before it's caught?"

Then the matter was dropped for the time being, and all went to bed. Next morning, being persuaded by Hawkins, the Colonel made drawings and specifications, and went down and applied for a patent for his toy puzzle, and Hawkins took the toy itself and started out to see what chance there might be to do something with it commercially. He did not have to go far. In a small old wooden shanty which had once been occupied as a dwelling by some humble negro family he found a keen-eyed Yankee engaged in repairing cheap chairs and other second-hand furniture. This man examined the toy indifferently; attempted to do the puzzle; found it not so easy as he had expected; grew more interested, and finally emphatically so; achieved a success at last, and asked:

"Is it patented?"

"Patent applied for."

"That will answer. What do you want for it?"

"What will it retail for?"

"Well, twenty-five cents, I should think."

"What will you give for the exclusive right?"

"I couldn't give twenty dollars if I had to pay cash down; but I'll tell you what I'll do. I'll make it and market it, and pay you five cents royalty on each one."

Washington sighed. Another dream disappeared; no money in the thing. So he said:

"All right; take it at that. Draw me a paper."

He went his way with the paper, and dropped the matter out of his mind—dropped it out to make room for further attempts to think out the most promising way to invest his half of the reward in case a partnership investment satisfactory to both beneficiaries could not be hit upon.

He had not been very long at home when Sellers arrived sodden with grief and booming with glad excitement—working both these emotions successfully, sometimes separately, sometimes together. He fell on Hawkins's neck sobbing, and said:

"Oh, mourn with me, my friend, mourn for my desolate house; death has smitten my last kinsman, and I am Earl of Rossmore—congratulate me!"

He turned to his wife, who had entered while this was going on, put his arms about her, and said: "You will bear up, for my sake, my lady—it had to happen, it was decreed."

She bore up very well, and said:

"It's no great loss. Simon Lathers was a poor, well-meaning, useless thing and no account, and his brother never was worth shucks."

The rightful earl continued:

"I am too much prostrated by these conflicting griefs and joys to be able to concentrate my mind upon affairs; I will ask our good friend here to break the news by wire or post to the Lady Gwendolen, and instruct her to—"

"*What* Lady Gwendolen?"

"Our poor daughter, who, alas!—"

"Sally Sellers? Mulberry Sellers, are you losing your mind?"

"There—please do not forget who you are, and who I am; remember your own dignity, be considerate also of mine. It were best to cease from using my family name now, Lady Rossmore."

"Goodness gracious! well, I never! What *am* I to call you, then?"

"In private, the ordinary terms of endearment will still be admissible, to some degree; but in public it will be more becoming if your ladyship will speak *to* me as my lord, or your lordship, and *of* me as Rossmore, or the Earl, or his Lordship, and—"

"Oh, scat! I can't ever do it, Berry."

"But, indeed, you must, my love—we must live up to our altered position, and submit with what grace we may to its requirements."

"Well, all right, have it your own way; I've never set my wishes against your commands yet, Mul—my lord, and it's late to begin now, though to my mind it's the rottenest foolishness that ever was."

"Spoken like my own true wife! There, kiss and be friends again."

"But—Gwendolen! I don't know how I am ever going to stand that name. Why, a body wouldn't *know* Sally Sellers in it. It's too large for her; kind of like a cherub in an ulster, and it's a most outlandish sort of a name anyway, to my mind."

"You'll not hear her find fault with it, my lady."

"That's a true word. She takes to any kind of romantic rubbish like she was born to it. She never got it from me, that's sure. And sending her to that silly college hasn't helped the matter any— just the other way."

"Now hear her, Hawkins! Rowena-Ivanhoe College is the

selectest and most aristocratic seat of learning for young ladies in our country. Under no circumstances can a girl get in there unless she is either very rich and fashionable or can prove four generations of what may be called American nobility. Castellated college-buildings—towers and turrets and an imitation moat—and everything about the place named out of Sir Walter Scott's books and redolent of royalty and state and style; and all the richest girls keep phaetons, and coachmen in livery, and riding-horses, with English grooms in plug hats and tight-buttoned coats, and top-boots, and a whip-handle without any whip to it, to ride sixty-three feet behind them—"

"And they don't learn a blessed thing, Washington Hawkins, not a single blessed thing but showy rubbish and un-American pretentiousness. But send for the Lady Gwendolen—do; for I reckon the peerage regulations require that she must come home and let on to go into seclusion and mourn for those Arkansas blatherskites she's lost."

"My darling! Blatherskites? Remember—*noblesse oblige.*"

"There, there—talk to me in your own tongue, Ross—you don't know any other, and you only botch it when you try. Oh, don't stare—it was a slip, and no crime; customs of a lifetime can't be dropped in a second. Ross*more*—there now, be appeased, and go along with you and attend to Gwendolen. Are you going to write, Washington?—or telegraph?"

"He will telegraph, dear."

"I thought as much," my lady muttered, as she left the room. "Wants it so the address will have to appear on the envelope. It will just make a fool of that child. She'll get it, of course, for if there are any other Sellerses there they'll not be able to claim it. And just leave her alone to show it around and make the most of it. . . . Well, maybe she's forgivable for that. She's so poor and they're so rich, of course she's had her share of snubs from the livery-flunky sort, and I reckon it's only human to want to get even."

Uncle Dan'l was sent with the telegram; for although a conspicuous object in a corner of the drawing-room was a telephone hanging on a transmitter, Washington found all attempts to raise

the central office vain. The Colonel grumbled something about
its being *"always* out of order when you've got particular and
especial use for it," but he didn't explain that one of the reasons
for this was that the thing was only a dummy and hadn't any
wire attached to it. And yet the Colonel often used it—when visitors were present—and seemed to get messages through it.
Mourning-paper and a seal were ordered; then the friends took
a rest.

Next afternoon, while Hawkins, by request, draped Andrew
Jackson's portrait with crape, the rightful earl wrote off the
family bereavement to the usurper in England—a letter which
we have already read. He also, by letter to the village authorities
at Duffy's Corners, Arkansas, gave order that the remains of the
late twins be embalmed by some St. Louis expert and shipped
at once to the usurper—with bill. Then he drafted out the Rossmore arms and motto on a great sheet of brown paper, and he
and Hawkins took it to Hawkins's Yankee furniture-mender, and
at the end of an hour came back with a couple of stunning hatchments, which they nailed up on the front of the house—attractions calculated to draw, and they did; for it was mainly an idle
and shiftless negro neighborhood, with plenty of ragged children
and indolent dogs to spare for a point of interest like that, and
keep on sparing them for it, days and days together.

The new earl found—without surprise—this society item in the
evening paper, and cut it out and scrap-booked it:

By a recent bereavement our esteemed fellow-citizen,
Colonel Mulberry Sellers, Perpetual Member-at-large of the
Diplomatic Body, succeeds, as rightful lord, to the great
earldom of Rossmore, third by order of precedence in the
earldoms of Great Britain, and will take early measures, by
suit in the House of Lords, to wrest the title and estates
from the present usurping holder of them. Until the season
of mourning is past, the usual Thursday evening receptions
at Rossmore Towers will be discontinued.

Lady Rossmore's comment—to herself:
"Receptions! People who don't rightly know him may think

he is commonplace, but to my mind he is one of the most unusual men I ever saw. As for suddenness and capacity in imagining things, his beat don't exist, I reckon. As like as not it wouldn't have occurred to anybody else to name this poor old rat-trap Rossmore Towers, but it just comes natural to him. Well, no doubt it's a blessed thing to have an imagination that can always make you satisfied, no matter how you are fixed. Uncle Dave Hopkins used to always say, 'Turn me into John Calvin, and I want to know which place I'm going to; turn me into Mulberry Sellers, and I don't care.'"

The rightful earl's comment—to himself:

"It's a beautiful name, beautiful. Pity I didn't think of it before I wrote the usurper. But I'll be ready for him when he answers."

5

Gwendolen's letter—Her arrival at home—Hawkins is introduced, to his great pleasure—Communication from the bank thief—Hawkins and Sellers have to wait ten days longer before getting the reward—Viscount Berkeley and the late Claimant's remains start simultaneously from England and America

No ANSWER to that telegram; no arriving daughter. Yet nobody showed any uneasiness or seemed surprised; that is, nobody but Washington. After three days of waiting he asked Lady Rossmore what she supposed the trouble was. She answered tranquilly:

"Oh, it's some notion of hers; you never can tell. She's a Sellers all through—at least, in some of her ways; and a Sellers can't tell you beforehand what he's going to do, because he don't know himself till he's done it. *She's* all right; no occasion to worry about *her.* When she's ready she'll come or she'll write, and you can't tell which till it's happened."

It turned out to be a letter. It was handed in at that moment, and was received by the mother without trembling hands or feverish eagerness, or any other of the manifestations common in the case of long-delayed answers to imperative telegrams. She polished her glasses with tranquillity and thoroughness, pleasantly gossiping along the while, then opened the letter and began to read aloud:

KENILWORTH KEEP, REDGAUNTLET HALL,
ROWENA-IVANHOE COLLEGE, THURSDAY.

DEAR PRECIOUS MAMMA ROSSMORE:

Oh, the joy of it!—you can't think. They had always turned up their noses at our pretensions, you know; and I had fought back as well as I could by turning up mine at theirs. They always said it might be something great and fine to be the rightful Shadow of an earldom, but to merely be shadow *of* a shadow, and two or three times removed at that—pooh-pooh! And I always retorted that not to be able to show four generations of American-Colonial-Dutch-Peddler-and-Salt-Cod-McAllister Nobility might be endurable, but to *have* to confess such an origin—pfew-few! Well, the telegram, it was just a cyclone! The messenger came right into the great Rob Roy Hall of Audience, as excited as he could be, singing out, "Despatch for Lady Gwendolen Sellers!" and you ought to have seen that simpering chattering assemblage of pinchbeck aristocrats turn to stone! I was off in the corner, of course, by myself—it's where Cinderella belongs. I took the telegram and read it, and tried to faint—and I could have done it if I had had any preparation, but it was all so sudden, you know—but no matter, I did the next best thing: I put my handkerchief to my eyes and fled sobbing to my room, dropping the telegram as I started. I released one corner of my eye a moment—just enough to see the herd swarm for the telegram—and then continued my broken-hearted flight just as happy as a bird.

Then the visits of condolence began, and I had to accept

the loan of Miss Augusta-Templeton-Ashmore Hamilton's quarters because the press was so great and there isn't room for three and a cat in mine. And I've been holding a Lodge of Sorrow ever since and defending myself against people's attempts to claim kin. And do you know, the very first girl to fetch her tears and sympathy to my market was that foolish Skimperton girl who has always snubbed me so shamefully and claimed lordship and precedence of the whole college because some ancestor of hers, some time or other, was a McAllister. Why, it was like the bottom bird in the menagerie putting on airs because its head ancestor was a pterodactyl.

But the ger-reatest triumph of all was—guess. But you'll never. This is it. That little fool and two others have always been fussing and fretting over which was entitled to precedence—by rank, you know. They've nearly starved themselves at it; for each claimed the right to take precedence of all the college in leaving the table, and so neither of them ever finished her dinner, but broke off in the middle and tried to get out ahead of the others. Well, after my first day's grief and seclusion—I was fixing up a mourning dress, you see—I appeared at the public table again, and then—what do you think? Those three fluffy goslings sat there contentedly, and squared up the long famine—lapped and lapped, munched and munched, ate and ate, till the gravy appeared in their eyes—humbly waiting for the Lady Gwendolen to take precedence and move out first, you see!

Oh, yes, I've been having a darling good time. And do you know, not one of these collegians has had the cruelty to ask me how I came by my new name. With some, this is due to charity, but with the others it isn't. They refrain, not from native kindness but from educated discretion. I educated them.

Well, as soon as I shall have settled up what's left of the old scores and snuffed up a few more of those pleasantly intoxicating clouds of incense, I shall pack and depart homeward. Tell papa I am as fond of him as I am of my new name. I couldn't put it stronger than that. What an inspiration it was! But inspirations come easy to him.

These, from your loving daughter,

GWENDOLEN.

Hawkins reached for the letter and glanced over it.

"Good hand," he said, "and full of confidence and animation, and goes racing right along. She's bright—that's plain."

"Oh, they're all bright—the Sellerses. Anyway, they would be, if there were any. Even those poor Latherses would have been bright if they had been Sellerses; I mean full blood. Of course they had a Sellers strain in them—a big strain of it, too—but being a Bland dollar don't make it a *dollar* just the same."

The seventh day after the date of the telegram Washington came dreaming down to breakfast and was set wide awake by an electrical spasm of pleasure. Here was the most beautiful young creature he had ever seen in his life. It was Sally Sellers Lady Gwendolen; she had come in the night. And it seemed to him that her clothes were the prettiest and the daintiest he had ever looked upon, and the most exquisitely contrived and fashioned and combined, as to decorative trimmings, and fixings, and melting harmonies of color. It was only a morning dress, and inexpensive, but he confessed to himself, in the English common to Cherokee Strip, that it was a "corker." And now, as he perceived, the reason why the Sellers household poverties and sterilities had been made to blossom like the rose, and charm the eye and satisfy the spirit, stood explained; here was the magician; here in the midst of her works, and furnishing in her own person the proper accent and climaxing finish of the whole.

"My daughter, Major Hawkins—come home to mourn; flown home at the call of affliction to help the authors of her being bear the burden of bereavement. She was very fond of the late earl—idolized him, sir, idolized him—"

"Why, father, I've never seen him."

"True—she's right, I was thinking of another—er—of her mother—"

"*I* idolized that smoked haddock?—that sentimental, spiritless—"

"I was thinking of myself! Poor noble fellow, we were inseparable com—"

"Hear the man! Mulberry Sel—Mul—Rossmore!—hang the

troublesome name, I can never—if I've heard you say once I've heard you say a thousand times that if that poor sheep—"

"I was thinking of—of—I don't know who I was thinking of, and it doesn't make any difference anyway; *some*body idolized him, I recollect it as if it were yesterday; and—"

"Father, I am going to shake hands with Major Hawkins, and let the introduction work along and catch up at its leisure. I remember you very well, indeed, Major Hawkins, although I was a little child when I saw you last; and I am very, very glad, indeed, to see you again and have you in our house as one of us"; and beaming in his face she finished her cordial shake with the hope that he had not forgotten her.

He was prodigiously pleased by her outspoken heartiness, and wanted to repay her by assuring her that he remembered her, and not only that but better even than he remembered his own children, but the facts would not quite warrant this; still, he stumbled through a tangled sentence which answered just as well, since the purport of it was an awkward and unintentional confession that her extraordinary beauty had so stupefied him that he hadn't got back to his bearings yet, and therefore couldn't be certain as to whether he remembered her at all or not. The speech made him her friend; it couldn't well help it.

In truth, the beauty of this fair creature was of a rare type, and may well excuse a moment of our time spent in its consideration. It did not consist in the *fact* that she had eyes, nose, mouth, chin, hair, ears; it consisted in their arrangement. In true beauty, more depends upon right location and judicious distribution of feature than upon multiplicity of them. So also as regards color. The very combination of colors which in a volcanic irruption would add beauty to a landscape might detach it from a girl. Such was Gwendolen Sellers.

The family circle being completed by Gwendolen's arrival, it was decreed that the official mourning should now begin; that it should begin at six o'clock every evening (the dinner hour) and end with the dinner.

"It's a grand old line, Major, a sublime old line, and deserves to be mourned for almost royally; almost imperially, I may say.

Er—Lady Gwendolen—but she's gone; never mind; I wanted my Peerage; I'll fetch it myself, presently, and show you a thing or two that will give you a realizing idea of what our house is. I've been glancing through *Burke,* and I find that of William the Conqueror's sixty-four natural ch— My dear, would you mind getting me that book? It's on the escritoire in our boudoir. Yes, as I was saying, there's only St. Albans, Buccleuch, and Grafton ahead of us on the list—all the rest of the British nobility are in procession behind us. Ah, thanks, my lady. Now then, we turn to William, and we find—letter for XYZ? Oh, splendid—when'd you get it?"

"Last night; but I was asleep before you came, you were out so late; and when I came to breakfast Miss Gwendolen—well, she knocked everything out of me, you know—"

"Wonderful girl, wonderful; her great origin is detectable in her step, her carriage, her features—but what does he *say?* Come, this is exciting."

"I haven't read it—er—Rossm—Mr. Rossm—er—"

"M'lord! Just cut it short like that. It's the English way. I'll open it. Ah, now let's see.

A. TO YOU KNOW WHO. Think I know you. Wait ten days. Coming to Washington.

The excitement died out of both men's faces. There was a brooding silence for a while; then the younger one said, with a sigh:

"Why, *we* can't wait ten days for the money."

"No—the man's unreasonable; we are down to the bed rock, financially speaking."

"If we could explain to him in some way that we are so situated that time is of the utmost importance to us—"

"Yes-yes, that's it—and so if it would be as convenient for him to come at once it would be a great accommodation to us, and one which we—which we—which we—wh—well, which we should sincerely appreciate—"

"That's it—and most gladly reciprocate—"

"Certainly—that 'll fetch him. Worded right, if he's a *man—*

got any of the *feelings* of a man, *sympathies* and all that, he'll be here inside of twenty-four hours. Pen and paper—come, we'll get right at it."

Between them they framed twenty-two different advertisements, but none was satisfactory. A main fault in all of them was urgency. That feature was very troublesome; if made prominent, it was calculated to excite Pete's suspicion; if modified below the suspicion-point it was flat and meaningless. Finally the Colonel resigned, and said:

"I have noticed, in such literary experiences as I have had, that one of the most taking things to do is to conceal your meaning when you are *trying* to conceal it. Whereas, if you go at literature with a free conscience and nothing to conceal, you can turn out a book, every time, that the very elect can't understand. They all do."

Then Hawkins resigned also, and the two agreed that they must manage to wait the ten days somehow or other. Next, they caught a ray of cheer; since they had something definite to go upon now they could probably borrow money on the reward— enough, at any rate, to tide them over till they got it; and meantime the materializing recipe would be perfected, and then goodby to trouble for good and all.

The next day, May the 10th, a couple of things happened— among others. The remains of the noble Arkansas twins left our shores for England, consigned to Lord Rossmore, and Lord Rossmore's son, Kirkcudbright Llanover Marjoribanks Sellers Viscount Berkeley, sailed from Liverpool for America to place the reversion of the earldom in the hands of the rightful peer, Mulberry Sellers, of Rossmore Towers in the District of Columbia, U. S. A.

These two impressive shipments would meet and part in mid-Atlantic five days later, and give no sign.

6

Arrival of the remains of late Claimant and brother in England—The usurping earl officiates as chief mourner, and they are laid with their kindred in Cholmondeley church—Sally Sellers a gifted costume-designer—Another communication from the bank thief—Locating him in the New Gadsby—The colonel's glimpse of one-armed Pete in the elevator—Arrival of Viscount Berkeley at the same hotel

IN THE COURSE of time the twins arrived and were delivered to their great kinsman. To try to describe the rage of that old man would profit nothing, the attempt would fall so far short of the purpose. However, when he had worn himself out and got quiet again, he looked the matter over and decided that the twins had some moral rights, although they had no legal ones; they were of his blood, and it could not be decorous to treat them as common clay. So he laid them with their majestic kin in the Cholmondeley church, with imposing state and ceremony, and added the supreme touch by officiating as chief mourner himself. But he drew the line at hatchments.

Our friends in Washington watched the weary days go by while they waited for Pete and covered his name with reproaches because of his calamitous procrastinations. Meantime, Sally Sellers, who was as practical and democratic as the Lady Gwendolen Sellers was romantic and aristocratic, was leading a life of intense interest and activity, and getting the most she could out of her double personality. All day long in the privacy of her work-room Sally Sellers earned bread for the Sellers family, and all the evening Lady Gwendolen Sellers supported the Rossmore dignity. All day she was American, practically, and proud of the work of her head and hands and its commercial result; all the evening she took holiday and dwelt in a rich shadowland peopled with titled and coroneted fictions. By day, to her, the place was a plain, unaffected, ramshackle old trap —just that, and nothing more; by night it was Rossmore Towers. At college she had learned a trade without knowing it. The girls had found out that she was the designer of her own gowns. She had no idle moments after that, and wanted none; for the exercise of an extraordinary gift is the supremest pleasure in life, and it was manifest that Sally Sellers possessed a gift of that sort in the matter of costume designing. Within three days after reaching home she had hunted up some work; before Pete was yet due in Washington, and before the twins were fairly asleep in English soil, she was already nearly swamped with work, and the sacrificing of the family chromos for debt had got an effective check.

"She's a brick," said Rossmore to the Major; "just her father all over; prompt to labor with head or hands, and not ashamed of it; capable, always capable, let the enterprise be what it may; successful by nature—don't know what defeat is; thus, intensely and practically American by inhaled nationalism, and at the same time intensely and aristocratically European by inherited nobility of blood. Just me, exactly; Mulberry Sellers in matter of finance and invention; after office hours, what do you find? The same clothes, yes, but what's in them? Rossmore of the peerage."

The two friends had haunted the general post-office daily. At last they had their reward. Toward evening on the 20th of May they got a letter for XYZ. It bore the Washington postmark; the note itself was not dated. It said:

Ash barrel back of lamp post Black horse Alley. If you are playing square go and set on it to-morrow morning 21st 10.22 not sooner not later wait till I come.

The friends cogitated over the note profoundly. Presently the earl said:

"Don't you reckon he's afraid we are a sheriff with a requisition?"

"Why, m'lord?"

"Because that's no place for a séance. Nothing friendly, nothing sociable about it. And at the same time, a body that wanted to know who was roosting on that ash-barrel without exposing himself by going near it, or seeming to be interested in it, could just stand on the street corner and take a glance down the alley and satisfy himself, don't you see?"

"Yes, his idea is plain now. He seems to be a man that can't *be* candid and straightforward. He acts as if he thought we—shucks, I wish he had come out like a man and told us what hotel he—"

"Now you've struck it! you've struck it sure, Washington; he has told us."

"Has he?"

"Yes, he has; but he didn't mean to. That alley is a lonesome little pocket that runs along one side of the New Gadsby. That's his hotel."

"What makes you think that?"

"Why, I just know it. He's got a room that's just across from that lamp-post. He's going to sit there perfectly comfortable behind his shutters at 10.22 to-morrow, and when he sees us sitting on the ash-barrel, he'll say to himself, 'I saw *one* of those fellows on the train'—and then he'll pack his satchel in half a minute and ship for the ends of the earth."

Hawkins turned sick with disappointment.

"Oh, dear, it's all up, Colonel—it's exactly what he'll do."

"Indeed, he won't!"

"Won't he? Why?"

"Because *you* won't be holding the ash-barrel down; it 'll be me. You'll be coming in with an officer and a requisition in plain clothes—the officer, I mean—the minute you see him arrive and open up a talk with me."

"Well, what a head you have got, Colonel Sellers! I never should have thought of that in the world."

"Neither would any earl of Rossmore, betwixt William's contribution and Mulberry—*as* earl; but it's office hours now, you see, and the earl in me sleeps. Come—I'll show you his very room."

They reached the neighborhood of the New Gadsby about nine in the evening, and passed down the alley to the lamp-post.

"There you are," said the Colonel, triumphantly, with a wave of his hand which took in the whole side of the hotel. "There it is—what did I tell you?"

"Well, but—why, Colonel, it's six stories high. I don't quite make out which window you—"

"All the windows, all of them. Let him have his choice—I'm indifferent now that I have located him. You go and stand on the corner and wait; I'll prospect the hotel."

The earl drifted here and there through the swarming lobby, and finally took a waiting position in the neighborhood of the elevator. During an hour crowds went up and crowds came down; and all complete as to limbs; but at last the watcher got a glimpse of a figure that was satisfactory—got a glimpse of the back of it, though he had missed his chance at the face through waning alertness. The glimpse revealed a cowboy hat and below it a plaided sack of rather loud pattern, and an empty sleeve pinned up to the shoulder. Then the elevator snatched the vision aloft, and the watcher fled away in joyful excitement and rejoined the fellow-conspirator.

"We've got him, Major—got him sure! I've seen him—seen him good; and I don't care where or when that man approaches me backwards, I'll recognize him every time. We're all right. Now for the requisition."

They got it, after the delays usual in such cases. By half-past eleven they were at home and happy, and went to bed full of dreams of the morrow's great promise.

Among the elevator load which had the suspect for fellow-passenger was a young kinsman of Mulberry Sellers, but Mulberry was not aware of it and didn't see him. It was Viscount Berkeley.

7

Viscount Berkeley jots down his "impressions" to date with
a quill pen—The destruction of the New Gadsby by fire—
Berkeley loses his bearings and escapes with his journaled
"impressions" only—Discovery and hasty donning of one-
armed Pete's abandoned wardrobe—Glowing and affecting
account in the morning papers of the heroic death of the
heir of Rossmore—He will take a new name and start out
"incog"

ARRIVED in his room Lord Berkeley made preparations for that
first and last and all-the-time duty of the visiting Englishman—
the jotting down in his diary of his "impressions" to date. His
preparations consisted in ransacking his "box" for a pen. There
was a plenty of steel pens on his table with the ink-bottle, but he
was English. The English people manufacture steel pens for
nineteen-twentieths of the globe, but they never use any themselves. They use exclusively the prehistoric quill. My lord not
only found a quill pen, but the best one he had seen in several
years—and after writing diligently for some time, closed with the
following entry:

But in one thing I have made an immense mistake. I ought
to have sunk my title and changed my name before I started.

He sat admiring that pen awhile, and then went on:

All attempts to mingle with the common people and become permanently one of them are going to fail, unless I
can get rid of it, disappear from it, and reappear with the
solid protection of a new name. I am astonished and pained
to see how eager the most of these Americans are to get

acquainted with a lord, and how diligent they are in pushing attentions upon him. They lack English servility, it is true—but they could acquire it, with practice. My quality travels ahead of me in the most mysterious way. I write my family name without additions, on the register of this hotel, and imagine that I am going to pass for an obscure and unknown wanderer, but the clerk promptly calls out, "Front! show his lordship to four-eighty-two!" and before I can get to the lift there is a reporter trying to interview me, as they call it. This sort of thing shall cease at once. I will hunt up the American Claimant the first thing in the morning, accomplish my mission, then change my lodging and vanish from scrutiny under a fictitious name.

He left his diary on the table, where it would be handy in case any new "impressions" should wake him up in the night, then he went to bed and presently fell asleep. An hour or two passed, and then he came slowly to consciousness with a confusion of mysterious and augmenting sounds hammering at the gates of his brain for admission; the next moment he was sharply awake, and those sounds burst with the rush and roar and boom of an undammed freshet into his ears. Banging and slamming of shutters; smashing of windows and the ringing clash of falling glass; clatter of flying feet along the halls; shrieks, supplications, dumb moanings of despair within, hoarse shouts of command outside; cracklings and snappings, and the windy roar of victorious flames!

Bang, bang ,bang! on the door, and a cry:

"Turn out—the house is on fire!"

The cry passed on, and the banging. Lord Berkeley sprang out of bed and moved with all possible speed toward the clothes-press in the darkness and the gathering smoke, but fell over a chair and lost his bearings. He groped desperately about on his hands, and presently struck his head against the table and was deeply grateful, for it gave him his bearings again, since it stood close by the door. He seized his most precious possession, his journaled Impressions of America, and darted from the room.

He ran down the deserted hall toward the red lamp which

he knew indicated the place of a fire-escape. The door of the
room beside it was open. In the room the gas was burning full
head; on a chair was a pile of clothing. He ran to the window,
could not get it up, but smashed it with a chair, and stepped out
on the landing of the fire-escape; below him was a crowd of men,
with a sprinkling of women and youth, massed in a ruddy light.
Must he go down in his spectral night-dress? No—this side of
the house was not yet on fire except at the farther end; he would
snatch on those clothes. Which he did. They fitted well enough,
though a trifle loosely, and they were just a shade loud as to
pattern. Also as to hat—which was of a new breed to him, Buffalo
Bill not having been to England yet. One side of the coat went
on, but the other side refused; one of its sleeves was turned up
and stitched to the shoulder. He started down without waiting
to get it loose, made the trip successfully, and was promptly
hustled outside the limit-rope by the police.

The cowboy hat and the coat but half on made him too much
of a center of attraction for comfort, although nothing could be
more profoundly respectful, not to say deferential, than was the
manner of the crowd toward him. In his mind he framed a discouraged remark for early entry in his diary: "It is of no use;
they know a lord through any disguise, and show awe of him—
even something very like fear, indeed."

Presently one of the gaping and adoring half-circle of boys
ventured a timid question. My lord answered it. The boys
glanced wonderingly at each other, and from somewhere fell the
comment:

"*English* cowboy! Well, if that ain't curious."

Another mental note to be preserved for the diary: "Cowboy.
Now what might a cowboy be? Perhaps—" But the viscount perceived that some more questions were about to be asked; so he
worked his way out of the crowd, released the sleeve, put on the
coat, and wandered away to seek a humble and obscure lodging.
He found it, and went to bed and was soon asleep.

In the morning he examined his clothes. They were rather
assertive, it seemed to him, but they were new and clean, at any
rate. There was considerable property in the pockets. Item, five

one-hundred-dollar bills. Item, near fifty dollars in small bills and silver. Plug of tobacco. Hymnbook, which refuses to open; found to contain whisky. Memorandum-book bearing no name. Scattering entries in it, recording in a sprawling, ignorant hand, appointments, bets, horse-trades, and so on, with people of strange, hyphenated name—Six-Fingered Jake, Young-Man-Afraid-of-his-Shadow, and the like. No letters, no documents.

The young man muses—maps out his course. His letter of credit is burned; he will borrow the small bills and the silver in these pockets, apply part of it to advertising for the owner, and use the rest for sustenance while he seeks work. He sends out for the morning paper next, and proceeds to read about the fire. The biggest line in the display-head announces his own death! The body of the account furnishes all the particulars; and tells how, with the inherited heroism of his caste, he went on saving women and children until escape for himself was impossible; then with the eyes of weeping multitudes upon him, he stood with folded arms and sternly awaited the approach of the devouring fiend; "and so standing, amid a tossing sea of flame and onrushing billows of smoke, the noble young heir of the great house of Rossmore was caught up in a whirlwind of fiery glory, and disappeared forever from the vision of men."

The thing was so fine and generous and knightly that it brought the moisture to his eyes. Presently he said to himself: "What to do is as plain as day now. My Lord Berkeley is dead—let him stay so. Died creditably, too; that will make the calamity the easier for my father. And I don't have to report to the American Claimant now. Yes, nothing could be better than the way matters have turned out. I have only to furnish myself with a new name, and take my new start in life totally untrammeled. Now I breathe my first breath of real freedom; and how fresh and breezy and inspiring it is! At last I am a man! a man on equal terms with my neighbor; and by my manhood, and by it alone, I shall rise and be seen of the world, or I shall sink from sight and deserve it. This *is* the gladdest day, and the proudest, that ever poured its sun upon my head!"

8

The colonel's grief at the loss of both Berkeley and one-armed Pete—Materialization—Breaking the news to the family—The colonel starts to identify and secure a body (or ashes) to send to the bereaved father

"God bless my soul, Hawkins!"

The morning paper dropped from the Colonel's nerveless grasp.

"What is it?"

"He's gone!—the bright, the young, the gifted, the noblest of his illustrious race—gone! gone up in flames and unimaginable glory!"

"Who?"

"My precious, precious young kinsman—Kirkcudbright Llanover Marjoribanks Sellers Viscount Berkeley, son and heir of usurping Rossmore."

"No!"

"It's true—too true."

"When?"

"Last night."

"Where?"

"Right here in Washington, where he arrived from England last night, the papers say."

"You don't say!"

"Hotel burned down."

"What hotel?"

"The New Gadsby!"

"Oh, my goodness! And have we lost *both* of them?"

"Both *who*?"

"One-Arm Pete."

"Oh, great guns! I forgot all about him. Oh, I hope not!"

"Hope! Well, I should say! Oh, we *can't* spare *him!* We can better afford to lose a million viscounts than our only support and stay."

They searched the paper diligently, and were appalled to find that a one-armed man had been seen flying along one of the halls of the hotel in his underclothing and apparently out of his head with fright, and as he would listen to no one and persisted in making for a stairway which would carry him to certain death, his case was given over as a hopeless one.

"Poor fellow," sighed Hawkins; "and he had friends so near. I wish we hadn't come away from there—maybe we could have saved him."

The earl looked up and said, calmly:

"His being dead doesn't matter. He was uncertain before. We've got him sure, this time."

"Got him? How?"

"I will materialize him."

"Rossmore, don't—don't trifle with me. Do you mean that? Can you do it?"

"I can do it, just as sure as you are sitting there. And I will."

"Give me your hand, and let me have the comfort of shaking it. I was perishing, and you have put new life into me. Get at it, oh, get at it right away."

"It will take a little time, Hawkins, but there's no hurry, none in the world—in the circumstances. And of course certain duties have devolved upon me now which necessarily claim my first attention. This poor young nobleman—"

"Why, yes, I am sorry for my heartlessness, and you smitten with this new family affliction. Of course you must materialize him first—I quite understand that."

"I—I—well, I wasn't meaning just that, but—why, what am I thinking of! Of course I must materialize him. Oh, Hawkins, selfishness is the bottom trait in human nature; I was only thinking that now, with the usurper's heir out of the way—But you'll forgive that momentary weakness, and forget it. Don't ever

remember it against me that Mulberry Sellers was once mean
enough to think the thought that I was thinking. I'll materialize
him—I will, on my honor—and I'd do it were he a thousand heirs
jammed into one and stretching in a solid rank from here to the
stolen estates of Rossmore, and barring the road forever to the
rightful earl!"

"There spoke the real Sellers—the other had a false ring, old
friend."

"Hawkins, my boy, it just occurs to me—a thing I keep forgetting to mention—a matter that we've got to be mighty careful
about."

"What is that?"

"We must keep absolutely still about these materializations.
Mind, not a hint of them must escape—not a hint. To say nothing
of how my wife and daughter—high-strung, sensitive organizations—might feel about them, the negroes wouldn't stay on the
place a minute."

"That's true, they wouldn't. It's well you spoke, for I'm not
naturally discreet with my tongue when I'm not warned."

Sellers reached out and touched a bell button in the wall, set
his eye upon the rear door and waited; touched it again and
waited; and just as Hawkins was remarking admiringly that the
Colonel was the most progressive and most alert man he had ever
seen, in the matter of impressing into his service every modern
convenience the moment it was invented, and always keeping
breast to breast with the drum-major in the great work of
material civilization, he forsook the button (which hadn't any
wire attached to it), rang a vast dinner-bell which stood on the
table, and remarked that he had tried that new-fangled dry
battery now to his entire satisfaction, and had got enough of it;
and added:

"Nothing would do Graham Bell but I must try it; said the
mere *fact* of my trying it would secure public confidence, and
get it a chance to show what it could do. I *told* him that in theory
a dry battery was just a curled darling and no mistake, but when
it come to *practice*, sho!—and here's the result. Was I right?

What should *you* say, Washington Hawkins? You've seen me try that button twice. Was I right?—that's the idea. Did I know what I was talking about, or didn't I?"

"Well, you know how I feel about you, Colonel Sellers, and always have felt. It seems to me that you always know everything about *every*thing. If that man had known you as I know you he would have taken your judgment at the start, and dropped his dry battery where it was."

"Did you ring, Marse Sellers?"

"No, Marse Sellers didn't"

"Den it was you, Marse Washington. I's heah, suh."

"No, it wasn't Marse Washington, either."

"De good lan'l who did ring her, den?"

"Lord Rossmore rang it!"

The old negro flung up his hands and exclaimed:

"Blame my skin if I hain't gone en forgit dat name agin! Come heah, Jinny—run heah, honey."

Jinny arrived.

"You take dish-yer order de lord gwine to give you. I's gwine down suller and study dat name tell I git it."

"I take de order! Who's yo' nigger las' year? De bell rung for *you*."

"Dat don't make no diffunce. When a bell ring for anybody, en old marster tell me to—"

"Clear out, and settle it in the kitchen!"

The noise of the quarreling presently sank to a murmur in the distance, and the earl added: "That's a trouble with old house-servants that were your slaves once and have been your personal friends always."

"Yes, and members of the family."

"Members of the family is just what they become—*the* members of the family, in fact. And sometimes master and mistress of the household. These two are mighty good and loving and faithful and honest, but, hang it, they do just about as they please, they chip into a conversation whenever they want to, and the plain fact is they ought to be killed."

It was a random remark, but it gave him an idea—however, nothing could happen without that result.

"What I wanted, Hawkins, was to send for the family and break the news to them."

"Oh, never mind bothering with the servants, then. I will go and bring them down."

While he was gone the earl worked his idea.

"Yes," he said to himself, "when I've got the materializing down to a certainty, I will get Hawkins to kill them, and after that they will be under better control. Without doubt a materialized negro could easily be hypnotized into a state resembling silence. And this could be made permanent—yes, and also modifiable, at will —sometimes *very* silent, sometimes turn on more talk, more action, more emotion, according to what you want. It's a prime good idea. Make it adjustable—with a screw or something."

The two ladies entered now with Hawkins, and the two negroes followed, uninvited, and fell to brushing and dusting around, for they perceived that there was matter of interest to the fore, and were willing to find out what it was.

Sellers broke the news with stateliness and ceremony, first warning the ladies, with gentle art, that a pang of peculiar sharpness was about to be inflicted upon their hearts—hearts still sore from a like hurt, still lamenting a like loss—then he took the paper, and with trembling lips and with tears in his voice he gave them that heroic death-picture.

The result was a very genuine outbreak of sorrow and sympathy from all the hearers. The elder lady cried, thinking how proud that great-hearted young hero's mother would be, if she were living, and how unappeasable her grief; and the two old servants cried with her, and spoke out their applauses and their pitying lamentations with the eloquent sincerity and simplicity native to their race. Gwendolen was touched, and the romantic side of her nature was strongly wrought upon. She said that such a nature as that young man's was rarely and truly noble, and nearly perfect; and that with nobility of birth added it was entirely perfect. For such a man she could endure all things, suffer all things, even to the sacrificing of her life. She wished she could have seen him; the slightest, the most momentary contact with such a spirit would have ennobled her whole character, and made ignoble thoughts and ignoble acts thereafter impossible to her forever.

"Have they found the body, Rossmore?" asked the wife.

"Yes; that is, they've found several. It must be one of them, but none of them are recognizable."

"What are you going to do?"

"I am going down there and identify one of them, and send it home to the stricken father."

"But, papa, did you ever see the young man?"

"No, Gwendolen—why?"

"How will you identify it?"

"I—well, you know, it says none of them are recognizable. I'll send his father one of them—there's probably no choice."

Gwendolen knew it was not worth while to argue the matter further, since her father's mind was made up, and there was a chance for him to appear upon that sad scene down yonder in an authentic and official way. So she said no more—till he asked for a basket.

"A basket, papa? What for?"

"It might be ashes."

9

The usual actress and her diamonds in the hotel fire—The colonel secures three baskets of ashes—Mrs. Sellers forbids their lying in state—Generous hatchments—The ashes to be sent only when the earl sends for them

THE EARL and Washington started on the sorrowful errand, talking as they walked.

"And as *usual!*"

"What, Colonel?"

"Seven of them in that hotel. Actresses. And all burnt out, of course."

"Any of them burnt *up?*"

"Oh, no, they escaped; they always do; but there's never a one of them that knows enough to fetch out her jewelry with her."

"That's strange."

"Strange—it's the most unaccountable thing in the world. Experience teaches them nothing; they can't seem to learn anything except out of a book. In some cases there's manifestly a fatality about it. For instance, take What's-her-name, that plays those sensational thunder-and-lightning parts. She's got a perfectly immense reputation—draws like a dogfight—and it all came from getting burnt out in hotels."

"Why, how could that give her a reputation as an actress?"

"It didn't—it only made her name familiar. People want to see her play because her name is familiar, but they don't know what made it familiar, because they don't remember. First, she was at the bottom of the ladder and absolutely obscure—wages thirteen dollars a week and find her own pads."

"Pads?"

"Yes—things to fat up her spindles with so as to be plump and attractive. Well, she got burnt out in a hotel and lost $30,000 worth of diamonds—"

"She? Where'd she get them?"

"Goodness knows—given to her, no doubt, by spoony young flats and sappy old baldheads in the front row. All the papers were full of it. She struck for higher pay and got it. Well, she got burnt out again and lost all her diamonds, and it gave her such a lift that she went starring."

"Well, if hotel fires are all she's got to depend on to keep up her name, it's a pretty precarious kind of a reputation, I should think."

"Not with her. No, anything but that. Because she's so lucky; born lucky, I reckon. Every time there's a hotel fire she's in it. She's always there—and if she can't be there herself, her diamonds are. Now you can't make anything out of that but just sheer luck."

"I never heard of such a thing. She must have lost quarts of diamonds."

"Quarts! she's lost bushels of them. It's got so that the hotels are superstitious about her. They won't let her in. They think there will be a fire; and, besides, if she's there it cancels the insurance. She's been waning a little lately, but this fire will set her up. She lost $60,000 worth last night."

"I think she's a fool. If I had $60,000 worth of diamonds I wouldn't trust them in a hotel."

"I wouldn't either; but you can't teach an actress that. This one's been burnt out thirty-five times. And yet if there's a hotel fire in San Francisco to-night she's got to bleed again, you mark my words. Perfect ass; they say she's got diamonds in every hotel in the country."

When they arrived at the scene of the fire the poor old earl took one glimpse at the melancholy morgue and turned away his face, overcome by the spectacle. He said:

"It is too true, Hawkins—recognition is impossible; not one of the five could be identified by its nearest friend. You make the selection; I can't bear it."

"Which one had I better—"

"Oh, take any of them. Pick out the best one."

However, the officers assured the earl—for they knew him, everybody in Washington knew him—that the position in which these bodies were found made it impossible that any one of them could be that of his noble young kinsman. They pointed out the spot where, if the newspaper account was correct, he must have sunk down to destruction; and at a wide distance from this spot they showed him where the young man must have gone down in case he was suffocated in his room; and they showed still a third place, quite remote, where he might possibly have found his death if perchance he tried to escape by the side exit toward the rear. The old Colonel brushed away a tear, and said to Hawkins:

"As it turns out, there was something prophetic in my fears. Yes, it's a matter of ashes. Will you kindly step to a grocery and fetch a couple more baskets?"

Reverently they got a basket of ashes from each of those now hallowed spots, and carried them home to consult as to the best manner of forwarding them to England, and also to give them an opportunity to "lie in state"—a mark of respect which the Colonel deemed obligatory, considering the high rank of the deceased.

They set the baskets on the table in what was formerly the library, drawing-room, and work-shop—now the Hall of Audience —and went up-stairs to the lumber-room to see if they could find a British flag to use as a part of the outfit proper to the lying in state. A moment later Lady Rossmore came in from the street and caught sight of the baskets just as old Jinny crossed her field of vision. She quite lost her patience, and said:

"Well, what will you do next? What in the world possessed you to clutter up the parlor table with these baskets of ashes?"

"Ashes?" And she came to look. She put up her hands in pathetic astonishment. "Well, I *never* see de like!"

"Didn't you do it?"

"Who? me? Clah to goodness it's de fust time I've sot eyes on 'em, Miss Polly. Dat's Dan'l. Dat ole moke is losin' his mine."

But it wasn't Dan'l, for he was called, and denied it.

"Dey ain't no way to 'splain dat. Wen hit's one er dese-yer common 'currences, a body kin reckon maybe de cat—"

"Oh!" and a shudder shook Lady Rossmore to her foundations. "I see it all. Keep away from them—they're *his.*"

"*His,* m'lady?"

"Yes—your young Marse Sellers from England that's burnt up."

She was alone with the ashes—alone before she could take half a breath. Then she went after Mulberry Sellers, purposing to make short work of his programme, whatever it might be; "for," said she, "when his sentimentals are up he's a numskull, and there's no knowing what extravagance he'll contrive if you let him alone." She found him. He had found the flag and was bringing it. When she heard that his idea was to have the remains "lie in state, and invite the government and the public," she broke it up. She said:

"Your intentions are all right—they always are—you want to do honor to the remains, and surely nobody can find any fault with that, for he was your kin; but you are going the wrong way about it, and you will see it yourself if you stop and think. You can't file around a basket of ashes trying to look sorry for it and make a sight that is really solemn, because the solemner it is, the more it isn't—anybody can see that. It would be so with one basket; it would be three times so with three. Well, it stands to reason that if it wouldn't be solemn with one mourner, it wouldn't be with a procession—and there would be five thousand people here. I don't know but it would be pretty near ridiculous; I think it would. No, Mulberry, they can't lie in state—it would be a mistake. Give that up and think of something else."

So he gave it up; and not reluctantly, when he had thought it over and realized how right her instinct was. He concluded to merely sit up with the remains—just himself and Hawkins. Even this seemed a doubtful attention, to his wife, but she offered no objection, for it was plain that he had a quite honest and simple-hearted desire to do the friendly and honorable thing by these forlorn poor relics which could command no hospitality in this far-off land of strangers but his. He draped the flag about the baskets, put some crape on the doorknob, and said, with satisfaction:

"There—he is as comfortable now as we can make him in the circumstances. Except—yes, we must strain a point there—one must do as one would wish to be done by—he must have it."

"Have what, dear?"

"Hatchment."

The wife felt that the house-front was standing about all it could well stand in that way; the prospect of another stunning decoration of that nature distressed her, and she wished the thing had not occurred to him. She said, hesitatingly:

"But I thought such an honor as that wasn't allowed to any but very, *very* near relations, who—"

"Right, you are quite right, my lady, perfectly right; but there aren't any nearer relatives than relatives by usurpation. We cannot avoid it; we are slaves of aristocratic custom, and must submit."

The hatchments were unnecessarily generous, each being as large as a blanket, and they were unnecessarily volcanic, too, as to variety and violence of color, but they pleased the earl's barbaric eye, and they satisfied his taste for symmetry and completeness, too, for they left no waste room to speak of on the house-front.

Lady Rossmore and her daughter assisted at the sitting-up till near midnight, and helped the gentlemen to consider what ought to be done next with the remains. Rossmore thought they ought to be sent home—with a committee and resolutions—at once. But the wife was doubtful. She said:

"Would you send all of the baskets?"

"Oh, yes, all."

"All at once?"

"To his father? Oh, no—by no means. Think of the shock. No—one at a time; break it to him by degrees."

"Would *that* have that effect, father?"

"Yes, my daughter. Remember, you are young and elastic, but he is old. To send him the whole at once might well be more than he could bear. But mitigated—one basket at a time, with restful intervals between, he would be used to it by the time he got all of him. And sending him in three ships is safer anyway. On account of wrecks and storms."

"I don't like the idea, father. If I were his father it would be dreadful to have him coming in that—in that—"

"On the instalment plan," suggested Hawkins, gravely, and proud of being able to help.

"Yes—dreadful to have him coming in that incoherent way. There would be the strain of suspense upon me all the time. To have so depressing a thing as a funeral impending, delayed, waiting, unaccomplished—"

"Oh, no, my child," said the earl, reassuringly, "there would be nothing of that kind; so old a gentleman could not endure a long-drawn suspense like that. There will be three funerals."

Lady Rossmore looked up surprised, and said:

"How is *that* going to make it easier for him? It's a total mistake, to my mind. He ought to be buried all at once; I'm sure of it."

"I should think so, too," said Hawkins.

"And certainly *I* should," said the daughter.

"You are all wrong," said the earl. "You will see it yourselves if you think. Only one of these baskets has got him in it."

"Very well, then," said Lady Rossmore, "the thing is perfectly simple—bury *that* one."

"Certainly," said Lady Gwendolen.

"But it is *not* simple," said the earl, "because we do not know which basket he is in. We know he is in *one* of them, but that is all we *do* know. You see now, I reckon, that I was right; it takes three funerals, there is no other way."

"And three graves and three monuments and three inscriptions?" asked the daughter.

"Well—yes—to do it right. That is what I should do."

"It could not be done so, father. Each of the inscriptions would give the same name and the same facts and say he was under each and all of these monuments, and that would not answer at all."

The earl nestled uncomfortably in his chair.

"No," he said, "that *is* an objection. That is a serious objection. I see no way out."

There was a general silence for a while. Then Hawkins said:

"It seems to me that if we mixed the three ramifications together—"

The earl grasped him by the hand and shook it gratefully.

"It solves the whole problem," he said. "One ship, one funeral, one grave, one monument—it is admirably conceived. It does you honor, Major Hawkins, it has relieved me of a most painful embarrassment and distress, and it will save that poor stricken old father much suffering. Yes, he shall go over in one basket."

"When?" asked the wife.

"To-morrow—immediately, of course."

"I would wait, Mulberry."

"Wait? Why?"

"*You* don't want to break that childless old man's heart."

"God knows I don't."

"Then wait till he sends for his son's remains. If you do that you will never have to give him the last and sharpest pain a parent can know—I mean, the *certainty* that his son is dead. For he will never send."

"Why won't he?"

"Because to send—and find out the truth—would rob him of the one precious thing left him: the *uncertainty*, the dim hope that maybe, after all, his boy escaped, and he will see him again some day."

"Why, Polly, he'll know by the *papers* that he was burnt up."

"He won't let himself *believe* the papers; he'll argue against anything and everything that proves his son is dead; and he will keep that up and live on it, and on nothing else till he dies. But if the *remains* should actually come, and be put before that poor old dim-hoping soul—"

"Oh, my God, they never shall! Polly, you've saved me from a crime, and I'll bless you for it always. *Now* we know what to do. We'll place them reverently away, and he shall never know."

10

Lord Berkeley deposits the $500 found in his appropriated clothes—Attends "Mechanics' Debating Club"—Berkeley (*alias* Tracy) is glad he came to this country

THE YOUNG Lord Berkeley, with the fresh air of freedom in his nostrils, was feeling invincibly strong for his new career; and yet —and yet—if the fight should prove a very hard one at first, very discouraging, very taxing on untoughened moral sinews, he might in some weak moment want to retreat. Not likely, of course, but possibly that might happen. And so, on the whole, it might be pardonable caution to burn his bridges behind him. Oh, without doubt. He must not stop with advertising for the owner of that money, but must put it where he could not borrow from it himself, meantime, under stress of circumstances. So he went downtown and put in his advertisement, then went to a bank and handed in $500 for deposit.

"What name?"

He hesitated and colored a little; he had forgotten to make a selection. He now brought out the first one that suggested itself:

"Howard Tracy."

When he was gone, the clerks, marveling, said:

"The cowboy blushed."

The first step was accomplished. The money was still under his command and at his disposal, but the next step would dispose of that difficulty. He went to another bank and drew upon the first bank for the $500 by check. The money was collected and deposited a second time to the credit of Howard Tracy. He was asked to leave a few samples of his signature, which he did. Then he went away, once more proud and of perfect courage, saying:

"No help for me now, for henceforth I couldn't draw that money without identification, and that is become legally impossible. No resources to fall back on. It is work or starve from now to the end. I am ready—and not afraid!"

Then he sent this cablegram to his father:

Escaped unhurt from burning hotel. Have taken fictitious name. Good-by.

During the evening, while he was wandering about in one of the outlying districts of the city, he came across a small brick church, with a bill posted there with these words printed on it: "MECHANICS' CLUB DEBATE. ALL INVITED." He saw people, apparently mainly of the working class, entering the place, and he followed and took his seat. It was a humble little church, quite bare as to ornamentation. It had painted pews without cushions, and no pulpit, properly speaking, but it had a platform. On the platform sat the chairman, and by his side sat a man who held a manuscript in his hand and had the waiting look of one who is going to perform the principal part. The church was soon filled with a quiet and orderly congregation of decently dressed and modest people. This is what the chairman said:

"The essayist for this evening is an old member of our club whom you all know, Mr. Parker, assistant editor of the *Daily Democrat*. The subject of his essay is the American Press, and he will use as his text a couple of paragraphs taken from Mr. Matthew Arnold's new book. He asks me to read these texts for him. The first is as follows:

"'Goethe says somewhere that "the thrill of awe," that is to say, REVERENCE, is the best thing humanity has.'

"Mr. Arnold's other paragraph is as follows:

"'I should say that if one were searching for the best means to efface and kill in a whole nation the discipline of respect, one could not do better than take the American newspapers.'"

Mr. Parker rose and bowed, and was received with warm applause. He then began to read in a good, round, resonant voice, with clear enunciation and careful attention to his pauses and emphases. His points were received with approval as he went on.

The essayist took the position that the most important function of a public journal in any country was the propagating of national feeling and pride in the national name—the keeping the people "in love with *their* country and *its* institutions, and shielded from the allurements of alien and inimical systems." He sketched the manner in which the reverent Turkish or Russian journalist fulfilled this function—the one assisted by the prevalent "discipline of respect" for the bastinado, the other for Siberia. Continuing, he said:

The chief function of an English journal is that of all other journals the world over: it must keep the public eye fixed admiringly upon certain things, and keep it diligently diverted from certain others. For instance, it must keep the public eye fixed admiringly upon the glories of England, a processional splendor stretching its receding line down the hazy vistas of time, with the mellowed lights of a thousand years glinting from its banners; and it must keep it diligently diverted from the fact that all these glories were for the enrichment and aggrandizement of the petted and privileged few, at cost of the blood and sweat and poverty of the unconsidered masses who achieved them, but might not enter in and partake of them. It must keep the public eye fixed in loving and awful reverence upon the throne as a sacred thing, and diligently divert it from the fact that no throne was ever set up by the unhampered vote of a majority of any nation; and that hence no throne exists that has a right to exist, and no symbol of it, flying from any flagstaff, is righteously entitled to wear any device but the skull and crossbones of that kindred industry which differs from royalty only business-wise—merely as retail differs from wholesale. It must keep the citizen's eye fixed in reverent docility upon that curious invention of machine politics, an Established Church, and upon that bald contradiction of common justice, a hereditary nobility; and diligently divert it from the fact that the one damns him if he doesn't wear its collar, and robs him under the gentle name of taxation whether he wears it or not, and the other gets all the honors while he does all the work.

The essayist thought that Mr. Arnold, with his trained eye and intelligent observation, ought to have perceived that the very quality which he so regretfully missed from our press—respect-fulness, reverence—was exactly the thing which would make our press useless to us if it had it—rob it of the very thing which dif-ferentiates it from all other journalism in the world and makes it distinctively and preciously American, its frank and cheerful ir-reverence being by all odds the most valuable of all its qualities. "For its mission—overlooked by Mr. Arnold—is to stand guard over a nation's liberties, not its humbugs and shams." He thought that if during fifty years the institutions of the old world could be exposed to the fire of a flouting and scoffing press like ours, "monarchy and its attendant crimes would disappear from Chris-tendom." Monarchists might doubt this; then "why not persuade the Czar to give it a trial in Russia?" Concluding, he said:

Well, the charge is, that our press has but little of that old-world quality, reverence. Let us be candidly grateful that it is so. With its limited reverence it at least reveres the things which this nation reveres, as a rule, and that is suffi-cient; what other people revere is fairly and properly matter of light importance to us. Our press does not reverence kings, it does not reverence so-called nobilities; it does not rever-ence established ecclesiastical slaveries, it does not reverence laws which rob a younger son to fatten an elder one, it does not reverence any fraud or sham or infamy, howsoever old or rotten or holy, which sets one citizen above his neighbor by accident of birth; it does not reverence any law or cus-tom, howsoever old or decayed or sacred, which shuts against the best man in the land the best place in the land and the divine right to prove property and go up and occupy it. In the sense of the poet Goethe—that meek idolater of provincial three-carat royalty and nobility—our press is certainly bankrupt in the "thrill of awe"—otherwise reverence; reverence for nickel plate and brummagem. Let us sincerely hope that this fact will remain a fact forever; for to my mind a discriminating irreverence is the creator and protector of human liberty—even as the other thing is the creator, nurse, and steadfast protector of all forms of human slavery, bodily and mental.

Tracy said to himself, almost shouted to himself, "I'm glad I came to this country. I was right. I was right to seek out a land where such healthy principles and theories are in men's hearts and minds. Think of the innumerable slaveries imposed by misplaced reverence! How well he brought that out, and how true it is. There's manifestly prodigious force in reverence. If you can get a man to reverence your ideals, he's your slave. Oh, yes; in all the ages the peoples of Europe have been diligently taught to avoid reasoning about the shams of monarchy and nobility, been taught to avoid examining them, been taught to reverence them; and now, as a natural result, to reverence them is a second nature. In order to shock them it is sufficient to inject a thought of the opposite kind into their dull minds. For ages, any expression of so-called irreverence from their lips has been sin and crime. The sham and swindle of all this is apparent the moment one reflects that he is himself the only legitimately qualified judge of what *is* entitled to reverence and what is not. Come, I hadn't thought of that before, but it is true, absolutely true. What right has Goethe, what right has Arnold, what right has any dictionary, to define the word Irreverence for me? What their ideals are is nothing to me. So long as I reverence my own ideals my whole duty is done, and I commit no profanation if I laugh at theirs. I may scoff at other people's ideals as much as I want to. It is my right and my privilege. No man has any right to deny it."

Tracy was expecting to hear the essay debated, but this did not happen. The chairman said, by way of explanation:

"I would say, for the information of the strangers present here, that in accordance with our custom the subject of this meeting will be debated at the next meeting of the club. This is in order to enable our members to prepare what they may wish to say upon the subject with pen and paper, for we are mainly mechanics and unaccustomed to speaking. We are obliged to write down what we desire to say."

Many brief papers were now read, and several offhand speeches made in discussion of the essay read at the last meeting of the club, which had been a laudation, by some visiting professor, of college culture, and the grand results flowing from it to the nation. One of the papers was read by a man approaching middle age, who said he hadn't had a college education, that he had got his education in a printing-office, and had graduated from there into the patent-office, where he had been a clerk now for a great many years. Then he continued to this effect:

The essayist contrasted the America of to-day with the America of bygone times, and certainly the result is the exhibition of a mighty progress. But I think he a little over-rated the college-culture share in the production of that result. It can no doubt be easily shown that the colleges have contributed the intellectual part of this progress, and that that part is vast; but that the material progress has been immeasurably vaster I think you will concede. Now I have been looking over a list of inventors—the creators of this amazing material development—and I find that they were not college-bred men. Of course there are exceptions—like Professor Henry of Princeton, the inventor of Mr. Morse's system of telegraphy—but these exceptions are few. It is not overstatement to say that the imagination-stunning material development of this century, the only century worth living in since time itself was invented, is the creation of men not college-bred. We think we see what these inventors have done; no, we see only the visible vast frontage of their work; behind it is their far vaster work, and it is invisible to the careless glance. They have reconstructed this nation—made it over, that is—and, metaphorically speaking, have multiplied its numbers almost beyond the power of figures to express. I will explain what I mean. What constitutes the population of a land? Merely the numberable packages of meat and bones in it called by courtesy men and women? Shall a million ounces of brass and a million ounces of gold be held to be of the same value? Take a truer standard: the measure of a man's contributing capacity to his time and

his people—the work he can do—and then number the population of this country to-day, as multiplied by what a man
can now do more than his grandfather could do. By this
standard of measurement, this nation, two or three generations ago, consisted of mere cripples, paralytics, dead men,
as compared with the men of to-day. In 1840 our population
was 17,000,000. By the way of rude but striking illustration,
let us consider, for argument's sake, that four of these
millions consisted of aged people, little children, and other
incapables, and that the remaining 13,000,000 were divided
and employed as follows:

2,000,000 as ginners of cotton.
6,000,000 (women) as stocking-knitters.
2,000,000 (women) as thread-spinners.
500,000 as screw-makers.
400,000 as reapers, binders, etc.
1,000,000 as corn-shellers.
40,000 as weavers.
1,000 as stitchers of shoe soles.

Now the deductions which I am going to append to these
figures may sound extravagant, but they are not. I take them
from Miscellaneous Documents No. 50, second session 45th
Congress, and they are official and trustworthy. To-day the
work of those 2,000,000 cotton-ginners is done by 2,000 men;
that of the 6,000,000 stocking-knitters is done by 3,000 boys;
that of the 2,000,000 thread-spinners is done by 1,000 girls;
that of the 500,000 screw-makers is done by 500 girls; that
of the 400,000 reapers, binders, etc., is done by 4,000 boys;
that of the 1,000,000 corn-shellers is done by 7,5000 men;
that of the 40,000 weavers is done by 1,200 men; and that of
the 1,000 stitchers of shoe soles is done by 6 men. To bunch
the figures, 17,000 persons to-day do the above work, whereas
fifty years ago it would have taken thirteen millions of persons to do it. Now then, how many of that ignorant race—our
fathers and grandfathers—with their ignorant methods,
would it take to do our work to-day? It would take forty
thousand millions—a hundred times the swarming population
of China—twenty times the present population of the globe.
You look around you and you see a nation of sixty millions—
apparently; but secreted in their hands and brains, and in-

visible to your eyes, is the true population of this Republic, and it numbers forty billions! It is the stupendous creation of those humble, unlettered, un-college-bred inventors—all honor to their name.

"How grand that is!" said Tracy, as he wended homeward. "What a civilization it is, and what prodigious results these are! and brought about almost wholly by common men; not by Oxford-trained aristocrats, but men who stand shoulder to shoulder in the humble ranks of life and earn the bread that they eat. Again I'm glad I came. I have found a country at last where one may start fair, and, breast to breast with his fellow-man, rise by his own efforts, and be something in the world and be proud of that something; not be something created by an ancestor three hundred years ago."

11

No work for Tracy—Cheaper lodgings secured—Sleeping on the roof—"My daughter Hattie"—Tracy receives further "impressions" from Hattie (otherwise "Puss")—Mr. Barrow appears—And offers to help Tracy find work

DURING the first few days he kept the fact diligently before his mind that he was in a land where there was "work and bread for all." In fact, for convenience' sake he fitted it to a little tune and hummed it to himself; but as time wore on the fact itself began to take on a doubtful look, and next the tune got fatigued and presently ran down and stopped. His first effort was to get an upper clerkship in one of the departments, where his Oxford education could come into play and do him service. But he stood no chance whatever. There competency was no recommendation; political backing, without competency, was worth six of it. He was glaringly English, and that was necessarily against him in the political center of a nation where both parties prayed for the Irish cause on the house-top and blasphemed it in the cellar. By his dress he was a cowboy; that won him respect—when his back was not turned—but it couldn't get a clerkship for him. But he had said, in a rash moment, that he would wear those clothes till the owner or the owner's friends caught sight of them and asked for that money, and his conscience would not let him retire from that engagement now.

At the end of a week things were beginning to wear rather a startling look. He had hunted everywhere for work, descending gradually the scale of quality, until apparently he had sued for all the various kinds of work a man without a special calling might hope to be able to do, except ditching and the other coarse manual sorts—and had got neither work nor the promise of it.

He was mechanically turning over the leaves of his diary meanwhile, and now his eye fell upon the first record made after he was burnt out:

I myself did not doubt my stamina before; nobody could doubt it now, if they could see how I am housed, and realize that I feel absolutely no disgust with these quarters, but am as serenely content with them as any dog would be in a similar kennel. Terms, twenty-five dollars a week. I said I would start at the bottom. I have kept my word.

A shudder went quaking through him, and he exclaimed:

"What have I been thinking of! *This* the bottom! Mooning along a whole week, and these terrific expenses climbing and climbing all the time! I must end this folly straightway."

He settled up at once and went forth to find less sumptuous lodgings. He had to wander far and seek with diligence, but he succeeded. They made him pay in advance—four dollars and a half; this secured both bed and food for a week. The good-natured, hard-worked landlady took him up three flights of narrow, uncarpeted stairs and delivered him into his room. There were two double bedsteads in it and one single one. He would be allowed to sleep alone in one of the double beds until some new boarder should come, but he wouldn't be charged extra.

So he would presently be required to sleep with some stranger! The thought of it made him sick. Mrs. Marsh, the landlady, was very friendly, and hoped he would like her house—they all liked it, she said.

"And they're a very nice set of boys. They carry on a good deal, but that's their fun. You see, this room opens right into this back one, and sometimes they're all in one and sometimes in the other; and hot nights they all sleep on the roof when it don't rain. They get out there the minute it's hot enough. The season's so early that they've already had a night or two up there. If you'd like to go up and pick out a place, you can. You'll find chalk in the side of the chimney where there's a brick wanting. You just take the chalk and—but, of course, you've done it before."

"Oh, no, I haven't."

"Why, of course, you haven't—what am I thinking of? Plenty of room on the Plains without chalking, I'll be bound. Well, you just chalk out a place the size of a blanket anywhere on the tin that ain't already marked off, you know, and that's your property. You and your bed-mate take turn-about carrying up the blanket and pillows and fetching them down again; or one carries them up and the other fetches them down; you fix it the way you like, you know. You'll like the boys; they're everlasting sociable—except the printer. He's the one that sleeps in that single bed—the strangest creature; why, I don't believe you could get that man to sleep with another man, not if the house was afire. Mind you, I'm not just talking, I *know*. The boys tried him to see. They took his bed out one night, and so when he got home about three in the morning—he was on a morning paper then, but he's on an evening one now—there wasn't any place for him but with the iron-molder; and if you'll believe me, he just set up the rest of the night—he did, honest. They say he's cracked, but it ain't so, he's English—they're awful particular. You won't mind my saying that. You—you're English?"

"Yes."

"I thought so. I could tell it by the way you mispronounce the words that's got *a*'s in them, you know; such as saying loff when you mean laff—but you'll get over that. He's a right down good fellow, and a little sociable with the photographer's boy and the caulker and the blacksmith that work in the navy-yard, but not so much with the others. The fact is, though it's private, and the others don't know it, he's a kind of an aristocrat, his father being a doctor, and *you* know what style *that* is—in England, I mean, because in this country a doctor ain't so *very* much, even if he's *that*. But over there, of course, it's different. So this chap had a falling out with his father, and was pretty high strung, and just cut for this country, and the first he knew he had to get to work or starve. Well, he'd been to college, you see, and so he judged *he* was all right—did you say anything?"

"No—I only sighed."

"And there's where he was mistaken. Why, he mighty near starved. And I reckon he would have starved sure enough if some jour' printer or other hadn't took pity on him and got him a place as apprentice. So he learned the trade, and then he was all right—but it was a close call. Once he thought he had *got* to haul in his pride and holler for his father, and—why, you're sighing again. Is anything the matter with you?—does my clatter—"

"Oh, *dear*-no. Pray go on—I like it."

"Yes, you see, he's been over here ten years; he's twenty-eight now, and he ain't pretty well satisfied in his mind, because he can't get reconciled to being a mechanic and associating with mechanics, he being, as he says to me, a *gentleman*, which is a pretty plain letting-on that the boys ain't, but of course I know enough not to let *that* cat out of the bag."

"Why—would there be any harm in it?"

"Harm in it? They'd lick him, wouldn't they? Wouldn't *you?* Of course you would. Don't you ever let a man say you ain't a gentleman in *this* country. But laws, what am I thinking about? I reckon a body would think twice before he said a cowboy wasn't a gentleman."

A trim, active, slender, and very pretty girl of about eighteen walked into the room now, in the most satisfied and unembarrassed way. She was cheaply but smartly and gracefully dressed, and the mother's quick glance at the stranger's face as he rose was of the kind which inquires what effect has been produced, and expects to find indications of surprise and admiration.

"This is my daughter Hattie—we call her Puss. It's the new boarder, Puss." This without rising.

The young Englishman made the awkward bow common to his nationality and time of life in circumstances of delicacy and difficulty, and these were of that sort; for, being taken by surprise, his natural, lifelong self sprang to the front, and that self, of course, would not know just how to act when introduced to a chambermaid, or to the heiress of a mechanics' boarding-house. His other self—the self which recognized the equality of all men —would have managed the thing better if it hadn't been caught off guard and robbed of its chance. The young girl paid no attention to the bow, but put out her hand frankly and gave the stranger a friendly shake, and said:

"How do you do?"

Then she marched to the one washstand in the room, tilted her head this way and that before the wreck of a cheap mirror that hung above it, dampened her fingers with her tongue, perfected the circle of a little lock of hair that was pasted against her forehead, then began to busy herself with the slops.

"Well, I must be going—it's getting toward suppertime. Make yourself at home, Mr. Tracy; you'll hear the bell when it's ready."

The landlady took her tranquil departure without commanding either of the young people to vacate the room. The young man wondered a little that a mother who seemed so honest and respectable should be so thoughtless, and was reaching for his hat, intending to disembarrass the girl of his presence; but she said:

"Where are you going?"

"Well—nowhere in particular, but as I am only in the way here—"

"Why, who said you were in the way? Sit down—I'll move you when you are in the way."

She was making the beds now. He sat down and watched her deft and diligent performance.

"What gave you that notion? Do you reckon I need a whole room just to make up a bed or two in?"

"Well, no, it wasn't that, exactly. We are away up here in an empty house, and your mother being gone—"

The girl interrupted him with an amused laugh, and said:

"Nobody to protect me? Bless you, I don't need it. I'm not afraid. I might be if I was alone, because I do hate ghosts, and I don't deny it. Not that I believe in them, for I don't. I'm only just afraid of them."

"How can you be afraid of them if you don't believe in them?"

"Oh, I don't know the *how* of it—that's too many for *me; I* only know it's *so*. It's the same with Maggie Lee."

"Who is that?"

"One of the boarders; young lady that works in the fact'ry."

"She works in a factory?"

"Yes. Shoe fact'ry."

"In a shoe factory; and you call her a young lady?"

"Why, she's only twenty-two; what should you call her?"

"I wasn't thinking of her age; I was thinking of the title. The fact is, I came away from England to get away from artificial forms—for artificial forms suit artificial people only—and here you've got them, too. I'm sorry. I hoped you had only men and women; everybody equal; no differences in rank."

The girl stopped with a pillow in her teeth and the case spread open below it, contemplating him from under her brows with a slightly puzzled expression. She released the pillow, and said:

"Why, they *are* all equal. Where's any difference in rank?"

"If you call a factory girl a young *lady*, what do you call the President's wife?"

"Call her an *old* one."

"Oh, you make age the only distinction?"

"There ain't any other to make as far as I can see."

"Then *all* women are ladies?"

"Certainly they are. All the respectable ones."

"Well, that puts a better face on it. Certainly there is no harm in a title when it is given to everybody. It is only an offense and a wrong when it is restricted to a favored few. But, Miss—er—"

"Hattie."

"Miss Hattie, be frank; confess that that title *isn't* accorded by everybody to everybody. The rich American doesn't call her cook a lady—isn't that so?"

"Yes, it's so. What of it?"

He was surprised and a little disappointed to see that his admirable shot had produced no perceptible effect.

"What *of* it?" he said. "Why, this: equality is *not* conceded here, after all, and the Americans are no better off than the English. In fact, there's no difference."

"Now *what* an idea. There's nothing in a title except what is *put* into it—you've said that yourself. Suppose the title is *clean*, instead of lady. You get that?"

"I believe so. Instead of speaking of a woman as *lady*, you substitute clean and say she's a clean person."

"That's it. In England the swell folks don't speak of the working people as gentlemen and ladies?"

"Oh, no."

"And the working people don't call *themselves* gentlemen and ladies?"

"Certainly not."

"So if you used the other word there wouldn't be any change. The swell people wouldn't call anybody but themselves 'clean,' and those others would drop sort of meekly into their way of talking and *they* wouldn't call themselves clean. We don't do that way here. Everybody calls himself a lady or gentleman, and thinks he *is*, and don't care what anybody else thinks him, so long as he don't say it out loud. You think there's no difference. You *knuckle down* and we *don't*. Ain't that a difference?"

"It is a difference I hadn't thought of; I admit that. Still—*calling* one's self a lady doesn't—er—"

"I wouldn't go on if I were you."

Howard Tracy turned his head to see who it might be that had introduced this remark. It was a short man about forty years old, with sandy hair, no beard, and a pleasant face badly freckled but alive and intelligent, and he wore slop-shop clothing which was neat but showed wear. He had come from the front room beyond the hall, where he had left his hat, and he had a chipped and cracked white washbowl in his hand. The girl came and took the bowl.

"I'll get it for you. You go right ahead and *give* it to him, Mr. Barrow. He's the new boarder—Mr. Tracy—and I'd just got to where it was getting too deep for me."

"Much obliged if you will, Hattie. I was coming to borrow of the boys." He sat down at his ease on an old trunk, and said, "I've been listening and got interested; and as I was saying, I wouldn't go on if I were you. You see where you are coming to, don't you? *Calling* yourself a lady doesn't elect you; that is what you were going to say; and you saw that if you said it you were going to run right up against another difference that you hadn't thought of: to wit, Whose *right* is it to do the electing? Over there, twenty thousand people in a million elect themselves gentlemen and ladies, and the nine hundred and eighty thousand *accept* that decree and swallow the affront which it puts upon them. Why, if they didn't accept it it wouldn't *be* an election; it would be a dead letter, and have no force at all. Over here the twenty thousand would-be exclusives come up to the polls and vote themselves to be ladies and gentlemen. But the thing doesn't stop there. The nine hundred and eighty thousand come and vote themselves to be ladies and gentlemen *too*, and that elects the whole nation. Since the whole million vote themselves ladies and gentlemen, there is no question about that election. It *does* make absolute equality, and there is no fiction about it; while over yonder the *inequality* (by decree of the infinitely feeble, and consent of the infinitely strong) is also absolute—as real and absolute as our equality."

Tracy had shrunk promptly into his English shell when this speech began, notwithstanding he had now been in severe training several weeks for contact and intercourse with the common herd on the common herd's terms; but he lost no time in pulling himself out again, and so by the time the speech was finished his valves were open once more, and he was forcing himself to accept without resentment the common herd's frank fashion of dropping sociably into other people's conversations unembarrassed and uninvited. The process was not very difficult this time, for the man's smile and voice and manner were persuasive and winning. Tracy would even have liked him on the spot but for the fact—fact which he was not really aware of—that the equality of men was not yet a reality to him; it was only a theory; the *mind* perceived, but the *man* failed to feel it. It was Hattie's ghost over again, merely turned around. Theoretically Barrow was his equal, but it was distinctly distasteful to see him exhibit it. He presently said:

"I hope in all sincerity that what you have said is true as regards the Americans, for doubts have crept into my mind several times. It seemed that the equality must be ungenuine where the sign-names of castes were still in vogue; but those sign-names have certainly lost their offense and are wholly neutralized, nullified, and harmless if they are the undisputed property of every individual in the nation. I think I realize that caste does not exist and cannot exist except by common consent of the masses outside of its limits. I thought caste created itself and perpetuated itself; but it seems quite true that it only creates itself, and is perpetuated by the people whom it despises, and who can dissolve it at any time by assuming its mere sign-names themselves."

"It's what I think. There isn't any power on earth that can prevent England's thirty millions from electing themselves dukes and duchesses to-morrow and calling themselves so. And within six months all the former dukes and duchesses would have retired from the business. I wish they'd try that. Royalty itself couldn't survive such a process. A handful of frowners against thirty million laughers in a state of eruption: Why, it's Herculaneum against Vesuvius; it would take another eighteen centuries to find that Herculaneum after the cataclysm. What's a Colonel in our South? He's a nobody; because they're all colonels down there. No, Tracy" (shudder from Tracy), "nobody in England would call you a gentleman, and you wouldn't call yourself one; and I tell you it's a state of things that makes a man put himself into most unbecoming attitudes sometimes—the broad and general recognition and acceptance of caste *as* caste does, I mean. Makes him do it unconsciously—being bred in him, you see, and never thought over and reasoned out. You couldn't conceive of the Matterhorn being flattered by the notice of one of your comely little English hills, could you?"

"Why, no."

"Well, then, let a man in his right mind try to conceive of Darwin feeling flattered by the notice of a princess. It's so grotesque that it—well, it paralyzes the imagination. Yet that Memnon *was* flattered by the notice of that statuette; he *says* so—says so himself. The system that can make a god disown his godship and profane it—oh, well, it's all wrong, it's all wrong and ought to be abolished, I should say."

The mention of Darwin brought on a literary discussion, and this topic roused such enthusiasm in Barrow that he took off his coat and made himself the more free and comfortable for it, and detained him so long that he was still at it when the noisy proprietors of the room came shouting and skylarking in, and began to romp, scuffle, wash, and otherwise entertain themselves. He lingered yet a little longer to offer the hospitalities of his room and his bookshelf to Tracy, and ask him a personal question or two:

"What is your trade?"

"They—well, they call me a cowboy, but that is a fancy; I'm not that. I haven't any trade."

"What do you work at for your living?"

"Oh, anything—I mean I *would* work at anything I could get to do, but thus far I haven't been able to find an occupation."

"Maybe I can help you; I'd like to try."

"I shall be very glad. I've tried, myself, to weariness."

"Well, of course, where a man hasn't a regular trade he's pretty bad off in this world. What you needed, I reckon, was less book-learning and more bread-and-butter-learning. I don't know what your father could have been thinking of. You ought to have had a trade, you ought to have had a trade, by *all* means. But never mind about that; we'll stir up *something* to do, I guess. And don't you get homesick; that's a bad business. We'll talk the thing over and look around a little. You'll come out all right. Wait for me—I'll go down to supper with you."

By this time Tracy had achieved a very friendly feeling for

Barrow, and would have *called* him a friend, maybe, if not taken
too suddenly on a straight-out requirement to realize on his theories. He was glad of his society, anyway, and was feeling lighter-
hearted than before. Also he was pretty curious to know what
vocation it might be which had furnished Barrow such a large
acquaintanceship with books and allowed him so much time to
read.

12

A boarding-house dinner—"No money, no dinner" for Mr.
Brady—"How did you come to mount that hat?"—A
glimpse of (the supposed) one-armed Pete—Extract from
Tracy's diary

PRESENTLY the supper-bell began to ring in the depths of the
house, and the sound proceeded steadily upward, growing in in-
tensity all the way up toward the upper floors. The higher it
came the more maddening was the noise, until at last what it
lacked of being absolutely deafening was made up of the sudden
crash and clatter of an avalanche of boarders down the uncarpeted stairway. The peerage did not go to meals in this fashion;
Tracy's training had not fitted him to enjoy this hilarious zoologi-
cal clamor and enthusiasm. He had to confess that there was
something about this extraordinary outpouring of animal spirits
which he would have to get inured to before he could accept it.
No doubt in time he would prefer it; but he wished the process
might be modified and made just a little more gradual, and not
quite so pronounced and violent. Barrow and Tracy followed the
avalanche down through an ever-increasing and ever more and

more aggressive stench of bygone cabbage and kindred smells; smells which are to be found nowhere but in a cheap private boarding-house; smells which once encountered can never be forgotten; smells which encountered generations later are instantly recognizable, but never recognizable with pleasure. To Tracy these odors were suffocating, horrible, almost unendurable; but he held his peace and said nothing. Arrived in the basement, they entered a large dining-room where thirty-five or forty people sat at a long table. They took their places. The feast had already begun, and the conversation was going on in the liveliest way from one end of the table to the other. The tablecloth was of very coarse material, and was liberally spotted with coffee-stains and grease. The knives and forks were iron, with bone handles. The spoons appeared to be iron or sheet iron, or something of the sort. The tea and coffee cups were of the commonest and heaviest and most durable stoneware. All the furniture of the table was of the commonest and cheapest sort. There was a single large, thick slice of bread by each boarder's plate, and it was observable that he economized it as if he were not expecting it to be duplicated. Dishes of butter were distributed along the table within reach of people's arms, if they had long ones, but there were no private butter-plates. The butter was perhaps good enough, and was quiet and well behaved; but it had more bouquet than was necessary, though nobody commented upon that fact or seemed in any way disturbed by it. The main feature of the feast was a piping-hot Irish stew made of the potatoes and meat left over from a procession of previous meals. Everybody was liberally supplied with this dish. On the table were a couple of great dishes of sliced ham, and there were some other eatables of minor importance—preserves and New Orleans molasses and such things. There was also plenty of tea and coffee of an infernal sort, with brown sugar and condensed milk, but the milk and sugar supply was not left at the discretion of the boarders, but was rationed out at headquarters—one spoonful of sugar and one of condensed milk to each cup, and no more. The table was waited upon by two stalwart negro women who raced back and forth from the bases of supplies with splendid dash and clatter and energy. Their labors were supplemented after a fashion by the young girl Puss. She carried coffee and tea back and forth among the boarders, but she made pleasure excursions rather than business ones in this way, to speak strictly. She made jokes with various people. She chaffed the young men pleasantly—and wittily, as she supposed, and as the rest also supposed, apparently, judging by the applause and laughter which she got by her efforts. Manifestly she was a favorite with most of the young fellows and sweetheart of the rest of them. Where she conferred notice she conferred happiness, as was seen by the face of the recipient; and at the same time she conferred unhappiness—one could see it fall and dim the faces of the other young fellows like a shadow. She never "Mistered" these friends of hers, but called them "Billy," "Tom," "John," and they called her "Puss" or "Hattie."

Mr. Marsh sat at the head of the table, his wife sat at the foot. Marsh was a man of sixty, and was an American; but if he had been born a month earlier he would have been a Spaniard. He was plenty good enough Spaniard as it was; his face was very dark, his hair very black, and his eyes were not only exceedingly black, but were very intense, and there was something about them that indicated that they could burn with passion upon occasion. He was stoop-shouldered and lean-faced, and the general aspect of him was disagreeable; he was evidently not a very companionable person. If looks went for anything, he was the very opposite of his wife, who was all motherliness and charity, good-will and good-nature. All the young men and the women called her Aunt Rachel, which was another sign. Tracy's wandering and interested eye presently fell upon one boarder who had been overlooked in the distribution of the stew. He was very pale, and looked as if he had but lately come out of a sick-bed, and also as if he ought to get back into it again as soon as possible. His face was very melancholy. The waves of laughter and conversation broke upon it without affecting it any more than if it had been a rock in the sea, and the words and the laughter veritable waters. He held his head down and looked ashamed. Some of the women cast glances of pity toward him from time to time in a furtive and half-afraid way, and some of the youngest of the men plainly had compassion on the young fellow—a compassion exhibited in their faces, but not in any more active or compromising way. But the great majority of the people present showed entire indifference to the youth and his sorrows. Marsh sat with his head down, but one could catch the malicious gleam of his eyes through his shaggy brows. He was watching that young fellow with evident relish. He had not neglected him through carelessness, and apparently the table understood that fact. The spectacle was making Mrs. Marsh very uncomfortable. She had the look of one who hopes against hope that the impossible may happen; but as the impossible did not happen, she finally ventured to speak up and remind her husband that Nat Brady hadn't been helped to the Irish stew.

Marsh lifted his head and gasped out, with mock courtliness, "Oh, he hasn't, hasn't he? What a pity that is. I don't know how I came to overlook him. Ah, he must pardon me. You must, indeed, Mr.—er—Baxter—Barker, you must pardon me. I—er—my attention was directed to some other matter, I don't know what. The thing that grieves me mainly is that it happens every meal now. But you must try to overlook these little things, Mr. Bunker, these little neglects on my part. They're always likely to happen with me in any case, and they are especially likely to happen where a person has—er—well, where a person is, say, about three weeks in arrears for his board. You get my meaning?—you get my idea? Here is your Irish stew, and—er—it gives me the greatest pleasure to send it to you, and I hope that you will enjoy the charity as much as I enjoy conferring it."

A blush rose in Brady's white cheeks and flowed slowly backward to his ears and upward toward his forehead, but he said nothing and began to eat his food under the embarrassment of a general silence and the sense that all eyes were fastened upon him. Barrow whispered to Tracy:

"The old man's been waiting for that. He wouldn't have missed that chance for anything."

"It's a brutal business," said Tracy. Then he said to himself, purposing to set the thought down in his diary later:

"Well, here in this very house is a republic where all are free and equal, if men are free and equal anywhere in the earth; therefore I have arrived at the place I started to find, and I am a man among men, and on the strictest equality possible to men, no doubt. Yet here on the threshold I find an inequality. There are people at this table who are looked up to for some reason or another, and here is a poor devil of a boy who is looked down upon, treated with indifference and shamed by humiliations, when he has committed no crime but that common one of being poor. Equality ought to make men noble-minded. In fact, I had supposed it did do that."

After supper Barrow proposed a walk, and they started. Barrow had a purpose. He wanted Tracy to get rid of that cowboy hat. He didn't see his way to finding mechanical or manual employment for a person rigged in that fashion. Barrow presently said:

"As I understand it, you're not a cowboy."

"No, I'm not."

"Well, now, if you will not think me too curious, how did you come to mount that hat? Where'd you get it?"

Tracy didn't know quite how to reply to this, but presently said:

"Well, without going into particulars, I exchanged clothes with a stranger under stress of weather, and I would like to find him and re-exchange."

"Well, why don't you find him? Where is he?"

"I don't know. I supposed the best way to find him would be to continue to wear his clothes, which are conspicuous enough to attract his attention if I should meet him on the street."

"Oh, very well," said Barrow; "the rest of the outfit is well enough, and while it's not too conspicuous, it isn't quite like the clothes that anybody else wears. Suppress the hat. When you meet your man he'll recognize the rest of his suit. That's a mighty embarrassing hat, you know, in a center of civilization like this. I don't believe an angel could get employment in Washington in a halo like that."

Tracy agreed to replace the hat with something of a modester form, and they stepped aboard a crowded car and stood with others on the rear platform. Presently, as the car moved swiftly along the rails, two men crossing the street caught sight of the backs of Barrow and Tracy, and both exclaimed at once, "There he is!" It was Sellers and Hawkins. Both were so paralyzed with joy that before they could pull themselves together and make an effort to stop the car it was gone too far, and they decided to wait for the next one. They waited awhile; then it occurred to Washington that there could be no use in chasing one horse-car with another, and he wanted to hunt up a hack. But the Colonel said:

"When you come to think of it, there's no occasion for that at all. Now that I've got him materialized, I can command his motions. I'll have him at the house by the time we get there."

Then they hurried off home in a state of great and joyful excitement.

The hat exchange accomplished, the two new friends started to walk back leisurely to the boarding-house. Barrow's mind was full of curiosity about this young fellow. He said:

"You've never been to the Rocky Mountains?"

"No."

"You've never been out on the plains?"

"No."

"How long have you been in this country?"

"Only a few days."

"You've never been in America before?"

"No."

Then Barrow communed with himself. "Now what odd shapes the notions of romantic people take. Here's a fellow who's read in England about cowboys and adventures on the plains. He comes here and buys a cowboy's suit. Thinks he can play himself on folks for a cowboy, all inexperienced as he is. Now the minute he's caught in this poor little game, he's ashamed of it and ready to retire from it. It is that exchange that he has put up as an explanation. It's rather thin, too thin altogether. Well, he's young, never been anywhere, knows nothing about the world, sentimental, no doubt. Perhaps it was the natural thing for him to do, but it was a most singular choice, curious freak, altogether."

Both men were busy with their thoughts for a time; then Tracy heaved a sigh and said:

"Mr. Barrow, the case of that young fellow troubles me."

"You mean Nat Brady?"

"Yes, Brady, or Baxter, or whatever it was. The old landlord called him by several different names."

"Oh, yes, he has been very liberal with names for Brady, since Brady fell into arrears for his board. Well, that's one of his sarcasms—the old man thinks he's great on sarcasm."

"Well, what is Brady's difficulty? What is Brady—who is he?"

"Brady is a tinner. He's a young journeyman tinner who was getting along all right till he fell sick and lost his job. He was very popular before he lost his job; everybody in the house liked Brady. The old man was rather especially fond of him, but you know that when a man loses his job and loses his ability to support himself and to pay his way as he goes, it makes a great difference in the way people look at him and feel about him."

"Is that so! *Is* it so?"

Barrow looked at Tracy in a puzzled way. "Why, of course it's so. Wouldn't you know that, naturally? Don't you know that the wounded deer is always attacked and killed by its companions and friends?"

Tracy said to himself, while a chilly and boding discomfort spread itself through his system, "In a republic of deer and men, where all are free and equal, misfortune is a crime, and the prosperous gore the unfortunate to death." Then he said aloud, "Here in the boarding-house, if one would have friends and be popular, instead of having the cold shoulder turned upon him, he must be prosperous."

"Yes," Barrow said, "that is so. It's their human nature. They do turn against Brady, now that he's unfortunate, and they don't like him as well as they did before; but it isn't because of any lack in Brady—he's just as he was before, has the same nature and the same impulses, but they—well, Brady is a thorn in their conscience, you see. They know they ought to help him and they're too stingy to do it, and they're ashamed of themselves for that, and they ought also to hate themselves on that account, but instead of that they hate Brady because he makes them ashamed of themselves. I say that's human nature; that occurs everywhere; this boarding-house is merely the world in little; it's the case all over—they're all alike. In prosperity we are popular; popularity comes easy in that case, but when the other thing comes our friends are pretty likely to turn against us."

Tracy's noble theories and high purposes were beginning to feel pretty damp and clammy. He wondered if by any possibility he had made a mistake in throwing his own prosperity to the winds and taking up the cross of other people's unprosperity. But he wouldn't listen to that sort of thing; he cast it out of his mind, and resolved to go ahead resolutely along the course he had mapped out for himself.

Extracts from his diary:

Have now spent several days in this singular hive. I don't know quite what to make out of these people. They have merits and virtues, but they have some other qualities, and some ways that are hard to get along with. I can't enjoy them. The moment I appeared in a hat of the period I noticed a change. The respect which had been paid me before passed suddenly away, and the people became friendly —more than that, they became familiar, and I'm not used to familiarity, and can't take to it right off; I find that out. These people's familiarity amounts to impudence, sometimes. I suppose it's all right; no doubt I can get used to it, but it's not a satisfactory process at all. I have accomplished my dearest wish; I am a man among men, on an equal footing with Tom, Dick, and Harry, and yet it isn't just exactly what I thought it was going to be. I—I miss home. Am obliged to say I am homesick. Another thing—and this is a confession—a reluctant one, but I will make it: The thing I miss most, and most severely, is the respect, the deference, with which I was treated all my life in England, and which seems to be somehow necessary to me. I get along very well without the luxury and the wealth and the sort of society I've been accustomed to, but I do miss the respect, and can't seem to get reconciled to the absence of it. There is respect, there is deference here, but it doesn't fall to my share. It is lavished on two men. One of them is a portly man of middle age who is a retired plumber. Everybody is pleased to have that man's notice. He's full of pomp and circumstance and self-complacency and bad grammar, and at table he is Sir Oracle, and when he opens his mouth not any dog in the kennel barks. The other person is a policeman at the Capitol building. He represents the government. The deference paid to these two men is not so very far short of that paid to an earl in England, though the method of it differs. Not so much courtliness, but the deference is all there.

Yes, and there is obsequiousness, too.

It does rather look as if in a republic where all are free and equal prosperity and position constitute *rank*.

13

Tracy and trades-unions—Unpopularity with fellow-boarders—Which changes to popularity on his punishing Allen—The cablegram

THE DAYS drifted by, and they grew ever more dreary. For Barrow's efforts to find work for Tracy were unavailing. Always the first question asked was, "What union do you belong to?"

Tracy was obliged to reply that he didn't belong to any trade-union.

"Very well, then, it's impossible to employ you. My men wouldn't stay with me if I should employ a 'scab,' or 'rat,'" or whatever the phrase was.

Finally, Tracy had a happy thought. He said, "Why, the thing for me to do, of course, is to *join* a trade-union."

"Yes," Barrow said; "that is the thing for you to do—if you can."

"If I *can?* Is it difficult?"

"Well, yes," Barrow said, "it's sometimes difficult—in fact, very difficult. But you can try, and of course it will be best to try."

Therefore Tracy tried; but he did not succeed. He was refused admission with a good deal of promptness, and was advised to go back home, where he belonged, not come here taking honest men's bread out of their mouths. Tracy began to realize that the situation was desperate, and the thought made him cold to the marrow. He said to himself, "So there is an aristocracy of position here, and an aristocracy of prosperity, and apparently there is also an aristocracy of the ins as opposed to the outs, and I am with the outs. So the ranks grow daily here. Plainly there are all kinds of castes here, and only one that I belong to—the outcasts." But he couldn't even smile at his small joke, although he was obliged to confess that he had a rather good opinion of it. He was feeling so defeated and miserable by this time that he could no longer look with philosophical complacency on the horse-play of the young fellows in the upper rooms at night. At first it had been pleasant to see them unbend and have a good time after having so well earned it by the labors of the day, but now it all rasped upon his feelings and his dignity. He lost patience with the spectacle. When they were feeling good they shouted, they scuffled, they sang songs, they romped about the place like cattle, and they generally wound up with a pillow-fight, in which they banged each other over the head, and threw the pillows in all directions, and every now and then he got a buffet himself; and they were always inviting him to join in. They called him "Johnny Bull," and invited him with excessive familiarity to take a hand. At first he had endured all this with good-nature, but latterly he had shown by his manner that it was distinctly distasteful to him, and very soon he saw a change in the manner of these young people toward him. They were souring on him, as they would have expressed it in their language. He had never been what might be called popular. That was hardly the phrase for it; he had merely been liked, but now dislike for him was growing. His case was not helped by the fact that he was out of luck, couldn't get work, didn't belong to a union, and couldn't gain admission to one. He got a good many slights of that small, ill-defined sort that you can't quite put your finger on, and it was manifest there was that only one thing which protected him from open insult, and that was his muscle. These young people had seen him exercising mornings, after his cold sponge bath, and they had perceived by his performance and the build of his body that he was athletic, and also versed in boxing. He felt pretty naked now, recognizing that he was shorn of all respect except respect for his fists. One night when he entered his room he found about a dozen of the young fellows there carrying on a very lively conversation punctuated with horse-laughter. The talking ceased instantly, and the frank affront of a dead silence followed. He said:

"Good evening, gentlemen," and sat down.

There was no response. He flushed to the temples, but forced himself to maintain silence. He sat there in this uncomfortable stillness some time, then got up and went out.

The moment he had disappeared he heard a prodigious shout of laughter break forth. He saw that their plain purpose had been to insult him. He ascended to the flat roof, hoping to be able to cool down his spirit there and get back his tranquillity. He found the young tinner up there, alone and brooding, and entered into conversation with him. They were pretty fairly matched now in unpopularity and general ill-luck and misery, and they had no trouble in meeting upon this common ground with advantage and something of comfort to both. But Tracy's movements had been watched, and in a few minutes the tormentors came straggling one after another to the roof, where they began to stroll up and down in an apparently purposeless way. But presently they fell to dropping remarks that were evidently aimed at Tracy, and some of them at the tinner. The ringleader of this little mob was a short-haired bully and amateur prize-fighter named Allen, who was accustomed to lording it over the upper floor, and had more than once shown a disposition to make trouble with Tracy. Now there was an occasional cat-call, and hootings, and whistlings, and finally the diversion of an exchange of connected remarks was introduced:

"How many does it take to make a pair?"

"Well, two generally makes a pair, but sometimes there ain't stuff enough in them to make a whole pair." General laugh.

"What were you saying about the English awhile ago?"

"Oh, nothing; the English are all right, only—I—"

"What was it you *said* about them?"

"Oh, I only said they swallow well."

"Swallow better than other people?"

"Oh, yes; the English swallow a good deal better than other people."

"What is it they swallow best?"

"Oh, insults." Another general laugh.

"Pretty hard to make 'em fight, ain't it?"

"No, 'tain't hard to make 'em fight."

"Ain't it, really?"

"No, 'tain't hard. It's impossible." Another laugh.

"This one's kind of spiritless, that's certain."

"*Couldn't* be the other way—in his case."

"Why?"

"Don't you know the secret of his birth?"

"No! Has *he* got a secret of his birth?"

"You bet he has."

"What is it?"

"His father was a wax-figger."

Allen came strolling by where the pair were sitting, stopped, and said to the tinner:

"How are you off for friends these days?"

"Well enough off."

"Got a good many?"

"Well, as many as I need."

"A friend is valuable, sometimes—as a protector, you know. What do you reckon would happen if I was to snatch your cap off and slap you in the face with it?"

"Please don't trouble me, Mr. Allen. I ain't doing anything to you."

"You answer me! What do you reckon would happen?"

"Well, I don't know."

Tracy spoke up with a good deal of deliberation, and said:

"Don't trouble the young fellow. I can tell you what would happen."

"Oh, you can, can you? Boys, Johnny Bull can tell us what would happen if I was to snatch this chump's cap off and slap him in the face with it. Now you'll see."

He snatched the cap and struck the youth in the face, and before he could inquire what was going to happen it had already happened, and he was warming the tin with the broad of his back. Instantly there was a rush, and shouts of "A ring! a ring! make a ring! Fair play all round! Johnny's grit; give him a chance."

The ring was quickly chalked on the tin, and Tracy found himself as eager to begin as he could have been if his antagonist had been a prince instead of a mechanic. At bottom he was a little surprised at this, because although his theories had been all in that direction for some time, he was not prepared to find himself actually eager to measure strength with quite so common a man as this ruffian. In a moment all the windows in the neighborhood were filled with people, and the roofs also. The men squared off, and the fight began. But Allen stood no chance whatever against the young Englishman. Neither in muscle nor in science was he his equal. He measured his length on the tin time and again; in fact, as fast as he could get up he went down again, and the applause was kept up in liberal fashion from all the neighborhood around. Finally, Allen had to be helped up. Then Tracy declined to punish him further and the fight was at an end. Allen was carried off by some of his friends in a very much humbled condition, his face black-and-blue and bleeding, and Tracy was at once surrounded by the young fellows, who congratulated him, and told him that he had done the whole house a service, and that from this out Mr. Allen would be a little more particular about how he handed slights and insults and maltreatment around among the boarders.

Tracy was a hero now, and exceedingly popular. Perhaps nobody had ever been quite so popular on that upper floor before.

But if being discountenanced by these young fellows had been hard to bear, their lavish commendations and approval and hero-worship were harder still to endure. He felt degraded, but he did not allow himself to analyze the reasons why too closely. He was content to satisfy himself with the suggestion that he looked upon himself as degraded by the public spectacle which he had made of himself, fighting on a tin roof for the delectation of everybody a block or two around. But he wasn't entirely satisfied with that explanation of it. Once he went a little too far, and wrote in his diary that his case was worse than that of the prodigal son. He said the prodigal son merely fed swine; he didn't have to chum with them. But he struck that out, and said, "All men are equal. I will not disown my principles. These men are as good as I am."

Tracy was become popular on the lower floors also. Everybody was grateful for Allen's reduction to the ranks, and for his trans-formation from a doer of outrages to a mere threatener of them. The young girls, of whom there were half a dozen, showed many attentions to Tracy, particularly that boarding-house pet Hattie, the landlady's daughter. She said to him, very sweetly:

"I think you're ever so nice."

And when he said, "I'm glad you think so, Miss Hattie," she said, still more sweetly:

"Don't call me Miss Hattie—call me Puss."

Ah, here was promotion! He had struck the summit. There were no higher heights to climb in that boarding-house. His popu-larity was complete.

In the presence of people Tracy showed a tranquil outside, but his heart was being eaten out of him by distress and despair.

In a little while he should be out of money, and then what should he do? He wished now that he had borrowed a little more liberally from that stranger's store. He found it impossible to sleep. A single torturing, terrifying thought went racking round and round in his head, wearing a groove in his brain: What should he do—what was to become of him? And along with it began to intrude a something presently which was very like a wish that he had not joined the great and noble ranks of martyr-dom, but had stayed at home and been content to be merely an earl and nothing better, with nothing more to do in this world of a useful sort than an earl finds to do. But he smothered that part of his thought as well as he could; he made every effort to drive it away, and with fair success, but he couldn't keep it from intruding a little now and then, and when it intruded it came suddenly and nipped him like a bite, a sting, a burn. He recognized that thought by the peculiar sharpness of its pang. The others were painful enough, but that one cut to the quick when it came. Night after night he lay tossing to the music of the hideous snoring of the honest breadwinners until two and three o'clock in the morning, then got up and took refuge on the roof, where he sometimes got a nap and sometimes failed entirely. His appetite was leaving him, and the zest of life was going along with it. Finally, one day, being near the imminent verge of total discouragement, he said to himself—and took occasion to blush privately when he said it, "If my father knew what my American name is—he—well, my duty to my father rather *requires* that I furnish him my name. I have no right to make his days and nights unhappy, I can do enough unhappiness for the family all by myself. Really he ought to know what my American name is." He thought over it awhile, and framed a cablegram in his mind to this effect:

"My American name is Howard Tracy."

That wouldn't be suggesting anything. His father could understand that as he chose, and doubtless he would understand it as it was meant, as a dutiful and affectionate desire on the part of a son to make his old father happy for a moment. Continuing his train of thought, Tracy said to himself, "Ah, but if he should cable me to come home! I—I—couldn't do that—I *mustn't* do that. I've started out on a mission, and I mustn't turn my back on it in cowardice. No, no, I couldn't go home, at—at—least I shouldn't want to go home." After a reflective pause: "Well, maybe—perhaps—it would be my *duty* to go in the circumstances; he's very old, and he does need me by him to stay his footsteps down the long hill that inclines westward toward the sunset of his life. Well, I'll think about that. Yes, of course it wouldn't be right to stay here. I—if I —well, perhaps I could just drop him a line and put it off a little while and satisfy him in that way. It would be—well, it would mar everything to have him require me to come instantly." Another reflective pause—then: "And yet if he should do that I don't know but—oh, dear me—*home!* how good it sounds! and a body is excusable for wanting to see his home again, now and then, anyway."

He went to one of the telegraph offices in the avenue and got the first end of what Barrow called the "usual Washington courtesy," where "they treat you as a tramp until they find out you're a Congressman, and then they slobber all over you." There was a boy of seventeen on duty there, tying his shoe. He had his foot on a chair and his back turned toward the wicket. He glanced over his shoulder, took Tracy's measure, turned back, and went on tying his shoe. Tracy finished writing his telegram and waited, still waited, and still waited for that performance to finish, but there didn't seem to be any finish to it; so finally Tracy said:

"Can't you take my telegram?"

The youth looked over his shoulder and said, by his manner, not his words:

"Don't you think you could wait a minute if you tried?"

However, he got the shoe tied at last, and came and took the telegram, glanced over it, then looked up surprised at Tracy. There was something in his look that bordered upon respect, almost reverence, it seemed to Tracy, although he had been so long without anything of this kind he was not sure that he knew the signs of it.

The boy read the address aloud with pleased expression in face and voice.

"The Earl of Rossmore! Cracky! Do you know him?"

"Yes."

"Is that so? Does he know you?"

"Well—yes."

"Well, I swear! Will he answer you?"

"I think he will."

"Will he, though? Where'll you have it sent?"

"Oh, nowhere. I'll call here and get it. When shall I call?"

"Oh, I don't know—I'll send it to you. Where shall I send it? Give me your address; I'll send it to you soon's it comes."

But Tracy didn't propose to do this. He had acquired the boy's admiration and deferential respect, and he wasn't willing to throw these precious things away, a result sure to follow if he should give the address of that boarding-house. So he said again that he would call and get the telegram, and went his way.

He idled along, reflecting. He said to himself, "There *is* something pleasant about being respected. I have acquired the respect of Mr. Allen and some of those others, and almost the deference of some of them on pure merit, for having thrashed Allen. While their respect and their deference—if it is deference—is pleasant, a deference based upon a sham, a shadow, does really seem pleasanter still. It's no real merit to be in correspondence with an earl, and yet, after all, that boy makes me feel as if there was."

The cablegram was actually gone home! The thought of it gave him an immense uplift. He walked with a lighter tread. His heart was full of happiness. He threw aside all hesitancies, and confessed to himself that he was glad through and through that he was going to give up this experiment and go back to his home again. His eagerness to get his father's answer began to grow now, and it grew with marvelous celerity after it began. He waited an hour, walking about, putting in his time as well as he could, but interested in nothing that came under his eye, and at last he presented himself at the office again and asked if any answer had come yet. The boy said:

"No, no answer yet"; then glanced at the clock and added, "I don't think it's likely you'll get one to-day."

"Why not?"

"Well, you see it's getting pretty late. You can't always tell where'bouts a man is when he's on the other side, and you can't always find him just the minute you want him, and you see it's getting about six o'clock now, and over there it's pretty late at night."

"Why, yes," said Tracy, "I hadn't thought of that."

"Yes, pretty late now—half-past ten or eleven. Oh, yes, you probably won't get any answer to-night."

14

"Mechanics' Debating Club" again—Tracy is comforted by
Barrow's remarks—"Fool or *no* fool, he would grab it"—
"Earldom! oh, yes, take it if it offers"

So Tracy went home to supper. The odors in that supper-room
seemed more strenuous and more horrible than ever before, and
he was happy in the thought that he was so soon to be free from
them again. When the supper was over he hardly knew whether
he had eaten any of it or not, and he certainly hadn't heard any
of the conversation. His heart had been dancing all the time, his
thoughts had been far away from these things, and in the visions
of his mind the sumptuous appointments of his father's castle had
risen before him without rebuke. Even the plushed flunky, that
walking symbol of a sham inequality, had not been unpleasant
to his dreaming view. After the meal Barrow said:

"Come with me. I'll give you a jolly evening."

"Very good. Where are you going?"

"To my club."

"What club is that?"

"Mechanics' Debating Club."

Tracy shuddered slightly. He didn't say anything about having
visited that place himself. Somehow he didn't quite relish the
memory of that time. The sentiments which had made his former
visit there so enjoyable, and filled him with such enthusiasm, had
undergone a gradual change, and they had rotted away to such
a degree that he couldn't contemplate another visit there with
anything strongly resembling delight; in fact, he was a little
ashamed to go. He didn't want to go there and find out by the
rude impact of the thought of those people upon his reorganized

condition of mind, how sharp the change had been. He would have preferred to stay away. He expected that now he should hear nothing except sentiments which would be a reproach to him in his changed mental attitude, and he rather wished he might be excused. And yet he didn't quite want to say that; he didn't want to show how he did feel, or show any disinclination to go; and so he forced himself to go along with Barrow, privately purposing to take an early opportunity to get away.

After the essayist of the evening had read his paper, the chairman announced that the debate would now be upon the subject of the previous meeting, "The American Press." It saddened the backsliding disciple to hear this announcement. It brought up too many reminiscences. He wished he had happened upon some other subject. But the debate began, and he sat still and listened.

In the course of the discussion one of the speakers—a blacksmith named Tompkins—arraigned all monarchs and all lords on the earth for their cold selfishness in retaining their unearned dignities. He said that no monarch and no son of a monarch, no lord and no son of a lord, ought to be able to look his fellow-man in the face without shame. Shame for consenting to keep his unearned titles, property, and privileges at the expense of other people; shame for consenting to remain, on any terms, in dishonorable possession of these things, which represented bygone robberies and wrongs inflicted upon the general people of the nation. He said: "If there were a lord or the son of a lord here I would like to reason with him, and try to show him how unfair and how selfish his position is. I would try to persuade him to relinquish it, take his place among men on equal terms, earn the bread he eats, and hold of slight value all deference paid him because of artificial position, all reverence not the just due of his own personal merits."

Tracy seemed to be listening to utterances of his own made in talks with his radical friends in England. It was as if some eavesdropping phonograph had treasured up his words and brought them across the Atlantic to accuse him with them in the hour of his defection and retreat. Every word spoken by this stranger seemed to leave a blister on Tracy's conscience, and by the time the speech was finished he felt that he was all conscience and one blister. This man's deep compassion for the enslaved and oppressed millions in Europe who had to bear with the contempt of that small class above them, throned upon shining heights whose paths were shut against them, was the very thing he had often uttered himself. The pity in this man's voice and words was the very twin of the pity that used to reside in his own heart and come from his own lips when he thought of these oppressed peoples.

The homeward tramp was accomplished in brooding silence. It was a silence most grateful to Tracy's feelings. He wouldn't have broken it for anything; for he was ashamed of himself all the way through to his spine. He kept saying to himself:

"How unanswerable it all is—how absolutely unanswerable! It *is* basely, degradingly selfish to keep those unearned honors, and —and—oh, hang it, nobody but a cur—"

"What an idiotic damned speech that Tompkins made!"

This outburst was from Barrow. It flooded Tracy's demoralized soul with waters of refreshment. These were the darlingest words the poor vacillating young apostate had ever heard—for they whitewashed his shame for him, and that is a good service to have when you can't get the best of all verdicts: self-acquittal.

"Come up to my room and smoke a pipe, Tracy."

Tracy had been expecting this invitation, and had had his declination all ready; but he was glad enough to accept now. Was it possible that a reasonable argument could be made against that man's desolating speech? He was burning to hear Barrow try it. He knew how to start him and keep him going; it was to seem to combat his positions—a process effective with most people.

"What is it you object to in Tompkins's speech, Barrow?"

"Oh, the leaving out of the factor of human nature; requiring another man to do what you wouldn't do yourself."

"Do you mean—"

"Why, here's what I mean; it's very simple. Tompkins is a black-smith; has a family; works for wages; and hard, too—fooling around won't furnish the bread. Suppose it should turn out that

by the death of somebody in England he is suddenly an earl—
income, half a million dollars a year. What would he do?"

"Well, I—I suppose he would have to decline to—"

"Man, he would grab it in a second!"

"Do you really think he would?"

"Think?—I don't think anything about it, I know it."

"Why?"

"Why? Because he's not a fool."

"So you think that if he were a fool, he—"

"No, I don't. Fool or *no* fool, he would grab it. Anybody would.
Anybody that's alive. And I've seen dead people that would get
up and go for it. I would myself."

This was balm, this was healing, this was rest and peace and
comfort.

"But I thought you were opposed to nobilities?"

"Transmissible ones, yes. But that's nothing. I'm opposed to
millionaires, but it would be dangerous to offer me the position."

"You'd take it?"

"I would leave the funeral of my dearest enemy to go and assume its burdens and responsibilities."

Tracy thought awhile, then said:

"I don't know that I quite get the bearings of your position.
You say you are opposed to hereditary nobilities, and yet if you
had the chance you would—"

"Take one? In a minute I would. And there isn't a mechanic in
that entire club that wouldn't. There isn't a lawyer, doctor, editor,
author, tinker, loafer, railroad president, saint—land, there isn't a
human *being* in the United States that wouldn't jump at the
chance!"

"Except me," said Tracy, softly.

"Except you!" Barrow could hardly get the words out, his scorn
so choked him. And he couldn't get any further than that form
of words; it seemed to dam his flow utterly. He got up and came
and glared upon Tracy in a kind of outraged and unappeasable
way, and said again, "Except *you!*" He walked around him—in-
specting him from one point of view and then another, and
relieving his soul now and then by exploding that formula at him:

"Except *you!*" Finally he slumped down into his chair with the air of one who gives it up, and said:

"He's straining his viscera and he's breaking his heart trying to get some low-down job that a good dog wouldn't have, and yet wants to let on that if he had a chance to scoop an earldom he wouldn't do it. Tracy, don't put this kind of a strain on me. Lately I'm not as strong as I was."

"Well, I wasn't meaning to put a strain on you, Barrow; I was only meaning to intimate that if an earldom ever does fall in my way—"

"There—I wouldn't give myself any worry about *that* if I was you. And, besides, I can settle what you would do. Are you any different from me?"

"Well—no."

"Are you any better than me?"

"Oh—er—why, certainly not."

"Are you as *good?* Come!"

"Indeed, I—the fact is you take me so suddenly—"

"Suddenly? What is there sudden about it? It isn't a difficult question, is it? Or doubtful? Just measure us on the only fair lines—the lines of merit—and of course you'll admit that a journeyman chair-maker that earns his twenty dollars a week, and has had the good and genuine culture of contact with men, and care, and hardship, and failure, and success, and downs and ups and ups and downs, is just a trifle the superior of a young fellow like you, who doesn't know how to do anything that's valuable, can't earn his living in any secure and steady way, hasn't had any experience of life and its seriousness, hasn't any culture but the artificial culture of books, which adorns but doesn't really educate—come! if *I* wouldn't scorn an earldom, what the devil right have *you* to do it?"

Tracy dissembled his joy, though he wanted to thank the chair-maker for that last remark. Presently a thought struck him, and he spoke up briskly and said:

"But look here, I really can't quite get the hang of your notions—your principles, if they are principles. You are inconsistent. You are opposed to aristocracies, yet you'd take an earldom if you could. Am I to understand that you don't blame an earl for being and remaining an earl?"

"I certainly don't."

"And you wouldn't blame Tompkins, or yourself, or me, or anybody, for accepting an earldom if it was offered?"

"Indeed, I wouldn't."

"Well, then, whom *would* you blame?"

"The whole nation—any bulk and mass of population anywhere, in any country, that will put up with the infamy, the outrage, the insult of a hereditary aristocracy which *they* can't enter—and on absolutely free and equal terms."

"Come, aren't you beclouding yourself with distinctions that are not differences?"

"Indeed, I am not. I am entirely clear-headed about this thing. If I could extirpate an aristocratic system by declining its honors, *then* I should be a rascal to accept them. And if enough of the mass would join me to make the extirpation possible, *then* I should be a rascal to do otherwise than help in the attempt."

"I believe I understand—yes, I think I get the idea. You have no blame for the lucky few who naturally decline to vacate the pleasant nest they were born into; you only despise the all-powerful and stupid mass of the nation for allowing the nest to exist."

"That's it, that's it! You *can* get a simple thing through your head if you work at it long enough."

"Thanks."

"Don't mention it. And I'll give you some sound advice: when you go back, if you find your nation up and ready to abolish that hoary affront, lend a hand; but if that isn't the state of things and you get a chance at an earldom, don't you be a fool—you take it."

Tracy responded with earnestness and enthusiasm:

"As I live, I'll do it!"

Barrow laughed.

"I never saw such a fellow. I begin to think you've got a good deal of imagination. With you, the idlest fancy freezes into a reality at a breath. Why, you looked, then, as if it wouldn't astonish you if you did tumble into an earldom." Tracy blushed.

Barrow added: "Earldom! Oh, yes, take it if it offers; but meantime we'll go on looking around, in a modest way, and if you get a chance to superintend a sausage-stuffer at six or eight dollars a week, you just trade off the earldom for a last year's almanac and stick to the sausage-stuffing."

15

"You forgot to pay your board"—"I've been robbed"—Mr. Allen among the missing, likewise other things—The cablegram: "Thanks"—Despair of Tracy—"You've got to amuse your mind"

TRACY WENT to bed happy once more, at rest in his mind once more. He had started out on a high emprise—that was to his credit, he argued; he had fought the best fight he could, considering the odds against him—that was to his credit; he had been defeated—certainly there was nothing discreditable in that. Being defeated, he had a right to retire with the honors of war and go back without prejudice to the position in the world's society to which he had been born. Why not? Even the rabid republican chair-maker would do that. Yes, his conscience was comfortable once more.

He woke refreshed, happy, and eager for his cablegram. He had been born an aristocrat, he had been a democrat for a time, he was now an aristocrat again. He marveled to find that this final change was not merely intellectual, it had invaded his feeling; and he also marveled to note that this feeling seemed a good deal less artificial than any he had entertained in his system for a long time. He could also have noted, if he had thought of it, that his bearing had stiffened overnight, and that his chin had lifted itself a shade. Arrived in the basement, he was about to enter the breakfast-room when he saw old Marsh in the dim light of a corner of the hall, beckoning him with his finger to approach. The blood welled slowly up in Tracy's cheek, and he said, with a grade of injured dignity almost ducal:

"Is that for me?"

"Yes."

"What is the purpose of it?"

"I want to speak to you—in private."

"This spot is private enough for me."

Marsh was surprised; and not particularly pleased. He approached and said:

"Oh, in public, then, if you prefer. Though it hasn't been my way."

The boarders gathered to the spot, interested.

"Speak out," said Tracy. "What is it you want?"

"Well, haven't you—er—forgot something?"

"I? I'm not aware of it."

"Oh, you're not? Now you stop and think a minute."

"I refuse to stop and think. It doesn't interest me. If it interests you, speak out."

"Well, then," said Marsh, raising his voice to a slightly angry pitch, "you forgot to pay your board yesterday—if you're *bound* to have it public."

Oh, yes; this heir to an annual million or so had been dreaming and soaring, and had forgotten that pitiful three or four dollars. For penalty he must have it coarsely flung in his face in the presence of these people—people in whose countenances was already beginning to dawn an uncharitable enjoyment of the situation.

"Is *that* all! Take your money and give your terrors a rest."

Tracy's hand went down into his pocket with angry decision. But—it didn't come out. The color began to ebb out of his face. The countenances about him showed a growing interest; and some of them a heightened satisfaction. There was an uncomfortable pause; then he forced out, with difficulty, the words:

"I've—been robbed!"

Old Marsh's eyes flamed up with Spanish fire, and he exclaimed:

"Robbed, is it? *That's* your tune? It's too old—been played in this house too often; everybody plays it that can't get work when he wants it, and won't work when he can get it. Trot out Mr. Allen, somebody, and let *him* take a toot at it. It's *his* turn next; *he* forgot, too, last night. I'm laying for him."

One of the negro women came scrambling down stairs as pale as a sorrel horse with consternation and excitement:

"Misto Marsh, Misto Allen's skipped out!"

"What!"

"Yes-sah, and cleaned out his room *clean;* tuck bofe towels en de soap!"

"You lie, you hussy!"

"It's jes' so, jes' as I tells you—en Misto Sumner's socks is gone, en Misto Naylor's yuther shirt."

Mr. Marsh was at boiling-point by this time. He turned upon Tracy.

"Answer up now—when are you going to settle?"

"To-day—since you seem to be in a hurry."

"*To-day*, is it? Sunday—and you out of work? I like that. Come —where are you going to get the money?"

Tracy's spirit was rising again. He proposed to impress these people.

"I am expecting a cablegram from home."

Old Marsh was caught out, with the surprise of it. The idea was so immense, so extravagant, that he couldn't get his breath at first. When he did get it, it came rancid with sarcasm.

"A *cablegram*—think of it, ladies and gents, he's expecting a cablegram! *He's* expecting a cablegram—this duffer, this scrub, this bilk! From his father—eh? Yes—without a doubt. A dollar or two a word—oh, that's nothing—*they* don't mind a little thing like that—*this* kind's fathers don't. Now his father is—er—well, I reckon his father—"

"My father is an English earl!"

The crowd fell back aghast—aghast at the sublimity of the young loafer's "cheek." Then they burst into a laugh that made the windows rattle. Tracy was too angry to realize that he had done a foolish thing. He said:

"Stand aside, please. I—"

"Wait a minute, your lordship," said Marsh, bowing low; "where is your lordship going?"

"For the cablegram. Let me pass."

"Excuse me, your lordship, you'll stay right where you are."

"What do you mean by that?"

"I mean that I didn't begin to keep boarding-house yesterday. It means that I am not the kind that can be taken in by every hack-driver's son that comes loafing over here because he can't bum a living at home. It means that you can't skip out on any such—"

Tracy made a step toward the old man, but Mrs. Marsh sprang between, and said:

"Don't, Mr. Tracy, please." She turned to her husband and said, "*Do* bridle your tongue. What has he done to be treated so? Can't you *see* he has lost his mind with trouble and distress? He's not responsible."

"Thank your kind heart, madam, but I've not lost my mind; and if I can have the mere privilege of stepping to the telegraph-office—"

"Well, you can't!" cried Marsh.

"—or sending—"

"Sending! That beats everything. If there's anybody that's fool enough to go on such a chuckle-headed errand—"

"Here comes Mr. Barrow—he will go for me. Barrow—"

A brisk fire of exclamation broke out:

"Say, Barrow, he's expecting a cablegram!"

"Cablegram from his father, you know!"

"Yes—cablegram from the wax-figger!"

"And say, Barrow, this fellow's an earl—take off your hat, pull down your vest!"

"Yes, he's come off and forgot his crown that he wears Sundays. He's cabled over to his poppy to send it."

"You step out and get that cablegram, Barrow; his majesty's a little lame to-day."

"Oh, stop," cried Barrow; "give the man a chance." He turned, and said with some severity: "Tracy, what's the matter with you? What kind of foolishness is this you've been talking? You ought to have more sense."

"I've not been talking foolishness; and if you'll go to the telegraph-office—"

"Oh, don't talk so. I'm your friend in trouble and out of it, before your face and behind your back, for anything in *reason:* but you've lost your head, you see, and this moonshine about a cablegram—"

"*I'll* go there and ask for it!"

"Thank you from the bottom of my heart, Brady. Here, I'll give you a written order for it. Fly now and fetch it. We'll soon see!"

Brady flew. Immediately the sort of quiet began to steal over the crowd which means dawning doubt, misgiving; and might be translated into the words, "Maybe he *is* expecting a cablegram— maybe he *has* got a father somewhere—maybe we've been just a little too fresh, just a shade too 'previous'!" Loud talk ceased; then the mutterings and low murmurings and whisperings died out. The crowd began to crumble apart. By ones and twos the fragments drifted to the breakfast-table. Barrow tried to bring Tracy in; but he said:

"Not yet, Barrow—presently."

Mrs. Marsh and Hattie tried, offering gentle and kindly persuasions; but he said:

"I would rather wait—till he comes."

Even old Marsh began to have suspicions that maybe he had been a trifle too "brash," as he called it in the privacy of his soul, and he pulled himself together and started toward Tracy with invitation in his eyes; but Tracy warned him off with a gesture which was quite positive and eloquent. Then followed the stillest quarter of an hour which had ever been known in that house at that time of day. It was so still, and so solemn withal, that when somebody's cup slipped from his fingers and landed in his plate the shock made people start, and the sharp sound seemed as indecorous there and as out of place as if a coffin and mourners were imminent and being waited for. And at last when Brady's feet came clattering down the stairs the sacrilege seemed unbearable. Everybody rose softly and turned toward the door, where stood Tracy; then, with a common impulse, moved a step or two in that direction, and stopped. While they gazed young Brady arrived, panting, and put into Tracy's hand—sure enough—an envelope. Tracy fastened a bland, victorious eye upon the gazers, and kept it there till one by one they dropped their eyes, vanquished and embarrassed. Then he tore open the telegram and glanced at its message. The yellow paper fell from his fingers and fluttered to the floor, and his face turned white. There was nothing there but one word:

"Thanks."

The humorist of the house, the tall, raw-boned Billy Nash, caulker from the navy yard, was standing in the rear of the crowd. In the midst of the pathetic silence that was now brooding over the place and moving some few hearts there toward compassion, he began to whimper, then he put his handkerchief to his eyes and buried his face in the neck of the bashfulest young fellow in the company, a navy-yard blacksmith, shrieked, "Oh, pappy, how *could* you!" and began to bawl like a teething baby, if one may imagine a baby with the energy and the devastating voice of a jackass.

So perfect was the imitation of a child's cry, and so vast the scale of it, and so ridiculous the aspect of the performer, that all gravity was swept from the place as if by a hurricane, and almost everybody there joined in the crash of laughter provoked by the exhibition. Then the small mob began to take its revenge—revenge for the discomfort and apprehension it had brought upon itself by its own too rash freshness of a little while before. It guyed its poor victim, baited him, worried him, as dogs do with a cornered cat. The victim answered back with defiances and challenges which included everybody, and which only gave the sport new spirit and variety; but when he changed his tactics and began to single out individuals and invite them by name, the fun lost its funniness and the interest of the show died out, along with the noise.

Finally Marsh was about to take an innings, but Barrow said:

"Never mind now—leave him alone. You've no account with him but a money account. I'll take care of that myself."

The distressed and worried landlady gave Barrow a fervently grateful look for his championship of the abused stranger; and the pet of the house, a very prism in her cheap but ravishing Sunday rig, blew him a kiss from the tips of her fingers and said, with the darlingest smile and a sweet little toss of her head:

"You're the only man here, and I'm going to set my cap for you, you dear old thing!"

"For shame, Puss! How you talk! I *never* saw such a child!"

It took a good deal of argument and persuasion—that is to say, petting, under these disguises—to get Tracy to entertain the idea of breakfast. He at first said he would never eat again in that house; and added that he had enough firmness of character, he trusted, to enable him to starve like a man when the alternative was to eat insult with his bread.

When he had finished his breakfast, Barrow took him to his room, furnished him a pipe, and said, cheerily:

"*Now*, old fellow, take in your battle-flag out of the wet; you're not in the hostile camp any more. You're a little upset by your troubles, and that's natural enough, but don't let your mind run on them any more than you can help; drag your thoughts away from your troubles—by the ears, by the heels, or any other way, so you manage it; it's the healthiest thing a body can do; dwelling on troubles is deadly, just deadly—and that's the softest name there is for it. You must keep your mind amused—you must, indeed."

"Oh, miserable me!"

"*Don't!* There's just pure heart-break in that tone. It's just as I say; you've got to get right down to it and amuse your mind, as if it was salvation."

"They're easy words to say, Barrow, but how am I going to amuse, entertain, divert a mind that finds itself suddenly assaulted and overwhelmed by disaster of a sort not dreamed of and not provided for? No-no, the bare idea of amusement is repulsive to my feelings. Let us talk of deaths and funerals."

"No—not yet. That would be giving up the ship. We'll not give up the ship yet. I'm going to amuse you; I sent Brady out for the wherewithal before you finished breakfast."

"You did? What is it?"

"Come, this is a good sign—curiosity. Oh, there's hope for you yet."

16

The collaborative art collection—The artists—"The cannon's our trademark"—Tracy's mind *is* amused

BRADY ARRIVED with a box, and departed, after saying:

"They're finishing one up, but they'll be along as soon as it's done."

Barrow took a frameless oil portrait a foot square from the box, set it up in a good light, without comment, and reached for another, taking a fugitive glance at Tracy meantime. The stony solemnity in Tracy's face remained as it was, and gave out no sign of interest. Barrow placed the second portrait beside the first, and stole another glance while reaching for a third. The stone image softened a shade. No. 3 forced the ghost of a smile, No. 4 swept indifference wholly away, and No. 5 started a laugh which was still in good and hearty condition when No. 14 took its place in the row.

"Oh, *you're* all right yet," said Barrow. "You see, you're not past amusement."

The pictures were fearful as to color, and atrocious as to drawing and expression; but the feature which squelched animosity and made them funny was a feature which could not achieve its full force in a single picture, but required the wonder-working assistance of repetition. One loudly dressed mechanic in stately attitude, with his hand on a cannon, ashore, and a ship riding at anchor in the offing—this is merely odd; but when one sees the same cannon and the same ship in fourteen pictures in a row, and a different mechanic standing watch in each, the thing gets to be funny.

"Explain—explain these aberrations," said Tracy.

"Well, they are not the achievement of a single intellect, a single talent—it takes two to do these miracles. They are collaborations; the one artist does the figure, the other the accessories. The figure-artist is a German shoemaker with an untaught passion for art, the other is a simple-hearted old Yankee sailor-man whose possibilities are strictly limited to his ship, his cannon, and his patch of petrified sea. They work these things up from twenty-five-cent tintypes; they get six dollars apiece for them, and they can grind out a couple a day when they strike what they call a boost—that is, an inspiration."

"People actually pay money for these calumnies?"

"They actually do—and quite willingly, too. And these abortionists could double their trade and work the women in if Captain Saltmarsh could whirl a horse in, or a piano, or a guitar, in place of his cannon. The fact is, he fatigues the market with that cannon. Even the male market, I mean. These fourteen in the procession are not all satisfied. One is an old "independent" fireman, and he wants an engine in place of the cannon; another is a mate of a tug, and wants a tug in place of the ship—and so on, and so on. But the captain can't make a tug that is deceptive, and a fire-engine is many flights beyond his power."

"This *is* a most extraordinary form of robbery. I never have heard of anything like it. It's interesting."

"Yes, and so are the artists. They are perfectly honest men, and sincere. And the old sailor-man is full of sound religion, and is as devoted a student of the Bible and misquoter of it as you can find anywhere. I don't know a better man or kinder-hearted old soul than Saltmarsh, although he does swear a little sometimes."

"He seems to be perfect. I want to know him, Barrow."

"You'll have the chance. I guess I hear them coming now. We'll draw them out on their art, if you like."

The artists arrived and shook hands with great heartiness. The German was forty and a little fleshy, with a shiny bald head and a kindly face and deferential manner. Captain Saltmarsh was sixty, tall, erect, powerfully built, with coal-black hair and whiskers, and he had a well-tanned complexion, and a gait and countenance that were full of command, confidence, and decision. His horny hands and wrists were covered with tattoo-marks, and when his lips parted his teeth showed up white and blemishless. His voice was the effortless deep bass of a church organ, and would disturb the tranquillity of a gas flame fifty yards away.

"They're wonderful pictures," said Barrow. "We've been examining them."

"It is very bleasant dot you like dem," said Handel, the German, greatly pleased. "Und you, Herr Tracy, you haf peen bleased mit dem, too, alretty?"

"I can honestly say I have never seen anything just like them before."

"Schön!" cried the German, delighted. "You hear, Gaptain? Here is a chentleman, yes, vot abbreciate unser aart."

The Captain was charmed, and said:

"Well, sir, we're thankful for a compliment yet, though they're not as scarce now as they used to be before we made a reputation."

"Getting the reputation is the uphill time in most things, Captain."

"It's so. It ain't enough to know how to reef a gasket, you got to make the mate know you know it. That's reputation. The good word, said at the right time, that's the word that makes us; and evil be to him that evil thinks, as Isaiah says."

"It's very relevant, and hits the point exactly," said Tracy. "Where did you study art, Captain?"

"I haven't studied; it's a natural gift."

"He is born mit dose cannon in him. He tondt haf to do noding, his chenius do all de vork. Of he is asleep, and take a pencil in his hand, out come a cannon. Py crashus, of he could do a clavier, of he could do a guitar, of he could do a vash-tub, it is a fortune; heiliger Yohanniss, it is yoost a fortune!"

"Well, it is an immense pity that the business is hindered and limited in this unfortunate way."

The Captain grew a trifle excited himself now.

"You've said it, Mr. Tracy! Hindered? Well, I should say so. Why, look here. This fellow here, No. 11, he's a hackman—a flourishing hackman, I may say. He wants his hack in this picture. Wants it where the cannon is. I got around that difficulty by telling him the cannon's our trade-mark, so to speak—proves that the picture's our work, and I was afraid if we left it out people wouldn't know for certain if it *was* a Saltmarsh-Handel—now you wouldn't yourself—"

"What, Captain? You wrong yourself, indeed you do. Any one who has once seen a genuine Saltmarsh-Handel is safe from imposture forever. Strip it, flay it, skin it out of every detail but the bare color and expression, and that man will still recognize it, still stop to worship—"

"Oh, how it makes me feel to hear dose oxpressions!"

—"still say to himself again, as he said a hundred times before, the art of the Saltmarsh-Handel is an art apart; there is nothing in the heavens above or in the earth beneath that resembles it—"

"Py chiminy, nur hören Sie einmal! In my life day haf I never heard so brecious worts."

"So I talked him out of the hack, Mr. Tracy, and he let up on that, and said put in a hearse, then—because he's chief mate of a hearse, but don't own it—stands a watch for wages, you know. But I can't do a hearse any more than I can a hack; so here we are—becalmed, you see. And it's the same with women and such. They come and they want a little johnry picture—"

"It's the accessories that make it a *genre?*"

"Yes—cannon, or cat, or any little thing like that, that you heave in to whoop up the effect. We could do a prodigious trade with the women if we could foreground the things they like, but they don't give a damn for artillery. Mine's the lack," continued the Captain, with a sigh. "Andy's end of the business is all right—I tell you, *he's* an artist from way back!"

"Yoost hear dot old man! He always talk 'poud me like dot," purred the pleased German.

"Look at his work yourself! Fourteen portraits in a row. And no two of them alike."

"Now that you speak of it, it is true; I hadn't noticed it before. It is very remarkable. Unique, I suppose."

"I should say so. That's the very *thing* about Andy—he *discriminates*. Discrimination's the thief of time—forty-ninth Psalm; but that ain't any matter; it's the honest thing, and it pays in the end."

"Yes, he certainly is great in that feature, one is obliged to admit it; but—now mind, I'm not really criticizing—don't you think he is just a trifle overstrong in technique?"

The Captain's face was knocked expressionless by this remark. It remained quite vacant while he muttered to himself: "Technique—technique—polytechnique—pyrotechnique; that's it, likely —fireworks—too much color." Then he spoke up with serenity and confidence, and said:

"Well, yes, he does pile it on pretty loud; but they all like it, you know—fact is, it's the life of the business. Take that No. 9 there—Evans the butcher. He drops into the stoodio as sober-colored as anything you ever see; *now* look at him. You can't tell him from scarlet-fever. Well, it pleases that butcher to death. I'm making a study of a sausage-wreath to hang on the cannon, and I don't really reckon I can do it right; but if I can, we can break the butcher."

"Unquestionably your confederate—I mean your—your fellow-craftsman—is a great colorist—"

"Oh, danke schön!—"

—"in fact, a quite extraordinary colorist; a colorist, I make bold to say, without imitator here or abroad—and with a most bold and effective touch, a touch like a battering-ram, and a manner so peculiar and romantic and extraneous and *ad libitum* and heart-searching that—that—he—he is an impressionist, I presume?"

"No," said the Captain, simply, "he is a Presbyterian."

"It accounts for it all—all—there's something divine about his art—soulful, unsatisfactory, yearning, dim-hearkening on the void horizon, vague-murmuring, to the spirit out of ultra-marine distances and far-sounding cataclysms of uncreated space—oh, if he —if he—has he ever tried distemper?"

The Captain answered up, with energy:

"Not if he knows himself! But his dog has, and—"

"Oh, no, it vas not *my* dog."

"Why, you *said* it was your dog."

"Oh, no, Captain, I—"

"It was a white dog, wasn't it, with his tail docked, and one ear gone, and—"

"Dot's him, dot's him!—der fery dog. Wy, py Chorge, dot dog he vould eat baint yoost de same like—"

"Well, never mind that now—'vast heaving—I never saw such a man. You start him on that dog and he'll dispute a year. Blamed if I haven't *seen* him keep it up a level two hours and a half."

"Why, Captain!" said Barrow. "I guess that must be hearsay."

"No, sir, no hearsay about it—he disputed with me."

"I don't see how you stood it."

"Oh, you've got to—if you run with Andy. But it's the only fault he's got."

"Ain't you afraid of acquiring it?"

"Oh, no," said the Captain, tranquilly; "no danger of that, I reckon."

The artists presently took their leave. Then Barrow put his hands on Tracy's shoulders and said:

"Look me in the eye, my boy. Steady, steady. There—it's just as I thought—hoped, anyway; *you're* all right, thank goodness. Nothing the matter with your mind. But don't do that again—even for fun. It isn't wise. They wouldn't have believed you if you'd *been* an earl's son. Why, they *couldn't*—don't you know that? What ever possessed you to take such a freak? But never mind about that; let's not talk of it. It was a mistake; you see that yourself."

"Yes—it *was* a mistake."

"Well, just drop it out of your mind; it's no harm; we all make them. Pull your courage together, and don't brood, and don't give up. I'm at your back, and we'll pull through, don't you be afraid."

When he was gone, Barrow walked the floor a good while, uneasy in his mind. He said to himself, "I'm troubled about him. He never would have made a break like that if he hadn't been a little off his balance. But I know what being out of work and no prospect ahead can do for a man. First it knocks the pluck out of him and drags his pride in the dirt; worry does the rest, and his mind gets shaky. I must talk to these people. No—if there's any humanity in them—and there is, at bottom—they'll be easier on him if they think his troubles have disturbed his reason. But I've *got* to find him some work; work's the only medicine for his disease. Poor devil! away off here, and not a friend."

17

No further cablegram—"If those ghastly artists want a confederate, I'm their man"—Tracy taken into partnership —Disappointments of materialization—The phonograph adapted to marine service—Utilization of wasted sewer gas

THE MOMENT Tracy was alone his spirits vanished away, and all the misery of his situation was manifest to him. To be moneyless and an object of the chair-maker's charity—this was bad enough; but his folly in proclaiming himself an earl's son to that scoffing and unbelieving crew, and, on top of that, the humiliating result —the recollection of these things was a sharper torture still. He made up his mind that he would never play earl's son again before a doubtful audience.

His father's answer was a blow he could not understand. At

times he thought his father imagined he could get work to do in America without any trouble, and was minded to let him try it and cure himself of his radicalism by hard, cold, disenchanting experience. That seemed the most plausible theory, yet he could not content himself with it. A theory that pleased him better was that this cablegram would be followed by another, of a gentler sort, requiring him to come home. Should he write and strike his flag and ask for a ticket home? Oh, no; that he couldn't *ever* do— at least, not yet. That cablegram would come, it certainly would. So he went from one telegraph-office to another every day for nearly a week, and asked if there was a cablegram for Howard Tracy. No, there wasn't any. So they answered him at first. Later, they said it before he had a chance to ask. Later still they merely shook their heads impatiently as soon as he came in sight. After that he was ashamed to go any more.

He was down in the lowest depths of despair now, for the harder Barrow tried to find work for him the more hopeless the possibilities seemed to grow. At last he said to Barrow:

"Look here. I want to make a confession. I have got down now to where I am not only willing to acknowledge to myself that I am a shabby creature and full of false pride, but am willing to acknowledge it to you. Well, I've been allowing you to wear your-self out hunting for work for me when there's been a chance open to me all the time. Forgive my pride—what was left of it. It is all gone now, and I've come to confess that if those ghastly artists want another confederate I'm their man—for at last I am dead to shame."

"No? Really, can you paint?"

"Not as badly as *they*. No, I don't claim that, for I am not a genius; in fact, I am a very indifferent amateur, a slouchy dabster, a mere artistic sarcasm; but drunk or asleep I can beat *those* buccaneers."

"Shake! I want to shout! Oh, I tell you, I am immensely de-lighted and relieved. Oh, just to work—that is life! No matter what the work is—that's of no consequence. Just work itself is bliss when a man's been starving for it. I've *been* there! Come right along, we'll hunt the old boys up. Don't you feel good? I tell you I do."

The freebooters were not at home. But their "works" were—displayed in profusion all about the little ratty studio. Cannon to the right of them, cannon to the left of them, cannon in front —it was Balaklava come again.

"Here's the uncontented hackman, Tracy. Buckle to—deepen the sea-green to turf, turn the ship into a hearse. Let the boys have a taste of your quality."

The artists arrived just as the last touch was put on. They stood transfixed with admiration.

"My souls, but she's a stunner, that hearse! The hackman will just go all to pieces when he sees that—won't he, Andy?"

"Oh, it is sphlennid, sphlennid! Herr Tracy, why haf you not said you vas a so sublime aartist? Lob' Gott, of you had lif'd in Paris you would be a Pree de Rome, dot's vot's de matter!"

The arrangements were soon made. Tracy was taken into full and equal partnership, and he went straight to work, with dash and energy, to reconstructing gems of art whose accessories had failed to satisfy. Under his hand, on that and succeeding days, artillery disappeared and the emblems of peace and commerce took its place—cats, hacks, sausages, tugs, fire-engines, pianos, guitars, rocks, gardens, flower-pots, landscapes—whatever was wanted, he flung it in; and the more out of place and absurd the required object was, the more joy he got out of fabricating it. The pirates were delighted, the customers applauded, the sex began to flock in, great was the prosperity of the firm. Tracy was obliged to confess to himself that there was something about work—even such grotesque and humble work as this—which most pleasantly satisfied a something in his nature which had never been satisfied before, and also gave him a strange new dignity in his own private view of himself.

The Unqualified Member from Cherokee Strip was in a state of deep dejection. For a good while now he had been leading a sort of life which was calculated to kill; for it had consisted in regularly alternating days of brilliant hope and black disappointment. The brilliant hopes were created by the magician Sellers, and they always promised that *now* he had got the trick sure, and would effectively influence that materialized cowboy to call at the Towers before night. The black disappointments consisted in the persistent and monotonous failure of these prophecies.

At the date which this history has now reached, Sellers was appalled to find that the usual remedy was inoperative, and that Hawkins's low spirits refused absolutely to lift. Something must be done, he reflected; it was heart-breaking, this woe, this smile-less misery, this dull despair that looked out from his poor friend's face. Yes, he must be cheered up. He mused awhile, then he saw his way. He said, in his most conspicuously casual vein:

"Er-uh—by the way, Hawkins, we are feeling disappointed about this thing—the way the materializee is acting, I mean—we are disappointed; you concede that?"

"Concede it? Why, yes, if you like the term."

"Very well; so far, so good. Now for the *basis* of the feeling. It is not that your heart, your affections are concerned; that is to say, it is not that you *want* the materializee *Itself*. You concede that?"

"Yes, I concede that, too—cordially."

"Very well, again; we are making progress. To sum up: The feeling, it is conceded, is not engendered by the mere conduct of the materializee; it is conceded that it does not arise from any pang which the *personality* of the materializee could assuage. Now, then," said the earl, with the light of triumph in his eye, "the inexorable logic of the situation narrows us down to this: our feeling has its source in the *money*-loss involved. Come—isn't that so?"

"Goodness knows I concede that with all my heart."

"Very well. When you've found out the source of a disease, you've also found out what remedy is required—just as in this case. In this case money is required. And *only* money."

The old, old seduction was in that airy, confident tone and those significant words—usually called pregnant words in books. The old answering signs of faith and hope showed up in Hawkins's countenance, and he said:

"*Only* money? Do you mean that you know a way to—"

"Washington, have you the impression that I have no resources but those I allow the public and my intimate friends to know about?"

"Well, I—er—"

"Is it *likely*, do you think, that a man moved by nature and taught by experience to keep his affairs to himself, and a cautious and reluctant tongue in his head, wouldn't be thoughtful enough to keep a few resources in reserve for a rainy day, when he's got as many as I have to select from?"

"Oh, you make me feel so much better already, Colonel!"

"Have you ever been in my laboratory?"

"Why, no."

"That's it. You see, you didn't even know that I had one. Come along. I've got a little trick there that I want to show you. I've kept it perfectly quiet, not fifty people know anything about it. But that's my way, always been my way. Wait till you're *ready*, that's the idea; and *when* you're ready, *zzip!*—let her go!"

"Well, Colonel, I've never seen a man that I've had such unbounded confidence in as you. When you say a thing right out, I always feel as if that ends it; as if that is evidence, and proof, and everything else."

The old earl was profoundly pleased and touched.

"I'm glad *you* believe in me, Washington; not everybody is so just."

"I always have believed in you; and I always shall as long as I live."

"Thank you, my boy. You sha'n't repent it. And you *can't.*" Arrived in the "laboratory," the earl continued, "Now, cast your eye around this room—what do you see? *Apparently* a junk-shop; *apparently* a hospital connected with a patent-office—in *reality*, the mines of Golconda in disguise! Look at that thing there. Now what would you take that thing to be?"

"I don't believe I could ever imagine."

"Of course you couldn't. It's my grand adaptation of the phonograph to the marine service. You store up profanity in it for use at sea. You know that sailors don't fly around worth a cent unless you swear at them—so the mate that can do the best job of swearing is the most valuable man. In great emergencies his talent saves the ship. But a ship is a large thing, and he can't be everywhere at once; so there have been times when one mate has lost a ship which could have been saved if they had had a hundred. Prodigious storms, you know. Well, a ship can't afford a hundred mates; but she can afford a hundred Cursing Phonographs, and distribute them all over the vessel—and there, you see, she's armed at every point. Imagine a big storm, and a hundred of my machines all cursing away at once—splendid spectacle, splendid!—you couldn't hear yourself think. Ship goes through that storm perfectly serene—she's just as safe as she'd be on shore."

"It's a wonderful idea. How do you prepare the thing?"

"Load it—simply load it."

"How?"

"Why, you just stand over it and swear into it."

"That loads it, does it?"

"Yes; because every word it collars it *keeps*—keeps it forever. Never wears out. Any time you turn the crank, out it 'll come. In times of great peril you can reverse it, and it 'll swear backwards. *That* makes a sailor hump himself!"

"Oh, I see. Who loads them?—the mate?"

"Yes, if he chooses. Or I'll furnish them already loaded. I can hire an expert for seventy-five dollars a month who will load a hundred and fifty phonographs in one hundred and fifty hours, and do it *easy*. And an expert can furnish a stronger article, of course, than the mere average uncultivated mate could. Then, you see, all the ships of the world will buy them ready loaded—for I shall have them loaded in any language a customer wants. Hawkins, it will work the grandest moral reform of the nineteenth century. Five years from now *all* the swearing will be done by machinery—you won't ever hear a profane word come from human lips on a ship. Millions of dollars have been spent by the churches in the effort to abolish profanity in the commercial marine. Think of it—my name will live forever in the affections of good men as the man who, solitary and alone, accomplished this noble and elevating reform."

"Oh, it *is* grand and beneficent and beautiful. How *did* you ever come to think of it? You have a wonderful mind. How did you say you loaded the machine?"

"Oh, it's no trouble—perfectly simple. If you want to load it up loud and strong, you stand right over it and shout. But if you leave it open and all set, it 'll *eavesdrop,* so to speak—that is to say, it will load itself up with any sounds that are made within six feet of it. Now I'll show you how it works. I had an expert come and load this one up yesterday. Hello, it's been left open —it's too bad—still I reckon it hasn't had much chance to collect irrelevant stuff. All you do is to press this button in the floor—so."

The phonograph began to sing in a plaintive voice:

> There is a boarding-house far far away,
> Where they have ham and eggs three times a day.

"Hang it, *that* ain't it. Somebody's been singing around here."

The plaintive song began again, mingled with a low, gradually rising wail of cats slowly warming up toward a fight:

> Oh, *how* the boarders yell,
> When they hear that dinner-bell—
> They give that landlord ——

(momentary outburst of terrific cat-fight which drowns out one word)

> Three times a day.

(Renewal of furious cat-fight for a moment. The plaintive voice on a high, fierce key, "*Scat,* you devils!" and a racket as of flying missiles.)

"Well, never mind—let it go. I've got some sailor profanity down in there somewhere, if I could get to it. But it isn't any matter; you see how the machine works."

Hawkins responded, with enthusiasm:

"Oh, it works admirably! I know there's a hundred fortunes in it."

"And mind, the Hawkins family get their share, Washington."

"Oh, thanks, thanks; you are just as generous as ever. Ah, it's the grandest invention of the age!"

"Ah, well, we live in wonderful times. The elements are crowded *full* of beneficent forces—always *have* been—and ours is the first generation to turn them to account and make them work for us. Why, Hawkins, *everything* is useful—*nothing* ought ever to be wasted. Now look at sewer-gas, for instance. Sewer-gas has always been wasted heretofore; nobody tried to save up sewer-gas—you can't name me a man. Ain't that so? You know perfectly well it's so."

"Yes, it is so—but I never—er—I don't quite see why a body—"

"Should *want* to save it up? Well, I'll tell you. Do you see this little invention here?—it's a decomposer—I call it a decomposer. I give you my word of honor that if you show me a house that produces a given quantity of sewer-gas in a day, I'll engage to set up my decomposer there and make that house produce a hundred times that quantity of sewer-gas in less than half an hour."

"Dear me, but why should you want to?"

"*Want* to? Listen, and you'll see. My boy, for illuminating purposes and economy combined, there's nothing in the world that begins with sewer-gas. And really it don't cost a cent. You put in a good inferior article of plumbing—such as you find everywhere —and add my decomposer, and there you are. Just use the ordinary gas-pipes—and there your expense ends. Think of it. Why, Major, in five years from now you won't see a house lighted with anything but sewer-gas. Every physician I talk to recommends it, and every plumber."

"But isn't it dangerous?"

"Oh, yes, more or less, but everything is—coal-gas, candles, electricity—there isn't anything that ain't."

"It lights up well, does it?"

"Oh, magnificently."

"Have you given it a good trial?"

"Well, no, not a first-rate one. Polly's prejudiced, and she won't let me put it in here; but I'm playing my cards to get it adopted in the President's house, and *then* it 'll go—don't you doubt it. I shall not need this one for the present, Washington; you may take it down to some boarding-house and give it a trial if you like."

18

The colonel's project to set Russia free—"I am going to buy Siberia"—The materializee turns up—Being an artist he is invited to restore the colonel's collection—Which he forth-with begins

WASHINGTON SHUDDERED slightly at the suggestion; then his face took on a dreamy look and he dropped into a trance of thought. After a little Sellers asked him what he was grinding in his mental mill.

"Well, this. Have you got some secret project in your head which requires a Bank of England back of it to make it succeed?"

The Colonel showed lively astonishment, and said:

"Why, Hawkins, are you a mind-reader?"

"I? I never thought of such a thing."

"Well, then, how did you happen to drop on to that idea in this curious fashion? It's just mind-reading—that's what it is, though you may not know it. Because I *have* got a private project that requires a Bank of England at its back. How could you divine that? What was the process? This is interesting."

"There wasn't any process. A thought like this happened to slip through my head by accident: How much would make you or me comfortable? A hundred thousand. Yet you are expecting two or three of these inventions of yours to turn out some billions of money—and you are *wanting* them to do that. If you wanted ten millions, I could understand that—it's inside the human limits. But billions! That's clear outside the limits. There must be a definite project back of that somewhere."

The earl's interest and surprise augmented with every word, and when Hawkins finished he said, with strong admiration:

"It's wonderfully reasoned out, Washington, it certainly is. It shows what I think is quite extraordinary penetration. For you've hit it; you've driven the center, you've plugged the bull's-eye of my dream. Now I'll tell you the whole thing, and you'll understand it. I don't need to ask you to keep it to yourself, because you'll see that the project will prosper all the better for being kept in the background till the right time. Have you noticed how many pamphlets and books I've got lying around relating to Russia?"

"Yes, I think most anybody would notice that—anybody who wasn't dead."

"Well, I've been posting myself a good while. That's a great and splendid nation, and deserves to be set free." He paused; then added, in a quite matter-of-fact way, "When I get this money I'm going to set it free."

"Great guns!"

"Why, what makes you jump like that?"

"Dear me, when you are going to drop a remark under a man's chair that is likely to blow him out through the roof, why don't you put some expression, some force, some noise into it that will prepare him? You shouldn't flip out such a gigantic thing as this in that colorless kind of a way. You do jolt a person up so. Go on now, I'm all right again. Tell me all about it. I'm all interest—yes, and sympathy, too."

"Well, I've looked the ground over, and concluded that the methods of the Russian patriots, while good enough, considering the way the boys are hampered, are not the best—at least, not the quickest. They are trying to revolutionize Russia from *within;* that's pretty slow, you know, and liable to interruption all the time, and is full of perils for the workers. Do you know how Peter the Great started his army? He didn't start it on the family premises under the noses of the Strelitzes; no, he started it away off yonder, privately—only just one regiment, you know, and he built to *that*. The first thing the Strelitzes knew, the regiment was an *army*, their position was turned, and they had to take a walk. Just that little idea *made* the biggest and worst of all the despotisms the world has seen. The same idea can *un*make it. I'm going to prove it. I'm going to get out to one side and work my scheme the way Peter did."

"This is mighty interesting, Rossmore. What is it you are going to do?"

"I am going to buy Siberia and start a republic."

"There—bang you go again without giving any notice! Going to *buy* it?"

"Yes, as soon as I get the money. I don't care what the price is, I shall take it. I can afford it, and I will. Now, then, consider this —and you've never thought of it, I'll warrant. Where is the place where there is twenty-five times more manhood, pluck, true heroism, unselfishness, devotion to high and noble ideals, adoration of liberty, wide education, and *brains,* per thousand of population, than any other domain in the whole world can show?"

"Siberia!"

"Right."

"It is true; it certainly is true, but I never thought of it before."

"Nobody ever thinks of it. But it's so, just the same. In those mines and prisons are gathered together the very finest and noblest and capablest multitude of human beings that God is able to create. Now if you had that kind of a population to sell, would you offer it to a despotism? No, the despotism has no use for it; you would lose money. A despotism has no use for anything but human cattle. But suppose you want to start a republic?"

"Yes, I see. It's just the material for it."

"Well, I should say so! There's Siberia, with just the very finest and choicest material on the globe for a republic, and more coming—more coming all the time, don't you see! It is being daily, weekly, monthly recruited by the most perfectly devised system that has ever been invented perhaps. By this system the whole of the hundred millions of Russia are being constantly and patiently sifted, sifted, sifted by myriads of trained experts, spies appointed by the emperor personally; and whenever they catch a man, woman, or child that has got any brains or education or character they ship that person straight to Siberia. It is admirable, it is wonderful. It is so searching and so effective that it keeps the general level of Russian intellect and education down to that of the Czar."

"Come, that sounds like exaggeration."

"Well, it's what they say, anyway. But I think, myself, it's a lie. And it doesn't seem right to slander a whole nation that way, anyhow. Now, then, you see what the material is, there in Siberia, for a republic." He paused, and his breast began to heave and his eye to burn under the impulse of strong emotion. Then his words began to stream forth with constantly increasing energy and fire, and he rose to his feet as if to give himself larger freedom. "The minute I organize that republic, the light of liberty, intelligence, justice, humanity, bursting from it, flooding from it, flaming from it, will concentrate the gaze of the whole astonished world as upon the miracle of a new sun; Russia's countless multitudes of slaves will rise up and march, march!—eastward, with that great light transfiguring their faces as they come, and far back of them you will see—what will you see?—a vacant throne in an empty land! It can be done, and by God I will do it!"

He stood a moment bereft of earthly consciousness by his exaltation; then consciousness returned, bringing him a slight shock, and he said, with grave earnestness:

"I must ask you to pardon me, Major Hawkins. I have never used that expression before, and I beg you will forgive it this time."

Hawkins was quite willing.

"You see, Washington, it is an error which I am by nature not liable to. Only excitable people, impulsive people, are exposed to it. But the circumstances of the present case—I being a democrat by birth and preference, and an aristocrat by inheritance and relish—"

The earl stopped suddenly, his frame stiffened, and he began to stare speechless through the curtainless window. Then he pointed, and gasped out a single rapturous word:

"Look!"

"What *is* it, Colonel?"

"*It!*"

"No!"

"Sure as you're born. Keep perfectly still. I'll apply the influence —I'll turn on all my force. I've brought It thus far—I'll fetch It right into the house. You'll see."

He was making all sorts of passes in the air with his hands.

"There! Look at that. I've made It smile! See?"

Quite true. Tracy, out for an afternoon stroll, had come unexpectedly upon his family arms displayed upon this shabby housefront. The hatchments made him smile; which was nothing—they had made the neighborhood cats do that.

"Look, Hawkins, look! I'm drawing It over!"

"You're drawing It sure, Rossmore. If I ever had any doubts about materialization, they're gone now, and gone for good. Oh, this is a joyful day!"

Tracy was sauntering over to read the door-plate. Before he was half-way over he was saying to himself, "Why, manifestly these are the American Claimant's quarters."

"It's coming—coming right along. I'll slide down and pull It in. You follow after me."

Sellers, pale and a good deal agitated, opened the door and confronted Tracy. The old man could not at once get his voice; then he pumped out a scattering and hardly coherent salutation, and followed it with:

"Walk in, walk right in, Mr.—er—"

"Tracy—Howard Tracy."

—"Tracy—thanks—walk right in, you're expected."

Tracy entered, considerably puzzled, and said:

"Expected? I think there must be some mistake."

"Oh, I judge not," said Sellers, who, noticing that Hawkins had arrived, gave him a sidewise glance intended to call his close attention to a dramatic effect which he was proposing to produce by his next remark. Then he said, slowly and impressively: "I am—*You Know Who*."

To the astonishment of both conspirators the remark produced no dramatic effect at all; for the new-comer responded, with a quite innocent and unembarrassed air:

"No, pardon me. I don't *know* who you are. I only suppose— but no doubt correctly—that you are the gentleman whose title is on the door-plate."

"Right, quite right—sit down, pray sit down." The earl was rattled, thrown off his bearings, his head was in a whirl. Then he noticed Hawkins standing apart and staring idiotically at what to him was the apparition of a defunct man, and a new idea was born to him. He said to Tracy, briskly:

"But a thousand pardons, dear sir; I am forgetting courtesies due to a guest and stranger. Let me introduce my friend General Hawkins—General Hawkins, our new Senator—Senator from the latest and grandest addition to the radiant galaxy of sovereign States, Cherokee Strip"—(to himself, "that name will shrivel him up!"—but it didn't in the least, and the Colonel resumed the introduction piteously disheartened and amazed)—"Senator Hawkins, Mr. Howard Tracy, of—er—"

"England."

"England!—Why, that's im—"

"England, yes, native of England."

"Recently from there?"

"Yes, quite recently."

Said the Colonel to himself, "This phantom lies like an expert. Purifying this kind by fire don't work. I'll sound him a little further, give him another chance or two to work his gift." Then aloud, with deep irony:

"Visiting our great country for recreation and amusement, no doubt. I suppose you find that traveling in the majestic expanses of our Far West is—"

"I haven't been West, and haven't been devoting myself to amusement with any sort of exclusiveness, I assure you. In fact, to merely live, an artist has got to work, not play."

"Artist!" said Hawkins to himself, thinking of the rifled bank; "that *is* a name for it!"

"Are *you* an artist?" asked the Colonel. And added to himself, "*Now* I'm going to catch him."

"In a humble way, yes."

"What line?" pursued the sly veteran.

"Oils."

"I've got him!" said Sellers to himself. Then aloud, "This is fortunate. Could I engage you to restore some of my paintings that need that attention?"

"I shall be very glad. Pray let me see them."

No shuffling, no evasion, no embarrassment, even under this crucial test. The Colonel was nonplussed. He led Tracy to a chromo which had suffered damage in a former owner's hands through being used as a lamp-mat, and said, with a flourish of his hand toward the picture:

"This del Sarto—"

"Is *that* a del Sarto?"

The Colonel bent a look of reproach upon Tracy, allowed it to sink home, then resumed as if there had been no interruption:

"This del Sarto is perhaps the only original of that sublime master in our country. You see, yourself, that the work is of such exceeding delicacy that the risk—could—er—would you mind giving me a little example of what you can do before we—"

"Cheerfully, cheerfully. I will copy one of these marvels."

Water-color materials—relics of Miss Sally's college life—were brought. Tracy said he was better in oils, but would take a chance with these. So he was left alone. He began his work, but the attractions of the place were too strong for him, and he got up and went drifting about, fascinated; also amazed.

19

The perplexities and nobilities of materialization—The materializee eats a couple of apples—Horror of Hawkins and Sellers—"It must be a mistake"

MEANTIME the earl and Hawkins were holding a troubled and anxious private consultation. The earl said:

"The mystery that bothers me is, Where did It get its other arm?"

"Yes; it worries me, too. And another thing troubles me—the apparition is English. How do you account for that, Colonel?"

"Honestly, I don't know, Hawkins, I don't really know. It is very confusing and awful."

"Don't you think maybe we've waked up the wrong one?"

"The wrong one? How do you account for the clothes?"

"The clothes *are* right, there's no getting around it. What are we going to do? We can't collect, as I see. The reward is for a one-armed American. This is a two-armed Englishman."

"Well, it may be that that is not objectionable. You see, it isn't *less* than is called for; it is *more*, and so—"

But he saw that this argument was weak, and dropped it. The friends sat brooding over their perplexities some time in silence. Finally the earl's face began to glow with an inspiration, and he said, impressively:

"Hawkins, this materialization is a grander and nobler science than we have dreamed of. We have little imagined what a solemn and stupendous thing we have done. The whole secret is perfectly clear to me now, clear as day. *Every man is made up of heredities,* long-descended atoms and particles of his ancestors.

This present materialization is incomplete. We have only brought it down to perhaps the beginning of this century."

"What do you mean, Colonel?" cried Hawkins, filled with vague alarms by the old man's awe-compelling words and manner.

"This: We've materialized this burglar's ancestor!"

"Oh, don't—don't say that. It's hideous."

"But it's true, Hawkins; I *know* it. Look at the facts. This apparition is distinctly English—note that. It uses good grammar—note that. It is an artist—note that. It has the manners and carriage of a gentleman—note that. Where's your cowboy? Answer me that."

"Rossmore, this is dreadful—it's too dreadful to think of!"

"Never resurrected a rag of that burglar but the clothes, not a solitary rag of him but the clothes."

"Colonel, do you really mean—"

The Colonel brought his fist down with emphasis, and said:

"I mean exactly this: This materialization was immature, the burglar has evaded us; this is nothing but a damned ancestor!"

He rose and walked the floor in great excitement. Hawkins said, plaintively:

"It's a bitter disappointment—bitter."

"I know it. I know it, Senator; I feel it as deeply as anybody could. But we've got to submit—on moral grounds. I need money, but God knows I am not poor enough or shabby enough to be an accessory to the punishing of a man's ancestor for crimes committed by that ancestor's posterity."

"But, Colonel!" implored Hawkins, "stop and think; don't be rash; you know it's the *only* chance we've got to get the money; and, besides, the Bible itself says posterity to the fourth generation shall be punished for the sins and crimes committed by ancestors four generations back that hadn't anything to do with them; and so it's only fair to turn the rule around and make it work both ways."

The Colonel was struck with the strong logic of this position. He strode up and down, and thought it painfully over. Finally he said:

"There's reason in it; yes, there's reason in it. And so, although it seems a piteous thing to sweat this poor ancient devil for a burglary he hadn't the least hand in, still if duty commands I suppose we must give him up to the authorities."

"*I* would," said Hawkins, cheered and relieved; "I'd give him up if he was a thousand ancestors compacted into one."

"Lord bless me, that's just what he is!" said Sellers, with something like a groan; "it's exactly what he is; there's a contribution in him from every ancestor he ever had. In him there's atoms of priests, soldiers, crusaders, poets, and sweet and gracious women —all kinds and conditions of folk who trod this earth in old, old centuries, and vanished out of it ages ago, and now by act of ours they are summoned from their holy peace to answer for gutting a one-horse bank away out on the borders of Cherokee Strip, and it's just a howling outrage!"

"Oh, don't talk like that, Colonel; it takes the heart all out of me, and makes me ashamed of the part I am proposing to—"

"Wait—I've got it!"

"A saving hope? Shout it out, I am perishing."

"It's perfectly simple; a child would have thought of it. He is all right, not a flaw in him, as far as I have carried the work. If I've been able to bring him as far as the beginning of this century, what's to stop me now? I'll go on and materialize him down to date."

"Land, I never thought of that!" said Hawkins, all ablaze with joy again. "It's the very thing. What a brain you have got! And will he shed the superfluous arm?"

"He will."

"And lose his English accent?"

"It will wholly disappear. He will speak Cherokee Strip—and other forms of profanity."

"Colonel, maybe he'll confess!"

"Confess? Merely that bank robbery?"

"Merely? Yes, but why 'merely'?"

The Colonel said, in his most impressive manner:

"Hawkins, he will be wholly under my command. I will make him confess every crime he ever committed. There must be a thousand. Do you get the idea?"

"Well—not quite."

"The rewards will come to us."

"Prodigious conception! I *never* saw such a head for seeing with a lightning glance all the outlying ramifications and possibilities of a central idea."

"It is nothing; it comes natural to me. When his time is out in one jail he goes to the next and the next, and we shall have nothing to do but collect the rewards as he goes along. It is a perfectly steady income as long as we live, Hawkins. And much better than other kinds of investments, because he is indestructible."

"It looks—it really does look the way you say; it does, indeed."

"Look?—why, it *is*. It will not be denied that I have had a pretty wide and comprehensive financial experience, and I do not hesitate to say that I consider this one of the most valuable properties I have ever controlled."

"Do you really think so?"

"I do, indeed."

"Oh, Colonel, the wasting grind and grief of poverty! If we could realize immediately. I don't mean sell it all, but sell part—enough, you know, to—"

"See how you tremble with excitement. That comes of lack of experience. My boy, when you have been familiar with vast operations as long as I have you'll be different. Look at me. Is my eye dilated? Do you notice a quiver anywhere? Feel my pulse: plunk—plunk—plunk—same as if I were asleep. And yet, what is passing through my calm, cold mind? A procession of figures which would make a financial novice drunk—just the sight of them. Now it is by keeping cool, and looking at a thing all around, that a man sees what's really in it, and saves himself from the novice's unfailing mistake—the one you just suggested—eagerness to *realize*. Listen to me. Your idea is to sell a part of him for ready cash. Now mine is—guess."

"I haven't an idea. What is it?"

"Stock him—of course."

"Well, I should never have thought of that."

"Because you are not a financier. Say he has committed a thousand crimes. Certainly that's a low estimate. By the look of him, even in his unfinished condition, he has committed all of a million. But call it only a thousand to be perfectly safe; five thousand reward, multiplied by a thousand, gives us a dead sure cash basis of—what? Five million dollars!"

"Wait—let me get my breath."

"And the property indestructible. Perpetually fruitful—perpetually; for a property with his disposition will go on committing crimes and winning rewards."

"You daze me, you make my head whirl!"

"Let it whirl, it won't do any harm. Now that matter is all fixed —leave it alone. I'll get up the company and issue the stock, all in good time. Just leave it in my hands. I judge you don't doubt my ability to work it up for all it is worth."

"Indeed, I don't. I can say that with truth."

"All right, then. That's disposed of. Everything in its turn. We old operators go by order and system—no helter-skelter business with us. What's the next thing on the docket? The carrying on of the materialization—the bringing it down to date. I will begin on that at once. I think—"

"Look here, Rossmore. You didn't lock It in. A hundred to one It has escaped!"

"Calm yourself as to that; don't give yourself any uneasiness."

"But why shouldn't It escape?"

"Let It, if It wants to. What of it?"

"Well, I should consider it a pretty serious calamity."

"Why, my dear boy, once in my power, always in my power. It may go and come freely. I can produce It here whenever I want It, just by the exercise of my will."

"Well, I am truly glad to hear that, I do assure you."

"Yes, I shall give It all the painting It wants to do, and we and the family will make It as comfortable and contented as we can. No occasion to restrain Its movements. I hope to persuade It to remain pretty quiet, though, because a materialization which is in a state of arrested development must of necessity be pretty soft and flabby and substanceless, and—er—by the way, I wonder where It comes from?"

"How? What do you mean?"

The earl pointed significantly—and interrogatively—toward the sky. Hawkins started; then settled into deep reflection; finally shook his head sorrowfully and pointed downward.

"What makes you think so, Washington?"

"Well, I hardly know, but really you can see yourself that he doesn't seem to be pining for his last place."

"It's well thought! Soundly deduced. We've done that Thing a favor. But I believe I will pump It a little, in a quiet way, and find out if we are right."

"How long is it going to take to finish him off and fetch him down to date, Colonel?"

"I wish I knew, but I don't. I am clear knocked out by this new detail—this unforeseen necessity of working a subject down gradually from his condition of ancestor to his ultimate result as posterity. But I'll make him hump himself, anyway."

"Rossmore!"

"Yes, dear. We're in the laboratory. Come—Hawkins is here. Mind now, Hawkins—he's a sound, living *human being* to all the family—*don't* forget that. Here she comes."

"Keep your seats, I'm not coming in. I just wanted to ask, who is it that's painting down there?"

"That? Oh, that's a young artist; young Englishman named Tracy; very promising—favorite pupil of Hans Christian Andersen or one of the other old masters—Andersen I'm pretty sure it is; he's going to half-sole some of our old Italian masterpieces. Been talking to him?"

"Well, only a word. I stumbled right in on him without expecting anybody was there. I tried to be polite to him; offered him a snack" (Sellers delivered a large wink to Hawkins from behind his hand), "but he declined, and said he wasn't hungry" (another sarcastic wink); "so I brought some apples" (double wink), "and he ate a couple of—"

"What!" And the Colonel sprang some yards toward the ceiling, and came down quaking with astonishment.

Lady Rossmore was smitten dumb with amazement. She gazed at the sheepish relic of Cherokee Strip, then at her husband, and then at the guest again. Finally she said:

"What is the matter with you, Mulberry?"

He did not answer immediately. His back was turned; he was bending over his chair, feeling the seat of it. But he answered next moment, and said:

"Ah, there it is; it was a tack."

The lady contemplated him doubtfully a moment, then said, pretty snappishly:

"All that for a tack! Praise goodness it wasn't a shingle nail; it would have landed you in the Milky Way. I do hate to have my nerves shook up so." And she turned on her heel and went her way.

As soon as she was safely out, the Colonel said in a suppressed voice:

"Come—we must see for ourselves. It *must* be a mistake."

They hurried softly down and peeped in. Sellers whispered, in a sort of despair:

"It *is* eating! What a grisly spectacle! Hawkins, it's horrible! Take me away—I can't stand it."

They tottered back to the laboratory.

20

Tracy's perplexities with regard to the Claimant's sanity—
The Claimant interviews him—Sally Sellers meets Tracy
—A violent case of love at first sight—Pinks

TRACY MADE slow progress with his work, for his mind wandered a good deal. Many things were puzzling him. Finally a light burst upon him all of a sudden—seemed to, at any rate—and he said to himself, "I've got the clue at last—this man's mind is off its balance; I don't know how much, but it's off a point or two, sure; off enough to explain this mess of perplexities, anyway. These dreadful chromos—which he takes for old masters; these villainous portraits—which to his frantic mind represent Rossmores; the hatchments; the pompous name of this ramshackle old crib— Rossmore Towers; and that odd assertion of his, that I was expected. How could I be expected? that is, Lord Berkeley. He knows by the papers that that person was burned up in the New Gadsby. Why, hang it, he really doesn't know *whom* he was expecting; for his talk showed that he was not expecting an Englishman, or yet an artist, yet I answer his requirements notwithstanding. He seems sufficiently satisfied with me. Yes, he is a little off; in fact, I am afraid he is a good deal off, poor old gentleman. But he's interesting—all people in about his condition are, I suppose. I hope he'll like my work; I would like to come every day and study him. And when I write my father—ah, that hurts! I mustn't get on that subject; it isn't good for my spirits. Somebody coming—I must get to work. It's the old gentleman again. He looks bothered. Maybe my clothes are suspicious; and they are—for an artist. If my conscience would allow me to make a change—but that is out of the question. I wonder what he's making those passes in the air for with his hands. I seem to be the object of them. Can he be trying to mesmerize me? I don't quite like it. There's something uncanny about it."

The Colonel muttered to himself, "It has an effect on him, I can see it myself. That's enough for one time, I reckon. He's not very solid yet, I suppose, and I might disintegrate him. I'll just put a sly question or two at him now, and see if I can find out what his condition is and where he's from."

He approached and said, affably:

"Don't let me disturb you, Mr. Tracy; I only want to take a little glimpse of your work. Ah, that's fine—that's very fine, indeed. You are doing it elegantly. My daughter will be charmed with this. May I sit down by you?"

"Oh, do; I shall be glad."

"It won't disturb you? I mean, won't dissipate your inspirations?"

Tracy laughed and said they were not ethereal enough to be very easily discommoded.

The Colonel asked a number of cautious and well-considered questions—questions which seemed pretty odd and flighty to Tracy—but the answers conveyed the information desired apparently, for the Colonel said to himself, with mixed pride and gratification:

"It's a good job as far as I've got with it. He's solid. Solid, and going to last; solid as the real thing. It's wonderful—wonderful. I believe I could petrify him."

After a little he asked, warily:

"Do you prefer being here, or—or there?"

"There? Where?"

"Why—er—where you've been?"

Tracy's thought flew to his boarding-house, and he answered with decision:

"Oh, *here,* much!"

The Colonel was startled, and said to himself, "There's no uncertain ring about that. It indicates where *he's* been to, poor fellow. Well, I am satisfied now. I'm glad I got him out."

He sat thinking and thinking, and watching the brush go. At length he said to himself, "Yes, it certainly seems to account for the failure of my endeavors in poor Berkeley's case. *He* went in the other direction. Well, it's all right. He's better off."

Sally Sellers entered from the street now, looking her divinest, and the artist was introduced to her. It was a violent case of mutual love at first sight, though neither party was entirely aware of the fact, perhaps. The Englishman made this irrelevant remark to himself: "Perhaps he is not insane, after all." Sally sat down and showed an interest in Tracy's work which greatly pleased him, and a benevolent forgiveness of it which convinced him that the girl's nature was cast in a large mold. Sellers was anxious to report his discoveries to Hawkins; so he took his leave, saying that if the two "young devotees of the colored Muse" thought they could manage without him, he would go and look after his affairs. The artist said to himself, "I think he *is* a little eccentric, perhaps, but that is all." He reproached himself for having injuriously judged a man without giving him any fair chance to show what he really was.

Of course the stranger was very soon at his ease and chatting along comfortably. The average American girl possesses the valuable qualities of naturalness, honesty, and inoffensive straightforwardness; she is nearly barren of troublesome conventions and artificialities; consequently, her presence and her ways are unembarrassing, and one is acquainted with her and on the pleasantest terms with her before he knows how it came about. This new acquaintanceship—friendship, indeed—progressed swiftly; and the unusual swiftness of it and the thoroughness of it are sufficiently evidenced and established by one noteworthy fact— that within the first half-hour both parties had ceased to be conscious of Tracy's clothes. Later this consciousness was reawakened; it was then apparent to Gwendolen that she was almost reconciled to them, and it was apparent to Tracy that he wasn't. The reawakening was brought about by Gwendolen's inviting the artist to stay to dinner. He had to decline because he wanted to live now—that is, now that there was something to live for—and he could not survive in those clothes at a gentleman's table. He thought he knew that. But he went away happy, for he saw that Gwendolen was disappointed.

And whither did he go? He went straight to a slop-shop and bought as neat and reasonably well-fitting a suit of clothes as an Englishman could be persuaded to wear. He said—*to* himself, but *at* his conscience—"I know it's wrong; but it would be wrong *not* to do it; and two wrongs do not make a right."

This satisfied him, and made his heart light. Perhaps it will also satisfy the reader—if he can make out what it means.

The old people were troubled about Gwendolen at dinner, because she was so distraught and silent. If they had noticed, they would have found that she was sufficiently alert and interested whenever the talk stumbled upon the artist and his work; but they didn't notice, and so the chat would swap around to some other subject, and then somebody would presently be privately worrying about Gwendolen again, and wondering if she were not well, or if something had gone wrong in the millinery line. Her mother offered her various reputable patent medicines and tonics with iron and other hardware in them, and her father even proposed to send out for wine, relentless prohibitionist and head of the order in the District of Columbia as he was, but these kindnesses were all declined—thankfully, but with decision. At bedtime, when the family were breaking up for the night, she privately looted one of the brushes, saying to herself, "It's the one he has used the most."

The next morning Tracy went forth wearing his new suit, and equipped with a pink in his buttonhole—a daily attention from Puss. His whole soul was full of Gwendolen Sellers, and this condition was an inspiration, art-wise. All the morning his brush pawed nimbly away at the canvases, almost without his awarity (awarity, in this sense, being the sense of being aware, though disputed by some authorities), turning out marvel upon marvel, in the way of decorative accessories to the portraits, with a felicity and celerity which amazed the veterans of the firm and fetched out of them continuous explosions of applause.

Meantime Gwendolen was losing her morning and many dollars. She supposed Tracy was coming in the forenoon—a conclusion which she had jumped to without outside help. So she tripped down-stairs every little while from her work-parlor to arrange the brushes and things over again and see if he had arrived. And when she was in her work-parlor it was not profitable, but just the other way—as she found out to her sorrow. She had put in her idle moments during the last little while back in designing a particularly rare and capable gown for herself, and this morning she set about making it up; but she was absent-minded, and made an irremediable botch of it. When she saw what she had done she knew the reason of it and the meaning of it, and she put her work away from her and said she would accept the sign. And from that time forth she came no more away from the Audience Chamber, but remained there and waited. After luncheon she waited again. A whole hour. Then a great joy welled up in her heart, for she saw him coming. So she flew back upstairs thankful, and could hardly wait for him to miss the principal brush, which she had mislaid down there, but knew where she had mislaid it. However, all in good time, the others were called in and couldn't find the brush, and then she was sent for, and she couldn't find it herself for some little time; but then she found it when the others had gone away to hunt in the kitchen and down cellar and in the woodshed, and all those other places where people look for things whose ways they are not familiar with. So she gave him the brush, and remarked that she ought to have seen that everything was ready for him, but it hadn't seemed necessary, because it was so early that she wasn't expecting—but she stopped there, surprised at herself for what she was saying; and he felt caught and ashamed, and said to himself, "I knew my impatience would drag me here before I was expected and betray me, and that is just what it has done; she sees straight through me—and is laughing at me inside, of course."

Gwendolen was very much pleased on one account, and a little the other way in another; pleased with the new clothes and the improvement which they had achieved; less pleased by the pink in the buttonhole. Yesterday's pink had hardly interested her; this one was just like it, but somehow it had got her immediate attention, and kept it. She wished she could think of some way of getting at its history in a properly colorless and indifferent way. Presently she made a venture. She said:

"Whatever a man's age may be, he can reduce it several years by putting a bright-colored flower in his buttonhole. I have often noticed that. Is that your sex's reason for wearing a boutonnière?"

"I fancy not, but certainly that reason would be a sufficient one. I've never heard of the idea before."

"You seem to prefer pinks. Is it on account of the color, or the form?"

"Oh, no," he said, simply, "they are given to me. I don't think I have any preference."

"They are given to him," she said to herself, and she felt a coldness toward that pink. "I wonder who it is, and what she is like." The flower began to take up a good deal of room; it obtruded itself everywhere; it intercepted all views, and marred them; it was becoming exceedingly annoying and conspicuous for a little thing. "I wonder if he cares for her." That thought gave her a quite definite pain.

21

Empty painting; empty millinerizing—Tracy's work satisfactory—Sellers's new picture of Lord Berkeley—"He is a
wobbler"—The unsuccessful dinner-parties—"They flung
their arms about each other's necks"

SHE HAD MADE everything comfortable for the artist; there was no further pretext for staying. So she said she would go now, and asked him to summon the servants in case he should need anything. She went away unhappy, and she left unhappiness behind her; for she carried away all the sunshine. The time dragged heavily for both now. He couldn't paint for thinking of her; she couldn't design or millinerize with any heart for thinking of him. Never before had painting seemed so empty to him, never before had millinerizing seemed so void of interest to her. She had gone without repeating that dinner invitation—an almost unendurable disappointment to him. On her part—well, she was suffering, too; for she had found she *couldn't* invite him. It was not hard yesterday, but it was impossible to-day. A thousand innocent privileges seemed to have been filched from her unawares in the past twenty-four hours. To-day she felt strangely hampered, restrained of her liberty. To-day she couldn't propose to herself to do anything or say anything concerning this young man without being instantly paralyzed into non-action by the fear that he might "suspect." Invite him to dinner *to-day?* It made her shiver to think of it.

And so her afternoon was one long fret—broken at intervals. Three times she had to go down-stairs on errands—that is, she thought she had to go down-stairs on errands. Thus, going and coming, she had six glimpses of him in the aggregate, without seeming to look in his direction; and she tried to endure these electric ecstasies without showing any sign, but they fluttered her up a good deal, and she felt that the naturalness she was putting on was overdone and quite too frantically sober and hysterically calm to deceive.

The painter had his share of the rapture; he had his six glimpses, and they smote him with waves of pleasure that assaulted him, beat upon him, washed over him deliciously, and drowned out all consciousness of what he was doing with his brush. So there were six places in his canvas which had to be done over again.

At last Gwendolen got some peace of mind by sending word to the Thompsons, in the neighborhood, that she was coming there to dinner. She wouldn't be reminded, at *that* table, that there was an absentee who ought to be a presentee—a word which she meant to look out in the dictionary at a calmer time.

About this time the old earl dropped in for a chat with the artist, and invited him to stay to dinner. Tracy cramped down his joy and gratitude by a sudden and powerful exercise of all his forces; and he felt that now that he was going to be close to Gwendolen, and hear her voice and watch her face during several precious hours, earth had nothing valuable to add to his life for the present.

The earl said to himself, "This specter can eat apples, apparently. We shall find out now if that is a specialty. I think, myself, it's a specialty. Apples, without doubt, constitute the spectral limit. It was the case with our first parents. No, I am wrong—at least, only partly right. The line *was* drawn at apples, just as in the present case, but it was from the other direction." The new clothes gave him a thrill of pleasure and pride. He said to himself, "I've got part of him down to date, anyway."

Sellers said he was pleased with Tracy's work; and he went on and engaged him to restore his old masters, and said he should also want him to paint his portrait and his wife's and possibly his daughter's. The tide of the artist's happiness was at flood now. The chat flowed pleasantly along while Tracy painted and Sellers carefully unpacked a picture which he had brought with him. It was a chromo; a new one, just out. It was the smirking, self-satisfied portrait of a man who was inundating the Union with advertisements inviting everybody to buy his specialty, which was a three-dollar shoe or a dress-suit or something of that kind. The old gentleman rested the chromo flat upon his lap and gazed down tenderly upon it, and became silent and meditative. Presently Tracy noticed that he was dripping tears on it. This touched the young fellow's sympathetic nature, and at the same time gave him the painful sense of being an intruder upon a sacred privacy, an observer of emotions which a stranger ought not to witness. But this pity rose superior to other considerations, and compelled him to try to comfort the old mourner with kindly words and a show of friendly interest. He said:

"I am very sorry—is it a friend whom—"

"Ah, more than that, far more than that—a relative, the dearest I had on earth, although I was never permitted to see him. Yes, it is young Lord Berkeley, who perished so heroically in the awful confla— Why, what is the matter?"

"Oh, nothing, nothing. It was a little startling to be so suddenly brought face to face, so to speak, with a person one has heard so much talk about. Is it a good likeness?"

"Without doubt, yes. I never saw him, but you can easily see the resemblance to his father," said Sellers, holding up the chromo, and glancing from it to the chromo misrepresenting the Usurping Earl, and back again with an approving eye.

"Well, no—I am not sure that I make out the likeness. It is plain that the Usurping Earl there has a great deal of character and a long face like a horse's, whereas his heir here is smirky, moon-faced, and characterless."

"We are all that way in the beginning—all the line," said Sellers, undisturbed. "We all start as moon-faced fools, then later we tadpole along into horse-faced marvels of intellect and character. It is by that sign and by that fact that I detect the resemblance here, and know this portrait to be genuine and perfect. Yes, all our family are fools at first."

"This young man seems to meet the hereditary requirement, certainly."

"Yes, yes, he was a fool, without any doubt. Examine the face, the shape of the head, the expression. It's all fool, fool, fool, straight through."

"Thanks," said Tracy, involuntarily.

"Thanks?"

"I mean for explaining it to me. Go on, please."

"As I was saying, fool is printed all over the face. A body can even read the *de*tails."

"What do they say?"

"Well, added up, he is a wobbler."

"A which?"

"Wobbler. A person that's always taking a firm stand about something or other—kind of a Gibraltar stand, *he* thinks, for unshakable fidelity and everlastingness—and then, inside of a little while, he begins to wobble; no more Gibraltar there; no, sir, a mighty ordinary commonplace weakling wobbling around on stilts. That's Lord Berkeley to a dot, you can *see* it—*look* at that sheep! But—why are you blushing like sunset? Dear sir, have I unwittingly offended in some way?"

"Oh, no indeed, no indeed. Far from it. But it always makes me blush to hear a man revile his own blood." He said to himself, How strangely his vagrant and unguided fancies have hit upon the truth. By accident he has described me. I am that contemptible thing. When I left England I thought I knew myself; I thought I was a very Frederick the Great for resolution and staying capacity; whereas in truth I am just a Wobbler, simply a Wobbler. Well—after all, it is at least creditable to *have* high ideals and give birth to lofty resolutions; I will allow myself that comfort." Then he said, aloud, "Could this sheep, as you call him, breed a great and self-sacrificing idea in his head, do you think? Could he meditate such a thing, for instance, as the renunciation of the earldom and its wealth and its glories, and voluntary retirement to the ranks of the commonalty, there to rise by his own merit or remain forever poor and obscure?"

"*Could* he? Why, look at him—look at this simpering, self-righteous mug! There is your answer. It's the very thing he would think of. And he would start in to do it, too."

"And then?"

"He'd wobble."

"And back down?"

"Every time."

"Is that to happen with *all* my—I mean would that happen to *all* his high resolutions?"

"Oh, certainly—certainly. It's the Rossmore of it."

"Then this creature was fortunate to die! Suppose, for argument's sake, that I was a Rossmore, and—"

"It can't be done."

"Why?"

"Because it's not a supposable case. To be a Rossmore at your age you'd have to be a fool, and you're not a fool. And you'd have to be a Wobbler, whereas anybody that is an expert in reading character can see at a glance that when you set your foot down once, it's there to stay; an earthquake can't wobble it." He added to himself, "That's enough to say to him, but it isn't half strong enough for the facts. The more I observe him now the more remarkable I find him. It is the strongest face I have ever examined. There is almost superhuman firmness here, immovable purpose, iron steadfastness of will. A most extraordinary young man."

He presently said, aloud:

"Some time I want to ask your advice about a little matter, Mr. Tracy. You see, I've got that young lord's remains—my goodness, how you jump!"

"Oh, it's nothing, pray go on. You've got his remains?"

"Yes."

"Are you sure they are his, and not somebody else's?"

"Oh, perfectly sure. Samples, I mean. Not all of him."

"Samples?"

"Yes—in baskets. Some time you will be going home; and if you wouldn't mind taking them along—"

"Who? I?"

"Yes—certainly. I don't mean *now;* but after a while; after—but look here, would you like to see them?"

"No! Most certainly not. I don't want to see them."

"Oh, very well. I only thought— Heyo, where are you going, dear?"

"Out to dinner, papa."

Tracy was aghast. The Colonel said, in a disappointed voice:

"Well, I'm sorry. Sho, I didn't know she was going out, Mr. Tracy." Gwendolen's face began to take on a sort of apprehensive What-have-I-done expression. "Three old people to one young one—well, it *isn't* a good team, that's a fact." Gwendolen's face betrayed a dawning hopefulness, and she said, with a tone of reluctance which hadn't the hallmark on it:

"If you prefer, I will send word to the Thompsons that I—"

"Oh, is it the Thompsons? That simplifies it—sets everything right. We can fix it without spoiling your arrangements, my child. You've got your heart set on—"

"But, papa, I'd *just* as soon go there some other—"

"No, I won't have it. You are a good, hard-working, darling child, and your father is not the man to disappoint you when you—"

"But, papa, I—"

"Go along, I won't hear a word. We'll get along, dear."

Gwendolen was ready to cry with vexation. But there was nothing to do but start; which she was about to do when her father hit upon an idea which filled him with delight because it so deftly covered all the difficulties of the situation, and made things smooth and satisfactory:

"I've got it, my love, so that you won't be robbed of your holiday, and at the same time we'll be pretty satisfactorily fixed for a good time here. You send Belle Thompson here—perfectly beautiful creature, Tracy, per-fectly beautiful. I want you to see that girl; why, you'll just go mad—you'll go mad inside of a minute. Yes, you send her right along, Gwendolen, and tell her— Why, she's gone!" He turned—she was already passing out at the gate. He muttered, "I wonder what's the matter; I don't know what her mouth's doing, but I think her shoulders are swearing. Well," said Sellers, blithely, to Tracy, "I shall miss her—parents always miss the children as soon as they're out of sight; it's only a natural and wisely ordained partiality; but you'll be all right, because Miss Belle will supply the youthful element for you and to your entire content; and we old people will do our best, too. We shall have a good enough time. And you'll have a chance to get better acquainted with Admiral Hawkins. That's a rare character, Mr. Tracy—one of the rarest and most engaging characters the world has produced. You'll find him worth studying. I've studied him ever since he was a child, and have always found him developing. I really consider that one of the main things that have enabled me to master the difficult science of character-reading was the vivid interest I always felt in that boy, and the baffling inscrutabilities of his ways and inspirations."

Tracy was not hearing a word. His spirits were gone, he was desolate.

"Yes, a most wonderful character. Concealment—that's the basis of it. Always the first thing you want to do is to find the keystone a man's character is built on—then you've got it. No misleading and apparently inconsistent peculiarities can fool you then. What do you read on the Senator's surface? Simplicity—a kind of rank and protuberant simplicity; whereas, in fact, that's one of the deepest minds in the world. A perfectly honest man—an absolutely honest and honorable man—and yet, without doubt, the profoundest master of dissimulation the world has ever seen."

"Oh, it's devilish!" This was wrung from the unlistening Tracy by the anguished thought of what might have been if only the dinner arrangemnts hadn't got mixed.

"No, I shouldn't call it that," said Sellers, who was now placidly walking up and down the room with his hands under his coat-tails and listening to himself talk. "One could quite properly call it devilish in another man, but not in the Senator. Your *term* is right, perfectly right—I grant that; but the application is wrong. It makes a great difference. Yes, he is a marvelous character. I do not suppose that any other statesman ever had such a colossal sense of humor, combined with the ability to totally conceal it. I may except George Washington and Cromwell, and perhaps Robespierre, but I draw the line there. A person not an expert might be in Judge Hawkins's company a lifetime and never find out he had any more sense of humor than a cemetery."

A deep-drawn, yard-long sigh from the distraught and dreaming artist, followed by a murmured "Miserable, oh, miserable!"

"Well, no, I shouldn't say *that* about it, quite. On the contrary, I admire his ability to conceal his humor even more if possible than I admire the gift itself, stupendous as it is. Another thing—General Hawkins is a thinker; a keen, logical, exhaustive, analytical thinker—perhaps the ablest of modern times. That is, of course, upon themes suited to his size, like the glacial period, and the correlation of forces, and the evolution of the Christian from the caterpillar—any of those things; give him a subject according to his size, and just stand back and watch him think! Why, you can see the place rock! Ah, yes, you must know him; you must get on the inside of him. Perhaps the most extraordinary mind since Aristotle."

Dinner was kept waiting for a while for Miss Thompson, but as Gwendolen had not delivered the invitation to her the waiting did no good, and the household presently went to the meal without her. Poor old Sellers tried everything his hospitable soul could devise to make the occasion an enjoyable one for the guest, and the guest tried his honest best to be cheery and chatty and happy for the old gentleman's sake; in fact, all hands worked hard in the interest of a mutual good time, but the thing was a failure from the start; Tracy's heart was lead in his bosom; there seemed to be only one prominent feature in the landscape, and that was a vacant chair; he couldn't drag his mind away from Gwendolen and his hard luck; consequently, his distractions allowed deadly pauses to slip in every now and then when it was his turn to say something, and of course this disease spread to the rest of the conversation—wherefore, instead of having a breezy sail in sunny waters, as anticipated, everybody was bailing out and praying for land. What *could* the matter be? Tracy alone could have told, the others couldn't even invent a theory.

Meanwhile they were having a similarly dismal time at the Thompson house; in fact, a twin experience. Gwendolen was ashamed of herself for allowing her disappointment to so depress her spirits, and make her so strangely and profoundly miserable; but feeling ashamed of herself didn't improve the matter any; it only seemed to aggravate the suffering. She explained that she was not feeling very well, and everybody could see that this was true; so she got sincere sympathy and commiseration; but that didn't help the case. Nothing helps that kind of a case. It is best to just stand off and let it fester. The moment the dinner was over the girl excused herself, and she hurried home, feeling unspeakably grateful to get away from that house and that intolerable captivity and suffering.

Will he be gone? The thought arose in her brain but took effect in her heels. She slipped into the house, threw off her things, and made straight for the dining-room. She stopped and listened. Her father's voice—with no life in it; presently her mother's—no life in that; a considerable vacancy, then a sterile remark from Washington Hawkins. Another silence; then, not Tracy's, but her father's voice again.

"He's gone," she said to herself, despairingly, and listlessly opened the door and stepped within.

"Why, my child," cried the mother, "how white you are! Are you—has anything—"

"White?" exclaimed Sellers. "It's gone like a flash; 'twasn't serious. Already she's as red as the soul of a watermelon! Sit down, dear, sit down—goodness knows you're welcome. Did you have a good time? We've had great times here—immense. Why didn't Miss Belle come? Mr. Tracy is not feeling well, and she'd have made him forget it."

She was content now; and out from her happy eyes there went a light that told a secret to another pair of eyes there and got a secret in return. In just that infinitely small fraction of a second those two great confessions were made, received, and perfectly understood. All anxiety, apprehension, uncertainty, vanished out of these young people's hearts and left them filled with a great peace.

Sellers had had the most confident faith that with the new reinforcement victory would be at this last moment snatched from the jaws of defeat, but it was an error. The talk was as stubbornly disjointed as ever. He was proud of Gwendolen, and liked to show her off, even against Miss Belle Thompson, and here had been a great opportunity, and what had she made of it? He felt a good deal put out. It vexed him to think that this Englishman, with the traveling Briton's everlasting disposition to generalize whole mountain ranges from single sample-grains of sand, would jump to the conclusion that American girls were as dumb as himself—generalizing the whole tribe from this single sample, and she at her poorest, there being nothing at that table to inspire her, give her a start, keep her from going to sleep. He made up his mind that for the honor of the country he would bring these two together again over the social board before long. There would be a different result another time, he judged. He said to himself, with a deep sense of injury, "He'll put in his diary —they all keep diaries—he'll put in his diary that she was miraculously uninteresting—dear, dear, but *wasn't* she!—I never saw the like—and yet looking as beautiful as Satan, too—and couldn't seem to do anything but paw bread-crumbs, and pick flowers to pieces, and look fidgety. And it isn't any better here in the Hall of Audience. I've had enough; I'll haul down my flag; the others may fight it out if they want to."

He shook hands all around and went off to do some work which he said was pressing. The idolaters were the width of the room apart, and apparently unconscious of each other's presence. The distance got shortened a little now. Very soon the mother withdrew. The distance narrowed again. Tracy stood before a chromo of some Ohio politician which had been retouched and chain-mailed for a crusading Rossmore, and Gwendolen was sitting on the sofa not far from his elbow, artificially absorbed in examining a photograph-album that hadn't any photographs in it.

The "Senator" still lingered. He was sorry for the young people; it had been a dull evening for them. In the goodness of his heart he tried to make it pleasant for them now; tried to remove the ill impression necessarily left by the general defeat; tried to be chatty, even tried to be gay. But the responses were sickly, there was no starting any enthusiasm; he would give it up and quit—it was a day specially picked out and consecrated to failures.

But when Gwendolen rose up promptly and smiled a glad smile, and said, with thankfulness and blessing, "*Must* you go?" it seemed cruel to desert, and he sat down again.

He was about to begin a remark when—when he didn't. We have all been there. He didn't know how he knew his concluding to stay longer had been a mistake, he merely knew it; and knew it for dead certain, too. And so he bade good night and went mooning out, wondering what he could have done that changed the atmosphere that way. As the door closed behind him those two were standing side by side, looking at the door—looking at it in a waiting, second-counting, but deeply grateful kind of way. And the instant it closed they flung their arms about each other's necks, and there, heart to heart and lip to lip—

"Oh, my God, she's kissing It!"

Nobody heard this remark, because Hawkins, who bred it, only thought it; he didn't utter it. He had turned the moment he had closed the door, and had pushed it open a little, intending to re-enter and ask what ill-advised thing he had done or said, and apologize for it. But he didn't re-enter; he staggered off stunned, terrified, distressed.

22

FIVE MINUTES LATER he was sitting in his room, with his head bowed within the circle of his arms, on the table—final attitude of grief and despair. His tears were flowing fast, and now and then a sob broke upon the stillness. Presently he said:

"I knew her when she was a little child and used to climb about my knees; I love her as I love my own, and now—oh, poor thing, poor thing, I cannot bear it!—she's gone and lost her heart to this mangy materializee! Why *didn't* we see that that might happen? But how could we? Nobody could; nobody could ever have dreamed of such a thing. You couldn't expect a person would fall in love with a wax-work. And this one doesn't even amount to that."

He went on grieving to himself, and now and then giving voice to his lamentations.

"It's done, oh, it's done, and there's no help for it, no undoing the miserable business. If I had the nerve, I would kill It. But that wouldn't do any good. *She* loves It; she thinks It's genuine and authentic. If she lost It she would grieve for It just as she would for a real person. And who's to break it to the family? Not I—I'll die first. Sellers is the best human being I ever knew, and I wouldn't any more think of—oh, dear, why, it 'll break his heart when he finds it out. And Polly's, too. *This* comes of meddling with such infernal matters! But for this the creature would still be roasting in Sheol, where It belongs. How is it that these people don't smell the brimstone? Sometimes I can't come into the same room with him without nearly suffocating."

After a while he broke out again:

"Well, there's *one* thing sure. The materializing has got to stop right where it is. If she's got to marry a specter, let her marry a decent one out of the Middle Ages, like this one—not a cowboy and a thief such as this protoplasmic tadpole's going to turn into if Sellers keeps on fussing at It. It costs five thousand dollars cash and shuts down on the incorporated company to stop the works at this point, but Sally Sellers's happiness is worth more than that."

He heard Sellers coming, and got himself to rights. Sellers took a seat, and said:

"Well, I've got to confess I'm a good deal puzzled. It did certainly eat, there's no getting around it. Not eat, exactly, either, but It nibbled; nibbled in an appetiteless way, but still It nibbled; and that's just a marvel. Now the question is, What does It do with those nibblings? That's it—what does It do with them? My idea is that we don't begin to know all there is to this stupendous discovery yet. But time will show—time and science—give us a chance, and don't get impatient."

But he couldn't get Hawkins interested; couldn't make him talk to amount to anything; couldn't drag him out of his depression. But at last he took a turn that arrested Hawkins's attention.

"I'm coming to like him, Hawkins. He is a person of stupendous character—absolutely gigantic. Under that placid exterior is concealed the most dare-devil spirit that was ever put into a man; he's just a Clive over again. Yes, I'm all admiration for him on account of his character, and liking naturally follows admiration, you know. I'm coming to like him immensely. Do you know, I haven't the heart to degrade such a character as that down to the burglar estate for money or for anything else; and I've come to ask if you are willing to let the reward go and leave this poor fellow—"

"Where he is?"

"Yes—not bring him down to date."

"Oh, there's my hand; and my heart's in it, too!"

"I'll never forget you for this, Hawkins," said the old gentleman, in a voice which he found it hard to control. "You are making a great sacrifice for me, and one which you can ill afford, but I'll never forget your generosity, and if I live you shall not suffer for it, be sure of that."

Sally Sellers immediately and vividly realized that she was become a new being; a being of a far higher and worthier sort than she had been such a little while before; an earnest being, in place of a dreamer; and supplied with a reason for her presence in the world, where merely a wistful and troubled curiosity about it had existed before. So great and so comprehensive was the change which had been wrought that she seemed to herself to be a real person who had lately been a shadow; a something, which had lately been a nothing; a purpose, which had lately been a fancy; a finished temple, with the altar-fires lit and the voice of worship ascending, where before had been but an architect's confusion of arid working plans, unintelligible to the passing eye and prophesying nothing.

"Lady" Gwendolen! The pleasantness of that sound was all gone; it was an offense to her ear now. She said:

"There—that sham belongs to the past; I will not be called by it any more."

"I may call you simply Gwendolen? You will allow me to drop the formalities straightway and name you by your dear first name without additions?"

She was dethroning the pink and replacing it with a rosebud.

"There—that is better. I hate pinks—some pinks. Indeed, yes, you are to call me by my first name without additions—that is— well, I don't mean without additions *entirely*, but—"

It was as far as she could get. There was a pause; his intellect was struggling to comprehend; presently it did manage to catch the idea in time to save embarrassment all around, and he said, gratefully:

"*Dear* Gwendolen! I may say that?"

"Yes—part of it. But—don't kiss me when I am talking; it makes me forget what I was going to say. You can call me by part of that form, but not the last part. Gwendolen is not my name."

"Not your name?" This in a tone of wonder and surprise.

The girl's soul was suddenly invaded by a creepy apprehension, a quite definite sense of suspicion and alarm. She put his arms away from her, looked searchingly in his eye, and said:

"Answer me truly, on your honor. You are not seeking to marry me on account of my *rank?*"

The shot almost knocked him through the wall, he was so little prepared for it. There was something so finely grotesque about the question and its parent suspicion that he stopped to wonder and admire, and thus was he saved from laughing. Then, without wasting precious time, he set about the task of convincing her that he had been lured by herself alone, and had fallen in love with her only, not her title and position; that he loved her with all his heart, and could not love her more if she were a duchess, or less if she were without home, name, or family. She watched his face wistfully, eagerly, hopefully, translating his words by its expression; and when he had finished there was gladness in her heart—a tumultuous gladness, indeed, though outwardly she was calm, tranquil, even judicially austere. She prepared a surprise for him now, calculated to put a heavy strain upon those disinterested protestations of his; and thus she delivered it, burning it away word by word as the fuse burns down to a bombshell, and watching to see how far the explosion would lift him.

"Listen—and do not doubt me—for I shall speak the exact truth. Howard Tracy, I am no more an earl's child than you are!"

To her joy—and secret surprise also—it never phased him. He was ready this time, and saw his chance. He cried out, with enthusiasm, "Thank Heaven for that!" and gathered her to his arms.

To express her happiness was almost beyond her gift of speech.

"You make me the proudest girl in all the earth," she said, with her head pillowed on his shoulder. "I thought it only natural that you should be dazzled by the title—maybe even unconsciously, you being English—and that you might be deceiving yourself in thinking you only loved me, and find you didn't love me when the deception was swept away; so it makes me proud that the revelation stands for nothing and that you *do* love just me, only me—oh, prouder than any words can tell!"

"It is only you, sweetheart; I never gave one envying glance toward your father's earldom. That is utterly true, dear Gwendolen."

"There—you mustn't call me that. I hate that false name. I told you it wasn't mine. My name is Sally Sellers—or Sarah, if you like. From this time I banish dreams, visions, imaginings, and will no more of them. I am going to be myself—my genuine self, my honest self, my natural self, clear and clean of sham and folly and fraud, and worthy of you. There is no grain of social inequality between us; I, like you, am poor; I, like you, am without position or distinction; you are a struggling artist; I am that, too, in my humbler way. Our bread is honest bread; we work for our living. Hand in hand we will walk hence to the grave, helping each other in all ways, living for each other, being and remaining one in heart and purpose, one in hope and aspiration, inseparable to the end. And though our place is low, judged by the world's eye, we will make it as high as the highest in the great essentials of honest work for what we eat and wear, and conduct above reproach. We live in a land, let us be thankful, where this is all-sufficient, and no man is better than his neighbor by the grace of God, but only by his own merit."

Tracy tried to break in, but she stopped him, and kept the floor herself.

"I am not through yet. I am going to purge myself of the last vestiges of artificiality and pretense, and then start fair on your own honest level, and be worthy mate to you thenceforth. My father honestly thinks he is an earl. Well, leave him his dream; it pleases him, and does no one any harm. It was the dream of his ancestors before him. It has made fools of the house of Sellers for generations, and it made something of a fool of me, but took no deep root. I am done with it now, and for good. Forty-eight hours ago I was privately proud of being the daughter of a pinchbeck earl, and thought the proper mate for me must be a man of like degree; but to-day—oh, how grateful I am for your love, which has healed my sick brain and restored my sanity!—I could make oath that no earl's son in all the world—"

"Oh—well, but—but—"

"Why, you look like a person in a panic. What is it? What is the matter?"

"Matter? Oh, nothing—nothing. I was only going to say"—but in his flurry nothing occurred to him to say for a moment; then by a lucky inspiration he thought of something entirely sufficient for the occasion, and brought it out with eloquent force: "Oh, how beautiful you are! You take my breath away when you look like that."

It was well conceived, well timed and cordially delivered— and it got its reward.

"Let me see. Where was I? Yes, my father's earldom is pure moonshine. Look at those dreadful things on the wall. You have of course supposed them to be portraits of his ancestors, earls of Rossmore. Well, they are not. They are chromos of distinguished Americans—all moderns; but he has carried them back a thousand years by relabeling them. Andrew Jackson there is doing what he can to be the late American earl; and the newest treasure in the collection is supposed to be the young English heir—I mean the idiot with the crape; but in truth it's a shoemaker, and not Lord Berkeley at all."

"Are you sure?"

"Why, of course I am. He wouldn't look like that."

"Why?"

"Because his conduct in his last moments, when the fire was sweeping around him, shows that he was a man. It shows that he was a fine, high-souled young creature."

Tracy was strongly moved by these compliments, and it seemed to him that the girl's lovely lips took on a new loveliness when they were delivering them. He said, softly:

"It is a pity he could not know what a gracious impression his behavior was going to leave with the dearest and sweetest stranger in the land of—"

"Oh, I almost loved him! Why, I think of him every day. He is always floating about in my mind."

Tracy felt that this was a little more than was necessary. He was conscious of the sting of jealousy. He said:

"It is quite right to think of him—at least, now and then—that is, at intervals—in perhaps an admiring way—but it seems to me that—"

"Howard Tracy, are you jealous of that dead man?"

He was ashamed—and at the same time he was not jealous. In a sense the dead man was himself; in that case compliments and affection lavished upon that corpse went into his own till and were clear profit. But in another sense the dead man was not himself; and in that case all compliments and affection lavished there were wasted, and a sufficient basis for jealousy. A tiff was the result of the dispute between the two. Then they made it up, and were more loving than ever. As an affectionate clincher of the reconciliation, Sally declared that she had now banished Lord Berkeley from her mind; and added, "And in order to make sure that he shall never make trouble between us again, I will teach myself to detest that name and all that have ever borne it or ever shall bear it."

This inflicted another pang, and Tracy was minded to ask her to modify that a little—just on general principles, and as practice in not overdoing a good thing—but perhaps he might better leave things as they were and not risk bringing on another tiff. He got away from that particular, and sought less tender ground for conversation.

"I suppose you disapprove wholly of aristocracies and nobilities, now that you have renounced your title and your father's earldom?"

"*Real* ones? Oh, dear, no; but I've thrown aside our sham one for good."

This answer fell just at the right time and just in the right place to save the poor, unstable young man from changing his political complexion once more. He had been on the point of beginning to totter again, but this prop shored him up and kept him from floundering back into democracy and re-renouncing aristocracy. So he went home glad that he had asked the fortunate question. The girl would accept a little thing like a genuine earldom; she was merely prejudiced against the brummagem article. Yes, he could have his girl and have his earldom, too; that question was a fortunate stroke.

Sally went to bed happy, too; and remained happy, deliriously happy, for nearly two hours; but at last, just as she was sinking into a contented and luxurious unconsciousness, the shady devil who lives and lurks and hides and watches inside of human beings and is always waiting for a chance to do the proprietor a malicious damage, whispered to her soul and said, "That question had a harmless look, but what was *back* of it?—what was the secret motive of it?—what suggested it?"

The shady devil had knifed her, and could retire now and take a rest; the wound would attend to business for him. And it did.

Why should Howard Tracy ask that question? If he was not trying to marry her for the sake of her rank, what should suggest that question to him? Didn't he plainly look gratified when she said her objections to aristocracy had their limitations? Ah, he is after that earldom, that gilded sham—it isn't poor me he wants.

So she argued, in anguish and tears. Then she argued the opposite theory, but made a weak, poor business of it, and lost the case. She kept the arguing up, one side and then the other, the rest of the night, and at last fell asleep at dawn; fell in the fire at dawn, one may say; for that kind of sleep resembles fire, and one comes out of it with his brain baked and his physical forces fried out of him.

23

TRACY WROTE his father before he sought his bed. He wrote a
letter which he believed would get better treatment than his
cablegram received, for it contained what ought to be welcome
news: namely, that he had tried equality and working for a
living; had made a fight which he could find no reason to be
ashamed of, and in the matter of earning a living had proved
that he was able to do it; but that on the whole he had arrived at
the conclusion that he could not reform the world single-handed,
and was willing to retire from the conflict with the fair degree of
honor which he had gained, and was also willing to return home
and resume his position and be content with it and thankful for it
for the future, leaving further experiment of a missionary sort to
other young people needing the chastening and quelling persuasions of experience, the only logic sure to convince a diseased
imagination and restore it to rugged health. Then he approached
the subject of marriage with the daughter of the American Claimant with a good deal of caution and much painstaking art. He
said praiseful and appreciative things about the girl, but didn't
dwell upon that detail or make it prominent. The thing which
he made prominent was the opportunity now so happily afforded
to reconcile York and Lancaster, graft the warring roses upon
one stem, and end forever a crying injustice which had already
lasted far too long. One could infer that he had thought this
thing all out and chosen this way of making all things fair and

right because it was sufficiently fair and considerably wiser than the renunciation scheme which he had brought with him from England. One could infer that, but he didn't say it. In fact, the more he read his letter over, the more he got to inferring it himself.

When the old earl received that letter the first part of it filled him with a grim and snarly satisfaction; but the rest of it brought a snort or two out of him that could be translated differently. He wasted no ink in this emergency, either in cablegrams or letters; he promptly took ship for America to look into the matter himself. He had stanchly held his grip all this long time, and given no sign of the hunger at his heart to see his son; hoping for the cure of his insane dream, and resolute that the process should go through all the necessary stages without assuaging telegrams or other nonsense from home, and here was victory at last—victory, but stupidly marred by this idiotic marriage project. Yes, he would step over and take a hand in this matter himself.

During the first ten days following the mailing of the letter Tracy's spirits had no idle time; they were always climbing up into the clouds or sliding down into the earth as deep as the law of gravitation reached. He was intensely happy or intensely miserable by turns, according to Miss Sally's moods. He never could tell when the mood was going to change, and when it changed he couldn't tell what it was that had changed it. Sometimes she was so in love with him that her love was tropical, torrid, and she could find no language fervent enough for its expression; then suddenly, and without warning or any apparent reason, the weather would change, and the victim would find himself adrift among the icebergs and feeling as lonesome and friendless as the north pole. It sometimes seemed to him that a man might better be dead than exposed to these devastating varieties of climate.

The case was simple. Sally *wanted* to believe that Tracy's preference was disinterested; so she was always applying little tests of one sort or another, hoping and expecting that they would bring out evidence which would confirm or fortify her belief. Poor Tracy did not know that these experiments were being made upon him, consequently he walked promptly into all the traps the girl set for him. These traps consisted in apparently casual references to social distinction, aristocratic title and privilege, and such things. Often Tracy responded to these references heedlessly and not much caring what he said, provided it kept the talk going and prolonged the séance. He didn't suspect that the girl was watching his face and listening for his words as one who watches the judge's face and listens for the words which will restore him to home and friends and freedom, or shut him away from the sun and human companionship forever. He didn't suspect that his careless words were being weighed, and so he often delivered sentence of death when it would have been just as handy and all the same to him to pronounce acquittal. Daily he broke the girl's heart, nightly he sent her to the rack for sleep. He couldn't understand it.

Some people would have put this and that together and perceived that the weather never changed until one particular subject was introduced, and that then it *always* changed. And they would have looked further, and perceived that that subject was always introduced by the one party, never the other. They would have argued then that this was done for a purpose. If they could not find out what that purpose was in any simpler or easier way they would *ask*.

But Tracy was not deep enough or suspicious enough to think of these things. He noticed only one particular: that the weather was always sunny when a visit *began*. No matter how much it might cloud up later, it always began with a clear sky. He couldn't explain this curious fact to himself; he merely knew it to be a fact. The truth of the matter was that by the time Tracy had been out of Sally's sight six hours she was so famishing for a sight of him that her doubts and suspicions were all consumed away in the fire of that longing, and so always she came into his presence as surprisingly radiant and joyous as she wasn't when she went out of it.

In circumstances like these a growing portrait runs a good many risks. The portrait of Sellers, by Tracy, was fighting along day by day through this mixed weather, and daily adding to itself ineradicable signs of the checkered life it was leading. It was the happiest portrait, in spots, that was ever seen; but in other spots a damned soul looked out from it; a soul that was suffering all the different kinds of distress there are, from stomach-ache to rabies. But Sellers liked it. He said it was just himself all over—a portrait that sweated moods from every pore, and no two moods alike. He said he had as many different kinds of emotions in him as a jug.

It was a kind of a deadly work of art, maybe, but it was a starchy picture for show; for it was life-size, full length, and represented the American earl in a peer's scarlet robe, with the three ermine bars indicative of an earl's rank, and on the gray head an earl's coronet tilted just a wee bit to one side in a most gallus and winsome way. When Sally's weather was sunny the portrait made Tracy chuckle, but when her weather was overcast it disordered his mind and stopped the circulation of his blood.

Late one night when the sweethearts had been having a flawless visit together, Sally's interior devil began to work his specialty, and soon the conversation was drifting toward the customary rock. Presently, in the midst of Tracy's serene flow of talk, he felt a shudder which he knew was not his shudder, but exterior to his breast although immediately against it. After the shudder came sobs: Sally was crying.

"Oh, my darling, what have I done—what have I said? It has happened again! What *have* I done to wound you?"

She disengaged herself from his arms and gave him a look of deep reproach.

"What have you done? I will tell you what you have done. You have unwittingly revealed—oh, for the twentieth time, though I *could* not believe it, *would* not believe it!—that it is not me you love, but that foolish sham, my father's imitation earldom; and you have broken my heart!"

"Oh, my child, what are you saying? I never dreamed of such a thing!"

"Oh, Howard! Howard! the things you have uttered when you were forgetting to guard your tongue have betrayed you!"

"Things I have uttered when I was *forgetting* to guard my tongue? These are hard words. When have I *remembered* to guard it? Never in one instance. It has no office but to speak the truth. It needs no guarding for that."

"Howard, I have noted your words and weighed them when you were not thinking of their significance—and they have told me more than you meant they should."

"Do you mean to say you have answered the trust I had in you by using it as an ambuscade from which you could set snares for my unsuspecting tongue and be safe from detection while you did it? You have not done this—surely you have not done this thing. Oh, one's enemy could not do it!"

This was an aspect of the girl's conduct which she had not clearly perceived before. Was it treachery? Had she abused a trust? The thought crimsoned her cheeks with shame and remorse.

"Oh, forgive me," she said; "I did not know what I was doing. I have been so tortured—you *will* forgive me, you *must;* I have suffered so much, and I am so sorry and so humble; you *do* forgive me, *don't* you? Don't turn away, don't refuse me; it is only my love that is at fault, and you *know* I love you—love you with all my heart; I couldn't bear to—oh, dear, dear, I am so miserable, and I *never* meant any harm, and I didn't see where this insanity was carrying me, and how it was wronging and abusing the dearest heart in all the world to me—and—and—oh, take me in your arms again; I have no other refuge, no other home and hope!"

There was reconciliation again—immediate, perfect, all-embracing—and with it utter happiness. This would have been a good time to adjourn. But no, now that the cloud-breeder was revealed at last, now that it was manifest that all the sour weather had come from this girl's dread that Tracy was lured by her rank and not herself, he resolved to lay that ghost immediately and permanently by furnishing the best possible proof that he *couldn't* have had back of him at any time the suspected motive. So he said:

"Let me whisper a little secret in your ear—a secret which I have kept shut up in my breast all this time. Your rank *couldn't* ever have been an enticement. I am son and heir to an English earl!"

The girl stared at him—one, two, three moments, maybe a dozen—then her lips parted.

"You?" she said, and moved away from him, still gazing at him in a kind of blank amazement.

"Why—why, certainly I am. Why do you act like this? What have I done *now?*"

"What have you done? You have certainly made a most strange statement. You must see that yourself."

"Well," with a timid little laugh, "it may be a strange enough statement; but of what consequence is that if it is true?"

"*If* it is true. You are already retiring from it."

"Oh, not for a moment! You should not say that. I have not deserved it. I have spoken the truth; why do you doubt it?"

Her reply was prompt.

"Simply because you didn't speak it earlier."

"Oh!" It wasn't a groan exactly, but it was an intelligible enough expression of the fact that he saw the point and recognized that there was reason in it.

"You have seemed to conceal nothing from me that I ought to know concerning yourself, and you were not privileged to keep back such a thing as this from me a moment after—after—well, after you had determined to pay your court to me."

"It's true, it's true, I know it! But there were circumstances—in —in the way—circumstances which—"

She waved the circumstances aside.

"Well, you see," he said, pleadingly, "you seemed so bent on our traveling the proud path of honest labor and honorable poverty that I was terrified—that is, I was afraid—of—of—well, *you* know how you talked."

"Yes, I know how I talked. And I also know that before the talk was finished you inquired how I stood as regards aristocracies, and my answer was calculated to relieve your fears."

He was silent awhile. Then he said, in a discouraged way:

"I don't see any way out of it. It was a mistake. That is in truth all it was, just a mistake. No harm was meant, no harm in the world. I didn't see how it might some time look. It is my way. I don't seem to see far."

The girl was almost disarmed for a moment. Then she flared up again.

"An earl's son! Do earls' sons go about working in lowly callings for their bread and butter?"

"God knows they don't! I have wished they did."

"Do earls' sons sink their degree in a country like this, and come sober and decent to sue for the hand of a born child of poverty when they can go drunk, profane, and steeped in dishonorable debt and buy the pick and choice of the millionaires' daughters of America? *You* an earl's son! Show me the signs."

"I thank God I am not able—if those are the signs. But yet I am an earl's son and heir. It is all I can say. I wish you would believe me, but you will not. I know no way to persuade you."

She was about to soften again, but his closing remark made her bring her foot down with smart vexation, and she cried out:

"Oh, you drive all patience out of me! Would you have one believe that you haven't your proofs at hand, and yet are what you say you are? You do not put your hand in your pocket *now* —for you have nothing there. You make a claim like this, and then venture to travel without credentials. These are simply incredibilities. Don't you see that yourself?"

He cast about in his mind for a defense of some kind or other —hesitated a little, and then said, with difficulty and diffidence:

"I will tell you just the truth, foolish as it will seem to you—to anybody, I suppose—but it *is* the truth. I had an ideal—call it a dream, a folly, if you will—but I wanted to renounce the privileges and unfair advantages enjoyed by the nobility and wrung from the nation by force and fraud, and purge myself of my share of those crimes against right and reason by thenceforth comrading with the poor and humble on equal terms, earning with my own hands the bread I ate, and rising by my own merit if I rose at all."

The young girl scanned his face narrowly while he spoke; and there was something about his simplicity of manner and statement which touched her—touched her almost to the danger-point; but she set her grip on the yielding spirit and choked it to quiescence; it could not be wise to surrender to compassion or any kind of sentiment yet; she must ask one or two more questions. Tracy was reading her face; and what he read there lifted his drooping hopes a little.

"An earl's son to do that! Why, he were a man! A man to love! —oh, more, a man to worship!"

"Why, I—"

"But he never lived! He is not born, he will not be born. The self-abnegation that could do that—even in utter folly, and hopeless of conveying benefit to any, beyond the mere example —could be mistaken for greatness; why, it would *be* greatness in this cold age of sordid ideals! A moment—wait—let me finish; I have one question more. Your father is earl of what?"

"Rossmore—and I am Viscount Berkeley."

The fat was in the fire again. The girl felt so outraged that it was difficult for her to speak.

"How *can* you venture such a brazen thing! You know that he is dead, and you know that I know it. Oh, to rob the living of name and honors for a selfish and temporary advantage is crime enough, but to rob the defenseless dead—why, it is more than crime: it *degrades* crime!"

"Oh, listen to me—just a word—don't turn away like that. Don't go—don't leave me so—stay one moment. On my honor—"

"Oh, on your honor!"

"On my honor I am what I say! And I will prove it, and you will believe, I know you will. I will bring you a message—a cablegram—"

"When?"

"To-morrow—next day—"

"Signed 'Rossmore'?"

"Yes—signed 'Rossmore.'"

"What will that prove?"

"What will it prove? What *should* it prove?"

"If you force me to say it—possibly the presence of a confederate somewhere."

This was a hard blow, and staggered him. He said, dejectedly:

"It is true. I did not think of it. Oh, my God, I do not know any way to do; I do everything wrong. You are going?—and you won't say even good night—or good-by? Ah, we have not parted like this before."

"Oh, I *want* to run and—no, go now." A pause—then she said, "You may bring the message when it comes."

"Oh, may I? God bless you."

He was gone; and none too soon; her lips were already quivering, and now she broke down. Through her sobbings her words broke from time to time.

"Oh, he is gone. I have lost him, I shall never see him any more. And he didn't kiss me good-by; never even offered to force a kiss from me, and he *knowing* it was the very, very last, and I expecting he would, and never *dreaming* he would treat me so after all we have been to each other. Oh, oh, oh, oh, what shall I do, what *shall* I do? He is a dear, poor, miserable, good-hearted, transparent liar and humbug, but oh, I *do* love him so!" After a little she broke into speech again. "How dear he is! and I shall miss him so, I shall miss him so! Why *won't* he ever think to *forge* a message and fetch it?—but no, he never will, he never thinks of anything; he's so honest and simple it wouldn't ever occur to him. Oh, what *did* possess him to think he could succeed as a fraud—and he hasn't the first requisite except duplicity that I can see. Oh, dear, I'll go to bed and give it all up. Oh, I *wish* I had told him to come and tell me whenever he didn't get any telegram—and now it's all my own fault if I never see him again. How my eyes must look!"

24

Time drags heavily for all concerned—Success of "Pigs in the Clover"—Sellers is "fixed" for his temperance lecture—Colonel and Mrs. Sellers start for Europe—Interview of Hawkins and Sally—Tracy an impostor

NEXT DAY, sure enough, the cablegram didn't come. This was an immense disaster; for Tracy couldn't go into the presence without that ticket, although it wasn't going to possess any value as evidence. But if the failure of the cablegram on that first day may be called an immense disaster, where is the dictionary that can turn out a phrase sizable enough to describe the tenth day's failure? Of course every day that the cablegram didn't come made Tracy all of twenty-four hours more ashamed of himself than he was the day before, and made Sally fully twenty-four hours more certain than ever that he not only hadn't any father anywhere, but hadn't even a confederate—and so it followed that he was a double-dyed humbug, and couldn't be otherwise.

These were hard days for Barrow and the art firm. All these had their hands full trying to comfort Tracy. Barrow's task was particularly hard, because he was made a confidant in full, and therefore had to humor Tracy's delusion that he had a father, and that the father was an earl, and that he was going to send a cablegram. Barrow early gave up the idea of trying to convince Tracy that he hadn't any father, because this had such a bad effect on the patient, and worked up his temper to such an alarming degree. He had tried, as an experiment, letting Tracy think he had a father; the result was so good that he went further, with proper caution, and tried letting him think his father was an earl; this wrought so well that he grew bold, and tried letting him think he had two fathers, if he wanted to, but he didn't want to, so Barrow withdrew one of them and substituted letting him think he was going to get a cablegram—which Barrow judged he wouldn't, and was right; but Barrow worked the cablegram daily for all it was worth, and it was the one thing that kept Tracy alive; that was Barrow's opinion.

And these were bitter, hard days for poor Sally, and mainly delivered up to private crying. She kept her furniture pretty damp, and so caught cold, and the dampness and the cold and the sorrow together undermined her appetite, and she was a pitiful enough object, poor thing! Her state was bad enough, as per statement of it above quoted; but all the forces of nature and circumstance seemed conspiring to make it worse—and succeeding. For instance, the morning after her dismissal of Tracy, Hawkins and Sellers read in the Associated Press despatches that a toy puzzle called Pigs in the Clover had come into sudden favor within the past few weeks, and that from the Atlantic to the Pacific all the populations of all the States had knocked off work to play with it, and that the business of the country had now come to a standstill by consequence; that judges, lawyers, burglars, parsons, thieves, merchants, mechanics, murderers, women, children, babies—everybody, indeed, could be seen from morning till midnight absorbed in one deep project and purpose, and only one: to pen those pigs, work out that puzzle successfully; that all gaiety, all cheerfulness, had departed from the nation, and in its place care, preoccupation, and anxiety sat upon every countenance, and all faces were drawn, distressed, and furrowed with the signs of age and trouble, and marked with the still sadder signs of mental decay and incipient madness; that factories were at work night and day in eight cities, and yet to supply the demand for the puzzle was thus far impossible. Hawkins was wild with joy, but Sellers was calm. Small matters could not disturb his serenity. He said:

"That's just the way things go. A man invents a thing which could revolutionize the arts, produce mountains of money, and bless the earth, and who will bother with it or show any interest in it?—and so you are just as poor as you were before. But you invent some worthless thing to amuse yourself with, and would throw it away if let alone, and all of a sudden the whole world makes a snatch for it and out crops a fortune. Hunt up that Yankee and collect, Hawkins—half is yours, you know. Leave me to potter at my lecture."

This was a temperance lecture. Sellers was head chief in the Temperance camp, and had lectured, now and then, in that interest, but had been dissatisfied with his efforts; wherefore he was now about to try a new plan. After much thought he had concluded that a main reason why his lectures lacked fire or something was that they were too transparently amateurish; that is to say, it was probably too plainly perceptible that the lecturer was trying to tell people about the horrid effects of liquor when he didn't really know anything about those effects except from hearsay, since he had hardly ever tasted an intoxicant in his life. His scheme now was to prepare himself to speak from bitter experience. Hawkins was to stand by with the bottle, calculate the doses, watch the effects, make notes of results, and otherwise assist in the preparation. Time was short, for the ladies would be along about noon—that is to say, the temperance organization called the Daughters of Siloam—and Sellers must be ready to head the procession.

The time kept slipping along—Hawkins did not return—Sellers could not venture to wait longer; so he attacked the bottle himself, and proceeded to note the effects. Hawkins got back at last; took one comprehensive glance at the lecturer, and went down and headed off the procession. The ladies were grieved to hear that the champion had been taken suddenly ill and violently so, but glad to hear that it was hoped he would be out again in a few days.

As it turned out, the old gentleman didn't turn over or show any signs of life worth speaking of for twenty-four hours. Then he asked after the procession, and learned what had happened about it. He was sorry; said he had been "fixed" for it. He remained abed several days, and his wife and daughter took turns in sitting with him and ministering to his wants. Often he patted Sally's head and tried to comfort her.

"Don't cry, my child, don't cry so; *you* know your old father did it by mistake, and didn't mean a bit of harm; you know he wouldn't intentionally do anything to make you ashamed for the world; you know he was trying to do good, and only made the mistake through ignorance, not knowing the right doses and Washington not there to help. Don't cry so, dear, it breaks my old heart to see you, and think I've brought this humiliation on you, and you so dear to me and so good. I won't ever do it again, indeed I won't; now be comforted, honey, that's a good child."

But when she wasn't on duty at the bedside the crying went on just the same; then the mother would try to comfort her, and say:

"Don't cry, dear, *he* never meant any harm; it was all one of those happens that you can't guard against when you are trying experiments that way. You see, *I* don't cry. It's because I know him so well. I could never look anybody in the face again if he had got into such an amazing condition as that a-purpose; but, bless you, his intention was pure and high, and that makes the *act* pure, though it was higher than was necessary. We're not humiliated, dear; he did it under a noble impulse, and we don't need to be ashamed. There, don't cry any more, honey."

Thus the old gentleman was useful to Sally during several days as an explanation of her tearfulness. She felt thankful to him for the shelter he was affording her, but often said to herself, "It's a shame to let him see in my crying a reproach—as if he could ever do anything that could make me reproach him! But I can't confess; I've got to go on using him for a pretext; he's the only one I've got in the world, and I do need one so much."

As soon as Sellers was out again, and found that stacks of money had been placed in bank for him and Hawkins by the Yankee, he said, "*Now* we'll soon see who's the Claimant and who's the Authentic. I'll just go over there and warm up that House of Lords." During the next few days he and his wife were so busy with preparations for the voyage that Sally had all the privacy she needed, and all the chance to cry that was good for her. Then the old pair left for New York—and England.

Sally had also had a chance to do another thing. That was, to make up her mind that life was not worth living upon the present terms. If she *must* give up her impostor and die, doubtless she must submit; but might she not lay her whole case before some disinterested person first, and see if there wasn't perhaps some saving way out of the matter? She turned this idea over in her mind a good deal. In her first visit with Hawkins after her parents were gone, the talk fell upon Tracy, and she was impelled to set her case before the statesman and take his counsel. So she poured out her heart, and he listened with painful solicitude. She concluded, pleadingly, with:

"*Don't* tell me he is an impostor. I suppose he is, but doesn't it look to you as if he isn't? You are cool, you know, and outside; and so, maybe it can look to you as if he isn't one, when it can't to me. *Doesn't* it look to you as if he isn't? Couldn't you—*can't* it look to you that way—for—for my sake?"

The poor man was troubled, but he felt obliged to keep in the neighborhood of the truth. He fought around the present detail a little while, then gave it up, and said he couldn't see his way to clearing Tracy.

"No," he said; "the truth is, he's an impostor."

"That is, you—you feel a little certain, but not entirely—oh, not *entirely*, Mr. Hawkins!"

"It's a pity to have to say it—I do hate to say it—but I don't think anything about it, I *know* he's an impostor."

"Oh, now, Mr. Hawkins, you *can't* go that far. A body *can't* really know it, you know. It isn't *proved* that he's not what he says he is."

Should he come out and make a clean breast of the whole wretched business? Yes—at least, the most of it—it ought to be done. So he set his teeth and went at the matter with determination, but purposing to spare the girl one pain—that of knowing that Tracy was a criminal.

"Now I am going to tell you a plain tale; one not pleasant for me to tell or for you to hear, but we've got to stand it. I know all about that fellow, and I *know* he is no earl's son."

The girl's eyes flashed, and she said:

"I don't care a snap for that—go on!"

This was so wholly unexpected that it at once obstructed the narrative; Hawkins was not even sure that he had heard aright. He said:

"I don't know that I quite understand. Do you mean to say that if he was all right and proper otherwise, you'd be indifferent about the earl part of the business?"

"Absolutely."

"You'd be entirely satisfied with him, and wouldn't *care* for his not being an earl's son—that *being* an earl's son wouldn't add any value to him?"

"Not the least value that I would care for. Why, Mr. Hawkins, I've gotten over all that day-dreaming about earldoms and aristocracies and all such nonsense, and am become just a plain ordinary nobody and content with it; and it is to *him* I owe my cure. And as to anything being able to add a value to him, nothing can do that. He is the whole world to me, just as he is; he comprehends *all* the values there are—then how can you *add* one?"

"She's pretty far gone." He said that to himself. He continued, still to himself, "I must change my plan again; I can't seem to strike one that will stand the requirements of this most variegated emergency five minutes on a stretch. Without making this fellow a criminal, I believe I will invent a name and a character for him calculated to disenchant her. If it fails to do it, then I'll know that the next rightest thing to do will be to help her to her fate, poor thing, not hinder her."

Then he said aloud:

"Well, Gwendolen—"

"I want to be called Sally."

"I'm glad of it; I like it better myself. Well, then, I'll tell you about this man Snodgrass."

"Snodgrass! Is *that* his name?"

"Yes—Snodgrass. The other's his *nom de plume*."

"It's hideous!"

"I know it is, but we can't help our names."

"And that is truly his real name—and not Howard Tracy?"

Hawkins answered, regretfully:

"Yes; it seems a pity."

The girl sampled the name musingly once or twice:

"Snodgrass! Snodgrass! No, I could not endure that. I could not get used to it. No, I should call him by his first name. What is his first name?"

"His—er—his initials are S. M."

"His initials? I don't care anything about his initials. I can't call him by his initials. What do they *stand* for?"

"Well, you see, his father was a physician, and he—he—well, he was an idolator of his profession, and he—well, he was a very eccentric man, and—"

"What do they *stand* for? What are you shuffling about?"

"They—well, they stand for Spinal Meningitis. His father being a phy—"

"I never heard such an infamous name! Nobody can ever call a person *that*—a person they love. I wouldn't call an enemy by such a name. It sounds like an epithet." After a moment she added, with a kind of consternation, "Why, it would be *my* name! Letters would come with it on."

"Yes—Mrs. Spinal Meningitis Snodgrass."

"Don't repeat it—don't; I can't bear it. Was the father a lunatic?"

"No, that is not charged."

"I am glad of that, because that is transmissible. What do you think *was* the matter with him, then?"

"Well, I don't really know. The family used to run a good deal to idiots, and so, maybe—"

"Oh, there isn't any maybe about it. This one was an idiot."

"Well, yes—he could have been. He was suspected."

"Suspected!" said Sally, with irritation. "Would one *suspect* there was going to be a dark time if he saw the constellations fall out of the sky? But that is enough about the idiot, I don't take any interest in idiots; tell me about the son."

"Very well, then; this one was the eldest, but not the favorite. His brother, Zylobalsamum—"

"Wait—give me a chance to realize that. It is perfectly stupefying. Zylo—what did you call it?"

"Zylobalsamum."

"I never heard such a name. It sounds like a disease. Is it a disease?"

"No, I don't think it's a disease. It's either Scriptural or—"

"Well, it's not Scriptural."

"Then it's anatomical. I knew it was one or the other. Yes, I remember now; it *is* anatomical. It's a ganglion—a nerve center—it is what is called the zylobalsamum process."

"Well, go on; and if you come to any more of them, omit the names; they make one feel so uncomfortable."

"Very well, then. As I said, this one was not a favorite in the family, and so he was neglected in every way—never sent to school, always allowed to associate with the worst and coarsest characters, and so of course he has grown up a rude, vulgar, ignorant, dissipated ruffian, and—"

"He? It's no such thing! You ought to be more generous than to make such a statement as that about a poor young stranger who —who—why, he is the very opposite of that! He is considerate, courteous, obliging, modest, gentle, refined, cultivated—*oh*, for shame! how can you say such things about him?"

"I don't blame you, Sally—indeed, I haven't a word of blame for you for being blinded by your affection—blinded to these minor defects which are so manifest to others who—"

"Minor defects? Do you call these minor defects? What are murder and arson, pray?"

"It is a difficult question to answer straight off—and of course estimates of such things vary with environment. With us, out our way, they would not necessarily attract as much attention as with you, yet they are often regarded with disapproval—"

"Murder and arson are regarded with disapproval?"

"Oh, frequently."

"With disapproval! Who *are* those Puritans you are talking

about? But wait—how did you come to know so much about this family? Where did you get all this hearsay evidence?"

"Sally, it isn't hearsay evidence. That is the serious part of it. I *knew* that family—personally."

This was a surprise.

"You? You actually knew them?"

"Knew Zylo, as we used to call him, and knew his father, Dr. Snodgrass. I didn't know your own Snodgrass, but have had glimpses of him from time to time, and I heard about him all the time. He was the common talk, you see, on account of his—"

"On account of his not being a house-burner or an assassin, I suppose. That would have made him commonplace. Where did you know these people?"

"In Cherokee Strip."

"Oh, how preposterous! There are not enough people in Cherokee Strip to *give* anybody a reputation, good or bad. There isn't a quorum. Why, the whole population consists of a couple of wagon-loads of horse thieves."

Hawkins answered, placidly:

"Our friend was one of those wagon-loads."

Sally's eyes burned, and her breath came quick and fast, but she kept a fairly good grip on her anger, and did not let it get the advantage of her tongue. The statesman sat still and waited for developments. He was content with his work. It was as handsome a piece of diplomatic art as he had ever turned out, he thought; and now let the girl make her own choice. He judged she would let her specter go; he hadn't a doubt of it, in fact; but anyway let the choice be made, and he was ready to ratify it and offer no further hindrance.

Meantime Sally had thought her case out and made up her mind. To the Major's disappointment the verdict was against him. Sally said:

"He has no friend but me, and I will not desert him now. I will not marry him if his moral character is bad; but if he can prove that it isn't, I will—and he shall have the chance. To me he seems utterly good and dear; I've never seen anything about him that looked otherwise—except, of course, his calling himself an earl's son. Maybe that is only vanity, and no real harm when you get to the bottom of it. I do *not* believe he is any such person as you have painted him. I want to see him. I want you to find him and send him to me. I will implore him to be honest with me, and tell me the whole truth, and not be afraid."

"Very well; if that is your decision, I will do it. But, Sally, you know he's poor, and—"

"Oh, *I* don't care anything about that. That's neither here nor there. Will you bring him to me?"

"I'll do it. When?"

"Oh, dear, it's getting toward dark now, and so you'll have to put it off till morning. But you *will* find him in the morning, *won't* you? Promise."

"I'll have him here by daylight."

"Oh, *now* you're your own old self again—and lovelier than ever!"

"I couldn't ask fairer than that. Good-by, dear."

Sally mused a moment alone; then said, earnestly, "I love him in *spite* of his name!" and went about her affairs with a light heart.

25

Telegram: "She's going to marry the materializee"—Interview between Tracy and Sally—Arrival of the usurping earl—"You can have him if you'll take him"—A quiet wedding at the Towers—Sellers does not join the party to England—Preparing to furnish climates to order

HAWKINS WENT straight to the telegraph-office and disburdened his conscience. He said to himself, "She's not going to give this galvanized cadaver up, that's plain. Wild horses can't pull her away from him. I've done my share; it's for Sellers to take an innings now." So he sent this message to New York:

Come back. Hire special train. She's going to marry the materializee.

Meantime a note came to Rossmore Towers to say that the Earl of Rossmore had just arrived from England, and would do himself the pleasure of calling in the evening. Sally said to herself, "It is a pity he didn't stop in New York; but it's no matter; he can go up to-morrow and see my father. He has come over here to tomahawk papa very likely, or buy out his claim. This thing would have excited me a while back, but it has only one interest for me now, and only one value. I can say to—to—Spine, Spiny, Spinal—I don't like any *form* of that name!—I can say to him to-morrow, '*Don't* try to keep it up any more, or I shall have to tell you whom I have been talking with last night, and then you will be embarrassed."

Tracy couldn't know he was to be invited for the morrow, or he might have waited. As it was, he was too miserable to wait any longer; for his last hope—a letter—had failed him. It was fully due to-day; it had not come. Had his father really flung him away? It looked so. It was not like his father, but it surely looked so. His father was a rather tough nut, in truth, but had never been so with his son—still, this implacable silence had a calamitous look. Anyway, Tracy would go to the Towers and—then what? He didn't know; his head was tired out with thinking—he wouldn't think about what he must do or say—let it all take care of itself. So that he saw Sally once more he would be satisfied, happen what might; he wouldn't care.

He hardly knew how he got to the Towers, or when. He knew and cared for only one thing—he was alone with Sally. She was kind, she was gentle, there was moisture in her eyes, and a yearning something in her face and manner which she could not wholly hide—but she kept her distance. They talked. By and by she said, watching his downcast countenance out of the corner of her eye:

"It's so lonesome—with papa and mamma gone. I try to read, but I can't seem to get interested in any book. I try the newspapers, but they do put such rubbish in them! You take up a paper and start to read something you think's interesting, and it goes on and on and on about how somebody—well, Dr. Snodgrass, for instance—"

Not a movement from Tracy, not the quiver of a muscle. Sally was amazed—what command of himself he must have! Being disconcerted, she paused so long that Tracy presently looked up wearily and said:

"Well?"

"Oh, I thought you were not listening. Yes, it goes on and on about this Dr. Snodgrass till you are *so* tired, and then about his younger son—the favorite son—Zylobalsamum Snodgrass—"

Not a sign from Tracy, whose head was drooping again. What supernatural self-possession! Sally fixed her eye on him and began again, resolved to blast him out of his serenity this time if she knew how to apply the dynamite that is concealed in certain forms of words when those words are properly loaded with unexpected meanings.

"And next it goes on and on and on about the eldest son—
not the favorite, this one—and how he is neglected in his poor
barren boyhood, and allowed to grow up unschooled, ignorant,
coarse, vulgar, the comrade of the community's scum, and become in his completed manhood a rude, profane, dissipated
ruffian—"

That head still drooped! Sally rose, moved softly and solemnly
a step or two, and stood before Tracy—his head came slowly up,
his meek eyes met her intense ones—then she finished, with deep
impressiveness:

"—named Spinal Meningitis Snodgrass!"

Tracy merely exhibited signs of increased fatigue. The girl was
outraged by this iron indifference and callousness, and cried
out:

"What *are* you made of?"

"I? Why?"

"Haven't you *any* sensitiveness? Don't these things touch any
poor *remnant* of delicate feeling in you?"

"N-no," he said, wonderingly, "they don't seem to. Why should
they?"

"Oh, dear me, *how* can you look so innocent, and foolish, and
good, and empty, and gentle, and all that, right in the hearing of
such things as those! Look me in the eye—straight in the eye.
There, now then, answer me without a flinch. Isn't Dr. Snodgrass
your father, and isn't Zylobalsamum your brother" (here Hawkins
was about to enter the room, but changed his mind upon hearing these words, and elected for a walk down-town, and so
glided swiftly away), "and isn't your name Spinal Meningitis,
and isn't your father a doctor and an idiot, like all the family
for generations, and doesn't he name all his children after poisons
and pestilences and abnormal anatomical eccentricities of the
human body? Answer me, some way or somehow—and quick.
Why do you sit there looking like an envelope without any
address on it and see me going mad before your face with
suspense?"

"Oh, I wish I could do—do—I wish I could do something,
anything that would give you peace again and make you happy;

but I know of nothing—I know of no way. I have never heard of these awful people before."

"What? Say it again!"

"I have never—never in my life till now."

"Oh, you *do* look so honest when you say that! It *must* be true—surely you *couldn't* look that way, you *wouldn't* look that way if it were not true—*would* you?"

"I couldn't and wouldn't. It *is* true. Oh, let us end this suffering—take me back into your heart and confidence—"

"Wait—one more thing. Tell me you told that falsehood out of mere vanity and are sorry for it; that you're *not* expecting to ever wear the coronet of an earl—"

"Truly I am cured—cured this very day—I am *not* expecting it!"

"Oh, now you *are* mine! I've got you back in the beauty and glory of your unsmirched poverty and your honorable obscurity, and nobody shall ever take you from me again but the grave! And if—"

"De Earl of Rossmore, fum Englan'!"

"My father!" The young man released the girl and hung his head.

The old gentleman stood surveying the couple—the one with a strongly complimentary right eye, the other with a mixed expression done with the left. This is difficult, and not often resorted to. Presently his face relaxed into a kind of constructive gentleness, and he said to his son:

"Don't you think you could embrace me, too?"

The young man did it with alacrity.

"Then you *are* the son of an earl, after all," said Sally, reproachfully.

"Yes, I—"

"Then I won't have you!"

"Oh, but you know—"

"No, I will not. You've told me another fib."

"She's right. Go away and leave us. I want to talk with her."

Berkeley was obliged to go. But he did not go far. He remained on the premises. At midnight the conference between the old gentleman and the young girl was still going blithely on, but it presently drew to a close, and the former said:

"I came all the way over here to inspect you, my dear, with the general idea of breaking off this match if there were *two* fools of you, but as there's only one, you can have him if you'll take him."

"Indeed, I will, then. May I kiss you?"

"You may. Thank you. Now you shall have that privilege whenever you are good."

Meantime Hawkins had long ago returned and slipped up into the laboratory. He was rather disconcerted to find his late invention, Snodgrass, there. The news was told him: that the English Rossmore was come, "and I'm his son, Viscount Berkeley, not Howard Tracy any more."

Hawkins was aghast. He said:

"Good gracious, then you're dead!"

"Dead?"

"Yes, you are—we've got your ashes."

"Hang those ashes, I'm tired of them; I'll give them to my father."

Slowly and painfully the statesman worked the truth into his head that this was really a flesh-and-blood young man, and not the insubstantial resurrection he and Sellers had so long supposed him to be. Then he said, with feeling:

"I'm so glad; so glad on Sally's account, poor thing. We took you for a departed materialized bank thief from Tahlequah. This will be a heavy blow to Sellers." Then he explained the whole matter to Berkeley, who said:

"Well, the Claimant must manage to stand the blow, severe as it is. But he'll get over the disappointment."

"Who—the Colonel? He'll get over it the minute he invents a new miracle to take its place. And he's already at it by this time. But look here—what do you suppose became of the man you've been *representing* all this time?"

"I don't know. I saved his clothes—it was all I could do. I am afraid he lost his life."

"Well, you must have found twenty or thirty thousand dollars in those clothes in money or certificates of deposit."

"No, I found only five hundred and a trifle. I borrowed the trifle and banked the five hundred."

"What 'll we do about it?"

"Return it to the owner."

"It's easy said, but not easy to manage. Let's leave it alone till we get Sellers's advice. And that reminds me. I've got to run and meet Sellers and explain who you are *not* and who you *are*, or he'll come thundering in here to stop his daughter from marrying a phantom. But—suppose your father came over here to break off the match?"

"Well, isn't he down-stairs getting acquainted with Sally? That's all safe."

So Hawkins departed to meet and prepare the Sellerses.

Rossmore Towers saw great times and late hours during the succeeding week. The two earls were such opposites in nature that they fraternized at once. Sellers said privately that Rossmore was the most extraordinary character he had ever met—a man just made out of the condensed milk of human kindness, yet with the ability to totally hide the fact from any but the most practised character-reader; a man whose whole being was sweetness, patience, and charity, yet with a cunning so profound, an ability so marvelous in the acting of a double part, that many a person of considerable intelligence might live with him for centuries and never suspect the presence in him of these characteristics.

Finally there was a quiet wedding at the Towers, instead of a big one at the British Embassy, with the militia and the fire brigades and the temperance organizations on hand in torchlight procession, as at first proposed by one of the earls. The art firm and Barrow were present at the wedding, and the tinner and Puss had been invited, but the tinner was ill and Puss was nursing him—for they were engaged.

The Sellerses were to go to England with their new allies for a brief visit, but when it was time to take the train from Washington the Colonel was missing. Hawkins was going as far as New

York with the party, and said he would explain the matter on the road. The explanation was in a letter left by the Colonel in Hawkins's hands. In it he promised to join Mrs. Sellers later in England, and then went on to say:

The truth is, my dear Hawkins, a mighty idea has been born to me within the hour, and I must not even stop to say good-by to my dear ones. A man's highest duty takes precedence of all minor ones, and must be attended to with his best promptness and energy, at whatsoever cost to his affections or his convenience. And first of all a man's duties is his duty to his own honor—he must keep that spotless. Mine is threatened. When I was feeling sure of my imminent future solidity, I forwarded to the Czar of Russia—perhaps prematurely—an offer for the purchase of Siberia, naming a vast sum. Since then an episode has warned me that the method by which I was expecting to acquire this money—materialization upon a scale of limitless magnitude—is marred by a taint of temporary uncertainty. His imperial majesty may accept my offer at any moment. If this should occur now, I should find myself painfully embarrassed—in fact, financially inadequate. I could not take Siberia. This would become known, and my credit would suffer.

Recently my private hours have been dark indeed, but the sun shines again now; I see my way; I shall be able to meet my obligation, and without having to ask an extension of the stipulated time, I think. This grand new idea of mine—the sublimest I have ever conceived—will save me whole, I am sure. I am leaving for San Francisco this moment to test it by the help of the great Lick telescope. Like all of my more notable discoveries and inventions, it is based upon hard, practical scientific laws; all other bases are unsound, and hence untrustworthy.

In brief, then, I have conceived the stupendous idea of reorganizing the climates of the earth according to the desire of the populations interested. That is to say, I will furnish climates to order, for cash or negotiable paper, taking the old climates in part payment, of course, at a fair discount, where they are in condition to be repaired at small cost and let out for hire to poor and remote communities not able to afford a good climate and not caring for an expensive one for mere display. My studies have convinced me that the regulation of climates and the breeding of new varieties at will from the old stock is a feasible thing; indeed, I am convinced that it has been done before, done in prehistoric times by now forgotten and unrecorded civilizations. Everywhere I find hoary evidences of artificial manipulation of climates in bygone times. Take the glacial period. Was that produced by accident? Not at all; it was done for money. I have a thousand proofs of it, and will some day reveal them.

I will confide to you an outline of my idea. It is to utilize the spots on the sun—get control of them, you understand, and apply the stupendous energies which they wield to beneficent purposes in the reorganization of our climates. At present they merely make trouble and do harm in the evoking of cyclones and other kinds of electric storms; but once under humane and intelligent control this will cease, and they will become a boon to man.

I have my plan all mapped out, whereby I hope and expect to acquire complete and perfect control of the sunspots, also details of the method whereby I shall employ the same commercially; but I will not venture to go into particulars before the patents shall have been issued. I shall hope and expect to sell shop-rights to the minor countries at a reasonable figure, and supply a good business article of climate to the great empires at special rate, together with fancy brands for coronations, battles, and other great and particular occasions. There are billions of money in this enterprise, no expensive plant is required, and I shall begin to realize in a few days—in a few weeks at furthest. I shall stand ready to pay cash for Siberia the moment it is delivered, and thus save my honor and my credit. I am confident of this.

I would like you to provide a proper outfit and start north as soon as I telegraph you, be it night or be it day. I wish you to take up all the country stretching away from the north pole on all sides for many degrees south, and buy Greenland and Iceland at the best figure you can get now while they are cheap. It is my intention to move one of the tropics up there and transfer the frigid zone to the equator.

I will have the entire Arctic Circle in the market as a summer resort next year, and will use the surplusage of the old climate, over and above what can be utilized on the equator, to reduce the temperature of opposition resorts. But I have said enough to give you an idea of the prodigious nature of my scheme and the feasible and enormously profitable character of it. I shall join all you happy people in England as soon as I shall have sold out some of my principal climates and arranged with the Czar about Siberia.

Meantime, watch for a sign from me. Eight days from now we shall be wide asunder; for I shall be on the border of the Pacific, and you far out on the Atlantic, approaching England. That day, if I am alive and my sublime discovery is proved and established, I will send you greeting, and my messenger shall deliver it where you are, in the solitudes of the sea; for I will waft a vast sun-spot across the disk like drifting smoke, and you will know it for my love-sign, and will say, "Mulberry Sellers throws us a kiss across the universe."

APPENDIX

WEATHER FOR USE IN THIS BOOK

Selected from the best authorities

A brief though violent thunder-storm which had raged over the city was passing away; but still, though the rain had ceased more than an hour before, wild piles of dark and coppery clouds, in which a fierce and rayless glow was laboring, gigantically overhung the grotesque and huddled vista of dwarf houses, while in the distance, sheeting high over the low, misty confusion of gables and chimneys, spread a pall of dead, leprous blue, suffused with blotches of dull, glistening yellow, and with black plague-spots of vapor floating and faint lightnings crinkling on its surface. Thunder, still muttering in the close and sultry air, kept the scared dwellers in the street within, behind their closed shutters; and all deserted, cowed, dejected, squalid, like poor, stupid, top-heavy things that had felt the wrath of the summer tempest, stood the drenched structures on either side of the narrow and crooked way, ghastly and picturesque under the giant canopy. Rain dripped wretchedly in slow drops of melancholy sound from their projecting eaves upon the broken flagging, lay there in pools or trickled into the swollen drains, where the fallen torrent sullenly gurgled on its way to the river.—*"The Brazen Android": W. D. O'Connor.*

The fiery mid-March sun a moment hung
Above the bleak Judean wilderness;
Then darkness swept upon us, and 'twas night.
        —*"Easter-Eve at Kerak-Moab": Clinton Scollard.*

The quick-coming winter twilight was already at hand. Snow was again falling, sifting delicately down, incidentally as it were.—*"Felicia": Fanny N. D. Murfree.*

Merciful heavens! The whole west, from right to left, blazes up with a fierce light, and next instant the earth reels and quivers with the awful shock of ten thousand batteries of artillery. It is the signal for the Fury to spring—for a thousand demons to scream and shriek—for innumerable serpents of fire to writhe and light up the blackness.

Now the rain falls—now the wind is let loose with a terrible shriek—now the lightning is so constant that the eyes burn, and the thunder-claps merge into an awful roar, as did the eight hundred cannon at Gettysburg. Crash! Crash! Crash! It is the cottonwood-trees falling to earth. Shriek! Shriek! Shriek! It is the Demon racing along the plain and uprooting even the blades of grass. Shock! Shock! Shock! It is the Fury flinging his fiery bolts into the bosom of the earth.—*"The Demon and the Fury": M. Quad.*

Away up the gorge all diurnal fancies trooped into the wide liberties of endless luminous vistas of azure sunlit mountains beneath the shining azure heavens. The sky, looking down in deep blue placidities, only here and there smote the water to azure emulations of its tint. —*"In the 'Stranger People's' Country:" Charles Egbert Craddock.*

There was every indication of a dust-storm, though the sun still shone brilliantly. The hot wind had become wild and rampant. It was whipping up the sandy coating of the plain in every direction. High in the air were seen whirling spires and cones of sand—a curious effect against the deep-blue sky. Below, puffs of sand were breaking out of the plain in every direction, as though the plain were alive with invisible horsemen. These sandy cloudlets were instantly dissipated by the wind; it was the larger clouds that were lifted whole into the air, and the larger clouds of sand were becoming more and more the rule.

Alfred's eye, quickly scanning the horizon, descried the roof of the boundary-rider's hut still gleaming in the sunlight. He remembered the hut well. It could not be farther than four miles, if as much as that, from this point of the track. He also knew these dust-storms of old; Bindarra was notorious for them. Without thinking twice, Alfred put spurs to his horse and headed for the hut. Before he had ridden half the distance the detached clouds of sand banded together in one dense whirlwind, and it was only owing to his horse's instinct that he did not ride wide of the hut altogether; for during the last half-mile he never saw the hut, until its outline loomed suddenly over his horse's ears; and by then the sun was invisible.—*"A Bride from the Bush."*

And the rain was upon the earth forty days and forty nights.— *Genesis.*

PUDD'NHEAD
WILSON

CONTENTS

A WHISPER TO THE READER

THERE IS no character, howsoever good and fine, but it can
be destroyed by ridicule, howsoever poor and witless. Observe the ass, for instance: his character is about perfect,
he is the choicest spirit among all the humbler animals, yet
see what ridicule has brought him to. Instead of feeling
complimented when we are called an ass, we are left in
doubt.—*Pudd'nhead Wilson's Calendar.*

A PERSON who is ignorant of legal matters is always liable to make
mistakes when he tries to photograph a court scene with his pen;
and so I was not willing to let the law chapters in this book
go to press without first subjecting them to rigid and exhausting
revision and correction by a trained barrister—if that is what
they are called. These chapters are right now in every detail, for
they were rewritten under the immediate eye of William Hicks,
who studied law part of a while in southwest Missouri thirty-five
years ago and then came over here to Florence for his health and
is still helping for exercise and board in Macaroni Vermicelli's
horse-feed shed which is up the back alley as you turn around
the corner out of the Piazza del Duomo just beyond the house
where that stone that Dante used to sit on six hundred years ago
is let into the wall when he let on to be watching them build
Giotto's campanile and yet always got tired looking as soon as
Beatrice passed along on her way to get a chunk of chestnut cake
to defend herself with in case of a Ghibelline outbreak before
she got to school, at the same old stand where they sell the same
old cake to this day and it is just as light and good as it was then,

too, and this is not flattery, far from it. He was a little rusty on his law, but he rubbed up for this book, and those two or three legal chapters are right and straight now. He told me so himself.

Given under my hand this second day of January, 1893, at the Villa Viviani, village of Settignano, three miles back of Florence, on the hills—the same certainly affording the most charming view to be found on this planet, and with it the most dream-like and enchanting sunsets to be found in any planet or even in any solar system—and given, too, in the swell room of the house, with the busts of Cerretani senators and other grandees of this line looking approvingly down upon me as they used to look down upon Dante, and mutely asking me to adopt them into my family, which I do with pleasure, for my remotest ancestors are but spring chickens compared with these robed and stately antiques, and it will be a great and satisfying lift for me, that six hundred years will.

MARK TWAIN.

1

Pudd'nhead Wins His Name

Tell the truth or trump—but get the trick.
—*Pudd'nhead Wilson's Calendar.*

THE SCENE of this chronicle is the town of Dawson's Landing, on the Missouri side of the Mississippi, half a day's journey, per steamboat, below St. Louis.

In 1830 it was a snug little collection of modest one and two-story frame dwellings whose whitewashed exteriors were almost concealed from sight by climbing tangles of rose vines, honeysuckles, and morning-glories. Each of these pretty homes had a garden in front fenced with white palings and opulently stocked with hollyhocks, marigolds, touch-me-nots, prince's-feathers, and other old-fashioned flowers; while on the window-sills of the houses stood wooden boxes containing moss-rose plants and terra-cotta pots in which grew a breed of geranium whose spread of intensely red blossoms accented the prevailing pink tint of the rose-clad house-front like an explosion of flame. When there was room on the ledge outside of the pots and boxes for a cat, the cat was there—in sunny weather—stretched at full length, asleep and blissful, with her furry belly to the sun and a paw curved over her nose. Then that house was complete, and its contentment and peace were made manifest to the world by this symbol, whose testimony is infallible. A home without a cat—and a well-fed, well-petted and properly revered cat—may be a perfect home, perhaps, but how can it prove title?

All along the streets, on both sides, at the outer edge of the brick sidewalks, stood locust-trees with trunks protected by wooden boxing, and these furnished shade for summer and a sweet fragrance in spring when the clusters of buds came forth. The main street, one block back from the river, and running parallel with it, was the sole business street. It was six blocks long, and in each block two or three brick stores three stories high towered above interjected bunches of little frame shops. Swinging signs creaked in the wind, the street's whole length. The candy-striped pole, which indicates nobility proud and ancient along the palace-bordered canals of Venice, indicated merely the humble barber shop along the main street of Dawson's Landing. On a chief corner stood a lofty unpainted pole wreathed from top to bottom with tin pots and pans and cups, the chief tinmonger's noisy notice to the world (when the wind blew) that his shop was on hand for business at that corner.

The hamlet's front was washed by the clear waters of the great river; its body stretched itself rearward up a gentle incline; its most rearward border fringed itself out and scattered its houses about the baseline of the hills; the hills rose high, inclosing the town in a half-moon curve, clothed with forests from foot to summit.

Steamboats passed up and down every hour or so. Those belonging to the little Cairo line and the little Memphis line always stopped; the big Orleans liners stopped for hails only, or to land passengers or freight; and this was the case also with the great flotilla of "transients." These latter came out of a dozen rivers—the Illinois, the Missouri, the Upper Mississippi, the Ohio, the Monongahela, the Tennessee, the Red River, the White River, and so on; and were bound every whither and stocked with every imaginable comfort or necessity which the Mississippi's communities could want, from the frosty Falls of St. Anthony down through nine climates to torrid New Orleans.

Dawson's Landing was a slaveholding town, with a rich slave-worked grain and pork country back of it. The town was sleepy and comfortable and contented. It was fifty years old, and was growing slowly—very slowly, in fact, but still it was growing. The chief citizen was York Leicester Driscoll, about forty years old, judge of the county court. He was very proud of his old Virginian ancestry, and in his hospitalities and his rather formal and stately manners he kept up its traditions. He was fine and just and generous. To be a gentleman—a gentleman without stain or blemish—was his only religion, and to it he was always faithful. He was respected, esteemed, and beloved by all the community. He was well off, and was gradually adding to his store. He and his wife were very nearly happy, but not quite, for they had no children. The longing for the treasure of a child had grown stronger and stronger as the years slipped away, but the blessing never came—and was never to come.

With this pair lived the Judge's widowed sister, Mrs. Rachel Pratt, and she also was childless—childless, and sorrowful for that reason, and not to be comforted. The women were good and commonplace people, and did their duty and had their reward in clear consciences and the community's approbation. They were Presbyterians, the Judge was a free-thinker.

Pembroke Howard, lawyer and bachelor, aged about forty, was another old Virginian grandee with proved descent from the First Families. He was a fine, brave, majestic creature, a gentleman according to the nicest requirements of the Virginia rule, a devoted Presbyterian, an authority on the "code," and a man always courteously ready to stand up before you in the field if any act or word of his had seemed doubtful or suspicious to you, and explain it with any weapon you might prefer from brad-awls to artillery. He was very popular with the people, and was the Judge's dearest friend.

Then there was Colonel Cecil Burleigh Essex, another F. F. V. of formidable caliber—however, with him we have no concern.

Percy Northumberland Driscoll, brother to the Judge, and younger than he by five years, was a married man, and had had children around his hearthstone; but they were attacked in detail by measles, croup, and scarlet fever, and this had given the doctor a chance with his effective antediluvian methods; so the cradles were empty. He was a prosperous man, with a good head for speculations, and his fortune was growing. On the 1st of

February, 1830, two boy babes were born in his house; one to him, the other to one of his slave girls, Roxana by name. Roxana was twenty years old. She was up and around the same day, with her hands full, for she was tending both babies.

Mrs. Percy Driscoll died within the week. Roxy remained in charge of the children. She had her own way, for Mr. Driscoll soon absorbed himself in his speculations and left her to her own devices.

In that same month of February, Dawson's Landing gained a new citizen. This was Mr. David Wilson, a young fellow of Sctoch parentage. He had wandered to this remote region from his birthplace in the interior of the state of New York, to seek his fortune. He was twenty-five years old, college-bred, and had finished a post-college course in an Eastern law school a couple of years before.

He was a homely, freckled, sandy-haired young fellow, with an intelligent blue eye that had frankness and comradeship in it and a covert twinkle of a pleasant sort. But for an unfortunate remark of his, he would no doubt have entered at once upon a successful career at Dawson's Landing. But he made his fatal remark the first day he spent in the village, and it "gaged" him. He had just made the acquaintance of a group of citizens when an invisible dog began to yelp and snarl and howl and make himself very comprehensively disagreeable, whereupon young Wilson said, much as one who is thinking aloud:

"I wish I owned half of that dog."

"Why?" somebody asked.

"Because I would kill my half."

The group searched his face with curiosity, with anxiety even, but found no light there, no expression that they could read. They fell away from him as from something uncanny, and went into privacy to discuss him. One said:

"'Pears to be a fool."

"'Pears?" said another. "*Is*, I reckon you better say."

"Said he wished he owned *half* of the dog, the idiot," said a third. "What did he reckon would become of the other half if he killed his half? Do you reckon he thought it would live?"

"Why, he must have thought it, unless he *is* the downrightest fool in the world; because if he hadn't thought it, he would have wanted to own the whole dog, knowing that if he killed his half and the other half died, he would be responsible for that half just the same as if he had killed that half instead of his own. Don't it look that way to you, gents?"

"Yes, it does. If he owned one half of the general dog, it would be so; if he owned one end of the dog and another person owned the other end, it would be so, just the same; particularly in the first case, because if you kill one half of a general dog, there ain't any man that can tell whose half it was, but if he owned one end of the dog, maybe he could kill his end of it and—"

"No, he couldn't, either; he couldn't and not be responsible if the other end died, which it would. In my opinion the man ain't in his right mind."

"In my opinion he hain't *got* any mind."

No. 3 said: "Well, he's a lummox, anyway."

"That's what he is," said No. 4, "he's a labrick—just a Simon-pure labrick, if ever there was one."

"Yes, sir, he's a dam fool, that's the way I put him up," said No. 5. "Anybody can think different that wants to, but those are my sentiments."

"I'm with you, gentlemen," said No. 6. "Perfect jackass—yes, and it ain't going too far to say he is a pudd'nhead. If he ain't a pudd'nhead, I ain't no judge, that's all."

Mr. Wilson stood elected. The incident was told all over the town, and gravely discussed by everybody. Within a week he had lost his first name; Pudd'nhead took its place. In time he came to be liked, and well liked, too; but by that time the nickname had got well stuck on, and it stayed. That first day's verdict made him a fool, and he was not able to get it set aside, or even modified. The nickname soon ceased to carry any harsh or unfriendly feeling with it, but it held its place, and was to continue to hold its place for twenty long years.

2

Driscoll Spares His Slaves

Adam was but human—this explains it all. He did not want
the apple for the apple's sake, he wanted it only because it
was forbidden. The mistake was in not forbidding the
serpent; then he would have eaten the serpent.
                                    —*Pudd'nhead Wilson's Calendar.*

PUDD'NHEAD WILSON had a trifle of money when he arrived, and
he bought a small house on the extreme western verge of the
town. Between it and Judge Driscoll's house there was only a
grassy yard, with a paling fence dividing the properties in the
middle. He hired a small office down in the town and hung out a
tin sign with these words on it:

DAVID WILSON
ATTORNEY AND COUNSELOR-AT-LAW
SURVEYING, CONVEYANCING, ETC.

But his deadly remark had ruined his chance—at least in the
law. No clients came. He took down his sign after a while and
put it up on his own house with the law features knocked out of
it. It offered his services now in the humble capacities of land-
surveyor and expert accountant. Now and then he got a job of
surveying to do, and now and then a merchant got him to
straighten out his books. With Scotch patience and pluck he resolved to live down his reputation and work his way into the
legal field yet. Poor fellow! he could not foresee that it was
going to take him such a weary long time to do it.

He had a rich abundance of idle time, but it never hung heavy
on his hands, for he interested himself in every new thing that

was born into the universe of ideas, and studied it and experimented upon it at his house. One of his pet fads was palmistry. To another one he gave no name, neither would he explain to anybody what its purpose was, but merely said it was an amusement. In fact, he had found that his fads added to his reputation as a pudd'nhead; therefore he was growing chary of being too communicative about them. The fad without a name was one which dealt with people's fingermarks. He carried in his coat pocket a shallow box with grooves in it, and in the grooves strips of glass five inches long and three inches wide. Along the lower edge of each strip was pasted a slip of white paper. He asked people to pass their hands through their hair (thus collecting upon them a thin coating of the natural oil) and then make a thumbmark on a glass strip, following it with the mark of the ball of each finger in succession. Under this row of faint greaseprints he would write a record on the strip of white paper—thus:

JOHN SMITH, *right hand—*

and add the day of the month and the year, then take Smith's left hand on another glass strip, and add name and date and the words "left hand." The strips were now returned to the grooved box, and took their place among what Wilson called his "records."

He often studied his records, examining and poring over them with absorbing interest until far into the night; but what he found there—if he found anything—he revealed to no one. Sometimes he copied on paper the involved and delicate pattern left by the ball of a finger, and then vastly enlarged it with a pantograph so that he could examine its web of curving lines with ease and convenience.

One sweltering afternoon—it was the first day of July, 1830—he was at work over a set of tangled account-books in his workroom, which looked westward over a stretch of vacant lots, when a conversation outside disturbed him. It was carried on in yells, which showed that the people engaged in it were not close together:

"Say, Roxy, how does yo' baby come on?" This from the distant voice.

"Fust-rate; how does *you* come on, Jasper?" This yell was from close by.

"Oh, I's middlin'; hain't got noth'n' to complain of. I's gwine to come a-court'n' you bimeby, Roxy."

"*You* is, you black mudcat! Yah—yah—yah! I got somep'n' better to do den 'sociat'n' wid niggers as black as you is. Is ole Miss Cooper's Nancy done give you de mitten?" Roxy followed this sally with another discharge of care-free laughter.

"You's jealous, Roxy, dat's what's de matter wid *you*, you hussy —yah—yah—yah! Dat's de time I got you!"

"Oh, yes, *you* got me, hain't you. 'Clah to goodness if dat conceit o' yo'n strikes in, Jasper, it gwine to kill you sho'. If you b'longed to me I'd sell you down de river 'fo' you git too fur gone. Fust time I runs acrost yo' marster, I's gwine to tell him so."

This idle and aimless jabber went on and on, both parties enjoying the friendly duel and each well satisfied with his own share of the wit exchanged—for wit they considered it.

Wilson stepped to the window to observe the combatants; he could not work while their chatter continued. Over in the vacant lots was Jasper, young, coal-black, and of magnificent build, sitting on a wheelbarrow in the pelting sun—at work, supposably, whereas he was in fact only preparing for it by taking an hour's rest before beginning. In front of Wilson's porch stood Roxy, with a local hand-made baby-wagon, in which sat her two charges— one at each end and facing each other. From Roxy's manner of speech, a stranger would have expected her to be black, but she was not. Only one-sixteenth of her was black, and that sixteenth did not show. She was of majestic form and stature, her attitudes were imposing and statuesque, and her gestures and movements distinguished by a noble and stately grace. Her complexion was very fair, with the rosy glow of vigorous health in the cheeks, her face was full of character and expression, her eyes were brown and liquid, and she had a heavy suit of fine soft hair which was also brown, but the fact was not apparent because her head was bound about with a checkered handkerchief and the hair was concealed under it. Her face was shapely, intelligent, and comely —even beautiful. She had an easy, independent carriage—when she was among her own caste—and a high and "sassy" way, withal; but of course she was meek and humble enough where white people were.

To all intents and purposes Roxy was as white as anybody, but the one-sixteenth of her which was black outvoted the other fifteen parts and made her a negro. She was a slave, and salable as such. Her child was thirty-one parts white, and he, too, was a slave, and by a fiction of law and custom a negro. He had blue eyes and flaxen curls like his white comrade, but even the father of the white child was able to tell the children apart— little as he had commerce with them—by their clothes; for the white babe wore ruffled soft muslin and a coral necklace, while the other wore merely a coarse tow-linen shirt which barely reached to its knees, and no jewelry.

The white child's name was Thomas à Becket Driscoll, the other's name was Valet de Chambre; no surname—slaves hadn't the privilege. Roxana had heard that phrase somewhere, the fine sound of it had pleased her ear, and as she had supposed it was a name, she loaded it onto her darling. It soon got shortened to "Chambers," of course.

Wilson knew Roxy by sight, and when the duel of wit began to play out, he stepped outside to gather in a record or two. Jasper went to work energetically, at once, perceiving that his leisure was observed. Wilson inspected the children and asked:

"How old are they, Roxy?"

"Bofe de same age, sir—five months. Bawn de fust o' Feb'uary."

"They're handsome little chaps. One's just as handsome as the other, too."

A delighted smile exposed the girl's white teeth, and she said:

"Bless yo' soul, Misto Wilson, it's pow'ful nice o' you to say dat, 'ca'se one of 'em ain't on'y a nigger. Mighty prime little nigger, *I* al'ays says, but dat's 'ca'se it's mine, o' course."

"How do you tell them apart, Roxy, when they haven't any clothes on?"

Roxy laughed a laugh proportioned to her size, and said:

"Oh, *I* kin tell 'em 'part, Misto Wilson, but I bet Marse Percy couldn't, not to save his life."

Wilson chatted along for a while, and presently got Roxy's finger-prints for his collection—right hand and left—on a couple of his glass strips; then labeled and dated them, and took the "records" of both children, and labeled and dated them also.

Two months later, on the 3d of September, he took this trio of finger-marks again. He liked to have a "series," two or three "takings" at intervals during the period of childhood, these to be followed by others at intervals of several years.

The next day—that is to say, on the 4th of September—something occurred which profoundly impressed Roxana. Mr. Driscoll missed another small sum of money—which is a way of saying that this was not a new thing, but had happened before. In truth, it had happened three times before. Driscoll's patience was exhausted. He was a fairly humane man toward slaves and other animals; he was an exceedingly humane man toward the erring of his own race. Theft he could not abide, and plainly there was a thief in his house. Necessarily the thief must be one of his negroes. Sharp measures must be taken. He called his servants before him. There were three of these, besides Roxy; a man, a woman, and a boy twelve years old. They were not related. Mr. Driscoll said:

"You have all been warned before. It has done no good. This time I will teach you a lesson. I will sell the thief. Which of you is the guilty one?"

They all shuddered at the threat, for here they had a good home, and a new one was likely to be a change for the worse. The denial was general. None had stolen anything—not money, anyway—a little sugar, or cake, or honey, or something like that, that "Marse Percy wouldn't mind or miss," but not money—never a cent of money. They were eloquent in their protestations, but Mr. Driscoll was not moved by them. He answered each in turn with a stern "Name the thief!"

The truth was, all were guilty but Roxana; she suspected that the others were guilty, but she did not know them to be so. She was horrified to think how near she had come to being guilty herself; she had been saved in the nick of time by a revival in the colored Methodist church, a fortnight before, at which time and place she "got religion." The very next day after that gracious experience, while her change of style was fresh upon her and she was vain of her purified condition, her master left a couple of dollars lying unprotected on his desk, and she happened upon that temptation when she was polishing around with a dust-rag. She looked at the money awhile with a steadily rising resentment, then she burst out with:

"Dad blame dat revival, I wisht it had 'a' be'n put off till to-morrow!"

Then she covered the tempter with a book, and another member of the kitchen cabinet got it. She made this sacrifice as a matter of religious etiquette; as a thing necessary just now, but by no means to be wrested into a precedent; no, a week or two would limber up her piety, then she would be rational again, and the next two dollars that got left out in the cold would find a comforter—and she could name the comforter.

Was she bad? Was she worse than the general run of her race? No. They had an unfair show in the battle of life, and they held it no sin to take military advantage of the enemy—in a small way; in a small way, but not in a large one. They would smouch provisions from the pantry whenever they got a chance; or a brass thimble, or a cake of wax, or an emery-bag, or a paper of needles, or a silver spoon, or a dollar bill, or small articles of clothing, or any other property of light value; and so far were they from considering such reprisals sinful, that they would go to church and shout and pray the loudest and sincerest with their plunder in their pockets. A farm smokehouse had to be kept heavily padlocked, for even the colored deacon himself could not resist a ham when Providence showed him in a dream, or otherwise, where such a thing hung lonesome and longed for some one to love. But with a hundred hanging before him the deacon would not take two—that is, on the same night. On frosty nights the humane negro prowler would warm the end of a plank and put it up under the cold claws of chickens roosting in a tree; a drowsy hen would step onto the comfortable board, softly clucking her gratitude, and the prowler would dump her into his bag, and later into his stomach, perfectly sure that in taking this trifle from the

man who daily robbed him of an inestimable treasure—his liberty
—he was not committing any sin that God would remember
against him in the Last Great Day.

"Name the thief!"

For the fourth time Mr. Driscoll had said it, and always in the
same hard tone. And now he added these words of awful import:

"I give you one minute"—he took out his watch. "If at the end
of that time you have not confessed, I will not only sell all four of
you, *but*—I will sell you DOWN THE RIVER!"

It was equivalent to condemning them to hell! No Missouri
negro doubted this. Roxy reeled in her tracks and the color
vanished out of her face; the others dropped to their knees as if
they had been shot; tears gushed from their eyes, their supplicating hands went up, and three answers came in the one instant:

"I done it!"

"I done it!"

"I done it!—have mercy, marster—Lord have mercy on us po'
niggers!"

"Very good," said the master, putting up his watch, "I will sell
you *here* though you don't deserve it. You ought to be sold
down the river."

The culprits flung themselves prone, in an ecstasy of gratitude,
and kissed his feet, declaring that they would never forget his
goodness and never cease to pray for him as long as they lived.
They were sincere, for like a god he had stretched forth his
mighty hand and closed the gates of hell against them. He knew,
himself, that he had done a noble and gracious thing, and was
privately well pleased with his magnanimity; and that night he
set the incident down in his diary, so that his son might read
it in after years, and be thereby moved to deeds of gentleness
and humanity himself.

3

Roxy Plays a Shrewd Trick

Whoever has lived long enough to find out what life is, knows how deep a debt of gratitude we owe to Adam, the first great benefactor of our race. He brought death into the world.—*Pudd'nhead Wilson's Calendar.*

PERCY DRISCOLL slept well the night he saved his house-minions from going down the river, but no wink of sleep visited Roxy's eyes. A profound terror had taken possession of her. Her child could grow up and be sold down the river! The thought crazed her with horror. If she dozed and lost herself for a moment, the next moment she was on her feet flying to her child's cradle to see if it was still there. Then she would gather it to her heart and pour out her love upon it in a frenzy of kisses, moaning, crying, and saying, "Dey sha'n't, oh, dey *sha'n't!*—yo' po' mammy will kill you fust!"

Once, when she was tucking it back in its cradle again, the other child nestled in its sleep and attracted her attention. She went and stood over it a long time communing with herself: "What has my po' baby done, dat he couldn't have yo' luck? He hain't done noth'n'. God was good to you; why warn't he good to him? Dey can't sell *you* down de river. I hates yo' pappy; he hain't got no heart—for niggers he hain't, anyways. I hates him, en I could kill him!" She paused awhile, thinking; then she burst into wild sobbings again, and turned away, saying, "Oh, I got to kill my chile, dey ain't no yuther way—killin' *him* wouldn't save de chile fum goin' down de river. Oh, I got to do it, yo' po' mammy's got to kill you to save you, honey"—she gathered her baby to her bosom now, and began to smother it with caresses—"Mammy's got to kill you—how *kin* I do it! But yo' mammy ain't gwine to desert you—no, no; *dah*, don't cry—she gwine *wid* you, she gwine to kill herself, too. Come along, honey, come along wid mammy; we gwine to jump in de river, den de troubles o' dis worl' is all over—dey don't sell po' niggers down the river over *yonder*."

She started toward the door, crooning to the child and hushing it; midway she stopped suddenly. She caught sight of her new Sunday gown—a cheap curtain-calico thing, a conflagration of gaudy colors and fantastic figures. She surveyed it wistfully, longingly.

"Hain't ever wore it yet," she said, "en it's jist lovely." Then she nodded her head in response to a pleasant idea, and added, "No, I ain't gwine to be fished out, wid everybody lookin' at me, in dis mis'able ole linsey-woolsey."

She put down the child and made the change. She looked in the glass and was astonished at her beauty. She resolved to make her death-toilet perfect. She took off her handkerchief-turban and dressed her glossy wealth of hair "like white folks"; she added some odds and ends of rather lurid ribbon and a spray of atrocious artificial flowers; finally she threw over her shoulders a fluffy thing called a "cloud" in that day, which was of a blazing red complexion. Then she was ready for the tomb.

She gathered up her baby once more; but when her eye fell upon its miserably short little gray towel-linen shirt and noted the contrast between its pauper shabbiness and her own volcanic irruption of infernal splendors, her mother-heart was touched, and she was ashamed.

"No, dolling, mammy ain't gwine to treat you so. De angels is gwine to 'mire you jist as much as dey does yo' mammy. Ain't gwine to have 'em putt'n' dey han's up 'fo' dey eyes en sayin' to David en Goliah en dem yuther prophets, 'Dat chile is dress' too indelicate fo' dis place.'"

By this time she had stripped off the shirt. Now she clothed the naked little creature in one of Thomas à Becket's snowy long baby gowns, with its bright blue bows and dainty flummery of ruffles.

"Dah—now you's fixed." She propped the child in a chair and

stood off to inspect it. Straightway her eyes began to widen with astonishment and admiration, and she clapped her hands and cried out, "Why, it do beat all!—I *never* knowed you was so lovely. Marse Tommy ain't a bit puttier—not a single bit."

She stepped over and glanced at the other infant; she flung a glance back at her own; then one more at the heir of the house. Now a strange light dawned in her eyes, and in a moment she was lost in thought. She seemed in a trance; when she came out of it she muttered, "When I 'uz a-washin' 'em in de tub, yistiddy, his own pappy asked me which of 'em was his'n."

She began to move about like one in a dream. She undressed Thomas à Becket, stripping him of everything, and put the tow-linen shirt on him. She put his coral necklace on her own child's neck. Then she placed the children side by side, and after earnest inspection she muttered:

"Now who would b'lieve clo'es could do de like o' dat? Dog my cats if it ain't all *I* kin do to tell t'other fum which, let alone his pappy."

She put her cub in Tommy's elegant cradle and said:

"You's young Marse *Tom* fum dis out, en I got to practise and git used to 'memberin' to call you dat, honey, or I's gwine to make a mistake some time en git us bofe into trouble. Dah—now you lay still en don't fret no mo', Marse Tom—oh, thank de good Lord in heaven, you's saved, you's saved!—dey ain't no man kin ever sell mammy's po' little honey down de river now!"

She put the heir of the house in her own child's unpainted pine cradle, and said, contemplating its slumbering form uneasily:

"I's sorry for you, honey; I's sorry, God knows I is,—but what *kin* I do, what *could* I do? Yo' pappy would sell him to somebody, some time, en den he'd go down de river, sho', en I couldn't, couldn't *couldn't* stan' it."

She flung herself on her bed and began to think and toss, toss and think. By and by she sat suddenly upright, for a comforting thought had flown through her worried mind:

"'Tain't no sin—*white* folks has done it! It ain't no sin, glory to goodness it ain't no sin! *Dey's* done it—yes, en dey was de biggest quality in de whole bilin', too—*kings!*"

She began to muse; she was trying to gather out of her memory the dim particulars of some tale she had heard some time or other. At last she said:

"Now I's got it; now I 'member. It was dat ole nigger preacher dat tole it, de time he come over here fum Illinois en preached in de nigger church. He said dey ain't nobody kin save his own self—can't do it by faith, can't do it by works, can't do it no way at all. Free grace is de *on'y* way, en dat don't come fum nobody but jis' de Lord; en *he* kin give it to anybody he please, saint or sinner—*he* don't kyer. He do jis' as he's a mineter. He s'lect out anybody dat suit him, en put another one in his place, en make de fust one happy forever en leave t'other one to burn wid Satan. De preacher said it was jist like dey done in Englan' one time, long time ago. De queen she lef' her baby layin' aroun' one day, en went out callin'; en one o' de niggers roun' 'bout de place dat was 'mos' white, she come in en see de chile layin' aroun', en tuck en put her own chile's clo'es on de queen's chile, en put de queen's chile's clo'es on her own chile, en den lef' her own chile layin' aroun' en tuck en toted de queen's chile home to de nigger quarter, en nobody ever foun' it out, en her chile was de king bimeby, en sole de queen's chile down de river one time when dey had to settle up de estate. Dah, now—de preacher said it his own self, en it ain't no sin, 'ca'se white folks done it. *Dey* done it—yes, *dey* done it; en not on'y jis' common white folks nuther, but de biggest quality dey is in de whole bilin'. Oh, I's *so* glad I 'member 'bout dat!"

She got up light-hearted and happy, and went to the cradles and spent what was left of the night "practising." She would give her own child a light pat and say humbly, "Lay still, Marse Tom," then give the real Tom a pat and say with severity, "Lay *still,* Chambers!—does you want me to take somep'n' *to* you?"

As she progressed with her practice, she was surprised to see how steadily and surely the awe which had kept her tongue reverent and her manner humble toward her young master was transferring itself to her speech and manner toward the usurper, and how similarly handy she was becoming in transferring her motherly curtness of speech and peremptoriness of manner to the unlucky heir of the ancient house of Driscoll.

She took occasional rests from practising, and absorbed herself in calculating her chances.

"Dey'll sell dese niggers to-day fo' stealin' de money, den dey'll buy some mo' dat don't know de chillen—so *dat's* all right. When I takes de chillen out to git de air, de minute I's roun' de corner I's gwine to gaum dey mouths all roun' wid jam, den dey can't *nobody* notice dey's changed. Yes, I gwineter do dat till I's safe, if it's a year.

"Dey ain't but one man dat I's afeard of, en dat's dat Pudd'n-head Wilson. Dey calls him a pudd'nhead, en says he's a fool. My lan', dat man ain't no mo' fool den I is! He's de smartes' man in dis town, less'n it's Jedge Driscoll or maybe Pem Howard. Blame dat man, he worries me wid dem ornery glasses o' his'n; I b'lieve he's a witch. But nemmine, I's gwine to happen aroun' dah one o' dese days en let on dat I reckon he wants to print de chillen's fingers ag'in; en if *he* don't notice dey's changed, I bound dey ain't nobody gwine to notice it, en den I's safe, sho'. But I reckon I'll tote along a hoss-shoe to keep off de witch work."

The new negroes gave Roxy no trouble, of course. The master gave her none, for one of his speculations was in jeopardy, and his mind was so occupied that he hardly saw the children when he looked at them, and all Roxy had to do was to get them both into a gale of laughter when he came about; then their faces were mainly cavities exposing gums, and he was gone again before the spasm passed and the little creatures resumed a human aspect.

Within a few days the fate of the speculation became so dubious that Mr. Percy went away with his brother the Judge, to see what could be done with it. It was a land speculation, as usual, and it had gotten complicated with a lawsuit. The men were gone seven weeks. Before they got back Roxy had paid her visit to Wilson, and was satisfied. Wilson took the finger-prints, labeled them with the names and the date—October the first—put them carefully away and continued his chat with Roxy, who seemed very anxious that he should admire the great advance in flesh and beauty which the babies had made since he took their finger-prints a month before. He complimented their improvement to her contentment; and as they were without any disguise of jam or other stain, she trembled all the while and was miserably frightened lest at any moment he—

But he didn't. He discovered nothing; and she went home jubilant, and dropped all concern about the matter permanently out of her mind.

4

The Ways of the Changelings

Adam and Eve had many advantages, but the principal one was, that they escaped teething.
—*Pudd'nhead Wilson's Calendar.*

There is this trouble about special providences—namely, there is so often a doubt as to which party was intended to be the beneficiary. In the case of the children, the bears, and the prophet, the bears got more real satisfaction out of the episode than the prophet did, because they got the children.—*Pudd'nhead Wilson's Calendar.*

THIS HISTORY must henceforth accommodate itself to the change which Roxana has consummated, and call the real heir "Chambers" and the usurping little slave "Thomas à Becket"—shortening this latter name to "Tom," for daily use, as the people about him did.

"Tom" was a bad baby from the very beginning of his usurpation. He would cry for nothing; he would burst into storms of devilish temper without notice, and let go scream after scream and squall after squall, then climax the thing with "holding his breath"—that frightful specialty of the teething nursling, in the throes of which the creature exhausts its lungs, then is convulsed with noiseless squirmings and twistings and kickings in the effort to get its breath, while the lips turn blue and the mouth stands wide and rigid, offering for inspection one wee tooth set in the lower rim of a hoop of red gums; and when the appalling stillness has endured until one is sure the lost breath will never return, a nurse comes flying, and dashes water in the child's face, and— presto! the lungs fill, and instantly discharge a shriek, or a yell, or a howl which bursts the listening ear and surprises the owner of it into saying words which would not go well with a halo if he had one. The baby Tom would claw anybody who came within reach of his nails, and pound anybody he could reach with his rattle. He would scream for water until he got it, and then throw cup and all on the floor and scream for more. He was indulged in all his caprices, howsoever troublesome and exasperating they might be; he was allowed to eat anything he wanted, particularly things that would give him the stomach-ache.

When he got to be old enough to begin to toddle about and say broken words and get an idea of what his hands were for, he was a more consummate pest than ever. Roxy got no rest while he was awake. He would call for anything and everything he saw, simply saying, "Awnt it!" (want it) which was a command. When it was brought, he said in a frenzy, and motioning it away with his hands, "Don't awnt it! don't awnt it!" and the moment it was gone he set up frantic yells of "Awnt it! awnt it! awnt it!" and Roxy had to give wings to her heels to get that thing back to him again before he could get time to carry out his intention of going into convulsions about it.

What he preferred above all other things was the tongs. This was because his "father" had forbidden him to have them lest he break windows and furniture with them. The moment Roxy's back was turned he would toddle to the presence of the tongs and say, "Like it!" and cock his eye to one side to see if Roxy was observing; then, "Awnt it!" and cock his eye again; then, "Hab it!" with another furtive glance; and finally, "Take it!"—and the prize was his. The next moment the heavy implement was raised aloft; the next, there was a crash and a squall, and the cat was off on three legs to meet an engagement; Roxy would arrive just as the lamp or a window went to irremediable smash.

Tom got all the petting, Chambers got none. Tom got all the delicacies, Chambers got mush and milk, and clabber without sugar. In consequence, Tom was a sickly child and Chambers wasn't. Tom was "fractious," as Roxy called it, and overbearing; Chambers was meek and docile.

With all her splendid common sense and practical every-day ability, Roxy was a doting fool of a mother. She was this toward her child—and she was also more than this; by the fiction created by herself, he was become her master; the necessity of recognizing this relation outwardly and of perfecting herself in the forms required to express the recognition, had moved her to such diligence and faithfulness in practising these forms that this exercise soon concreted itself into habit; it became automatic and unconscious; then a natural result followed; deceptions intended solely for others gradually grew practically into self-deceptions as well; the mock reverence became real reverence, the mock obsequiousness real obsequiousness, the mock homage real homage; the little counterfeit rift of separation between imitation slave and imitation master widened and widened, and became an abyss, and a very real one—and on one side of it stood Roxy, the dupe of her own deceptions, and on the other stood her child, no longer a usurper to her, but her accepted and recognized master. He was her darling, her master, and her deity all in one, and in her worship of him she forgot who she was and what he had been.

In babyhood Tom cuffed and banged and scratched Chambers unrebuked, and Chambers early learned that between meekly bearing it and resenting it, the advantage all lay with the former policy. The few times that his persecutions had moved him beyond control and made him fight back had cost him very dear at headquarters; not at the hands of Roxy, for if she ever went beyond scolding him sharply for "forgitt'n' who his young marster was," she at least never extended her punishment beyond a box on the ear. No, Percy Driscoll was the person. He told Chambers that under no provocation whatever was he privileged to lift his hand against his little master. Chambers overstepped the line three times, and got three such convincing canings from the man who was his father and didn't know it, that he took Tom's cruelties in all humility after that, and made no more experiments.

Outside of the house the two boys were together all through their boyhood. Chambers was strong beyond his years, and a good fighter; strong because he was coarsely fed and hard-worked about the house, and a good fighter because Tom furnished him plenty of practice—on white boys whom he hated and was afraid of. Chambers was his constant body-guard, to and from school; he was present on the playground at recess to protect his charge. He fought himself into such a formidable reputation, by and by, that Tom could have changed clothes with him, and "ridden in peace," like Sir Kay in Launcelot's armor.

He was good at games of skill, too. Tom staked him with marbles to play "keeps" with, and then took all the winnings away from him. In the winter season Chambers was on hand, in Tom's worn-out clothes, with "holy" red mittens, and "holy" shoes, and pants "holy" at the knees and seat, to drag a sled up the hill for Tom, warmly clad, to ride down on; but he never got a ride himself. He built snow men and snow fortifications under Tom's directions. He was Tom's patient target when Tom wanted to do some snowballing, but the target couldn't fire back. Chambers carried Tom's skates to the river and strapped them on him, then trotted around after him on the ice, so as to be on hand when wanted; but he wasn't ever asked to try the skates himself.

In summer the pet pastime of the boys of Dawson's Landing was to steal apples, peaches, and melons from the farmers' fruit-wagons—mainly on account of the risk they ran of getting their heads laid open with the butt of the farmer's whip. Tom was a distinguished adept at these thefts—by proxy. Chambers did his stealing, and got the peach-stones, apple-cores, and melon-rinds for his share.

Tom always made Chambers go in swimming with him, and stay by him as a protection. When Tom had had enough, he would slip out and tie knots in Chambers's shirt, dip the knots in the water to make them hard to undo, then dress himself and sit by and laugh while the naked shiverer tugged at the stubborn knots with his teeth.

Tom did his humble comrade these various ill turns partly out of native viciousness, and partly because he hated him for his superiorities of physique and pluck, and for his manifold clevernesses. Tom couldn't dive, for it gave him splitting headaches. Chambers could dive without inconvenience, and was fond of doing it. He excited so much admiration, one day, among a crowd of white boys, by throwing back somersaults from the stern of a canoe, that it wearied Tom's spirit, and at last he shoved the canoe underneath Chambers while he was in the air —so he came down on his head in the canoe-bottom; and while he lay unconscious, several of Tom's ancient adversaries saw that their long-desired opportunity was come, and they gave the false heir such a drubbing that with Chambers's best help he was hardly able to drag himself home afterward.

When the boys were fifteen and upward, Tom was "showing off" in the river one day, when he was taken with a cramp, and shouted for help. It was a common trick with the boys—particularly if a stranger was present—to pretend a cramp and howl for help; then when the stranger came tearing hand over hand to the rescue, the howler would go on struggling and howling till he was close at hand, then replace the howl with a sarcastic smile and swim blandly away, while the town boys assailed the dupe with a volley of jeers and laughter. Tom had never tried this joke as yet, but was supposed to be trying it now, so the boys held warily back; but Chambers believed his master was in earnest, therefore he swam out, and arrived in time, unfortunately, and saved his life.

This was the last feather. Tom had managed to endure everything else, but to have to remain publicly and permanently under such an obligation as this to a nigger, and to this nigger of all niggers—this was too much. He heaped insults upon Chambers for "pretending" to think he was in earnest in calling for help, and said that anybody but a block-headed nigger would have known he was funning and left him alone.

Tom's enemies were in strong force here, so they came out with their opinions quite freely. They laughed at him, and called him coward, liar, sneak, and other sorts of pet names, and told him they meant to call Chambers by a new name after this, and make it common in the town—"Tom Driscoll's niggerpappy" —to signify that he had had a second birth into this life, and that Chambers was the author of his new being. Tom grew frantic under these taunts, and shouted:

"Knock their heads off, Chambers! knock their heads off! What do you stand there with your hands in your pockets for?"

Chambers expostulated, and said, "But, Marse Tom, dey's too many of 'em—dey's—"

"Do you hear me?"

"Please, Marse Tom, don't make me! Dey's so many of 'em dat—"

Tom sprang at him and drove his pocket-knife into him two or three times before the boys could snatch him away and give the wounded lad a chance to escape. He was considerably hurt, but not seriously. If the blade had been a little longer his career would have ended there.

Tom had long ago taught Roxy "her place." It had been many a day now since she had ventured a caress or a fondling epithet in his quarter. Such things, from a "nigger," were repulsive to him, and she had been warned to keep her distance and remember who she was. She saw her darling gradually cease from being her son, she saw *that* detail perish utterly; all that was left was master—master, pure and simple, and it was not a gentle mastership, either. She saw herself sink from the sublime height of motherhood to the somber depths of unmodified slavery. The abyss of separation between her and her boy was complete. She was merely his chattel now, his convenience, his dog, his cringing and helpless slave, the humble and unresisting victim of his capricious temper and vicious nature.

Sometimes she could not go to sleep, even when worn out with fatigue, because her rage boiled so high over the day's experiences with her boy. She would mumble and mutter to herself:

"He struck me, en I warn't no way to blame—struck me in de face, right before folks. En he's al'ays callin' me nigger-wench, en hussy, en all dem mean names, when I's doin' de very bes' I kin. Oh, Lord, I done so much for him—I lift' him away up to what he is—en dis is what I git for it."

Sometimes when some outrage of peculiar offensiveness stung her to the heart, she would plan schemes of vengeance and revel in the fancied spectacle of his exposure to the world as an impostor and a slave; but in the midst of these joys fear would strike her; she had made him too strong; she could prove nothing, and—heavens, she might get sold down the river for her pains! So her schemes always went for nothing, and she laid them aside in impotent rage against the fates, and against herself for playing the fool on that fatal September day in not providing herself with a witness for use in the day when such a thing might be needed for the appeasing of her vengeance-hungry heart.

And yet the moment Tom happened to be good to her, and kind—and this occurred every now and then—all her sore places were healed, and she was happy; happy and proud, for this was her son, her nigger son, lording it among the whites and securely avenging their crimes against her race.

There were two grand funerals in Dawson's Landing that fall —the fall of 1845. One was that of Colonel Cecil Burleigh Essex, the other that of Percy Driscoll.

On his death-bed Driscoll set Roxy free and delivered his idolized ostensible son solemnly into the keeping of his brother the Judge, and his wife. Those childless people were glad to get him. Childless people are not difficult to please.

Judge Driscoll had gone privately to his brother, a month before, and bought Chambers. He had heard that Tom had been trying to get his father to sell the boy down the river, and he wanted to prevent the scandal—for public sentiment did not approve of that way of treating family servants for light cause or for no cause.

Percy Driscoll had worn himself out in trying to save his great speculative landed estate, and had died without succeeding. He was hardly in his grave before the boom collapsed and left his hitherto envied young devil of an heir a pauper. But that was nothing; his uncle told him he should be his heir and have all his fortune when he died; so Tom was comforted.

Roxy had no home now; so she resolved to go around and say good-by to her friends and then clear out and see the world—that is to say, she would go chambermaiding on a steamboat, the darling ambition of her race and sex.

Her last call was on the black giant, Jasper. She found him chopping Pudd'nhead Wilson's winter provision of wood.

Wilson was chatting with him when Roxy arrived. He asked her how she could bear to go off chambermaiding and leave her boys; and chaffingly offered to copy off a series of their finger-prints, reaching up to their twelfth year, for her to remember them by; but she sobered in a moment, wondering if he suspected anything; then she said she believed she didn't want them. Wilson said to himself, "The drop of black blood in her is superstitious; she thinks there's some devilry, some witch business about my glass mystery somewhere; she used to come here with an old horseshoe in her hand; it could have been an accident, but I doubt it."

5

The Twins Thrill Dawson's Landing

Training is everything. The peach was once a bitter almond; cauliflower is nothing but cabbage with a college education.—*Pudd'nhead Wilson's Calendar.*

Remark of Dr. Baldwin's, concerning upstarts: We don't care to eat toadstools that think they are truffles.
—*Pudd'nhead Wilson's Calendar.*

MRS. YORK DRISCOLL enjoyed two years of bliss with that prize, Tom—bliss that was troubled a little at times, it is true, but bliss nevertheless; then she died, and her husband and his childless sister, Mrs. Pratt, continued the bliss business at the old stand. Tom was petted and indulged and spoiled to his entire content—or nearly that. This went on till he was nineteen, then he was sent to Yale. He went handsomely equipped with "conditions," but otherwise he was not an object of distinction there. He remained at Yale two years, and then threw up the struggle. He came home with his manners a good deal improved; he had lost his surliness and brusqueness, and was rather pleasantly soft and smooth now: he was furtively, and sometimes openly, ironical of speech, and given to gently touching people on the raw, but he did it with a good-natured semiconscious air that carried it off safely, and kept him from getting into trouble. He was as indolent as ever and showed no very strenuous desire to hunt up an occupation. People argued from this that he preferred to be supported by his uncle until his uncle's shoes should become vacant. He brought back one or two new habits with him, one of which he rather openly practised—tippling—but concealed another, which was gambling. It would not do to gamble where his uncle could hear of it; he knew that quite well.

Tom's Eastern polish was not popular among the young people. They could have endured it, perhaps, if Tom had stopped there; but he wore gloves, and that they couldn't stand, and wouldn't; so he was mainly without society. He brought home with him a suit of clothes of such exquisite style and cut and fashion—Eastern fashion, city fashion—that it filled everybody with anguish and was regarded as a peculiarly wanton affront. He enjoyed the feeling which he was exciting, and paraded the town serene and happy all day; but the young fellows set a tailor to work that night, and when Tom started out on his parade next morning he found the old deformed negro bell-ringer straddling along in his wake tricked out in a flamboyant curtain-calico exaggeration of his finery, and imitating his fancy Eastern graces as well as he could.

Tom surrendered, and after that clothed himself in the local fashion. But the dull country-town was tiresome to him since his acquaintanceship with livelier regions, and it grew daily more and more so. He began to make little trips to St. Louis for refreshment. There he found companionship to suit him, and pleasures to his taste, along with more freedom, in some particulars, than he could have at home. So, during the next two years his visits to the city grew in frequency and his tarryings there grew steadily longer in duration.

He was getting into deep waters. He was taking chances, privately, which might get him into trouble some day—in fact, *did*.

Judge Driscoll had retired from the bench and from all business activities in 1850, and had now been comfortably idle three years. He was president of the Free-thinkers' Society, and Pudd'nhead Wilson was the other member. The society's weekly discussions were now the old lawyer's main interest in life. Pudd'nhead was still toiling in obscurity at the bottom of the ladder, under the blight of that unlucky remark which he had let fall twenty-three years before about the dog.

Judge Driscoll was his friend, and claimed that he had a mind above the average, but that was regarded as one of the Judge's whims, and it failed to modify the public opinion. Or, rather, that was one of the reasons why it failed, but there was another and better one. If the Judge had stopped with bare assertion, it would have had a good deal of effect; but he made the mistake of trying to prove his position. For some years Wilson had been privately at work on a whimsical almanac, for his amusement—a calendar, with a little dab of ostensible philosophy, usually in ironical form, appended to each date; and the Judge thought that these quips and fancies of Wilson's were neatly turned and cute; so he carried a handful of them around one day, and read them to some of the chief citizens. But irony was not for those people; their mental vision was not focused for it. They read those playful trifles in the solidest earnest, and decided without hesitancy that if there had ever been any doubt that Dave Wilson was a pudd'nhead—which there hadn't—this revelation removed that doubt for good and all. That is just the way in this world; an enemy can partly ruin a man, but it takes a good-natured injudicious friend to complete the thing and make it perfect. After this the Judge felt tenderer than ever toward Wilson, and surer than ever that his calendar had merit.

Judge Driscoll could be a free-thinker and still hold his place in society, because he was the person of most consequence in the community, and therefore could venture to go his own way and follow out his own notions. The other member of his pet organization was allowed the like liberty because he was a cipher in the estimation of the public, and nobody attached any importance to what he thought or did. He was liked, he was welcome enough all around, but he simply didn't count for anything.

The widow Cooper—affectionately called "Aunt Patsy" by everybody—lived in a snug and comely cottage with her daughter Rowena, who was nineteen, romantic, amiable, and very pretty, but otherwise of no consequence. Rowena had a couple of young brothers—also of no consequence.

The widow had a large spare room which she let to a lodger, with board, when she could find one, but this room had been empty for a year now, to her sorrow. Her income was only sufficient for the family support, and she needed the lodging-money for trifling luxuries. But now, at last, on a flaming June day, she found herself happy; her tedious wait was ended; her year-worn advertisement had been answered; and not by a village applicant, oh, no!—this letter was from away off yonder in the dim great world to the north; it was from St. Louis. She sat on her porch gazing out with unseeing eyes upon the shining reaches of the mighty Mississippi, her thoughts steeped in her good fortune. Indeed, it was specially good fortune, for she was to have two lodgers instead of one.

She had read the letter to the family, and Rowena had danced away to see to the cleaning and airing of the room by the slave woman Nancy, and the boys had rushed abroad in the town to spread the great news, for it was matter of public interest, and the public would wonder and not be pleased if not informed. Presently Rowena returned, all ablush with joyous excitement, and begged for a rereading of the letter. It was framed thus:

> HONORED MADAM: My brother and I have seen your advertisement, by chance, and beg leave to take the room you offer. We are twenty-four years of age and twins. We are Italians by birth, but have lived long in the various countries of Europe, and several years in the United States. Our names are Luigi and Angelo Capello. You desire but one guest; but, dear Madam, if you will allow us to pay for two, we will not incommode you. We shall be down Thursday.

"Italians! How romantic! Just think, ma—there's never been one in this town, and everybody will be dying to see them and they're all *ours!* Think of that!"

"Yes, I reckon they'll make a grand stir."

"Oh, indeed they will. The whole town will be on its head! Think—they've been in Europe and everywhere! There's never been a traveler in this town before. Ma, I shouldn't wonder if they've seen kings!"

"Well, a body can't tell; but they'll make stir enough, without that."

"Yes, that's of course. Luigi—Angelo. They're lovely names; and so grand and foreign—not like Jones and Robinson and such.

Thursday they are coming, and this is only Tuesday; it's a cruel long time to wait. Here comes Judge Driscoll in at the gate. He's heard about it. I'll go and open the door."

The Judge was full of congratulations and curiosity. The letter was read and discussed. Soon Justice Robinson arrived with more congratulations, and there was a new reading and a new discussion. This was the beginning. Neighbor after neighbor, of both sexes, followed, and the procession drifted in and out all day and evening, and all Wednesday and Thursday. The letter was read and reread until it was nearly worn out; everybody admired its courtly and gracious tone, and smooth and practised style, everybody was sympathetic and excited, and the Coopers were steeped in happiness all the while.

The boats were very uncertain in low water in these primitive times. This time the Thursday boat had not arrived at ten at night—so the people had waited at the landing all day for nothing; they were driven to their homes by a heavy storm without having had a view of the illustrious foreigners.

Eleven o'clock came; and the Cooper house was the only one in the town that still had lights burning. The rain and thunder were booming yet, and the anxious family were still waiting, still hoping. At last there was a knock at the door and the family jumped to open it. Two negro men entered, each carrying a trunk, and proceeded up-stairs toward the guest-room. Then entered the twins—the handsomest, the best dressed, the most distinguished-looking pair of young fellows the West had ever seen. One was a little fairer than the other, but otherwise they were exact duplicates.

6

Swimming in Glory

Let us endeavor so to live that when we come to die even
the undertaker will be sorry.
                    —*Pudd'nhead Wilson's Calendar.*

Habit is habit, and not to be flung out of the window by
any man, but coaxed down-stairs a step at a time.
                    —*Pudd'nhead Wilson's Calendar.*

AT BREAKFAST in the morning the twins' charm of manner and
easy and polished bearing made speedy conquest of the family's
good graces. All constraint and formality quickly disappeared,
and the friendliest feeling succeeded. Aunt Patsy called them
by their Christian names almost from the beginning. She was
full of the keenest curiosity about them, and showed it; they
responded by talking about themselves, which pleased her greatly.
It presently appeared that in their early youth they had known
poverty and hardship. As the talk wandered along the old lady
watched for the right place to drop in a question or two concerning that matter, and when she found it she said to the blond
twin who was now doing the biographies in his turn while
the brunette one rested:

"If it ain't asking what I ought not to ask, Mr. Angelo, how
did you come to be so friendless and in such trouble when you
were little? Do you mind telling? But don't if you do."

"Oh, we don't mind it at all, madam; in our case it was merely
misfortune, and nobody's fault. Our parents were well to do,
there in Italy, and we were their only child. We were of the
old Florentine nobility"—Rowena's heart gave a great bound, her
nostrils expanded, and a fine light played in her eyes— "and when

the war broke out my father was on the losing side and had to fly for his life. His estates were confiscated, his personal property seized, and there we were, in Germany, strangers, friendless, and, in fact, paupers. My brother and I were ten years old, and well educated for that age, very studious, very fond of our books, and well grounded in the German, French, Spanish, and English languages. Also, we were marvelous musical prodigies—if you will allow me to say it, it being only the truth.

"Our father survived his misfortunes only a month, our mother soon followed him, and we were alone in the world. Our parents could have made themselves comfortable by exhibiting us as a show, and they had many large offers; but the thought revolted their pride, and they said they would starve and die first. But what they wouldn't consent to do we had to do without the formality of consent. We were seized for the debts occasioned by their illness and their funerals, and placed among the attractions of a cheap museum in Berlin to earn the liquidation money. It took us two years to get out of that slavery. We traveled all about Germany receiving no wages, and not even our keep. We had to be exhibited for nothing, and beg our bread.

"Well, madam, the rest is not of much consequence. When we escaped from that slavery at twelve years of age, we were in some respects men. Experience had taught us some valuable things; among others, how to take care of ourselves, how to avoid and defeat sharks and sharpers, and how to conduct our own business for our own profit and without other people's help. We traveled everywhere—years and years—picking up smatterings of strange tongues, familiarizing ourselves with strange sights and strange customs, accumulating an education of a wide and varied and curious sort. It was a pleasant life. We went to Venice —to London, Paris, Russia, India, China, Japan—"

At this point Nancy, the slave woman, thrust her head in at the door and exclaimed:

"Ole Missus, de house is plum' jam full o' people, en dey's jes' a-spi'lin to see de gen'lmen!" She indicated the twins with a nod of her head, and tucked it back out of sight again.

It was a proud occasion for the widow, and she promised herself high satisfaction in showing off her fine foreign birds before her neighbors and friends—simple folk who had hardly ever seen a foreigner of any kind, and never one of any distinction or style. Yet her feeling was moderate indeed when contrasted with Rowena's. Rowena was in the clouds, she walked on air; this was to be the greatest day, the most romantic episode, in the colorless history of that dull country-town. She was to be familiarly near the source of its glory and feel the full flood of it pour over her and about her; the other girls could only gaze and envy, not partake.

The widow was ready, Rowena was ready, so also were the foreigners.

The party moved along the hall, the twins in advance, and entered the open parlor door, whence issued a low hum of conversation. The twins took a position near the door, the widow stood at Luigi's side, Rowena stood beside Angelo, and the march-past and the introductions began. The widow was all smiles and contentment. She received the procession and passed it on to Rowena.

"Good mornin', Sister Cooper"—handshake.

"Good morning, Brother Higgins—Count Luigi Capello, Mr. Higgins"—handshake, followed by a devouring stare and "I'm glad to see ye," on the part of Higgins, and a courteous inclination of the head and a pleasant "Most happy!" on the part of Count Luigi.

"Good mornin', Roweny"—handshake.

"Good morning, Mr. Higgins—present you to Count Angelo Capello." Handshake, admiring stare, "Glad to see ye,"—courteous nod, smily "Most happy!" and Higgins passes on.

None of these visitors was at ease, but, being honest people, they didn't pretend to be. None of them had ever seen a person bearing a title of nobility before, and none had been expecting to see one now, consequently the title came upon them as a kind of pile-driving surprise and caught them unprepared. A few tried to rise to the emergency, and got out an awkward "My lord," or "Your lordship," or something of that sort, but the great majority were overwhelmed by the unaccustomed word and its dim and awful associations with gilded courts and stately ceremony and anointed kingship, so they only fumbled through the handshake and passed on speechless. Now and then, as happens at all receptions everywhere, a more than ordinarily friendly soul blocked the procession and kept it waiting while he inquired how the brothers liked the village, and how long they were going to stay, and if their families were well, and dragged in the weather, and hoped it would get cooler soon, and all that sort of thing, so as to be able to say, when they got home, "I had quite a long talk with them"; but nobody did or said anything of a regrettable kind, and so the great affair went through to the end in a creditable and satisfactory fashion.

General conversation followed, and the twins drifted about from group to group, talking easily and fluently and winning approval, compelling admiration and achieving favor from all. The widow followed their conquering march with a proud eye, and every now and then Rowena said to herself with deep satisfaction, "And to think they are ours—all ours!"

There were no idle moments for mother or daughter. Eager inquiries concerning the twins were pouring into their enchanted ears all the time; each was the constant center of a group of breathless listeners; each recognized that she knew now for the first time the real meaning of that great word Glory, and perceived the stupendous value of it, and understood why men in all ages had been willing to throw away meaner happinesses, treasure, life itself, to get a taste of its sublime and supreme joy. Napoleon and all his kind stood accounted for—and justified.

When Rowena had at last done all her duty by the people in the parlor, she went up-stairs to satisfy the longings of an overflow-meeting there, for the parlor was not big enough to hold all the comers. Again she was besieged by eager questioners and again she swam in sunset seas of glory. When the forenoon was nearly gone, she recognized with a pang that this most splendid episode of her life was almost over, that nothing could prolong it, that nothing quite its equal could ever fall to her fortune again. But never mind, it was sufficient unto itself, the grand occasion had moved on an ascending scale from the start, and was a noble and memorable success. If the twins could but do some crowning act now to climax it, something unusual, something startling, something to concentrate upon themselves the company's loftiest admiration, something in the nature of an electric surprise—

Here a prodigious slam-banging broke out below, and everybody rushed down to see. It was the twins knocking out a classic four-handed piece on the piano in great style. Rowena was satisfied—satisfied down to the bottom of her heart.

The young strangers were kept long at the piano. The villagers were astonished and enchanted with the magnificence of their performance, and could not bear to have them stop. All the music that they had ever heard before seemed spiritless prenticework and barren of grace or charm when compared with these intoxicating flood of melodious sound. They realized that for once in their lives they were hearing masters.

7

The Unknown Nymph

One of the most striking differences between a cat and a lie is that a cat has only nine lives.
—*Pudd'nhead Wilson's Calendar.*

THE COMPANY broke up reluctantly, and drifted toward their several homes, chatting with vivacity, and all agreeing that it would be many a long day before Dawson's Landing would see the equal of this one again. The twins had accepted several invitations while the reception was in progress, and had also volunteered to play some duets at an amateur entertainment for the benefit of a local charity. Society was eager to receive them to its bosom. Judge Driscoll had the good fortune to secure them for an immediate drive, and to be the first to display them in public. They entered his buggy with him, and were paraded down the main street, everybody flocking to the windows and sidewalks to see.

The Judge showed the strangers the new graveyard, and the jail, and where the richest man lived, and the Freemasons' hall, and the Methodist church, and the Presbyterian church, and where the Baptist church was going to be when they got some money to build it with, and showed them the town hall and the slaughter-house, and got out the independent fire company in uniform and had them put out an imaginary fire; then he let them inspect the muskets of the militia company, and poured out an exhaustless stream of enthusiasm over all these splendors, and seemed very well satisfied with the responses he got, for the twins admired his admiration, and paid him back the best they could, though they could have done better if some fifteen or sixteen hundred thousand previous experiences of this sort in various countries had not already rubbed off a considerable part of the novelty of it.

The Judge laid himself out hospitably to make them have a good time, and if there was a defect anywhere it was not his fault. He told them a good many humorous anecdotes, and always forgot the nub, but they were always able to furnish it, for these yarns were of a pretty early vintage, and they had had many a rejuvenating pull at them before. And he told them all about his several dignities, and how he had held this and that and the other place of honor or profit, and had once been to the legislature, and was now president of the Society of Free-thinkers. He said the society had been in existence four years, and already had two members, and was firmly established. He would call for the brothers in the evening if they would like to attend a meeting of it.

Accordingly he called for them, and on the way he told them all about Pudd'nhead Wilson, in order that they might get a favorable impression of him in advance and be prepared to like him. This scheme succeeded—the favorable impression was achieved. Later it was confirmed and solidified when Wilson proposed that out of courtesy to the strangers the usual topics be put aside and the hour be devoted to conversation upon ordinary subjects and the cultivation of friendly relations and good-fellowship—a proposition which was put to vote and carried.

The hour passed quickly away in lively talk, and when it was ended the lonesome and neglected Wilson was richer by two friends than he had been when it began. He invited the twins to look in at his lodgings, presently, after disposing of an intervening engagement, and they accepted with pleasure.

Toward the middle of the evening they found themselves on the road to his house. Pudd'nhead was at home waiting for them and putting in his time puzzling over a thing which had come under his notice that morning. The matter was this: He happened to be up very early—at dawn, in fact; and he crossed the hall which divided his cottage through the center, and entered a room to get something there. The window of the room had no curtains, for that side of house had long been unoccupied, and through this window he caught sight of something which surprised and interested him. It was a young woman—a young woman where properly no young woman belonged; for she was in Judge Driscoll's house, and in the bedroom over the Judge's private study or sitting-room. This was young Tom Driscoll's bedroom. He and the Judge, the Judge's widowed sister, Mrs. Pratt, and three negro servants were the only people who belonged in the house. Who, then, might this young lady be? The two houses were separated by an ordinary yard, with a low fence running back through its middle from the street in front to the lane in the rear. The distance was not great, and Wilson was able to see the girl very well, the window-shades of the room she was in being up, and the window also. The girl had on a neat and trim summer dress, patterned in broad stripes of pink and white, and her bonnet was equipped with a pink veil. She was practising steps, gaits, and attitudes, apparently; she was doing the thing gracefully, and was very much absorbed in her work. Who could she be, and how came she to be in young Tom Driscoll's room?

Wilson had quickly chosen a position from which he could watch the girl without running much risk of being seen by her, and he remained there hoping she would raise her veil and betray her face. But she disappointed him. After a matter of twenty minutes she disappeared, and although he stayed at his post half an hour longer, she came no more.

Toward noon he dropped in at the Judge's and talked with Mrs. Pratt about the great event of the day, the levee of the distinguished foreigners at Aunt Patsy Cooper's. He asked after her nephew Tom, and she said he was on his way home, and that she was expecting him to arrive a little before night; and added that she and the Judge were gratified to gather from his letters that he was conducting himself very nicely and creditably —at which Wilson winked to himself privately. Wilson did not ask if there was a newcomer in the house, but he asked questions that would have brought light-throwing answers as to that matter if Mrs. Pratt had had any light to throw; so he went away satisfied that he knew of things that were going on in her house of which she herself was not aware.

He was now waiting for the twins, and still puzzling over the problem of who that girl might be, and how she happened to be in that young fellow's room at daybreak in the morning.

8

Marse Tom Tramples His Chance

> The holy passion of Friendship is of so sweet and steady
> and loyal and enduring a nature that it will last through a
> whole lifetime, if not asked to lend money.
> > —*Pudd'nhead Wilson's Calendar.*

> Consider well the proportions of things. It is better to be a
> young June-bug than an old bird of paradise.
> > —*Pudd'nhead Wilson's Calendar.*

IT IS NECESSARY now to hunt up Roxy.

At the time she was set free and went away chambermaiding,
she was thirty-five. She got a berth as second chambermaid on a
Cincinnati boat in the New Orleans trade, the *Grand Mogul.* A
couple of trips made her wonted and easy-going at the work, and
infatuated her with the stir and adventure and independence of
steamboat life. Then she was promoted and became head chambermaid. She was a favorite with the officers, and exceedingly
proud of their joking and friendly ways with her.

During eight years she served three parts of the year on that
boat, and the winters on a Vicksburg packet. But now for two
months she had had rheumatism in her arms, and was obliged
to let the wash-tub alone. So she resigned. But she was well fixed
—rich, as she would have described it; for she had lived a steady
life, and had banked four dollars every month in New Orleans as
a provision for her old age. She said in the start that she had
"put shoes on one bar'footed nigger to tromple on her with," and
that one mistake like that was enough; she would be independent of the human race thenceforth forevermore if hard work and
economy could accomplish it. When the boat touched the levee

at New Orleans she bade good-by to her comrades on the *Grand Mogul* and moved her kit ashore.

But she was back in an hour. The bank had gone to smash and carried her four hundred dollars with it. She was a pauper, and homeless. Also disabled bodily, at least for the present. The officers were full of sympathy for her in her trouble, and made up a little purse for her. She resolved to go to her birthplace; she had friends there among the negroes, and the unfortunate always help the unfortunate, she was well aware of that; those lowly comrades of her youth would not let her starve.

She took the little local packet at Cairo, and now she was on the home-stretch. Time had worn away her bitterness against her son, and she was able to think of him with serenity. She put the vile side of him out of her mind, and dwelt only on recollections of his occasional acts of kindness to her. She gilded and otherwise decorated these, and made them very pleasant to contemplate. She began to long to see him. She would go and fawn upon him, slave-like—for this would have to be her attitude, of course —and maybe she would find that time had modified him, and that he would be glad to see his long-forgotten old nurse and treat her gently. That would be lovely; that would make her forget her woes and her poverty.

Her poverty! That thought inspired her to add another castle to her dream; maybe he would give her a trifle now and then— maybe a dollar, once a month, say; any little thing like that would help, oh, ever so much.

By the time she reached Dawson's Landing she was her old self again; her blues were gone, she was in high feather. She would get along, surely; there were many kitchens where the servants would share their meals with her, and also steal sugar and apples and other dainties for her to carry home—or give her a chance to pilfer them herself, which would answer just as well. And there was the church. She was a more rabid and devoted Methodist than ever, and her piety was no sham, but was strong and sincere. Yes, with plenty of creature comforts and her old place in the amen-corner in her possession again, she would be perfectly happy and at peace thenceforward to the end.

She went to Judge Driscoll's kitchen first of all. She was received there in great form and with vast enthusiasm. Her wonderful travels, and the strange countries she had seen and the adventures she had had, made her a marvel, and a heroine of romance. The negroes hung enchanted upon the great story of her experiences, interrupting her all along with eager questions, with laughter, exclamations of delight and expressions of applause; and she was obliged to confess to herself that if there was anything better in this world than steamboating, it was the glory to be got by telling about it. The audience loaded her stomach with their dinners, and then stole the pantry bare to load up her basket.

Tom was in St. Louis. The servants said he had spent the best part of his time there during the previous two years. Roxy came every day, and had many talks about the family and its affairs. Once she asked why Tom was away so much. The ostensible "Chambers" said:

"De fac' is, ole marster kin git along better when young marster's away den he kin when he's in de town; yes, en he love him better, too; so he gives him fifty dollahs a month—"

"No, is dat so? Chambers, you's a-jokin', ain't you?"

"'Clah to goodness I ain't, mammy; Marse Tom tole me so his own self. But nemmine, 't ain't enough."

"My lan', what de reason 't ain't enough?"

"Well, I's gwine to tell you, if you gimme a chanst, mammy. De reason it ain't enough is 'ca'se Marse Tom gambles."

Roxy threw up her hands in astonishment and Chambers went on:

"Ole marster found it out, 'ca'se he had to pay two hundred dollahs for Marse Tom's gamblin' debts, en dat's true, mammy, jes as dead certain as you's bawn."

"Two—hund'd—dollahs! Why, what is you talkin' 'bout? Two —hund'd—dollahs. Sakes alive, it's 'mos' enough to buy a tol'able good second-hand nigger wid. En you ain't lyin', honey?—you wouldn't lie to yo' ole mammy?"

"It's God's own truth, jes as I tell you—two hund'd dollahs—I wisht I may never stir outen my tracks if it ain't so. En, oh, my

lan', ole Marse was jes a-hoppin'! he was b'ilin' mad, I tell you!
He tuck 'n' dissenhurrit him."

He licked his chops with relish after that stately word. Roxy
struggled with it a moment, then gave it up and said:

"Dissen*whiched* him?"

"Dissenhurrit him."

"What's dat? What do it mean?"

"Means he bu'sted de will."

"Bu's—ted de will! He wouldn't *ever* treat him so! Take it back,
you mis'able imitation nigger dat I bore in sorrow en tribbilation."

Roxy's pet castle—an occasional dollar from Tom's pocket—
was tumbling to ruin before her eyes. She could not abide such a
disaster as that; she couldn't endure the thought of it. Her remark
amused Chambers:

"Yah-yah-yah! jes listen to dat! If I's imitation, what is you?
Bofe of us is imitation *white*—dat's what we is—en pow'ful good
imitation, too—yah-yah-yah!—we don't 'mount to noth'n' as imitation niggers; and as for—"

"Shet up yo' foolin', 'fo' I knock you side de head, en tell me
'bout de will. Tell me 'tain't bu'sted—do, honey, en I'll never
forgit you."

"Well, *'tain't*—'ca'se dey's a new one made, en Marse Tom's all
right ag'in. But what is you in sich a sweat 'bout it for, mammy?
'Tain't none o' your business I don't reckon."

"'Tain't none o' my business? Whose business is it den, I'd like
to know? Wuz I his mother tell he was fifteen years old, or wusn't
I?—you answer me dat. En you speck I could see him turned out
po' en ornery on de worl' en never care noth'n' 'bout it? I reckon
if you'd ever be'n a mother yo'self, Valet de Chambers, you
wouldn't talk sich foolishness as dat."

"Well, den, ole Marse forgive him en fixed up de will ag'in—do
dat satisfy you?"

Yes, she was satisfied now, and quite happy and sentimental
over it. She kept coming daily, and at last she was told that Tom
had come home. She began to tremble with emotion, and
straightway sent to beg him to let his "po' ole nigger mammy
have jes one sight of him en die for joy."

Tom was stretched at his lazy ease on a sofa when Chambers brought the petition. Time had not modified his ancient detestation of the humble drudge and protector of his boyhood; it was still bitter and uncompromising. He sat up and bent a severe gaze upon the fair face of the young fellow whose name he was unconsciously using and whose family rights he was enjoying. He maintained the gaze until the victim of it had become satisfactorily pallid with terror, then he said:

"What does the old rip want with me?"

The petition was meekly repeated.

"Who gave you permission to come and disturb me with the social attentions of niggers?"

Tom had risen. The other young man was trembling now, visibly. He saw what was coming, and bent his head sideways, and put up his left arm to shield it. Tom rained cuffs upon the head and its shield, saying no word; the victim received each blow with a beseeching "Please, Marse Tom!—oh, please, Marse Tom!" Seven blows—then Tom said, "Face the door—march!" He followed behind with one, two, three solid kicks. The last one helped the pure-white slave over the door-sill, and he limped away mopping his eyes with his old ragged sleeve. Tom shouted after him, "Send her in!"

Then he flung himself panting on the sofa again, and rasped out the remark, "He arrived just at the right moment; I was full to the brim with bitter thinkings, and nobody to take it out of. How refreshing it was! I feel better."

Tom's mother entered now, closing the door behind her, and approached her son with all the wheedling and supplicating servilities that fear and interest can impart to the words and attitudes of the born slave. She stopped a yard from her boy and made two or three admiring exclamations over his manly stature and general handsomeness, and Tom put an arm under his head and hoisted a leg over the sofa-back in order to look properly indifferent.

"My lan', how you is growed, honey! 'Clah to goodness, I wouldn't 'a' knowed you, Marse Tom! 'deed I wouldn't! Look at me good; does you 'member old Roxy?—does you know yo' old nigger mammy, honey? Well, now, I kin lay down en die in peace, 'ca'se I's seed—"

"Cut it short, —— it, cut it short! What is it you want?"

"You heah dat? Jes de same old Marse Tom, al'ays so gay and funnin' wid de old mammy. I 'uz jes as shore—"

"Cut it short, I tell you, and get along! What do you want?"

This was a bitter disappointment. Roxy had for so many days nourished and fondled and petted her notion that Tom would be glad to see his old nurse, and would make her proud and happy to the marrow with a cordial word or two, that it took two rebuffs to convince her that he was not funning, and that her beautiful dream was a fond and foolish vanity, a shabby and pitiful mistake. She was hurt to the heart, and so ashamed that for a moment she did not quite know what to do or how to act. Then her breast began to heave, the tears came, and in her forlornness she was moved to try that other dream of hers—an appeal to her boy's charity; and so, upon the impulse, and without reflection, she offered her supplication:

"Oh, Marse Tom, de po' ole mammy is in sich hard luck dese days; en she's kinder crippled in de arms en can't work, en if you could gimme a dollah—on'y jes one little dol—"

Tom was on his feet so suddenly that the supplicant was startled into a jump herself.

"A dollar!—give you a dollar! I've a notion to strangle you! Is *that* your errand here? Clear out! and be quick about it!"

Roxy backed slowly toward the door. When she was half-way she stopped, and said mournfully:

"Marse Tom, I nussed you when you was a little baby, en I raised you all by myself tell you was 'most a young man; en now you is young en rich, en I is po' en gitt'n ole, en I come heah b'lievin' dat you would he'p de ole mammy 'long down de little road dat's lef' 'twix' her en de grave, en—"

Tom relished this tune less than any that had preceded it, for it began to wake up a sort of echo in his conscience; so he interrupted and said with decision, though without asperity, that he was not in a situation to help her, and wasn't going to do it.

"Ain't you ever gwine to he'p me, Marse Tom?"

"No! Now go away and don't bother me any more."

Roxy's head was down, in an attitude of humility. But now the fires of her old wrongs flamed up in her breast and began to burn fiercely. She raised her head slowly, till it was well up, and at the same time her great frame unconsciously assumed an erect and masterful attitude, with all the majesty and grace of her vanished youth in it. She raised her finger and punctuated with it:

"You has said de word. You has had yo' chance, en you has trompled it under yo' foot. When you git another one, you'll git down on yo' knees en *beg* for it!"

A cold chill went to Tom's heart, he didn't know why; for he did not reflect that such words, from such an incongruous source, and so solemnly delivered, could not easily fail of that effect. However, he did the natural thing; he replied with bluster and mockery:

"*You'll* give me a chance—*you!* Perhaps I'd better get down on my knees now! But in case I don't—just for argument's sake—what's going to happen, pray?"

"Dis is what is gwine to happen. I's gwine as straight to yo' uncle as I kin walk, en tell him every las' thing I knows 'bout you."

Tom's cheek blenched, and she saw it. Disturbing thoughts began to chase each other through his head. "How can she know? And yet she must have found out—she looks it. I've had the will back only three months, and am already deep in debt again, and moving heaven and earth to save myself from exposure and destruction, with a reasonably fair show of getting the thing covered up if I'm let alone, and now this fiend has gone and found me out somehow or other. I wonder how much she knows? Oh, oh, oh, it's enough to break a body's heart! But I've got to humor her—there's no other way."

Then he worked up a rather sickly sample of a gay laugh and a hollow chipperness of manner, and said:

"Well, well, Roxy dear, old friends like you and me mustn't quarrel. Here's your dollar—now tell me what you know."

He held out the wildcat bill; she stood as she was, and made no movement. It was her turn to scorn persuasive foolery now, and she did not waste it. She said, with a grim implacability in voice and manner which made Tom almost realize that even a former slave can remember for ten minutes insults and injuries returned for compliments and flatteries received, and can also enjoy taking revenge for them when the opportunity offers:

"What does I know? I'll tell you what I knows. I knows enough to bu'st dat will to flinders—en more, mind you, *more!*"

Tom was aghast.

"More?" he said. "What do you call more? Where's there any room for more?"

Roxy laughed a mocking laugh, and said scoffingly, with a toss of her head, and her hands on her hips:

"Yes!—oh, I reckon! *Co'se* you'd like to know—wid yo' po' little ole rag dollah. What you reckon I's gwine to tell *you* for?—you ain't got no money. I's gwine to tell yo' uncle—en I'll do it dis minute, too—he'll gimme *five* dollahs for de news, en mighty glad, too."

She swung herself around disdainfully, and started away. Tom was in a panic. He seized her skirts, and implored her to wait. She turned and said, loftily:

"Look-a-heah, what 'uz it I tole you?"

"You—you—I don't remember anything. What was it you told me?"

"I tole you dat de next time I give you a chance you'd git down on yo' knees en beg for it."

Tom was stupefied for a moment. He was panting with excitement. Then he said:

"Oh, Roxy, you wouldn't require your young master to do such a horrible thing. You can't mean it."

"I'll let you know mighty quick whether I means it or not! You call me names, en as good as spit on me when I comes here po' en ornery en 'umble, to praise you for bein' growed up so fine en handsome, en tell you how I used to nuss you en tend you en watch you when you 'uz sick en hadn't no mother but me in de whole worl', en beg you to give de po' ole nigger a dollah for to git her som'n' to eat, en you call me names—*names*, dad blame you! Yassir, I gives you jes one chance mo', and dat's *now*, en it las' on'y a half a second—yo hear?'"

Tom slumped to his knees and began to beg, saying:

"You see, I'm begging, and it's honest begging, too! Now tell me, Roxy, tell me!"

The heir of two centuries of unatoned insult and outrage looked down on him and seemed to drink in deep draughts of satisfaction. Then she said:

"Fine nice young white gen'l'man kneelin' down to a nigger wench! I's wanted to see dat jes once befo' I's called. Now, Gabr'el, blow de hawn, I's ready. . . . Git up!"

Tom did it. He said, humbly:

"Now, Roxy, don't punish me any more. I deserved what I've got, but be good and let me off with that. Don't go to uncle. Tell me—I'll give you the five dollars."

"Yes, I bet you will; en you won't stop dah, nuther. But I ain't gwine to tell you heah—"

"Good gracious, no!"

"Is you 'feared o' de ha'nted house?"

"N-no."

"Well, den, you come to de ha'nted house 'bout ten or 'leven to-night, en climb up de ladder, 'ca'se de sta'r-steps is broke down, en you'll find me. I's a-roostin' in de ha'nted house 'ca'se I can't 'ford to roos' nowhers' else." She started toward the door, but stopped and said, "Gimme de dollah bill!" He gave it to her. She examined it and said, "H'm—like enough de bank's bu'sted." She started again, but halted again. "Has you got any whisky?"

"Yes, a little."

"Fetch it!"

He ran to his room overhead and brought down a bottle which was two-thirds full. She tilted it up and took a drink. Her eyes sparkled with satisfaction and she tucked the bottle under her shawl, saying, "It's prime. I'll take it along."

Tom humbly held the door for her, and she marched out as grim and erect as a grenadier.

9

Tom Practises Sycophancy

Why is it that we rejoice at a birth and grieve at a funeral?
It is because we are not the person involved.
—*Pudd'nhead Wilson's Calendar.*

It is easy to find fault, if one has that disposition. There
was once a man who, not being able to find any other fault
with his coal, complained that there were too many prehistoric toads in it.—*Pudd'nhead Wilson's Calendar.*

TOM FLUNG HIMSELF on the sofa, and put his throbbing head in
his hands, and rested his elbows on his knees. He rocked himself
back and forth and moaned.

"I've knelt to a nigger wench!" he muttered. "I thought I had
struck the deepest depths of degradation before, but oh, dear, it
was nothing to this. . . . Well, there is one consolation, such as
it is—I've struck bottom this time; there's nothing lower."

But that was a hasty conclusion.

At ten that night he climbed the ladder in the haunted house,
pale, weak, and wretched. Roxy was standing in the door of one
of the rooms, waiting, for she had heard him.

This was a two-story log house which had acquired the reputation a few years before of being haunted, and that was the end of
its usefulness. Nobody would live in it afterward, or go near it by
night, and most people even gave it a wide berth in the daytime.
As it had no competition, it was called *the* haunted house. It was
getting crazy and ruinous now from long neglect. It stood three
hundred yards beyond Pudd'nhead Wilson's house, with nothing
between but vacancy. It was the last house in the town at that
end.

Tom followed Roxy into the room. She had a pile of clean straw in the corner for a bed, some cheap but well-kept clothing was hanging on the wall, there was a tin lantern freckling the floor with little spots of light, and there were various soap and candle boxes scattered about, which served for chairs. The two sat down. Roxy said:

"Now den, I'll tell you straight off, en I'll begin to k'leck de money later on; I ain't in no hurry. What does you reckon I's gwine to tell you?"

"Well, you—you—oh, Roxy, don't make it too hard for me! Come right out and tell me you've found out somehow what a shape I'm in on account of dissipation and foolishness."

"Disposition en foolishness! *No*, sir, dat ain't it. Dat jist ain't nothin' at all, 'longside o' what *I* knows."

Tom stared at her, and said:

"Why, Roxy, what do you mean?"

She rose, and gloomed above him like a Fate.

"I mean dis—en it's de Lord's truth. You ain't no more kin to ole Marse Driscoll den I is!—*dat's* what I means!" and her eyes flamed with triumph.

"What!"

"Yassir, en *dat* ain't all! You's a *nigger!—bawn* a nigger en a *slave!*—en you's a nigger en a slave dis minute; en if I opens my mouf ole Marse Driscoll 'll sell you down de river befo' you is two days older den what you is now!"

"It's a thundering lie, you miserable old blatherskite!"

"It ain't no lie, nuther. It's jes de truth, en nothin' *but* de truth, so he'p me. Yassir—you's my *son—*"

"You devil!"

"En dat po' boy dat you's be'n a-kicken' en a-cuffin' to-day is Percy Driscoll's son en yo' *marster—*"

"You beast!"

"En *his* name's Tom Driscoll, en yo' name's Valet de Chambers, en you ain't *got* no fambly name, beca'se niggers don't *have* em!"

Tom sprang up and seized a billet of wood and raised it; but his mother only laughed at him, and said:

"Set down, you pup! Does you think you kin skyer me? It ain't in you, nor de likes of you. I reckon you'd shoot me in de back, maybe, if you got a chance, for dat's jist yo' style—*I* knows you, throo en throo—but I don't mind gitt'n killed, beca'se all dis is down in writin' en it's in safe hands, too, en de man dat's got it knows whah to look for de right man when I gits killed. Oh, bless yo' soul, if you puts yo' mother up for as big a fool as *you* is, you's pow'ful mistaken, I kin tell you! Now den, you set still en behave yo'self; en don't you git up ag'in till I tell you!"

Tom fretted and chafed awhile in a whirlwind of disorganizing sensations and emotions, and finally said, with something like settled conviction:

"The whole thing is moonshine; now then, go ahead and do your worst; I'm done with you."

Roxy made no answer. She took the lantern and started toward the door. Tom was in a cold panic in a moment.

"Come back, come back!" he wailed. "I didn't mean it, Roxy; I take it all back, and I'll never say it again! Please come back, Roxy!"

The woman stood a moment, then she said gravely:

"Dat's one thing you's got to stop, Valet de Chambers. You can't call me *Roxy*, same as if you was my equal. Chillen don't speak to dey mammies like dat. You'll call me ma or mammy, dat's what you'll call me—leastways when dey ain't nobody aroun'. *Say* it!"

It cost Tom a struggle, but he got it out.

"Dat's all right. Don't you ever forget it ag'in, if you knows what's good for you. Now den, you has said you wouldn't ever call it lies en moonshine ag'in. I'll tell you dis, for a warnin': if you ever does say it ag'in, it's de *las'* time you'll ever say it to me; I'll tramp as straight to de Judge as I kin walk, en tell him who you is, en *prove* it. Does you b'lieve me when I says dat?"

"Oh," groaned Tom, "I more than believe it; I *know* it."

Roxy knew her conquest was complete. She could have proved nothing to anybody, and her threat about the writings was a lie; but she knew the person she was dealing with, and had made both statements without any doubt as to the effect they would produce.

She went and sat down on her candle-box, and the pride and pomp of her victorious attitude made it a throne. She said:

"Now den, Chambers, we's gwine to talk business, en dey ain't gwine to be no mo' foolishness. In de fust place, you gits fifty dollahs a month; you's gwine to han' over half of it to yo' ma. Plank it out!"

But Tom had only six dollars in the world. He gave her that, and promised to start fair on next month's pension.

"Chambers, how much is you in debt?"

Tom shuddered, and said:

"Nearly three hundred dollars."

"How is you gwine to pay it?"

Tom groaned out— "Oh, I don't know; don't ask me such awful questions."

But she stuck to her point until she wearied a confession out of him: he had been prowling about in disguise, stealing small valuables from private houses; in fact, had made a good deal of a raid on his fellow-villagers a fortnight before, when he was supposed to be in St. Louis; but he doubted if he had sent away enough stuff to realize the required amount, and was afraid to make a further venture in the present excited state of the town. His mother approved of his conduct, and offered to help, but this frightened him. He tremblingly ventured to say that if she would retire from the town he should feel better and safer, and could hold his head higher—and was going on to make an argument, but she interrupted and surprised him pleasantly by saying she was ready; it didn't make any difference to her where she stayed, so that she got her share of the pension regularly. She said she would not go far, and would call at the haunted house once a month for her money. Then she said:

"I don't hate you so much now, but I've hated you a many a year—and anybody would. Didn't I change you off, en give you a good fambly en a good name, en made you a white gen'l'man en rich, wid store clothes on—en what did I git for it? You despised me all de time, en was al'ays sayin' mean hard things to me befo' folks, en wouldn't ever let me forgit I's a nigger—en —en—"

She fell to sobbing, and broke down. Tom said:

"But you know I didn't know you were my mother; and besides—"

"Well, nemmine 'bout dat, now; let it go. I's gwine to fo'git it." Then she added fiercely, "En don't ever make me remember it ag'in, or you'll be sorry, *I* tell you."

When they were parting, Tom said, in the most persuasive way he could command:

"Ma, would you mind telling me who was my father?"

He had supposed he was asking an embarrassing question. He was mistaken. Roxy drew herself up with a proud toss of her head, and said:

"Does I mine tellin' you? No, dat I don't! You ain't got no 'casion to be shame' o' yo' father, *I* kin tell you. He wuz the highest quality in dis whole town—ole Virginny stock. Fust famblies, he wuz. Jes as good stock as de Driscolls en de Howards, de bes' day dey ever seed." She put on a little prouder air, if possible, and added impressively: "Does you 'member Cunnel Cecil Burleigh Essex, dat died de same year yo' young Marse Tom Driscoll's pappy died, en all de Masons en Odd Fellers en Churches turned out en give him de bigges' funeral dis town ever seed? Dat's de man."

Under the inspiration of her soaring complacency the departed graces of her earlier days returned to her, and her bearing took to itself a dignity and state that might have passed for queenly if her surroundings had been a little more in keeping with it.

"Dey ain't another nigger in dis town dat's as high-bawn as you is. Now den, go 'long! En jes you hold yo' head up as high as you want to—you has de right, en dat I kin swah."

10

The Nymph Revealed

All say, "How hard it is that we have to die"—a strange complaint to come from the mouths of people who have had to live.—*Pudd'nhead Wilson's Calendar.*

When angry, count four; when very angry, swear.
—*Pudd'nhead Wilson's Calendar.*

EVERY now and then, after Tom went to bed, he had sudden wakings out of his sleep, and his first thought was, "Oh, joy, it was all a dream!" Then he laid himself heavily down again, with a groan and the muttered words, "A nigger! I am a nigger! Oh, I wish I was dead!"

He woke at dawn with one more repetition of this horror, and then he resolved to meddle no more with that treacherous sleep. He began to think. Sufficiently bitter thinkings they were. They wandered along something after this fashion:

"Why were niggers *and* whites made? What crime did the un-created first nigger commit that the curse of birth was decreed for him? And why is this awful difference made between white and black? . . . How hard the nigger's fate seems, this morning! —yet until last night such a thought never entered my head."

He sighed and groaned an hour or more away. Then "Chambers" came humbly in to say that breakfast was nearly ready. "Tom" blushed scarlet to see this aristocratic white youth cringe to him, a nigger, and call him "Young Marster." He said roughly:

"Get out of my sight!" and when the youth was gone, he muttered, "He has done me no harm, poor wretch, but he is an eye-sore to me now, for he is Driscoll the young gentleman, and I am a—oh, I wish I was dead!"

A gigantic eruption, like that of Krakatoa a few years ago, with the accompanying earthquakes, tidal waves, and clouds of volcanic dust, changes the face of the surrounding landscape beyond recognition, bringing down the high lands, elevating the low, making fair lakes where deserts had been, and deserts where green prairies had smiled before. The tremendous catastrophe which had befallen Tom had changed his moral landscape in much the same way. Some of his low places he found lifted to ideals, some of his ideals had sunk to the valleys, and lay there with the sackcloth and ashes of pumice-stone and sulphur on their ruined heads.

For days he wandered in lonely places, thinking, thinking, thinking—trying to get his bearings. It was new work. If he met a friend, he found that the habit of a lifetime had in some mysterious way vanished—his arm hung limp, instead of involuntarily extending the hand for a shake. It was the "nigger" in him asserting its humility, and he blushed and was abashed. And the "nigger" in him was surprised when the white friend put out his hand for a shake with him. He found the "nigger" in him involuntarily giving the road, on the sidewalk, to the white rowdy and loafer. When Rowena, the dearest thing his heart knew, the idol of his secret worship, invited him in, the "nigger" in him made an embarrassed excuse and was afraid to enter and sit with the dread white folks on equal terms. The "nigger" in him went shrinking and skulking here and there and yonder, and fancying it saw suspicion and maybe detection in all faces, tones, and gestures. So strange and uncharacteristic was Tom's conduct that people noticed it, and turned to look after him when he passed on; and when he glanced back—as he could not help doing, in spite of his best resistance—and caught that puzzled expression in a person's face, it gave him a sick feeling, and he took himself out of view as quickly as he could. He presently came to have a hunted sense and a hunted look, and then he fled away to the hilltops and the solitudes. He said to himself that the curse of Ham was upon him.

He dreaded his meals; the "nigger" in him was ashamed to sit at the white folks' table, and feared discovery all the time; and once when Judge Driscoll said, "What's the matter with you? You look as meek as a nigger," he felt as secret murderers are said to feel when the accuser says, "Thou art the man!" Tom said he was not well, and left the table.

His ostensible "aunt's" solicitudes and endearments were become a terror to him, and he avoided them.

And all the time, hatred of his ostensible "uncle" was steadily growing in his heart; for he said to himself, "He is white; and I am his chattel, his property, his goods, and he can sell me, just as he could his dog."

For as much as a week after this, Tom imagined that his character had undergone a pretty radical change. But that was because he did not know himself.

In several ways his opinions were totally changed, and would never go back to what they were before, but the main structure of his character was not changed, and could not be changed. One or two very important features of it were altered, and in time effects would result from this, if opportunity offered—effects of a quite serious nature, too. Under the influence of a great mental and moral upheaval his character and habits had taken on the appearance of complete change, but after a while with the subsidence of the storm both began to settle toward their former places. He dropped gradually back into his old frivolous and easy-going ways and conditions of feeling and manner of speech, and no familiar of his could have detected anything in him that differentiated him from the weak and careless Tom of other days.

The theft-raid which he had made upon the village turned out better than he had ventured to hope. It produced the sum necessary to pay his gaming debts, and saved him from exposure to his uncle and another smashing of the will. He and his mother learned to like each other fairly well. She couldn't love him, as yet, because there "warn't nothing *to* him," as she expressed it, but her nature needed something or somebody to rule over, and he was better than nothing. Her strong character and aggressive and commanding ways compelled Tom's admiration in spite of the fact that he got more illustrations of them than he needed for his comfort. However, as a rule her conversation was made up of racy tattle about the privacies of the chief families of the town (for she went harvesting among their kitchens every time she came to the village), and Tom enjoyed this. It was just in his line. She always collected her half of his pension punctually, and he was always at the haunted house to have a chat with her on these occasions. Every now and then she paid him a visit there on between-days also.

Occasionally he would run up to St. Louis for a few weeks, and at last temptation caught him again. He won a lot of money, but lost it, and with it a deal more besides, which he promised to raise as soon as possible.

For this purpose he projected a new raid on his town. He never meddled with any other town, for he was afraid to venture into the houses whose ins and outs he did not know and the habits of whose households he was not acquainted with. He arrived at the haunted house in disguise on the Wednesday before the advent of the twins—after writing his aunt Pratt that he would not arrive until two days after—and lay in hiding there with his mother until toward daylight Friday morning, when he went to his uncle's house and entered by the back way with his own key, and slipped up to his room, where he could have the use of mirror and toilet articles. He had a suit of girl's clothes with him in a bundle as a disguise for his raid, and was wearing a suit of his mother's clothing, with black gloves and veil. By dawn he was tricked out for his raid, but he caught a glimpse of Pudd'nhead Wilson through the window over the way, and knew that Pudd'nhead had caught a glimpse of him. So he entertained Wilson with some airs and graces and attitudes for a while, then stepped out of sight and resumed the other disguise, and by and by went down and out the back way, and started down-town to reconnoiter the scene of his intended labors.

But he was ill at ease. He had changed back to Roxy's dress, with the stoop of age added to the disguise, so that Wilson would not bother himself about a humble old woman leaving a neighbor's house by the back way in the early morning, in case he was still spying. But supposing Wilson had seen him leave, and had thought it suspicious, and had also followed him? The thought

made Tom cold. He gave up the raid for the day, and hurried
back to the haunted house by the obscurest route he knew. His
mother was gone; but she came back, by and by, with the news
of the grand reception at Patsy Cooper's, and soon persuaded
him that the opportunity was like a special providence, it was so
inviting and perfect. So he went raiding, after all, and made a
nice success of it while everybody was gone to Patsy Cooper's.
Success gave him nerve and even actual intrepidity; insomuch,
indeed, that after he had conveyed his harvest to his mother in a
back alley, he went to the reception himself, and added several
of the valuables of that house to his takings.

After this long digression we have now arrived once more at
the point where Pudd'nhead Wilson, while waiting for the arrival
of the twins on that same Friday evening, sat puzzling over the
strange apparition of that morning—a girl in young Tom Driscoll's
bedroom; fretting, and guessing, and puzzling over it, and wondering who the shameless creature might be.

11

Pudd'nhead's Startling Discovery

There are three infallible ways of pleasing an author, and the three form a rising scale of compliment: 1, to tell him you have read one of his books; 2, to tell him you have read all of his books; 3, to ask him to let you read the manuscript of his forthcoming book. No. 1 admits you to his respect; No. 2 admits you to his admiration; No. 3 carries you clear into his heart.
— *Pudd'nhead Wilson's Calendar.*

As to the Adjective: when in doubt, strike it out.
— *Pudd'nhead Wilson's Calendar.*

THE TWINS arrived presently, and talk began. It flowed along chattily and sociably, and under its influence the new friendship gathered ease and strength. Wilson got out his Calendar, by request, and read a passage or two from it, which the twins praised quite cordially. This pleased the author so much that he complied gladly when they asked him to lend them a batch of the work to read at home. In the course of their wide travels they had found out that there are three sure ways of pleasing an author; they were now working the best of the three.

There was an interruption, now. Young Tom Driscoll appeared, and joined the party. He pretended to be seeing the distinguished strangers for the first time when they rose to shake hands; but this was only a blind, as he had already had a glimpse of them, at the reception, while robbing the house.

The twins made mental note that he was smooth-faced and rather handsome, and smooth and undulatory in his movements —graceful, in fact. Angelo thought he had a good eye; Luigi thought there was something veiled and sly about it. Angelo thought he had a pleasant free-and-easy way of talking; Luigi thought it was more so than was agreeable. Angelo thought he was a sufficiently nice young man; Luigi reserved his decision. Tom's first contribution to the conversation was a question which he had put to Wilson a hundred times before. It was always cheerily and good-naturedly put, and always inflicted a little pang, for it touched a secret sore; but this time the pang was sharp, since strangers were present.

"Well, how does the law come on? Had a case yet?"

Wilson bit his lip, but answered, "No—not yet," with as much indifference as he could assume. Judge Driscoll had generously left the law feature out of the Wilson biography which he had furnished to the twins. Young Tom laughed pleasantly, and said:

"Wilson's a lawyer, gentlemen, but he doesn't practise now."

The sarcasm bit, but Wilson kept himself under control, and said without passion:

"I don't practise, it is true. It is true that I have never had a case, and have had to earn a poor living for twenty years as an expert accountant in a town where I can't get hold of a set of books to untangle as often as I should like. But it is also true that I did fit myself well for the practice of the law. By the time I was your age, Tom, I had chosen a profession, and was soon competent to enter upon it." Tom winced. "I never got a chance to try my hand at it, and I may never get a chance; and yet if I ever do get it I shall be found ready, for I have kept up my law studies all these years."

"That's it; that's good grit! I like to see it. I've a notion to throw all my business your way. My business and your law practice ought to make a pretty gay team, Dave," and the young fellow laughed again.

"If you will throw—" Wilson had thought of the girl in Tom's bedroom, and was going to say, "If you will throw the surreptitious and disreputable part of your business my way, it may amount to something"; but thought better of it and said, "However, this matter doesn't fit well in a general conversation."

"All right, we'll change the subject; I guess you were about to give me another dig, anyway, so I'm willing to change. How's the Awful Mystery flourishing these days? Wilson's got a scheme for driving plain window-glass out of the market by decorating it with greasy finger-marks, and getting rich by selling it at famine prices to the crowned heads over in Europe to outfit their palaces with. Fetch it out, Dave."

Wilson brought three of his glass strips, and said:

"I get the subject to pass the fingers of his right hand through his hair, so as to get a little coating of the natural oil on them, and then press the balls of them on the glass. A fine and delicate print of the lines in the skin results, and is permanent, if it doesn't come in contact with something able to rub it off. You begin, Tom."

"Why, I think you took my finger-marks once or twice before."

"Yes, but you were a little boy the last time, only about twelve years old."

"That's so. Of course I've changed entirely since then, and variety is what the crowned heads want, I guess."

He passed his fingers through his crop of short hair, and pressed them one at a time on the glass. Angelo made a print of his fingers on another glass, and Luigi followed with the third. Wilson marked the glasses with names and date, and put them away. Tom gave one of his little laughs, and said:

"I thought I wouldn't say anything, but if variety is what you are after, you have wasted a piece of glass. The hand-print of one twin is the same as the hand-print of the fellow twin."

"Well, it's done now, and I like to have them both, anyway," said Wilson, returning to his place.

"But look here, Dave," said Tom, "you used to tell people's fortunes, too, when you took their finger-marks. Dave's just an all-round genius—a genius of the first water, gentlemen; a great scientist running to seed here in this village, a prophet with the kind of honor that prophets generally get at home—for here they don't give shucks for his scientifics, and they call his skull a notion factory—hey, Dave, ain't it so? But never mind; he'll make his mark some day—finger-mark, you know, he-he! But really, you want to let him take a shy at your palms once; it's worth twice the price of admission or your money's returned at the door. Why, he'll read your wrinkles as easy as a book, and not only tell you fifty or sixty things that's going to happen to you, but fifty or sixty thousand that ain't. Come, Dave, show the gentlemen what an inspired Jack-at-all-science we've got in this town, and don't know it."

Wilson winced under this nagging and not very courteous chaff, and the twins suffered with him and for him. They rightly judged, now, that the best way to relieve him would be to take the thing in earnest and treat it with respect, ignoring Tom's rather overdone raillery; so Luigi said:

"We have seen something of palmistry in our wanderings, and know very well what astonishing things it can do. If it isn't a science, and one of the greatest of them, too, I don't know what its other name ought to be. In the Orient—"

Tom looked surprised and incredulous. He said:

"That juggling a science? But really, you ain't serious, are you?"

"Yes, entirely so. Four years ago we had our hands read out to us as if our palms had been covered with print."

"Well, do you mean to say there was actually anything in it?" asked Tom, his incredulity beginning to weaken a little.

"There was this much in it," said Angelo; "what was told us of our characters was minutely exact—we could not have bettered it ourselves. Next, two or three memorable things that had happened to us were laid bare—things which no one present but ourselves could have known about."

"Why, it's rank sorcery!" exclaimed Tom, who was now becoming very much interested. "And how did they make out with what was going to happen to you in the future?"

"On the whole, quite fairly," said Luigi. "Two or three of the most striking things foretold have happened since; much the most striking one of all happened within that same year. Some of the minor prophecies have come true; some of the minor and some of the major ones have not been fulfilled yet, and of course may never be: still, I should be more surprised if they failed to arrive than if they didn't."

Tom was entirely sobered, and profoundly impressed. He said, apologetically:

"Dave, I wasn't meaning to belittle that science; I was only chaffing—chattering, I reckon I'd better say. I wish you would look at their palms. Come, won't you?"

"Why, certainly, if you want me to; but you know I've had no chance to become an expert, and don't claim to be one. When a past event is somewhat prominently recorded in the palm I can generally detect that, but minor ones often escape me—not always, of course, but often—but I haven't much confidence in myself when it comes to reading the future. I am talking as if palmistry was a daily study with me, but that is not so. I haven't examined half a dozen hands in the last half-dozen years; you see, the people got to joking about it, and I stopped to let the talk die down. I'll tell you what we'll do, Count Luigi: I'll make a try at your past, and if I have any success there—no, on the whole, I'll let the future alone; that's really the affair of an expert."

He took Luigi's hand. Tom said:

"Wait—don't look yet, Dave! Count Luigi, here's paper and pencil. Set down that thing that you said was the most striking one that was foretold to you, and happened less than a year afterward, and give it to me so I can see if Dave finds it in your hand."

Luigi wrote a line privately, and folded up the piece of paper, and handed it to Tom, saying:

"I'll tell you when to look at it, if he finds it."

Wilson began to study Luigi's palm, tracing life lines, heart lines, head lines, and so on, and noting carefully their relations with the cobweb of finer and more delicate marks and lines that enmeshed them on all sides; he felt of the fleshy cushion at the base of the thumb, and noted its shape; he felt of the fleshy side of the hand between the wrist and the base of the little finger, and noted its shape also; he painstakingly examined the fingers, observing their form, proportions, and natural manner of disposing themselves when in repose. All this process was watched by the three spectators with absorbing interest, their heads bent together over Luigi's palm, and nobody disturbing the stillness with a word. Wilson now entered upon a close survey of the palm again, and his revelations began.

He mapped out Luigi's character and disposition, his tastes, aversions, proclivities, ambitions, and eccentricities in a way which sometimes made Luigi wince and the others laugh, but both twins declared that the chart was artistically drawn and was correct.

Next, Wilson took up Luigi's history. He proceeded cautiously and with hesitation, now, moving his finger slowly along the great lines of the palm, and now and then halting it at a "star" or some such landmark, and examining that neighborhood minutely. He proclaimed one or two past events, Luigi confirmed his correctness, and the search went on. Presently Wilson glanced up suddenly with a surprised expression—

"Here is record of an incident which you would perhaps not wish me to—"

"Bring it out," said Luigi, good-naturedly; "I promise you it sha'n't embarrass me."

But Wilson still hesitated, and did not seem quite to know what to do. Then he said:

"I think it is too delicate a matter to—to—I believe I would rather write it or whisper it to you, and let you decide for yourself whether you want it talked out or not."

"That will answer," said Luigi; "write it."

Wilson wrote something on a slip of paper and handed it to Luigi, who read it to himself and said to Tom:

"Unfold your slip and read it, Mr. Driscoll."

Tom read:

"It was prophesied that I would kill a man. It came true before the year was out."

Tom added, "Great Scott!"

Luigi handed Wilson's paper to Tom, and said:

"Now read this one."

Tom read:

"You have killed some one, but whether man, woman, or child, I do not make out."

"Cæsar's ghost!" commented Tom, with astonishment. "It beats anything that was ever heard of! Why, a man's own hand is his deadliest enemy! Just think of that—a man's own hand keeps a record of the deepest and fatalest secrets of his life, and is treacherously ready to expose him to any black-magic stranger that comes along. But what do you let a person look at your hand for, with that awful thing printed in it?"

"Oh," said Luigi, reposefully, "I don't mind it. I killed the man for good reasons, and I don't regret it."

"What were the reasons?"

"Well, he needed killing."

"I'll tell you why he did it, since he won't say himself," said Angelo, warmly. "He did it to save my life, that's what he did it for. So it was a noble act, and not a thing to be hid in the dark."

"So it was, so it was," said Wilson; "to do such a thing to save a brother's life is a great and fine action."

"Now come," said Luigi, "it is very pleasant to hear you say these things, but for unselfishness, or heroism, or magnanimity, the circumstances won't stand scrutiny. You overlook one detail; suppose I hadn't saved Angelo's life, what would have become of mine? If I had let the man kill him, wouldn't he have killed me, too? I saved my own life, you see."

"Yes; that is your way of talking," said Angelo, "but I know you —I don't believe you thought of yourself at all. I keep that weapon yet that Luigi killed the man with, and I'll show it to you sometime. That incident makes it interesting, and it had a history before it came into Luigi's hands which adds to its interest. It was given to Luigi by a great Indian prince, the Gaikowar of Baroda, and it had been in his family two or three centuries. It killed a good many disagreeable people who troubled that hearthstone at one time or another. It isn't much to look at, except that it isn't shaped like other knives, or dirks, or whatever it may be called—here, I'll draw it for you." He took a sheet of paper and made a rapid sketch. "There it is—a broad and murderous blade, with edges like a razor for sharpness. The devices engraved on it are the ciphers or names of its long line of possessors—I had Luigi's name added in Roman letters myself with our coat of arms,

as you see. You notice what a curious handle the thing has. It is
solid ivory, polished like a mirror, and is four or five inches long
—round, and as thick as a large man's wrist, with the end squared
off flat, for your thumb to rest on; for you grasp it, with your
thumb resting on the blunt end—so—and lift it aloft and strike
downward. The Gaikowar showed us how the thing was done
when he gave it to Luigi, and before that night was ended Luigi
had used the knife, and the Gaikowar was a man short by reason
of it. The sheath is magnificently ornamented with gems of great
value. You will find the sheath more worth looking at than the
knife itself, of course."

Tom said to himself:

"It's lucky I came here. I would have sold that knife for a song;
I supposed the jewels were glass."

"But go on; don't stop," said Wilson. "Our curiosity is up now,
to hear about the homicide. Tell us about that."

"Well, briefly, the knife was to blame for that, all around. A
native servant slipped into our room in the palace in the night, to
kill us and steal the knife on account of the fortune incrusted on
its sheath, without a doubt. Luigi had it under his pillow; we
were in bed together. There was a dim night light burning. I was
asleep, but Luigi was awake, and he thought he detected a vague
form nearing the bed. He slipped the knife out of the sheath and
was ready, and unembarrassed by hampering bedclothes, for the
weather was hot and we hadn't any. Suddenly that native rose at
the bedside, and bent over me with his right hand lifted and a
dirk in it aimed at my throat; but Luigi grabbed his wrist, pulled
him downward, and drove his own knife into the man's neck.
That is the whole story."

Wilson and Tom drew deep breaths, and after some general
chat about the tragedy, Pudd'nhead said, taking Tom's hand:

"Now, Tom, I've never had a look at your palms, as it happens;
perhaps you've got some little questionable privacies that need
—hel-lo!"

Tom had snatched away his hand, and was looking a good deal
confused.

"Why, he's blushing!" said Luigi.

Tom darted an ugly look at him, and said, sharply:

"Well, if I am, it ain't because I'm a murderer!" Luigi's dark face flushed, but before he could speak or move, Tom added with anxious haste: "Oh, I beg a thousand pardons. I didn't mean that; it was out before I thought, and I'm very, very sorry—you must forgive me!"

Wilson came to the rescue, and smoothed things down as well as he could; and in fact was entirely successful as far as the twins were concerned, for they felt sorrier for the affront put upon him by his guest's outburst of ill manners than for the insult offered to Luigi. But the success was not so pronounced with the offender. Tom tried to seem at his ease, and he went through the motions fairly well, but at bottom he felt resentful toward all the three witnesses of his exhibition; in fact, he felt so annoyed at them for having witnessed it and noticed it that he almost forgot to feel annoyed at himself for placing it before them. However, something presently happened which made him almost comfortable, and brought him nearly back to a state of charity and friendliness. This was a little spat between the twins; not much of a spat, but still a spat; and before they got far with it they were in a decided condition of irritation with each other. Tom was charmed; so pleased, indeed, that he cautiously did what he could to increase the irritation while pretending to be actuated by more respectable motives. By his help the fire got warmed up to the blazing-point, and he might have had the happiness of seeing the flames show up, in another moment, but for the interruption of a knock on the door—an interruption which fretted him as much as it gratified Wilson. Wilson opened the door. The visitor was a good-natured, ignorant, energetic, middle-aged Irishman named John Buckstone, who was a great politician in a small way, and always took a large share in public matters of every sort. One of the town's chief excitements, just now, was over the matter of rum. There was a strong rum party and a strong anti-rum party. Buckstone was training with the rum party, and he had been sent to hunt up the twins and invite them to attend a mass-meeting of that faction. He delivered his errand, and said the clans were already gathering in the big hall over the market-house. Luigi accepted the invitation cordially, Angelo less cordially, since he disliked crowds, and did not drink the powerful intoxicants of America. In fact, he was even a teetotaler sometimes—when it was judicious to be one.

The twins left with Buckstone, and Tom Driscoll joined company with them uninvited.

In the distance one could see a long wavering line of torches drifting down the main street, and could hear the throbbing of the bass drum, the clash of cymbals, the squeaking of a fife or two, and the faint roar of remote hurrahs. The tail end of this procession was climbing the market-house stairs when the twins arrived in its neighborhood; when they reached the hall it was full of people, torches, smoke, noise, and enthusiasm. They were conducted to the platform by Buckstone—Tom Driscoll still following—and were delivered to the chairman in the midst of a prodigious explosion of welcome. When the noise had moderated a little, the chair proposed that "our illustrious guests be at once elected, by complimentary acclamation, to membership in our ever-glorious organization, the paradise of the free and the perdition of the slave."

This eloquent discharge opened the flood-gates of enthusiasm again, and the election was carried with thundering unanimity. Then arose a storm of cries:

"Wet them down! Wet them down! Give them a drink!"

Glasses of whisky were handed to the twins. Luigi waved his aloft, then brought it to his lips; but Angelo set his down. There was another storm of cries:

"What's the matter with the other one?" "What is the blond one going back on us for?" "Explain! Explain!"

The chairman inquired, and then reported:

"We have made an unfortunate mistake, gentlemen. I find that the Count Angelo Capello is opposed to our creed—is a teetotaler, in fact, and was not intending to apply for membership with us. He desires that we reconsider the vote by which he was elected. What is the pleasure of the house?"

There was a general burst of laughter, plentifully accented with whistlings and cat-calls, but the energetic use of the gavel presently restored something like order. Then a man spoke from the crowd, and said that while he was very sorry that the mistake had been made, it would not be possible to rectify it at the present meeting. According to the by-laws it must go over to the next regular meeting for action. He would not offer a motion, as none was required. He desired to apologize to the gentleman in the name of the house, and begged to assure him that as far as it might lie in the power of the Sons of Liberty, his temporary membership in the order would be made pleasant to him.

This speech was received with great applause, mixed with cries of:

"That's the talk!" "He's a good fellow, anyway, if he *is* a teetotaler!" "Drink his health!" "Give him a rouser, and no heeltaps!"

Glasses were handed around, and everybody on the platform drank Angelo's health, while the house bellowed forth in song:

> For he's a jolly good fel-low,
> For he's a jolly good fel-low,
> For he's a jolly good fe-el-low,—
> Which nobody can deny.

Tom Driscoll drank. It was his second glass, for he had drunk Angelo's the moment that Angelo had set it down. The two drinks made him very merry—almost idiotically so—and he began to take a most lively and prominent part in the proceedings, particularly in the music and cat-calls and side remarks.

The chairman was still standing at the front, the twins at his side. The extraordinarily close resemblance of the brothers to each other suggested a witticism to Tom Driscoll, and just as the chairman began a speech he skipped forward and said with an air of tipsy confidence to the audience:

"Boys, I move that he keeps still and lets this human philopena snip you out a speech."

The descriptive aptness of the phrase caught the house, and a mighty burst of laughter followed.

Luigi's southern blood leaped to the boiling-point in a moment under the sharp humiliation of this insult delivered in the presence of four hundred strangers. It was not in the young man's

nature to let the matter pass, or to delay the squaring of the
account. He took a couple of strides and halted behind the unsuspecting joker. Then he drew back and delivered a kick of
such titanic vigor that it lifted Tom clear over the footlights and
landed him on the heads of the front row of the Sons of Liberty.

Even a sober person does not like to have a human being emp-
tied on him when he is not doing any harm; a person who is not
sober cannot endure such an attention at all. The nest of Sons of
Liberty that Driscoll landed in had not a sober bird in it; in fact,
there was probably not an entirely sober one in the auditorium.
Driscoll was promptly and indignantly flung onto the heads of
Sons in the next row, and these Sons passed him on toward the
rear, and then immediately began to pummel the front-row Sons
who had passed him to them. This course was strictly followed
by bench after bench as Driscoll traveled in his tumultuous and
airy flight toward the door; so he left behind him an ever-
lengthening wake of raging and plunging and fighting and swearing humanity. Down went group after group of torches, and
presently above the deafening clatter of the gavel, roar of angry
voices, and crash of succumbing benches, rose the paralyzing cry
of "FIRE!"

The fighting ceased instantly; the cursing ceased; for one distinctly defined moment there was a dead hush, a motionless calm,
where the tempest had been; then with one impulse the multitude awoke to life and energy again, and went surging and struggling and swaying, this way and that, its outer edges melting
away through windows and doors and gradually lessening the
pressure and relieving the mass.

The fire-boys were never on hand so suddenly before; for there
was no distance to go, this time, their quarters being in the rear
end of the market-house. There was an engine company and a
hook-and-ladder company. Half of each was composed of rum-
mies and the other half of anti-rummies, after the moral and
political share-and-share-alike fashion of the frontier town of the
period. Enough anti-rummies were loafing in quarters to man the
engine and the ladders. In two minutes they had their red shirts
and helmets on—they never stirred officially in unofficial costume

—and as the mass-meeting overhead smashed through the long row of windows and poured out upon the roof of the arcade, the deliverers were ready for them with a powerful stream of water which washed some of them off the roof and nearly drowned the rest. But water was preferable to fire, and still the stampede from the windows continued, and still the pitiless drenching assailed it until the building was empty; then the fire-boys mounted to the hall and flooded it with water enough to annihilate forty times as much fire as there was there; for a village fire company does not often get a chance to show off, and so when it does get a chance it makes the most of it. Such citizens of that village as were of a thoughtful and judicious temperament did not insure against fire; they insured against the fire company.

12

The Shame of Judge Driscoll

Courage is resistance to fear, mastery of fear—not absence
of fear. Except a creature be part coward it is not a compliment to say it is brave; it is merely a loose misapplica-
tion of the word. Consider the flea!—incomparably the
bravest of all the creatures of God, if ignorance of fear
were courage. Whether you are asleep or awake he will
attack you, caring nothing for the fact that in bulk and
strength you are to him as are the massed armies of the
earth to a sucking child; he lives both day and night and
all days and nights in the very lap of peril and the immediate presence of death, and yet is no more afraid than is the
man who walks the streets of a city that was threatened by
an earthquake ten centuries before. When we speak of
Clive, Nelson, and Putnam as men who "didn't know what
fear was," we ought always to add the flea—and put him
at the head of the procession.

        —*Pudd'nhead Wilson's Calendar.*

JUDGE DRISCOLL was in bed and asleep by ten o'clock on Friday
night, and he was up and gone a-fishing before daylight in the
morning with his friend Pembroke Howard. These two had been
boys together in Virginia when that state still ranked as the chief
and most imposing member of the Union, and they still coupled
the proud and affectionate adjective "old" with her name when
they spoke of her. In Missouri a recognized superiority attached
to any person who hailed from Old Virginia; and this superiority
was exalted to supremacy when a person of such nativity could
also prove descent from the First Families of that great common-
wealth. The Howards and Driscolls were of this aristocracy. In
their eyes it was a nobility. It had its unwritten laws, and they

were as clearly defined and as strict as any that could be found among the printed statutes of the land. The F. F. V. was born a gentleman; his highest duty in life was to watch over that great inheritance and keep it unsmirched. He must keep his honor spotless. Those laws were his chart; his course was marked out on it; if he swerved from it by so much as half a point of the compass it meant shipwreck to his honor; that is to say, degradation from his rank as a gentleman. These laws required certain things of him which his religion might forbid: then his religion must yield—the laws could not be relaxed to accommodate religions or anything else. Honor stood first; and the laws defined what it was and wherein it differed in certain details from honor as defined by church creeds and by the social laws and customs of some of the minor divisions of the globe that had got crowded out when the sacred boundaries of Virginia were staked out.

If Judge Driscoll was the recognized first citizen of Dawson's Landing, Pembroke Howard was easily its recognized second citizen. He was called "the great lawyer"—an earned title. He and Driscoll were of the same age—a year or two past sixty.

Although Driscoll was a free-thinker and Howard a strong and determined Presbyterian, their warm intimacy suffered no impairment in consequence. They were men whose opinions were their own property and not subject to revision and amendment, suggestion or criticism, by anybody, even their friends.

The day's fishing finished, they came floating down-stream in their skiff, talking national politics and other high matters, and presently met a skiff coming up from town, with a man in it who said:

"I reckon you know one of the new twins gave your nephew a kicking last night, Judge?"

"Did *what?*"

"Gave him a kicking."

The old Judge's lips paled, and his eyes began to flame. He choked with anger for a moment, then he got out what he was trying to say:

"Well—well—go on! give me the details."

The man did it. At the finish the Judge was silent a minute,

turning over in his mind the shameful picture of Tom's flight over
the footlights; then he said, as if musing aloud—"H'm—I don't
understand it. I was asleep at home. He didn't wake me. Thought
he was competent to manage his affair without my help, I
reckon." His face lit up with pride and pleasure at that thought,
and he said with a cheery complacency, "I like that—it's the true
old blood—hey, Pembroke?"

Howard smiled an iron smile, and nodded his head approvingly.
Then the news-bringer spoke again:

"But Tom beat the twin on the trial."

The Judge looked at the man wonderingly, and said:

"The trial? What trial?"

"Why, Tom had him up before Judge Robinson for assault and
battery."

The old man shrank suddenly together like one who had received a death-stroke. Howard sprang for him as he sank forward
in a swoon, and took him in his arms, and bedded him on his back
in the boat. He sprinkled water in his face, and said to the startled
visitor:

"Go, now—don't let him come to and find you here. You see
what an effect your heedless speech has had; you ought to have
been more considerate than to blurt out such a cruel piece of
slander as that."

"I'm right down sorry I did it now, Mr. Howard, and I wouldn't
have done it if I had thought: but it ain't slander; it's perfectly
true, just as I told him."

He rowed away. Presently the old Judge came out of his faint
and looked up piteously into the sympathetic face that was bent
over him.

"Say it ain't true, Pembroke; tell me it ain't true!" he said in
a weak voice.

There was nothing weak in the deep organ-tones that responded:

"You know it's a lie as well as I do, old friend. He is of the
best blood of the Old Dominion."

"God bless you for saying it!" said the old gentleman, fervently.
"Ah, Pembroke, it was such a blow!"

Howard stayed by his friend, and saw him home, and entered the house with him. It was dark, and past supper-time, but the Judge was not thinking of supper; he was eager to hear the slander refuted from headquarters, and as eager to have Howard hear it, too. Tom was sent for, and he came immediately. He was bruised and lame, and was not a happy-looking object. His uncle made him sit down, and said:

"We have been hearing about your adventure, Tom, with a handsome lie added to it for embellishment. Now pulverize that lie to dust! What measures have you taken? How does the thing stand?"

Tom answered guilelessly: "It don't stand at all; it's all over. I had him up in court and beat him. Pudd'nhead Wilson defended him—first case he ever had, and lost it. The judge fined the miserable hound five dollars for the assault."

Howard and the Judge sprang to their feet with the opening sentence—why, neither knew; then they stood gazing vacantly at each other. Howard stood a moment, then sat mournfully down without saying anything. The Judge's wrath began to kindle, and he burst out:

"You cur! You scum! You vermin! Do you mean to tell me that blood of my race has suffered a blow and crawled to a court of law about it? Answer me!"

Tom's head dropped, and he answered with an eloquent silence. His uncle stared at him with a mixed expression of amazement and shame and incredulity that was sorrowful to see. At last he said:

"Which of the twins was it?"

"Count Luigi."

"You have challenged him?"

"N—no," hesitated Tom, turning pale.

"You will challenge him to-night. Howard will carry it."

Tom began to turn sick, and to show it. He turned his hat round and round in his hand, his uncle glowering blacker and blacker upon him as the heavy seconds drifted by; then at last he began to stammer, and said piteously:

"Oh, please don't ask me to do it, uncle! He is a murderous devil—I never could—I—I'm afraid of him!"

Old Driscoll's mouth opened and closed three times before he could get it to perform its office; then he stormed out:

"A coward in my family! A Driscoll a coward! Oh, what have I done to deserve this infamy!" He tottered to his secretary in the corner repeating that lament again and again in heartbreaking tones, and got out of a drawer a paper, which he slowly tore to bits, scattering the bits absently in his track as he walked up and down the room, still grieving and lamenting. At last he said:

"There it is, shreds and fragments once more—my will. Once more you have forced me to disinherit you, you base son of a most noble father! Leave my sight! Go—before I spit on you!"

The young man did not tarry. Then the Judge turned to Howard:

"You will be my second, old friend?"

"Of course."

"There is pen and paper. Draft the cartel, and lose no time."

"The Count shall have it in his hands in fifteen minutes," said Howard.

Tom was very heavy-hearted. His appetite was gone with his property and his self-respect. He went out the back way and wandered down the obscure lane grieving, and wondering if any course of future conduct, however discreet and carefully perfected and watched over, could win back his uncle's favor and persuade him to reconstruct once more that generous will which had just gone to ruin before his eyes. He finally concluded that it could. He said to himself that he had accomplished this sort of triumph once already, and that what had been done once could be done again. He would set about it. He would bend every energy to the task, and he would score that triumph once more, cost what it might to his convenience, limit as it might his frivolous and liberty-loving life.

"To begin," he said to himself, "I'll square up with the proceeds of my raid, and then gambling has got to be stopped—and stopped short off. It's the worst vice I've got—from my standpoint, anyway, because it's the one he can most easily find out, through the impatience of my creditors. He thought it expensive to have to pay two hundred dollars to them for me once. Expensive—*that!* Why, it cost me the whole of his fortune—but of course he never thought of that; some people can't think of any but their own side of a case. If he had known how deep I am in, now, the will would have gone to pot without waiting for a duel to help. Three hundred dollars! It's a pile! But he'll never hear of it, I'm thankful to say. The minute I've cleared it off, I'm safe; and I'll never touch a card again. Anyway, I won't while he lives, I make oath to that. I'm entering on my last reform—I know it— yes, and I'll win; but after that, if I ever slip again I'm gone."

13

Tom Stares at Ruin

When I reflect upon the number of disagreeable people who I know have gone to a better world, I am moved to lead a different life.—*Pudd'nhead Wilson's Calendar.*

October. This is one of the peculiarly dangerous months to speculate in stocks in. The others are July, January, September, April, November, May, March, June, December, August, and February.—*Pudd'nhead Wilson's Calendar.*

THUS mournfully communing with himself Tom moped along the lane past Pudd'nhead Wilson's house, and still on and on between fences inclosing vacant country on each hand till he neared the haunted house, then he came moping back again, with many sighs and heavy with trouble. He sorely wanted cheerful company. Rowena! His heart gave a bound at the thought, but the next thought quieted it—the detested twins would be there.

He was on the inhabited side of Wilson's house, and now as

he approached it he noticed that the sitting-room was lighted. This would do; others made him feel unwelcome sometimes, but Wilson never failed in courtesy toward him, and a kindly courtesy does at least save one's feelings, even if it is not professing to stand for a welcome. Wilson heard footsteps at his threshold, then the clearing of a throat.

"It's that fickle-tempered, dissipated young goose—poor devil, he finds friends pretty scarce to-day, likely, after the disgrace of carrying a personal-assault case into a law-court."

A dejected knock. "Come in!"

Tom entered, and drooped into a chair, without saying anything. Wilson said kindly:

"Why, my boy, you look desolate. Don't take it so hard. Try and forget you have been kicked."

"Oh, dear," said Tom, wretchedly, "it's not that, Pudd'nhead— it's not that. It's a thousand times worse than that—oh, yes, a million times worse."

"Why, Tom, what do you mean? Has Rowena—"

"Flung me? No, but the old man has."

Wilson said to himself, "Aha!" and thought of the mysterious girl in the bedroom. "The Driscolls have been making discoveries!" Then he said aloud, gravely:

"Tom, there are some kinds of dissipation which—"

"Oh, shucks, this hasn't got anything to do with dissipation. He wanted me to challenge that derned Italian savage, and I wouldn't do it."

"Yes, of course he would do that," said Wilson in a meditative matter-of-course way, "but the thing that puzzled me was, why he didn't look to that last night, for one thing, and why he let you carry such a matter into a court of law at all, either before the duel or after it. It's no place for it. It was not like him. I couldn't understand it. How did it happen?"

"It happened because he didn't know anything about it. He was asleep when I got home last night."

"And you didn't wake him? Tom, is that possible?"

Tom was not getting much comfort here. He fidgeted a moment, then said:

"I didn't choose to tell him—that's all. He was going a-fishing before dawn, with Pembroke Howard, and if I got the twins into the common calaboose—and I thought sure I could—I never dreamed of their slipping out on a paltry fine for such an outrageous offense—well, once in the calaboose they would be disgraced, and uncle wouldn't want any duels with that sort of characters, and wouldn't allow any."

"Tom, I am ashamed of you! I don't see how you could treat your good old uncle so. I am a better friend of his than you are; for if I had known the circumstances I would have kept that case out of court until I got word to him and let him have a gentleman's chance."

"You would?" exclaimed Tom, with lively surprise. "And it your first case! And you know perfectly well there never would have *been* any case if he had got that chance, don't you? And you'd have finished your days a pauper nobody, instead of being an actually launched and recognized lawyer to-day. And you would really have done that, would you?"

"Certainly."

Tom looked at him a moment or two, then shook his head sorrowfully and said:

"I believe you—upon my word I do. I don't know why I do, but I do. Pudd'nhead Wilson, I think you're the biggest fool I ever saw."

"Thank you."

"Don't mention it."

"Well, he has been requiring you to fight the Italian and you have refused. You degenerate remnant of an honorable line! I'm thoroughly ashamed of you, Tom!"

"Oh, that's nothing! I don't care for anything, now that the will's torn up again."

"Tom, tell me squarely—didn't he find any fault with you for anything but those two things—carrying the case into court and refusing to fight?"

He watched the young fellow's face narrowly, but it was entirely reposeful, and so also was the voice that answered:

"No, he didn't find any other fault with me. If he had had

any to find, he would have begun yesterday, for he was just in the humor for it. He drove that jack-pair around town and showed them the sights, and when he came home he couldn't find his father's old silver watch that don't keep time and he thinks so much of, and couldn't remember what he did with it three or four days ago when he saw it last, and so when I arrived he was all in a sweat about it, and when I suggested that it probably wasn't lost but stolen, it put him in a regular passion and he said I was a fool—which convinced me, without any trouble, that that was just what he was afraid *had* happened, himself, but did not want to believe it, because lost things stand a better chance of being found again than stolen ones."

"Whe-ew!" whistled Wilson; "score another on the list."

"Another what?"

"Another theft!"

"Theft?"

"Yes, theft. That watch isn't lost, it's stolen. There's been another raid on the town—and just the same old mysterious sort of thing that has happened once before, as you remember."

"You don't mean it!"

"It's as sure as you are born! Have you missed anything yourself?"

"No. That is, I did miss a silver pencil-case that Aunt Mary Pratt gave me last birthday—"

"You'll find it stolen—that's what you'll find."

"No, I sha'n't; for when I suggested theft about the watch and got such a rap, I went and examined my room, and the pencil-case was missing, but it was only mislaid, and I found it again."

"You are sure you missed nothing else?"

"Well, nothing of consequence. I missed a small plain gold ring worth two or three dollars, but that will turn up. I'll look again."

"In my opinion you'll not find it. There's been a raid, I tell you. Come *in!*"

Mr. Justice Robinson entered, followed by Buckstone and the town constable, Jim Blake. They sat down, and after some wandering and aimless weather conversation Wilson said:

"By the way, we've just added another to the list of thefts, maybe two. Judge Driscoll's old silver watch is gone, and Tom here has missed a gold ring."

"Well, it is a bad business," said the Justice, "and gets worse the further it goes. The Hankses, the Dobsons, the Pilligrews, the Ortons, the Grangers, the Hales, the Fullers, the Holcombs, in fact everybody that lives around about Patsy Cooper's has been robbed of little things like trinkets and teaspoons and such-like small valuables that are easily carried off. It's perfectly plain that the thief took advantage of the reception at Patsy Cooper's when all the neighbors were in her house and all their niggers hanging around her fence for a look at the show, to raid the vacant houses undisturbed. Patsy is miserable about it; miserable on account of the neighbors, and particularly miserable on account of her foreigners, of course; so miserable on their account that she hasn't any room to worry about her own little losses."

"It's the same old raider," said Wilson. "I suppose there isn't any doubt about that."

"Constable Blake doesn't think so."

"No, you're wrong there," said Blake; "the other times it was a man; there was plenty of signs of that, as we know, in the profession, though we never got hands on him; but this time it's a woman."

Wilson thought of the mysterious girl straight off. She was always in his mind now. But she failed him again. Blake continued:

"She's a stoop-shouldered old woman with a covered basket on her arm, in a black veil, dressed in mourning. I saw her going aboard the ferry-boat yesterday. Lives in Illinois, I reckon; but I don't care where she lives, I'm going to get her—she can make herself sure of that."

"What makes you think she's the thief?"

"Well, there ain't any other, for one thing; and for another, some of the nigger draymen that happened to be driving along saw her coming out of or going into houses, and told me so—and it just happens that they was *robbed* houses, every time."

It was granted that this was plenty good enough circumstantial evidence. A pensive silence followed, which lasted some moments, then Wilson said:

"There's one good thing, anyway. She can't either pawn or sell Count Luigi's costly Indian dagger."

"My!" said Tom, "is *that* gone?"

"Yes."

"Well, that was a haul! But why can't she pawn it or sell it?"

"Because when the twins went home from the Sons of Liberty meeting last night, news of the raid was sifting in from everywhere, and Aunt Patsy was in distress to know if they had lost anything. They found that the dagger was gone, and they notified the police and pawnbrokers everywhere. It was a great haul, yes, but the old woman won't get anything out of it, because she'll get caught."

"Did they offer a reward?" asked Buckstone.

"Yes; five hundred dollars for the knife, and five hundred dollars for the thief."

"What a leather-headed idea!" exclaimed the constable. "The thief da'sn't go near them, nor send anybody. Whoever goes is going to get himself nabbed, for there ain't any pawnbroker that's going to lose the chance to—"

If anybody had noticed Tom's face at that time, the gray-green color of it might have provoked curiosity; but nobody did. He said to himself: "I'm gone! I never can square up; the rest of the plunder won't pawn or sell for half of the bill. Oh, I know it— I'm gone, I'm gone—and this time it's for good. Oh, this is awful— I don't know what to do, nor which way to turn!"

"Softly, softly," said Wilson to Blake. "I planned their scheme for them at midnight last night, and it was all finished up shipshape by two this morning. They'll get their dagger back, and then I'll explain to you how the thing was done."

There were strong signs of a general curiosity, and Buckstone said:

"Well, you have whetted us up pretty sharp, Wilson, and I'm free to say that if you don't mind telling us in confidence—"

"Oh, I'd as soon tell as not, Buckstone, but as long as the twins and I agreed to say nothing about it, we must let it stand so. But you can take my word for it you won't be kept waiting three days. Sombody will apply for that reward pretty promptly, and I'll show you the thief and the dagger both very soon afterward."

The constable was disappointed, and also perplexed. He said:

"It may all be—yes, and I hope it will, but I'm blamed if I can see my way through it. It's too many for yours truly."

The subject seemed about talked out. Nobody seemed to have anything further to offer. After a silence the justice of the peace informed Wilson that he and Buckstone and the constable had come as a committee, on the part of the Democratic party, to ask him to run for mayor—for the little town was about to become a city and the first charter election was approaching. It was the first attention which Wilson had ever received at the hands of any party; it was a sufficiently humble one, but it was a recognition of his début into the town's life and activities at last; it was a step upward, and he was deeply gratified. He accepted, and the committee departed, followed by young Tom.

14

Roxana Insists Upon Reform

The true Southern watermelon is a boon apart, and not to
be mentioned with commoner things. It is chief of this
world's luxuries, king by the grace of God over all the
fruits of the earth. When one has tasted it, he knows what
the angels eat. It was not a Southern watermelon that Eve
took; we know it because she repented.

—Pudd'nhead Wilson's Calendar.

ABOUT THE TIME that Wilson was bowing the committee out, Pembroke Howard was entering the next house to report. He found
the old Judge sitting grim and straight in his chair, waiting.

"Well, Howard—the news?"

"The best in the world."

"Accepts, does he?" and the light of battle gleamed joyously in
the Judge's eye.

"Accepts? Why, he jumped at it."

"Did, did he? Now that's fine—that's very fine. I like that. When
is it to be?"

"Now! Straight off! To-night! An admirable fellow—admirable!"

"Admirable? He's a darling! Why, it's an honor as well as a
pleasure to stand up before such a man. Come—off with you!
Go and arrange everything—and give him my heartiest compliments. A rare fellow, indeed; an admirable fellow, as you have
said!"

Howard hurried away, saying:

"I'll have him in the vacant stretch between Wilson's and the
haunted house within the hour, and I'll bring my own pistols."

Judge Driscoll began to walk the floor in a state of pleased
excitement; but presently he stopped, and began to think—began

to think of Tom. Twice he moved toward the secretary, and twice he turned away again; but finally he said:

"This may be my last night in the world—I must not take the chance. He is worthless and unworthy, but it is largely my fault. He was intrusted to me by my brother on his dying bed, and I have indulged him to his hurt, instead of training him up severely, and making a man of him. I have violated my trust, and I must not add the sin of desertion to that. I have forgiven him once already, and would subject him to a long and hard trial before forgiving him again, if I could live; but I must not run that risk. No, I must restore the will. But if I survive the duel, I will hide it away, and he will not know, and I will not tell him until he reforms, and I see that his reformation is going to be permanent."

He redrew the will, and his ostensible nephew was heir to a fortune again. As he was finishing his task, Tom, wearied with another brooding tramp, entered the house and went tiptoeing past the sitting-room door. He glanced in, and hurried on, for the sight of his uncle had nothing but terrors for him to-night. But his uncle was writing! That was unusual at this late hour. What could he be writing? A chill of anxiety settled down upon Tom's heart. Did that writing concern him? He was afraid so. He reflected that when ill luck begins, it does not come in sprinkles, but in showers. He said he would get a glimpse of that document or know the reason why. He heard some one coming and stepped out of sight and hearing. It was Pembroke Howard. What could be hatching?

Howard said, with great satisfaction:

"Everything's right and ready. He's gone to the battle-ground with his second and the surgeon—also with his brother. I've arranged it all with Wilson—Wilson's his second. We are to have three shots apiece."

"Good! How is the moon?"

"Bright as day, nearly. Perfect, for the distance—fifteen yards. No wind—not a breath; hot and still."

"All good; all first-rate. Here, Pembroke, read this, and witness it."

Pembroke read and witnessed the will, then gave the old man's hand a hearty shake and said:

"Now that's right, York—but I knew you would do it. You couldn't leave that poor chap to fight along without means or profession, with certain defeat before him, and I knew you wouldn't, for his father's sake if not for his own."

"For his dead father's sake I couldn't, I know; for poor Percy —but you know what Percy was to me. But mind—Tom is not to know of this unless I fall to-night."

"I understand. I'll keep the secret."

The Judge put the will away, and the two started for the battle-ground. In another minute the will was in Tom's hands. His misery vanished, his feelings underwent a tremendous revulsion. He put the will carefully back in its place, and spread his mouth and swung his hat once, twice, three times around his head, in imitation of three rousing huzzas, no sound issuing from his lips. He fell to communing with himself excitedly and joyously, but every now and then he let off another volley of dumb hurrahs.

He said to himself: "I've got the fortune again, but I'll not let on that I know about it. And this time I'm going to hang onto it. I take no more risks. I'll gamble no more, I'll drink no more, because—well, because I'll not go where there is any of that sort of thing going on, again. It's the sure way, and the only sure way; I might have thought of that sooner—well, yes, if I had wanted to. But now—dear me, I've had a scare this time, and I'll take no more chances. Not a single chance more. Land! I persuaded myself this evening that I could fetch him around without any great amount of effort, but I've been getting more and more heavy-hearted and doubtful straight along, ever since. If he tells me about this thing, all right; but if he doesn't, I sha'n't let on. I—well, I'd like to tell Pudd'nhead Wilson, but—no, I'll think about that; perhaps I won't." He whirled off another dead huzza, and said, "I'm reformed, and this time I'll stay so, sure!"

He was about to close with a final grand silent demonstration, when he suddenly recollected that Wilson had put it out of his power to pawn or sell the Indian knife, and that he was once more in awful peril of exposure by his creditors for that reason. His joy collapsed utterly, and he turned away and moped toward the door moaning and lamenting over the bitterness of his luck. He dragged himself upstairs, and brooded in his room a long time disconsolate and forlorn, with Luigi's Indian knife for a text. At last he sighed and said:

"When I supposed these stones were glass and this ivory bone, the thing hadn't any interest for me because it hadn't any value, and couldn't help me out of my trouble. But now—why, now it is full of interest; yes, and of a sort to break a body's heart. It's a bag of gold that has turned to dirt and ashes in my hands. It could save me, and save me so easily, and yet I've got to go to ruin. It's like drowning with a life-preserver in my reach. All the hard luck comes to me, and all the good luck goes to other people —Pudd'nhead Wilson, for instance; even his career has got a sort of a little start at last, and what has he done to deserve it, I should like to know? Yes, he has opened his own road, but he isn't content with that, but must block mine. It's a sordid, selfish world, and I wish I was out of it." He allowed the light of the candle to play upon the jewels of the sheath, but the flashings and sparklings had no charm for his eye; they were only just so many pangs to his heart. "I must not say anything to Roxy about this thing," he said, "she is too daring. She would be for digging these stones out and selling them, and then—why, she would be arrested and the stones traced, and then—" The thought made him quake, and he hid the knife away, trembling all over and glancing furtively about, like a criminal who fancies that the accuser is already at hand.

Should he try to sleep? Oh, no, sleep was not for him; his trouble was too haunting, too afflicting for that. He must have somebody to mourn with. He would carry his despair to Roxy.

He had heard several distant gunshots, but that sort of thing was not uncommon, and they had made no impression upon him. He went out at the back door, and turned westward. He passed Wilson's house and proceeded along the lane, and presently saw several figures approaching Wilson's place through the vacant lots. These were the duelists returning from the fight; he thought he recognized them, but as he had no desire for white people's company, he stooped down behind the fence until they were out of his way.

Roxy was feeling fine. She said:

"Whah was you, child? Warn't you in it?"

"In what?"

"In de duel."

"Duel? Has there been a duel?"

"'Co'se dey has. De old Jedge has be'n havin' a duel wid one o' dem twins."

"Great Scott!" Then he added to himself: "That's what made him remake the will; he thought he might get killed, and it softened him toward me. And that's what he and Howard were so busy about. . . . Oh dear, if the twin had only killed him, I should be out of my—"

"What is you mumblin' 'bout, Chambers? Whah was you? Didn't you know dey was gwyne to be a duel?"

"No, I didn't. The old man tried to get me to fight one with Count Luigi, but he didn't succeed, so I reckon he concluded to patch up the family honor himself."

He laughed at the idea, and went rambling on with a detailed account of his talk with the Judge, and how shocked and ashamed the Judge was to find that he had a coward in his family. He glanced up at last, and got a shock himself. Roxana's bosom was heaving with suppressed passion, and she was glowering down upon him with measureless contempt written in her face.

"En you refuse' to fight a man dat kicked you, 'stid o' jumpin' at de chance! En you ain't got no mo' feelin' den to come en tell me, dat fetched sich a po' low-down ornery rabbit into de worl'! Pah! it makes me sick! It's de nigger in you, dat's what it is. Thirty-one parts o' you is white, en on'y one part nigger, en dat po' little one part is yo' *soul*. 'Tain't wuth savin'; 'tain't wuth totin' out on a shovel en throwin' in de gutter. You has disgraced yo' birth. What would yo' pa think o' you? It's enough to make him turn in his grave."

The last three sentences stung Tom into a fury, and he said to himself that if his father were only alive and in reach of assassination his mother would soon find that he had a very clear notion of the size of his indebtedness to that man, and was willing to pay it up in full, and would do it too, even at risk of his life; but he kept his thought to himself; that was safest in his mother's present state.

"Whatever has come o' yo' Essex blood? Dat's what I can't understan'. En it ain't on'y jist Essex blood dat's in you, not by a long sight—'deed it ain't! My great-great-great-gran'father en yo' great-great-great-great-gran'father was Ole Cap'n John Smith, de highest blood dat Ole Virginny ever turned out, en *his* great-great-gran'mother or somers along back dah, was Pocahontas de Injun queen, en her husbun' was a nigger king outen Africa—en yit here you is, a-slinkin' outen a duel en disgracin' our whole line like a ornery low-down hound! Yes, it's de nigger in you!"

She sat down on her candle-box and fell into a reverie. Tom did not disturb her; he sometimes lacked prudence, but it was not in circumstances of this kind. Roxana's storm went gradually down, but it died hard, and even when it seemed to be quite gone, it would now and then break out in a distant rumble, so to speak, in the form of muttered ejaculations. One of these was, "Ain't nigger enough in him to show in his finger-nails, en dat takes mighty little—yit dey's enough to paint his soul."

Presently she muttered, "Yassir, enough to paint a whole thimbleful of 'em." At last her ramblings ceased altogether, and her countenance began to clear—a welcome sign to Tom, who had learned her moods, and knew she was on the threshold of good humor, now. He noticed that from time to time she unconsciously carried her finger to the end of her nose. He looked closer and said:

"Why, mammy, the end of your nose is skinned. How did that come?"

She sent out the sort of whole-hearted peal of laughter which God has vouchsafed in its perfection to none but the happy angels in heaven and the bruised and broken black slave on the earth, and said:

"Dad fetch dat duel, I be'n in it myself."

"Gracious, did a bullet do that?"

"Yassir, you bet it did!"

"Well, I declare! Why, how did that happen?"

"Happened dis-away. I 'uz a-sett'n' here kinder dozin' in de dark, en *che-bang!* goes a gun, right out dah. I skips along out towards t'other end o' de house to see what's gwyne on, en stops by de old winder on de side towards Pudd'nhead Wilson's house dat ain't got no sash in it—but dey ain't none of 'em got any sashes, fur as dat's concerned,—en I stood dah in de dark en look out, en dar in de moonlight, right down under me, 'uz one o' de twins a-cussin'—not much, but jist a-cussin' soft—it 'uz de brown one dat 'uz cussin', 'ca'se he 'uz hit in de shoulder. E'n Dr. Claypool he 'uz a-workin' at him, en Pudd'nhead Wilson he 'uz a-he'pin', en old Jedge Driscoll en Pem Howard 'uz a-standin' out yonder a little piece waitin' for 'em to git ready ag'in. En treckly dey squared off en give de word, en *bang-bang* went de pistols, en de twin he say, 'Ouch!'—hit him on de han' dis time—en I hear dat same bullet go *spat!* ag'in de logs under de winder; en de nex' time dey shoot, de twin say, 'Ouch!' ag'in, en I done it too, 'ca'se de bullet glance on his cheek-bone en skip up here en glance on de side o' de winder en whiz right acrost my face en tuck de hide off'n my nose—why, if I'd 'a' be'n jist a inch or a inch en a half furder 'twould 'a' tuck de whole nose en disfiggered me. Here's de bullet; I hunted her up."

"Did you stand there all the time?"

"Dat's a question to ask, ain't it! What else would I do? Does I git a chance to see a duel every day?"

"Why, you were right in range! Weren't you afraid?"

The woman gave a sniff of scorn.

"'Fraid! De Smith-Pocahontases ain't 'fraid o' nothin', let alone bullets."

"They've got pluck enough, I suppose; what they lack is judgment. *I* wouldn't have stood there."

"Nobody's accusin' you!"

"Did anybody else get hurt?"

"Yes, we all got hit 'cep' de blon' twin en de doctor en de

seconds. De Jedge didn't git hurt, but I hear Pudd'nhead say de bullet snip some o' his ha'r off."

" 'George!" said Tom to himself, "to come so near being out of my trouble, and miss it by an inch. Oh dear, dear, he will live to find me out and sell me to some nigger-trader yet—yes, and he would do it in a minute." Then he said aloud, in a grave tone:

"Mother, we are in an awful fix."

Roxana caught her breath with a spasm, and said:

"Chile! What you hit a body so sudden for, like dat? What's be'n en gone en happen'?"

"Well, there's one thing I didn't tell you. When I wouldn't fight, he tore up the will again, and—"

Roxana's face turned a dead white, and she said:

"Now you's *done!*—done forever! Dat's de end. Bofe un us is gwyne to starve to—"

"Wait and hear me through, can't you! I reckon that when he resolved to fight, himself, he thought he might get killed and not have a chance to forgive me any more in this life, so he made the will again, and I've seen it, and it's all right. But—"

"Oh, thank goodness, den we's safe ag'in!—safe! en so what did you want to come here en talk sich dreadful—"

"Hold *on,* I tell you, and let me finish. The swag I gathered won't half square me up, and the first thing we know, my creditors —well, you know what 'll happen."

Roxana dropped her chin, and told her son to leave her alone —she must think this matter out. Presently she said impressively:

"You got to go mighty keerful now, I tell you! En here's what you got to do. He didn't git killed, en if you gives him de least reason, he'll bust de will ag'in, en dat's de *las'* time, now you hear me! So—you's got to show him what you kin do in de nex' few days. You's got to be pison good, en let him see it; you got to do everything dat 'll make him b'lieve in you, en you got to sweeten aroun' old Aunt Pratt, too—she's pow'ful strong wid de Jedge, en de bes' frien' you got. Nex', you'll go 'long away to Sent Louis, en dat 'll *keep* him in yo' favor. Den you go en make a bargain wid dem people. You tell 'em he ain't gwyne to live long—en dat's de fac', too—en tell 'em you'll pay 'em intrust, en big intrust, too—ten per—what you call it?"

"Ten per cent. a month?"

"Dat's it. Den you take and sell yo' truck aroun', a little at a time, en pay de intrust. How long will it las'?"

"I think there's enough to pay the interest five or six months."

"Den you's all right. If he don't die in six months, dat don't make no diff'rence—Providence 'll provide. You's gwyne to be safe—if you behaves." She bent an austere eye on him and added, "En you *is* gwyne to behave—does you know dat?"

He laughed and said he was going to try, anyway. She did not unbend. She said gravely:

"Tryin' ain't de thing. You's gwyne to *do* it. You ain't gwyne to steal a pin—'ca'se it ain't safe no mo'; en you ain't gwyne into no bad company—not even once, you understand; en you ain't gwyne to drink a drop—nary single drop; en you ain't gwyne to gamble one single gamble—not one! Dis ain't what you's gwyne to *try* to do, it's what you's gwyne to *do*. En I'll tell you how I knows it. Dis is how. I's gwyne to foller along to Sent Louis my own self; en you's gwyne to come to me every day o' yo' life, en I'll look you over; en if you fails in one single one o' dem things—jist *one*—I take my oath I'll come straight down to dis town en tell de Jedge you's a nigger en a slave—en *prove* it!" She paused to let her words sink home. Then she added, "Chambers, does you b'lieve me when I says dat?"

Tom was sober enough now. There was no levity in his voice when he answered:

"Yes, mother, I know, now, that I am reformed—and permanently. Permanently—and beyond the reach of any human temptation."

"Den g' long home en begin!"

15

The Robber Robbed

Nothing so needs reforming as other people's habits.
—Pudd'nhead Wilson's Calendar.

Behold, the fool saith, "Put not all thine eggs in the one
basket"—which is but a manner of saying, "Scatter your
money and your attention"; but the wise man saith, "Put
all your eggs in the one basket and—WATCH THAT BASKET."
—Pudd'nhead Wilson's Calendar.

WHAT A TIME of it Dawson's Landing was having! All its life it had
been asleep, but now it hardly got a chance for a nod, so swiftly
did big events and crashing surprises come along in one another's
wake: Friday morning, first glimpse of Real Nobility, also grand
reception at Aunt Patsy Cooper's, also great robber raid; Friday
evening, dramatic kicking of the heir of the chief citizen in presence of four hundred people; Saturday morning, emergence as
practising lawyer of the long-submerged Pudd'nhead Wilson;
Saturday night, duel between chief citizen and titled stranger.

The people took more pride in the duel than in all the other
events put together, perhaps. It was a glory to their town to have
such a thing happen there. In their eyes the principals had
reached the summit of human honor. Everybody paid homage
to their names; their praises were in all mouths. Even the
duelists' subordinates came in for a handsome share of the public
approbation: wherefore Pudd'nhead Wilson was suddenly become
a man of consequence. When asked to run for the mayoralty
Saturday night he was risking defeat, but Sunday morning found
him a made man and his success assured.

The twins were prodigiously great, now; the town took them

to its bosom with enthusiasm. Day after day, and night after
night, they went dining and visiting from house to house, making
friends, enlarging and solidifying their popularity, and charming
and surprising all with their musical prodigies, and now and then
heightening the effects with samples of what they could do in
other directions, out of their stock of rare and curious accomplish-
ments. They were so pleased that they gave the regulation thirty
days' notice, the required preparation for citizenship, and resolved to finish their days in this pleasant place. That was the
climax. The delighted community rose as one man and applauded;
and when the twins were asked to stand for seats in the forthcoming aldermanic board, and consented, the public contentment was rounded and complete.

Tom Driscoll was not happy over these things; they sunk deep,
and hurt all the way down. He hated the one twin for kicking
him, and the other one for being the kicker's brother.

Now and then the people wondered why nothing was heard of
the raider, or of the stolen knife or the other plunder, but nobody
was able to throw any light on that matter. Nearly a week had
drifted by, and still the thing remained a vexed mystery.

On Saturday Constable Blake and Pudd'nhead Wilson met on
the street, and Tom Driscoll joined them in time to open their
conversation for them. He said to Blake: "You are not looking
well, Blake; you seem to be annoyed about something. Has anything gone wrong in the detective business? I believe you fairly
and justifiably claim to have a pretty good reputation in that line,
isn't it so?"—which made Blake feel good, and look it; but Tom
added, "for a country detective"—which made Blake feel the other
way, and not only look it, but betray it in his voice:

"Yes, sir, I *have* got a reputation; and it's as good as anybody's
in the profession, too, country or no country."

"Oh, I beg pardon; I didn't mean any offense. What I started
out to ask was only about the old woman that raided the town—
the stoop-shouldered old woman, you know, that you said you
were going to catch; and I knew you would, too, because you
have the reputation of never boasting, and—well, you—you've
caught the old woman?"

"D——the old woman!"

"Why, sho! you don't mean to say you haven't caught her?"

"No; I haven't caught her. If anybody could have caught her, I could; but nobody couldn't, I don't care who he is."

"I am sorry, real sorry—for your sake; because, when it gets around that a detective has expressed himself so confidently, and then—"

"Don't you worry, that's all—don't you worry; and as for the town, the town needn't worry, either. She's my meat—make yourself easy about that. I'm on her track; I've got clues that—"

"That's good! Now if you could get an old veteran detective down from St. Louis to help you find out what the clues mean, and where they lead to, and then—"

"I'm plenty veteran enough myself, and I don't need anybody's help. I'll have her inside of a we—inside of a month. That I'll swear to!"

Tom said carelessly:

"I suppose that will answer—yes, that will answer. But I reckon she is pretty old, and old people don't often outlive the cautious pace of the professional detective when he has got his clues together and is out on his still-hunt."

Blake's dull face flushed under this gibe, but before he could set his retort in order Tom had turned to Wilson, and was saying, with placid indifference of manner and voice:

"Who got the reward, Pudd'nhead?"

Wilson winced slightly, and saw that his own turn was come.

"What reward?"

"Why, the reward for the thief, and the other one for the knife."

Wilson answered—and rather uncomfortably, to judge by his hesitating fashion of delivering himself:

"Well, the—well, in fact, nobody has claimed it yet."

Tom seemed surprised.

"Why, is that so?"

Wilson showed a trifle of irritation when he replied:

"Yes, it's so. And what of it?"

"Oh, nothing. Only I thought you had struck out a new idea,

and invented a scheme that was going to revolutionize the time-worn and ineffectual methods of the—" He stopped, and turned to Blake, who was happy now that another had taken his place on the gridiron: "Blake, didn't you understand him to intimate that it wouldn't be necessary for you to hunt the old woman down?"

"B'George, he said he'd have thief and swag both inside of three days—he did, by hokey! and that's just about a week ago. Why, I said at the time that no thief and no thief's pal was going to try to pawn or sell a thing where he knowed the pawnbroker could get both rewards by taking *him* into camp *with* the swag. It was the blessedest idea that ever *I* struck!"

"You'd change your mind," said Wilson, with irritated bluntness, "if you knew the entire scheme instead of only part of it."

"Well," said the constable, pensively, "I had the idea that it wouldn't work, and up to now I'm right anyway."

"Very well, then, let it stand at that, and give it a further show. It has worked at least as well as your own methods, you perceive."

The constable hadn't anything handy to hit back with, so he discharged a discontented sniff, and said nothing.

After the night that Wilson had partly revealed his scheme at his house, Tom had tried for several days to guess out the secret of the rest of it, but had failed. Then it occurred to him to give Roxana's smarter head a chance at it. He made up a supposititious case, and laid it before her. She thought it over, and delivered her verdict upon it. Tom said to himself, "She's hit it, sure!" He thought he would test that verdict, now, and watch Wilson's face; so he said reflectively:

"Wilson, you're not a fool—a fact of recent discovery. Whatever your scheme was, it had sense in it, Blake's opinion to the contrary notwithstanding. I don't ask you to reveal it, but I will suppose a case—a case which will answer as a starting-point for the real thing I am going to come at, and that's all I want. You offered five hundred dollars for the knife, and five hundred for the thief. We will suppose, for argument's sake, that the first reward is *advertised* and the second offered by *private letter* to pawnbrokers and—"

Blake slapped his thigh, and cried out:

"By Jackson, he's got you, Pudd'nhead! Now why couldn't I or *any* fool have thought of that?"

Wilson said to himself, "Anybody with a reasonably good head would have thought of it. I am not surprised that Blake didn't detect it; I am only surprised that Tom did. There is more to him than I supposed." He said nothing aloud, and Tom went on:

"Very well. The thief would not suspect that there was a trap, and he would bring or send the knife, and say he bought it for a song, or found it in the road, or something like that, and try to collect the reward, and be arrested—wouldn't he?"

"Yes," said Wilson.

"I think so," said Tom. "There can't be any doubt of it. Have you ever seen that knife?"

"No."

"Has any friend of yours?"

"Not that I know of."

"Well, I begin to think I understand why your scheme failed."

"What do you mean, Tom? What are you driving at?" asked Wilson, with a dawning sense of discomfort.

"Why, that there *isn't* any such knife."

"Look here, Wilson," said Blake, "Tom Driscoll's right, for a thousand dollars—if I had it."

Wilson's blood warmed a little, and he wondered if he had been played upon by those strangers; it certainly had something of that look. But what could they gain by it? He threw out that suggestion. Tom replied:

"Gain? Oh, nothing that you would value, maybe. But they are strangers making their way in a new community. Is it nothing to them to appear as pets of an Oriental prince—at no expense? Is it nothing to them to be able to dazzle this poor little town with thousand-dollar rewards—at no expense? Wilson, there isn't any such knife, or your scheme would have fetched it to light. Or if there is any such knife, they've got it yet. I believe, myself, that they've seen such a knife, for Angelo pictured it out with his pencil too swiftly and handily for him to have been inventing it, and of course I can't swear that they've never had it; but this

I'll go bail for—if they had it when they came to this town, they've got it yet."

Blake said:

"It looks mighty reasonable, the way Tom puts it; it most certainly does."

Tom responded, turning to leave:

"You find the old woman, Blake, and if she can't furnish the knife, go and search the twins!"

Tom sauntered away. Wilson felt a good deal depressed. He hardly knew what to think. He was loath to withdraw his faith from the twins, and was resolved not to do it on the present indecisive evidence; but—well, he would think, and then decide how to act.

"Blake, what do you think of this matter?"

"Well, Pudd'nhead, I'm bound to say I put it up the way Tom does. They hadn't the knife; or if they had it, they've got it yet."

The men parted. Wilson said to himself:

"I believe they had it; if it had been stolen, the scheme would have restored it, that is certain. And so I believe they've got it yet."

Tom had no purpose in his mind when he encountered those two men. When he began his talk he hoped to be able to gall them a little and get a trifle of malicious entertainment out of it. But when he left, he left in great spirits, for he perceived that just by pure luck and no troublesome labor he had accomplished several delightful things: he had touched both men on a raw spot and seen them squirm; he had modified Wilson's sweetness for the twins with one small bitter taste that he wouldn't be able to get out of his mouth right away; and, best of all, he had taken the hated twins down a peg with the community; for Blake would gossip around freely, after the manner of detectives, and within a week the town would be laughing at them in its sleeve for offering a gaudy reward for a bauble which they either never possessed or hadn't lost. Tom was very well satisfied with himself.

Tom's behavior at home had been perfect during the entire week. His uncle and aunt had seen nothing like it before. They could find no fault with him anywhere.

Saturday evening he said to the Judge:

"I've had something preying on my mind, uncle, and as I am going away, and might never see you again, I can't bear it any longer. I made you believe I was afraid to fight that Italian adventurer. I had to get out of it on some pretext or other, and maybe I chose badly, being taken unawares, but no honorable person could consent to meet him in the field, knowing what I know about him."

"Indeed? What was that?"

"Count Luigi is a confessed assassin."

"Incredible!"

"It is perfectly true. Wilson detected it in his hand, by palmistry, and charged him with it, and cornered him up so close that he had to confess; but both twins begged us on their knees to keep the secret, and swore they would lead straight lives here; and it was all so pitiful that we gave our word of honor never to expose them while they kept that promise. You would have done it yourself, uncle."

"You are right, my boy; I would. A man's secret is still his own property, and sacred, when it has been surprised out of him like that. You did well, and I am proud of you." Then he added mournfully, "But I wish I could have been saved the shame of meeting an assassin on the field of honor."

"It couldn't be helped, uncle. If I had known you were going to challenge him I should have felt obliged to sacrifice my pledged word in order to stop it, but Wilson couldn't be expected to do otherwise than keep silent."

"Oh, no; Wilson did right, and is in no way to blame. Tom, Tom, you have lifted a heavy load from my heart; I was stung to the very soul when I seemed to have discovered that I had a coward in my family."

"You may imagine what it cost *me* to assume such a part, uncle."

"Oh, I know it, poor boy, I know it. And I can understand how much it has cost you to remain under that unjust stigma to this time. But it is all right now, and no harm is done. You have restored my comfort of mind, and with it your own; and both of us had suffered enough."

The old man sat awhile plunged in thought; then he looked up with a satisfied light in his eye, and said: "That this assassin should have put the affront upon me of letting me meet him on the field of honor as if he were a gentleman is a matter which I will presently settle—but not now. I will not shoot him until after election. I see a way to ruin them both before; I will attend to that first. Neither of them shall be elected, that I promise. You are sure that the fact that he is an assassin has not got abroad?"

"Perfectly certain of it, sir."

"It will be a good card. I will fling a hint at it from the stump on the polling day. It will sweep the ground from under both of them."

"There's not a doubt of it. It will finish them."

"That and outside work among the voters will, to a certainty. I want you to come down here by an by and work privately among the rag-tag and bob-tail. You shall spend money among them; I will furnish it."

Another point scored against the detested twins! Really it was a great day for Tom. He was encouraged to chance a parting shot, at the same target, and did it.

"You know that wonderful Indian knife that the twins have been making such a to-do about? Well, there's no track or trace of it yet; so the town is beginning to sneer and gossip and laugh. Half the people believe they never had any such knife, the other half believe they had it and have got it still. I've heard twenty people talking like that to-day."

Yes, Tom's blemishless week had restored him to the favor of his aunt and uncle.

His mother was satisfied with him, too. Privately, she believed she was coming to love him, but she did not say so. She told him to go along to St. Louis, now, and she would get ready and follow. Then she smashed her whisky bottle and said:

"Dah now! I's a-gwyne to make you walk as straight as a string, Chambers, en so I's bown' you ain't gwyne to git no bad example out o' yo' mammy. I tole you you couldn't go into no bad comp'ny. Well, you's gwyne into my comp'ny, en I's gwyne to fill de bill. Now, den, trot along, trot along!"

Tom went aboard one of the big transient boats that night with his heavy satchel of miscellaneous plunder, and slept the sleep of the unjust, which is serener and sounder than the other kind, as we know by the hanging-eve history of a million rascals. But when he got up in the morning, luck was against him again: A brother thief had robbed him while he slept, and gone ashore at some intermediate landing.

16

Sold Down the River

If you pick up a starving dog and make him prosperous, he will not bite you. This is the principal difference between a dog and a man.—*Pudd'nhead Wilson's Calendar.*

We know all about the habits of the ant, we know all about the habits of the bee, but we know nothing at all about the habits of the oyster. It seems almost certain that we have been choosing the wrong time for studying the oyster.
                    —*Pudd'nhead Wilson's Calendar.*

WHEN Roxana arrived, she found her son in such despair and misery that her heart was touched and her motherhood rose up strong in her. He was ruined past hope, now; his destruction would be immediate and sure, and he would be an outcast and friendless. That was reason enough for a mother to love a child; so she loved him, and told him so. It made him wince, secretly—for she was a "nigger." That he was one himself was far from reconciling him to that despised race.

Roxana poured out endearments upon him, to which he responded uncomfortably, but as well as he could. And she tried to comfort him, but that was not possible. These intimacies quickly became horrible to him, and within the hour he began to try to get up courage enough to tell her so, and require that they be discontinued or very considerably modified. But he was afraid of her; and besides, there came a lull, now, for she had begun to think. She was trying to invent a saving plan. Finally she started up, and said she had found a way out. Tom was almost suffocated by the joy of this sudden good news. Roxana said:

"Here is de plan, en she'll win, sure. I's a nigger, en nobody ain't gwyne to doubt it dat hears me talk. I's wuth six hund'd dollahs. Take en sell me, en pay off dese gamblers."

Tom was dazed. He was not sure he had heard aright. He was dumb for a moment; then he said:

"Do you mean that you would be sold into slavery to save me?"

"Ain't you my chile? En does you know anything dat a mother won't do for her chile? Dey ain't nothin' a white mother won't do for her chile. Who made 'em so? De Lord done it. En who made de niggers? De Lord made 'em. In de inside, mothers is all de same. De good Lord he made 'em so. I's gwyne to be sole into slavery, en in a year you's gwyne to buy yo' ole mammy free ag'in. I'll show you how. Dat's de plan."

Tom's hopes began to rise, and his spirits along with them. He said:

"It's lovely of you, mammy—it's just—"

"Say it ag'in! En keep on sayin' it! It's all de pay a body kin want in dis worl', en it's mo' den enough. Laws bless you, honey, when I's slavin' aroun', en dey 'buses me, if I knows you's a-sayin' dat, 'way off yonder somers, it 'll heal up all de sore places, en I kin stan' 'em."

"I do say it again, mammy, and I'll keep on saying it, too. But how am I going to sell you? You're free, you know."

"Much diff'rence dat make! White folks ain't partic'lar. De law kin sell me now if dey tell me to leave de state in six months en I don't go. You draw up a paper—bill o' sale—en put it 'way off yonder, down in de middle o' Kaintuck somers, en sign some names to it, en say you'll sell me cheap 'ca'se you's hard up;

you'll find you ain't gwyne to have no trouble. You take me up de country a piece, en sell me on a farm; dem people ain't gwyne to ask no questions if I's a bargain."

Tom forged a bill of sale and sold his mother to an Arkansas cotton-planter for a trifle over six hundred dollars. He did not want to commit this treachery, but luck threw the man in his way, and this saved him the necessity of going up country to hunt up a purchaser, with the added risk of having to answer a lot of questions, whereas this planter was so pleased with Roxy that he asked next to none at all. Besides, the planter insisted that Roxy wouldn't know where she was, at first, and that by the time she found out she would already have become contented.

So Tom argued with himself that it was an immense advantage for Roxy to have a master who was as pleased with her, as this planter manifestly was. In almost no time his flowing reasonings carried him to the point of even half believing he was doing Roxy a splendid surreptitious service in selling her "down the river." And then he kept diligently saying to himself all the time: "It's for only a year. In a year I buy her free again; she'll keep that in mind, and it 'll reconcile her." Yes, the little deception could do no harm, and everything would come out right and pleasant in the end, anyway. By agreement, the conversation in Roxy's presence was all about the man's "up-country" farm, and how pleasant a place it was, and how happy the slaves were there; so poor Roxy was entirely deceived; and easily, for she was not dreaming that her own son could be guilty of treason to a mother who, in voluntarily going into slavery—slavery of any kind, mild or severe, or of any duration, brief or long—was making a sacrifice for him compared with which death would have been a poor and commonplace one. She lavished tears and loving caresses upon him privately, and then went away with her owner—went away broken-hearted, and yet proud of what she was doing, and glad that it was in her power to do it.

Tom squared his accounts, and resolved to keep to the very letter of his reform, and never to put that will in jeopardy again. He had three hundred dollars left. According to his mother's plan, he was to put that safely away, and add her half of his pension to it monthly. In one year this fund would buy her free again.

For a whole week he was not able to sleep well, so much the villainy which he had played upon his trusting mother preyed upon his rag of a conscience; but after that he began to get comfortable again, and was presently able to sleep like any other miscreant.

The boat bore Roxy away from St. Louis at four in the afternoon, and she stood on the lower guard abaft the paddle-box and watched Tom through a blur of tears until he melted into the throng of people and disappeared; then she looked no more, but sat there on a coil of cable crying till far into the night. When she went to her foul steerage bunk at last, between the clashing engines, it was not to sleep, but only to wait for the morning, and, waiting, grieve.

It had been imagined that she "would not know," and would think she was traveling up-stream. She! Why, she had been steamboating for years. At dawn she got up and went listlessly and sat down on the cable-coil again. She passed many a snag whose "break" could have told her a thing to break her heart, for it showed a current moving in the same direction that the boat was going; but her thoughts were elsewhere, and she did not notice. But at last the roar of a bigger and nearer break than usual brought her out of her torpor, and she looked up, and her practised eye fell upon that telltale rush of water. For one moment her petrified gaze fixed itself there. Then her head dropped upon her breast, and she said:

"Oh, de good Lord God have mercy on po' sinful me—*I's sole down de river!*"

17

The Judge Utters Dire Prophecy

Even popularity can be overdone. In Rome, along at first, you are full of regrets that Michelangelo died; but by and by you only regret that you didn't see him do it.

—*Pudd'nhead Wilson's Calendar.*

July 4. Statistics show that we lose more fools on this day than in all the other days of the year put together. This proves, by the number left in stock, that one Fourth of July per year is now inadequate, the country has grown so.

—*Pudd'nhead Wilson's Calendar.*

THE SUMMER weeks dragged by, and then the political campaign opened—opened in pretty warm fashion, and waxed hotter and hotter daily. The twins threw themselves into it with their whole heart, for their self-love was engaged. Their popularity, so general at first, had suffered afterward; mainly because they had been *too* popular, and so a natural reaction had followed. Besides, it had been diligently whispered around that it was curious—indeed, *very* curious—that that wonderful knife of theirs did not turn up—*if* it was so valuable, or *if* it had ever existed. And with the whisperings went chucklings and nudgings and winks, and such things have an effect. The twins considered that success in the election would reinstate them, and that defeat would work them irreparable damage. Therefore they worked hard, but not harder than Judge Driscoll and Tom worked against them in the closing days of the canvass. Tom's conduct had remained so letter-perfect during two whole months, now, that his uncle not only trusted him with money with which to persuade voters, but trusted him to go and get it himself out of the safe in the private sitting-room.

The closing speech of the campaign was made by Judge Driscoll, and he made it against both of the foreigners. It was disastrously effective. He poured out rivers of ridicule upon them, and forced the big mass-meeting to laugh and applaud. He scoffed at them as adventurers, mountebanks, side-show riffraff, dime-museum freaks; he assailed their showy titles with measureless derision; he said they were back-alley barbers disguised as nobilities, peanut-peddlers masquerading as gentlemen, organ-grinders bereft of their brother monkey. At last he stopped and stood still. He waited until the place had become absolutely silent and expectant, then he delivered his deadliest shot; delivered it with ice-cold seriousness and deliberation, with a significant emphasis upon the closing words: he said that he believed that the reward offered for the lost knife was humbug and buncombe, and that its owner would know where to find it whenever he should have occasion *to assassinate somebody.*

Then he stepped from the stand, leaving a startled and impressive hush behind him instead of the customary explosion of cheers and party cries.

The strange remark flew far and wide over the town and made an extraordinary sensation. Everybody was asking, "What could he mean by that?"

And everybody went on asking that question, but in vain; for the Judge only said he knew what he was talking about, and stopped there; Tom said he hadn't any idea what his uncle meant, and Wilson, whenever he was asked what he thought it meant, parried the question by asking the questioner what *he* thought it meant.

Wilson was elected, the twins were defeated—crushed, in fact, and left forlorn and substantially friendless. Tom went back to St. Louis happy.

Dawson's Landing had a week of repose, now, and it needed it. But it was in an expectant state, for the air was full of rumors of a new duel. Judge Driscoll's election labors had prostrated him, but it was said that as soon as he was well enough to entertain a challenge he would get one from Count Luigi.

The brothers withdrew entirely from society, and nursed their humiliation in privacy. They avoided the people, and went out for exercise only late at night, when the streets were deserted.

18

Roxana Commands

Gratitude and treachery are merely the two extremities of the same procession. You have seen all of it that is worth staying for when the band and the gaudy officials have gone by.—*Pudd'nhead Wilson's Calendar.*

Thanksgiving Day. Let all give humble, hearty, and sincere thanks, now, but the turkeys. In the island of Fiji they do not use turkeys; they use plumbers. It does not become you and me to sneer at Fiji.
—*Pudd'nhead Wilson's Calendar.*

THE FRIDAY after the election was a rainy one in St. Louis. It rained all day long, and rained hard, apparently trying its best to wash that soot-blackened town white, but of course not succeeding. Toward midnight Tom Driscoll arrived at his lodgings from the theater in the heavy downpour, and closed his umbrella and let himself in; but when he would have shut the door, he found that there was another person entering—doubtless another lodger; this person closed the door and tramped up-stairs behind Tom. Tom found his door in the dark, and entered it and turned up the gas. When he faced about, lightly whistling, he saw the back of a man. The man was closing and locking his door for him. His whistle faded out and he felt uneasy. The man turned around, a wreck of shabby old clothes, sodden with rain and all a-drip, and showed a black face under an old slouch hat. Tom was frightened. He tried to order the man out, but the words refused to come, and the other man got the start. He said, in a low voice:

"Keep still—I's yo' mother!"

Tom sunk in a heap on a chair, and gasped out:

"It was mean of me, and base—I know it; but I meant it for the best, I did indeed—I can swear it."

Roxana stood awhile looking mutely down on him while he writhed in shame and went on incoherently babbling self-accusations mixed with pitiful attempts at explanation and palliation of his crime; then she seated herself and took off her hat, and her unkempt masses of long brown hair tumbled down about her shoulders.

"It ain't no fault o' yo'n dat dat ain't gray," she said sadly, noticing the hair.

"I know it, I know it! I'm a scoundrel. But I swear I meant it for the best. It was a mistake, of course, but I thought it was for the best, I truly did."

Roxy began to cry softly, and presently words began to find their way out between her sobs. They were uttered lamentingly, rather than angrily:

"Sell a pusson down de river—*down de river!*—for de bes'! I wouldn't treat a dog so! I is all broke down en wore out, now, en so I reckon it ain't in me to storm aroun' no mo', like I used to when I 'uz trompled on en 'bused. I don't know—but maybe it's so. Leastways, I's suffered so much dat mournin' seem to come mo' handy to me now den stormin'."

These words should have touched Tom Driscoll, but, if they did, that effect was obliterated by a stronger one—one which removed the heavy weight of fear which lay upon him, and gave his crushed spirit a most grateful rebound, and filled all his small soul with a deep sense of relief. But he kept prudently still, and ventured no comment. There was a voiceless interval of some duration, now, in which no sounds were heard but the beating of the rain upon the panes, the sighing and complaining of the winds, and now and then a muffled sob from Roxana. The sobs became more and more infrequent, and at last ceased. Then the refugee began to talk again.

"Shet down dat light a little. More. More yit. A pusson dat is hunted don't like de light. Dah—dat 'll do. I kin see whah you is, en dat's enough. I's gwyne to tell you de tale, en cut it jes as short as I kin, en den I'll tell you what you's got to do. Dat man dat bought me ain't a bad man; he's good enough, as planters goes; en if he could 'a' had his way I'd 'a' be'n a house-servant in his fambly en be'n comfortable: but his wife she was a Yank, en not right down good-lookin', en she riz up agin me straight off; so den dey sent me out to de quarter 'mongst de common fiel' han's. Dat woman warn't satisfied even wid dat, but she worked up de overseer ag'in' me, she 'uz dat jealous en hateful; so de overseer he had me out befo' day in de mawnin's en worked me de whole long day as long as dey 'uz any light to see by; en many's de lashin's I got 'ca'se I couldn't come up to de work o' de stronges'. Dat overseer wuz a Yank, too, outen New Englan', en anybody down South kin tell you what dat mean. *Dey* knows how to work a nigger to death, en dey knows how to whale 'em, too—whale 'em till dey backs is welted like a washboard. 'Long at fust my marster say de good word for me to de overseer, but dat 'uz bad for me; for de mistis she fine it out, en arter dat I jis ketched it at every turn—dey warn't no mercy for me no mo'."

Tom's heart was fired—with fury against the planter's wife; and he said to himself, "But for that meddlesome fool, everything would have gone all right." He added a deep and bitter curse against her.

The expression of this sentiment was fiercely written in his face, and stood thus revealed to Roxana by a white glare of lightning which turned the somber dusk of the room into dazzling day at that moment. She was pleased—pleased and grateful; for did not that expression show that her child was capable of grieving for his mother's wrongs and of feeling resentment toward her persecutors?—a thing which she had been doubting. But her flash of happiness was only a flash, and went out again and left her spirit dark; for she said to herself, "He sole me down de river—he can't feel for a body long: dis 'll pass en go." Then she took up her tale again.

"'Bout ten days ago I 'uz sayin' to myself dat I couldn't las' many mo' weeks I 'uz so wore out wid de awful work en de

lashin's, en so downhearted en misable. En I didn't care no
mo', nuther—life warn't wuth noth'n' to me, if I got to go on like
dat. Well, when a body is in a frame o' mine like dat, what do a
body care what a body do? Dey was a little sickly nigger wench
'bout ten year ole dat 'uz good to me, en hadn't no mammy, po'
thing, en I loved her en she loved me; en she come out whah I
'uz workin', en she had a roasted tater, en tried to slip it to me—
robbin' herself, you see, 'ca'se she knowed de overseer didn't
gimme enough to eat—en he ketched her at it, en give her a lick
acrost de back wid his stick, which 'uz as thick as a broom-handle,
en she drop' screamin' on de groun', en squirmin' en wallerin'
aroun' in de dust like a spider dat's got crippled. I couldn't stan'
it. All de hell-fire dat 'uz ever in my heart flame' up, en I snatch
de stick outen his han' en laid him flat. He laid dah moanin' en
cussin', en all out of his head, you know, en de niggers 'uz plumb
sk'yerd to death. Dey gathered roun' him to he'p him, en I
jumped on his hoss en took out for de river as tight as I could go.
I knowed what dey would do wid me. Soon as he got well he
would start in en work me to death if marster let him; en if dey
didn't do dat, dey'd sell me furder down de river, en dat's de
same thing. So I 'lowed to drown myself en git out o' my troubles.
It 'uz gitt'n' towards dark. I 'uz at de river in two minutes. Den
I see a canoe, en I says dey ain't no use to drown myself tell I
got to; so I ties de hoss in de edge o' de timber en shove out
down de river, keepin' in under de shelter o' de bluff bank en
prayin' for de dark to shet down quick. I had a pow'ful good
start, 'ca'se de big house 'uz three mile back f'om de river en
on'y de work-mules to ride dah on, en on'y niggers to ride 'em, en
dey warn't gwyne to hurry—dey'd gimme all de chance dey could.
Befo' a body could go to de house en back it would be long pas'
dark, en dey couldn't track de hoss en fine out which way I went
tell mawnin', en de niggers would tell 'em all de lies dey could
'bout it.

"Well, de dark come, en I went on a-spinnin' down de river. I
paddled mo'n two hours, den I warn't worried no mo', so I quit
paddlin', en floated down de current, considerin' what I 'uz
gwyne to do if I didn't have to drown myself. I made up some

plans, en floated along, turnin' 'em over in my mine. Well, when it 'uz a little pas' midnight, as I reckoned, en I had come fifteen or twenty mile, I see de lights o' a steamboat layin' at de bank, whah dey warn't no town en no wood-yard, en putty soon I ketched de shape o' de chimbly-tops ag'in' de stars, en de good gracious me, I 'most jumped out o' my skin for joy! It 'uz *Gran' Mogul*—I 'uz chambermaid on her for eight seasons in de Cincinnati en Orleans trade. I slid 'long pas'—don't see nobody stirrin' nowhah—hear 'em a-hammerin' away in de engine-room, den I knowed what de matter was—some o' de machinery's broke. I got asho' below de boat en turn' de canoe loose, den I goes 'long up, en dey 'uz jes one plank out, en I step' 'board de boat. It 'uz pow'ful hot, deck-han's en roustabouts 'uz sprawled aroun' asleep on the fo'cas'l, de second mate, Jim Bangs, he sot dah on de bitts wid his head down, asleep—'ca'se dat's de way de second mate stan' de cap'n's watch!—en de ole watchman, Billy Hatch, he 'uz a-noddin' on de companionway;—en I knowed 'em all; 'en, lan', but dey did look good! I says to myself, I wished old marster'd come along *now* en try to take me—bless yo' heart, I's 'mong frien's, I is. So I tromped right along 'mongst 'em, en went up on de b'iler-deck en 'way back aft to de ladies' cabin guard, en sot down dah in de same cheer dat I'd sot in 'mos' a hund'd million times, I reckon; en it 'uz jist home ag'in, I tell you!

"In 'bout an hour I heard de ready-bell jingle, en den de racket begin. Putty soon I hear de gong strike. 'Set her back on de outside,' I says to myself—'I reckon I knows dat music!' I hear de gong ag'in. 'Come ahead on de inside,' I says. Gong ag'in. 'Stop de outside.' Gong ag'in. 'Come ahead on de outside—now we's pinted for Sent Louis, en I's outer de woods en ain't got to drown myself at all.' I knowed de *Mogul* 'uz in de Sent Louis trade now, you see. It 'uz jes fair daylight when we passed our plantation, en I seed a gang o' niggers en white folks huntin' up en down de sho', en troublin' deyselves a good deal 'bout me; but I warn't troublin' myself none 'bout dem.

"'Bout dat time Sally Jackson, dat used to be my second chambermaid en 'uz head chambermaid now, she come out on de guard, en 'uz pow'ful glad to see me, en so 'uz all de officers;

en I tole 'em I'd got kidnapped en sole down de river, en dey made me up twenty dollahs en give it to me, en Sally she rigged me out wid good clo'es, en when I got here I went straight to whah you used to wuz, en den I come to dis house, en dey say you's away but 'spected back every day; so I didn't dast to go down de river to Dawson's, 'ca'se I might miss you.

"Well, las' Monday I 'uz pass'n' by one o' dem places in Fourth Street whah deh sticks up runaway-nigger bills, en he'ps to ketch 'em, en I seed my marster! I 'mos' flopped down on de groun', I felt so gone. He had his back to me, en 'uz talkin' to de man en givin' him some bills—nigger-bills, I reckon, en I's de nigger. He's offerin' a reward—dat's it. Ain't I right, don't you reckon?"

Tom had been gradually sinking into a state of ghastly terror, and he said to himself, now: "I'm lost, no matter what turn things take! This man has said to me that he thinks there was something suspicious about that sale. He said he had a letter from a passenger on the *Grand Mogul* saying that Roxy came here on that boat and that everybody on board knew all about the case; so he says that her coming here instead of flying to a free state looks bad for me, and that if I don't find her for him, and that pretty soon, he will make trouble for me. I never believed that story; I couldn't believe she would be so dead to all motherly instincts as to come here, knowing the risk she would run of getting me into irremediable trouble. And after all, here she is! And I stupidly swore I would help him find her, thinking it was a perfectly safe thing to promise. If I venture to deliver her up, she—she—but how can I help myself? I've got to do that or pay the money, and where's the money to come from? I—I—well, I should think that if he would swear to treat her kindly hereafter —and she says, herself, that he is a good man—and if he would swear to never allow her to be overworked, or ill fed, or—"

A flash of lightning exposed Tom's pallid face, drawn and rigid with these worrying thoughts. Roxana spoke up sharply now, and there was apprehension in her voice:

"Turn up dat light! I want to see yo' face better. Dah now— lemme look at you. Chambers, you's as white as yo' shirt! Has you seen dat man? Has he be'n to see you?"

"Ye-s."

"When?"

"Monday noon."

"Monday noon! Was he on my track?"

"He—well, he thought he was. That is, he hoped he was. This is the bill you saw." He took it out of his pocket.

"Read it to me!"

She was panting with excitement, and there was a dusky glow in her eyes that Tom could not translate with certainty, but there seemed to be something threatening about it. The handbill had the usual rude woodcut of a turbaned negro woman running, with the customary bundle on a stick over her shoulder, and the heading in bold type, "$100 REWARD." Tom read the bill aloud— at least the part that described Roxana and named the master and his St. Louis address and the address of the Fourth Street agency; but he left out the item that applicants for the reward might also apply to Mr. Thomas Driscoll.

"Gimme de bill!"

Tom had folded it and was putting it in his pocket. He felt a chilly streak creeping down his back, but said as carelessly as he could:

"The bill? Why, it isn't any use to you, you can't read it. What do you want with it?"

"Gimme de bill!" Tom gave it to her, but with a reluctance which he could not entirely disguise. "Did you read it *all* to me?"

"Certainly I did."

"Hole up yo' han' en swah to it."

Tom did it. Roxana put the bill carefully away in her pocket, with her eyes fixed upon Tom's face all the while; then she said:

"Yo's lyin'!"

"What would I want to lie about it for?"

"I don't know—but you is. Dat's my opinion, anyways. But nemmine 'bout dat. When I seed dat man I 'uz dat sk'yerd dat I could sca'cely wabble home. Den I give a nigger man a dollar for dese clo'es, en I ain't be'n in a house sence, night ner day, till now. I blackened my face en laid hid in de cellar of a ole house dat's burnt down, daytimes, en robbed de sugar hogsheads en grain-sacks on de wharf, nights, to git somethin' to eat, en never dast to try to buy noth'n', en I's mos' starved. En I never dast come near dis place till dis rainy night, when dey ain't no people roun' sca'cely. But tonight I be'n a-stannin' in de dark alley ever sence night come, waitin' for you to go by. En here I is."

She fell to thinking. Presently she said:

"You seed dat man at noon, las' Monday?"

"Yes."

"I seed him de middle o' dat arternoon. He hunted you up, didn't he?"

"Yes."

"Did he give you de bill dat time?"

"No, he hadn't got it printed yet."

Roxana darted a suspicious glance at him.

"Did you he'p him fix up de bill?"

Tom cursed himself for making that stupid blunder, and tried to rectify it by saying he remembered, now, that it *was* at noon Monday that the man gave him the bill. Roxana said:

"You's lyin' ag'in, sho'." Then she straightened up and raised her finger:

"Now den! I's gwine to ask you a question, en I wants to know how you's gwine to git aroun' it. You knowed he 'uz arter me; en if you run off, 'stid o' stayin' here to he'p him, he'd know dey 'uz somethin' wrong 'bout dis business, en den he would inquire 'bout you, en dat would take him to yo' uncle, en yo' uncle would read de bill en see dat you be'n sellin' a free nigger down de river, en you know *him*, I reckon! He'd t'ar up de will en kick you outen de house. Now, den, you answer me dis question: Hain't you tole dat man dat I would be sho' to come here, and den you would fix it so he could set a trap en ketch me?"

Tom recognized that neither lies nor arguments could help him any longer—he was in a vise, with the screw turned on, and out of it there was no budging. His face began to take on an ugly look, and presently he said, with a snarl:

"Well, what could I do? You see, yourself, that I was in his grip and couldn't get out."

Roxy scorched him with a scornful gaze awhile, then she said:

"What could you do? You could be Judas to yo' own mother to save yo' wuthless hide! Would anybody b'lieve it? No— a dog couldn't! You is de low-downest orneriest hound dat was ever pup'd into dis worl'—en I's 'sponsible for it!"—and she spat on him.

He made no effort to resent this. Roxy reflected a moment, then she said:

"Now I'll tell you what you's gwine to do. You's gwine to give dat man de money dat you's got laid up, en make him wait till you kin go to de Jedge en git de res' en buy me free ag'in."

"Thunder! what are you thinking of? Go and ask him for three hundred dollars and odd? What would I tell him I want with it, pray?"

Roxy's answer was delivered in a serene and level voice:

"You'll tell him you's sole me to pay yo' gamblin' debts en dat you lied to me en was a villain, en dat I 'quires you to git dat money en buy me back ag'in."

"Why, you've gone stark mad! He would tear the will to shreds in a minute—don't you know that?"

"Yes, I does."

"Then you don't believe I'm idiot enough to go to him, do you?"

"I don't b'lieve nothin' 'bout it—I *knows* you's a-goin'. I knows it 'ca'se you knows dat if you don't raise dat money I'll go to him myself, en den he'll sell *you* down de river, en you kin see how you like it!"

Tom rose, trembling and excited, and there was an evil light in his eye. He strode to the door and said he must get out of this suffocating place for a moment and clear his brain in the fresh air so that he could determine what to do. The door wouldn't open. Roxy smiled grimly, and said:

"I's got de key, honey—set down. You needn't cle'r up yo' brain none to fine out what you gwine to do. I knows what you's gwine to do." Tom sat down and began to pass his hands through his hair with a helpless and desperate air. Roxy said, "Is dat man in dis house?"

Tom glanced up with a surprised expression, and asked:

"What gave you such an idea?"

"You done it. Gwine out to cle'r yo' brain! In de fust place you ain't got none to cle'r, en in the second place yo' ornery eye tole on you. You's de low-downest hound dat ever—but I done tole you dat befo'. Now den, dis is Friday. You kin fix it up wid dat man, en tell him you's gwine away to git de res' o' de money, en dat you'll be back wid it nex' Tuesday, or maybe Wednesday. You understan'?"

Tom answered sullenly:

"Yes."

"En when you gits de new bill o' sale dat sells me to my own self, take en send it in de mail to Mr. Pudd'nhead Wilson, en write on de back dat he's to keep it tell I come. You understan'?"

"Yes."

"Dat's all den. Take yo' umbreller, en put on yo' hat."

"Why?"

"Beca'se you's gwine to see me home to de wharf. You see dis knife? I's toted it aroun' sence de day I seed dat man en bought dese clo'es en it. If he ketch me, I's gwine to kill myself wid it. Now start along, en go sof', en lead de way; en if you gives a sign in dis house, or if anybody comes up to you in de street, I's gwine to jam it right into you. Chambers, does you b'lieve me when I says dat?"

"It's no use to bother me with that question. I know your word's good."

"Yes, it's diff'rent from yo'n! Shet de light out en move along—here's de key."

They were not followed. Tom trembled every time a late straggler brushed by them on the street, and half expected to feel the cold steel in his back. Roxy was right at his heels and always in reach. After tramping a mile they reached a wide vacancy on the deserted wharves, and in this dark and rainy desert they parted.

As Tom trudged home his mind was full of dreary thoughts and wild plans; but at last he said to himself, wearily:

"There is but the one way out. I must follow her plan. But with a variation—I will not ask for the money and ruin myself; I will *rob* the old skinflint."

19

The Prophecy Realized

Few things are harder to put up with than the annoyance
of a good example.—*Pudd'nhead Wilson's Calendar.*

It were not best that we should all think alike; it is difference of opinion that makes horse-races.
       —*Pudd'nhead Wilson's Calendar.*

DAWSON'S LANDING was comfortably finishing its season of dull
repose and waiting patiently for the duel. Count Luigi was waiting, too; but not patiently, rumor said. Sunday came, and Luigi
insisted on having his challenge conveyed. Wilson carried it.
Judge Driscoll declined to fight with an assassin—"that is," he
added significantly, "in the field of honor."

Elsewhere, of course, he would be ready. Wilson tried to convince him that if he had been present himself when Angelo told
about the homicide committed by Luigi, he would not have
considered the act discreditable to Luigi; but the obstinate old
man was not to be moved.

Wilson went back to his principal and reported the failure of
his mission. Luigi was incensed, and asked how it could be that
the old gentleman, who was by no means dull-witted, held his
trifling nephew's evidence and inferences to be of more value
than Wilson's. But Wilson laughed, and said:

"That is quite simple; that is easily explicable. I am not his
doll—his baby—his infatuation: his nephew is. The Judge and
his late wife never had any children. The Judge and his wife
were past middle age when this treasure fell into their lap. One
must make allowances for a parental instinct that has been starving for twenty-five or thirty years. It is famished, it is crazed

with hunger by that time, and will be entirely satisfied with anything that comes handy; its taste is atrophied, it can't tell mudcat from shad. A devil born to a young couple is measurably recognizable by them as a devil before long, but a devil adopted by an old couple is an angel to them, and remains so, through thick and thin. Tom is this old man's angel; he is infatuated with him. Tom can persuade him into things which other people can't —not all things; I don't mean that, but a good many—particularly one class of things: the things that create or abolish personal partialities or prejudices in the old man's mind. The old man liked both of you. Tom conceived a hatred for you. That was enough; it turned the old man around at once. The oldest and strongest friendship must go to the ground when one of these late-adopted darlings throws a brick at it."

"It's a curious philosophy," said Luigi.

"It ain't a philosophy at all—it's a fact. And there is something pathetic and beautiful about it, too. I think there is nothing more pathetic than to see one of these poor old childless couples taking a menagerie of yelping little worthless dogs to their hearts; and then adding some cursing and squawking parrots and a jackass-voiced macaw; and next a couple of hundred screeching song-birds, and presently some fetid guinea-pigs and rabbits, and a howling colony of cats. It is all a groping and ignorant effort to construct out of base metal and brass filings, so to speak, something to take the place of that golden treasure denied them by Nature, a child. But this is a digression. The unwritten law of this region requires you to kill Judge Driscoll on sight, and he and the community will expect that attention at your hands—though of course your own death by his bullet will answer every purpose. Look out for him! Are you heeled—that is, fixed?"

"Yes; he shall have his opportunity. If he attacks me I will respond."

As Wilson was leaving, he said:

"The Judge is still a little used up by his campaign work, and will not get out for a day or so; but when he does get out, you want to be on the alert."

About eleven at night the twins went out for exercise, and started on a long stroll in the veiled moonlight.

Tom Driscoll had landed at Hackett's Store, two miles below Dawson's, just about half an hour earlier, the only passenger for that lonely spot, and had walked up the shore road and entered Judge Driscoll's house without having encountered any one either on the road or under the roof.

He pulled down his window-blinds and lighted his candle. He laid off his coat and hat and began his preparations. He unlocked his trunk and got his suit of girl's clothes out from under the male attire in it, and laid it by. Then he blacked his face with burnt cork and put the cork in his pocket. His plan was, to slip down to his uncle's private sitting-room below, pass into the bedroom, steal the safe-key from the old gentleman's clothes, and then go back and rob the safe. He took up his candle to start. His courage and confidence were high, up to this point, but both began to waver a little, now. Suppose he should make a noise, by some accident, and get caught—say, in the act of opening the safe? Perhaps it would be well to go armed. He took the Indian knife from its hiding-place, and felt a pleasant return of his wandering courage. He slipped stealthily down the narrow stair, his hair rising and his pulses halting at the slightest creak. When he was half-way down, he was disturbed to perceive that the landing below was touched by a faint glow of light. What could that mean? Was his uncle still up? No, that was not likely; he must have left his night taper there when he went to bed. Tom crept on down, pausing at every step to listen. He found the door standing open, and glanced in. What he saw pleased him beyond measure. His uncle was asleep on the sofa; on a small table at the head of the sofa a lamp was burning low, and by it stood the old man's small tin cash-box, closed. Near the box was a pile of bank-notes and a piece of paper covered with figures in pencil. The safe-door was not open. Evidently the sleeper had wearied himself with work upon his finances, and was taking a rest.

Tom set his candle on the stairs, and began to make his way toward the pile of notes, stooping low as he went. When he was passing his uncle, the old man stirred in his sleep, and Tom stopped instantly—stopped, and softly drew the knife from its sheath, with his heart thumping, and his eyes fastened upon his benefactor's face. After a moment or two he ventured forward again—one step—reached for his prize and seized it, dropping the knife-sheath. Then he felt the old man's strong grip upon him, and a wild cry of "Help! help!" rang in his ear. Without hesitation he drove the knife home—and was free. Some of the notes escaped from his left hand and fell in the blood on the floor. He dropped the knife and snatched them up and started to fly; transferred them to his left hand, and seized the knife again, in his fright and confusion, but remembered himself and flung it from him, as being a dangerous witness to carry away with him.

He jumped for the stair-foot, and closed the door behind him; and as he snatched his candle and fled upward, the stillness of the night was broken by the sound of urgent footsteps approaching the house. In another moment he was in his room and the twins were standing aghast over the body of the murdered man!

Tom put on his coat, buttoned his hat under it, threw on his suit of girl's clothes, dropped the veil, blew out his light, locked the room door by which he had just entered, taking the key, passed through his other door into the back hall, locked that door and kept the key, then worked his way along in the dark and descended the back stairs. He was not expecting to meet anybody, for all interest was centered in the other part of the house, now; his calculation proved correct. By the time he was passing through the back yard, Mrs. Pratt, her servants, and a dozen half-dressed neighbors had joined the twins and the dead, and accessions were still arriving at the front door.

As Tom, quaking as with a palsy, passed out at the gate, three women came flying from the house on the opposite side of the lane. They rushed by him and in at the gate, asking him what the trouble was there, but not waiting for an answer. Tom said to himself, "Those old maids waited to dress—they did the same thing the night Stevens' house burned down next door." In a few minutes he was in the haunted house. He lighted a candle and took off his girl clothes. There was blood on him all down his left side, and his right hand was red with the stains of the blood-stained notes which he had crushed in it; but otherwise he was free from this sort of evidence. He cleansed his hand on the straw, and cleaned most of the smut from his face. Then he burned his male and female attire to ashes, scattered the ashes, and put on a disguise proper for a tramp. He blew out his light, went below, and was soon loafing down the river road with the intent to borrow and use one of Roxy's devices. He found a canoe and paddled off down-stream, setting the canoe adrift as dawn approached, and making his way by land to the next village, where he kept out of sight till a transient steamer came along, and then took deck-passage for St. Louis. He was ill at ease until Dawson's Landing was behind him; then he said to himself, "All the detectives on earth couldn't trace me now; there's not a vestige of a clue left in the world; that homicide will take its place with the permanent mysteries, and people won't get done trying to guess out the secret of it for fifty years."

In St. Louis, next morning, he read this brief telegram in the papers—dated at Dawson's Landing:

> Judge Driscoll, an old and respected citizen, was assassinated here about midnight by a profligate Italian nobleman or barber on account of a quarrel growing out of the recent election. The assassin will probably be lynched.

"One of the twins!" soliloquized Tom. "How lucky! It is the knife that has done him this grace. We never know when fortune is trying to favor us. I actually cursed Pudd'nhead Wilson in my heart for putting it out of my power to sell that knife. I take it back, now."

Tom was now rich and independent. He arranged with the planter, and mailed to Wilson the new bill of sale which sold Roxana to herself; then he telegraphed his Aunt Pratt:

> Have seen the awful news in the papers and am almost prostrated with grief. Shall start by packet to-day. Try to bear up till I come.

When Wilson reached the house of mourning and had gathered such details as Mrs. Pratt and the rest of the crowd could tell him, he took command as mayor, and gave orders that nothing should be touched, but everything left as it was until Justice Robinson should arrive and take the proper measures as coroner. He cleared everybody out of the room but the twins and himself. The sheriff soon arrived and took the twins away to jail. Wilson told them to keep heart, and promised to do his best in their defense when the case should come to trial. Justice Robinson came presently, and with him Constable Blake. They examined the room thoroughly. They found the knife and the sheath. Wilson noticed that there were finger-prints on the knife-handle. That pleased him, for the twins had required the earliest comers to make a scrutiny of their hands and clothes, and neither these people nor Wilson himself had found any blood-stains upon them. Could there be a possibility that the twins had spoken the truth when they said they found the man dead when they ran into the house in answer to the cry for help? He thought of that mysterious girl at once. But this was not the sort of work for a girl to be engaged in. No matter; Tom Driscoll's room must be examined.

After the coroner's jury had viewed the body and its surroundings, Wilson suggested a search up-stairs, and he went along. The jury forced an entrance to Tom's room, but found nothing, of course.

The coroner's jury found that the homicide was committed by Luigi, and that Angelo was accessory to it.

The town was bitter against the unfortunates, and for the first few days after the murder they were in constant danger of being lynched. The grand jury presently indicted Luigi for murder in the first degree, and Angelo as accessory before the fact. The twins were transferred from the city jail to the county prison to await trial.

Wilson examined the finger-marks on the knife-handle and said to himself, "Neither of the twins made those marks." Then manifestly there was another person concerned, either in his own interest or as hired assassin.

But who could it be? That, he must try to find out. The safe was not open, the cash-box was closed, and had three thousand dollars in it. Then robbery was not the motive, and revenge was. Where had the murdered man an enemy except Luigi? There was but that one person in the world with a deep grudge against him.

The mysterious girl! The girl was a great trial to Wilson. If the motive had been robbery, the girl might answer; but there wasn't any girl that would want to take this old man's life for revenge. He had no quarrels with girls; he was a gentleman.

Wilson had perfect tracings of the finger-marks of the knife-handle; and among his glass records he had a great array of the finger-prints of women and girls, collected during the last fifteen or eighteen years; but he scanned them in vain, they successfully withstood every test; among them were no duplicates of the prints on the knife.

The presence of the knife on the stage of the murder was a worrying circumstance for Wilson. A week previously he had as good as admitted to himself that he believed Luigi had possessed such a knife, and that he still possessed it notwithstanding his pretense that it had been stolen. And now here was the knife, and with it the twins. Half the town had said the twins were humbugging when they claimed that they had lost their knife, and now these people were joyful, and said, "I told you so!"

If their finger-prints had been on the handle—but it was useless to bother any further about that; the finger-prints on the handle were *not* theirs—that he knew perfectly.

Wilson refused to suspect Tom; for first, Tom couldn't murder anybody—he hadn't character enough; secondly, if he could murder a person he wouldn't select his doting benefactor and nearest relative; thirdly, self-interest was in the way; for while the uncle lived, Tom was sure of a free support and a chance to get the destroyed will revived again, but with the uncle gone, that chance was gone, too. It was true the will had really been revived, as was now discovered, but Tom could not have been aware of it, or he would have spoken of it, in his native talky, unsecretive way. Finally, Tom was in St. Louis when the murder was done, and got the news out of the morning journals, as was shown by his telegram to his aunt. These speculations were unemphasized sensations rather than articulated thoughts, for Wilson would have laughed at the idea of seriously connecting Tom with the murder.

Wilson regarded the case of the twins as desperate—in fact, about hopeless. For he argued that if a confederate was not found, an enlightened Missouri jury would hang them, sure; if a confederate was found, that would not improve the matter, but simply furnish one more person for the sheriff to hang. Nothing could save the twins but the discovery of a person who did the murder on his sole personal account—an undertaking which had all the aspect of the impossible. Still, the person who made the finger-prints must be sought. The twins might have no case *with* him, but they certainly would have none without him.

So Wilson mooned around, thinking, thinking, guessing, guessing, day and night, and arriving nowhere. Whenever he ran across a girl or a woman he was not acquainted with, he got her finger-prints, on one pretext or another; and they always cost him a sigh when he got home, for they never tallied with the finger-marks on the knife-handle.

As to the mysterious girl, Tom swore he knew no such girl, and did not remember ever seeing a girl wearing a dress like the one described by Wilson. He admitted that he did not always lock his room, and that sometimes the servants forgot to lock the house doors; still, in his opinion the girl must have made but few visits or she would have been discovered. When Wilson tried to connect her with the stealing-raid, and thought she might have been the old woman's confederate, if not the very thief herself disguised as an old woman, Tom seemed struck, and also much interested, and said he would keep a sharp eye out for this person or persons, although he was afraid that she or they would be too smart to venture again into a town where everybody would now be on the watch for a good while to come.

Everybody was pitying Tom, he looked so quiet and sorrowful, and seemed to feel his great loss so deeply. He was playing a part, but it was not all a part. The picture of his alleged uncle, as he had last seen him, was before him in the dark pretty frequently, when he was awake, and called again in his dreams, when he was asleep. He wouldn't go into the room where the tragedy had happened. This charmed the doting Mrs. Pratt, who realized now, "as she had never done before," she said, what a sensitive and delicate nature her darling had, and how he adored his poor uncle.

20

The Murderer Chuckles

> Even the clearest and most perfect circumstantial evidence is likely to be at fault, after all, and therefore ought to be received with great caution. Take the case of any pencil, sharpened by any woman: if you have witnesses, you will find she did it with a knife; but if you take simply the aspect of the pencil, you will say she did it with her teeth.—*Pudd'nhead Wilson's Calendar.*

THE WEEKS dragged along, no friend visiting the jailed twins but their counsel and Aunt Patsy Cooper, and the day of trial came at last—the heaviest day in Wilson's life; for with all his tireless diligence he had discovered no sign or trace of the missing confederate. "Confederate" was the term he had long ago privately accepted for that person—not as being unquestionably the right term, but as being at least possibly the right one, though he was never able to understand why the twins did not vanish and escape, as the confederate had done, instead of remaining by the murdered man and getting caught there.

The court-house was crowded, of course, and would remain so to the finish, for not only in the town itself, but in the country for miles around, the trial was the one topic of conversation among the people. Mrs. Pratt, in deep mourning, and Tom with a weed on his hat, had seats near Pembroke Howard, the public prosecutor, and back of them sat a great array of friends of the family. The twins had but one friend present to keep their counsel in countenance, their poor old sorrowing landlady. She sat near Wilson, and looked her friendliest. In the "nigger corner" sat Chambers; also Roxy, with good clothes on, and her bill of sale in her pocket. It was her most precious possession, and she never parted with it, day or night. Tom had allowed her thirty-five dollars a month ever since he came into his property, and had said that he and she ought to be grateful to the twins for making them rich; but had roused such a temper in her by this speech that he did not repeat the argument afterward. She said the old Judge had treated her child a thousand times better than he deserved, and had never done her an unkindness in his life; so she hated these outlandish devils for killing him, and shouldn't ever sleep satisfied till she saw them hanged for it. She was here to watch the trial, now, and was going to lift up just one "hooraw" over it if the County Judge put her in jail a year for it. She gave her turbaned head a toss and said, "When dat verdic' comes, I's gwyne to lif' dat *roof*, now, I *tell* you."

Pembroke Howard briefly sketched the State's case. He said he would show by a chain of circumstantial evidence without break or fault in it anywhere, that the principal prisoner at the bar committed the murder; that the motive was partly revenge, and partly a desire to take his own life out of jeopardy, and that his brother, by his presence, was a consenting accessory to the crime; a crime which was the basest known to the calendar of human misdeeds—assassination; that it was conceived by the blackest of hearts and consummated by the cowardliest of hands; a crime which had broken a loving sister's heart, blighted the happiness of a young nephew who was as dear as a son, brought inconsolable grief to many friends, and sorrow and loss to the whole community. The utmost penalty of the outraged law would be exacted, and upon the accused, now present at the bar, that penalty would unquestionably be executed. He would reserve further remark until his closing speech.

He was strongly moved, and so also was the whole house; Mrs.

Pratt and several other women were weeping when he sat down, and many an eye that was full of hate was riveted upon the unhappy prisoners.

Witness after witness was called by the State, and questioned at length; but the cross-questioning was brief. Wilson knew they could furnish nothing valuable for his side. People were sorry for Pudd'nhead; his budding career would get hurt by this trial.

Several witnesses swore they heard Judge Driscoll say in his public speech that the twins would be able to find their lost knife again when they needed it to assassinate somebody with. This was not news, but now it was seen to have been sorrowfully prophetic, and a profound sensation quivered through the hushed court-room when those dismal words were repeated.

The public prosecutor rose and said that it was within his knowledge, through a conversation held with Judge Driscoll on the last day of his life, that counsel for the defense had brought him a challenge from the person charged at this bar with murder; that he had refused to fight with a confessed assassin—"that is, on the field of honor," but had added significantly, that he would be ready for him elsewhere. Presumably, the person here charged with murder was warned that he must kill or be killed the first time he should meet Judge Driscoll. If counsel for the defense chose to let the statement stand so, he would not call him to the witness-stand. Mr. Wilson said he would offer no denial. [Murmurs in the house—"It is getting worse and worse for Wilson's case."]

Mrs. Pratt testified that she heard no outcry, and did not know what woke her up, unless it was the sound of rapid footsteps approaching the front door. She jumped up and ran out in the hall just as she was, and heard the footsteps flying up the front steps and then following behind her as she ran to the sitting-room. There she found the accused standing over her murdered brother. [Here she broke down and sobbed. Sensation in the court.] Resuming, she said the persons entering behind her were Mr. Rogers and Mr. Buckstone.

Cross-examined by Wilson, she said the twins proclaimed their innocence; declared that they had been taking a walk, and had hurried to the house in response to a cry for help which was so loud and strong that they had heard it at a considerable distance; that they begged her and the gentlemen just mentioned to examine their hands and clothes—which was done, and no blood-stains found.

Confirmatory evidence followed from Rogers and Buckstone.

The finding of the knife was verified, the advertisement minutely describing it and offering a reward for it was put in evidence, and its exact correspondence with that description proved. Then followed a few minor details, and the case for the State was closed.

Wilson said that he had three witnesses, the Misses Clarkson, who would testify that they met a veiled young woman leaving Judge Driscoll's premises by the back gate a few minutes after the cries for help were heard, and that their evidence, taken with certain circumstantial evidence which he would call the court's attention to, would in his opinion convince the court that there was still one person concerned in this crime who had not yet been found, and also that a stay of proceedings ought to be granted, in justice to his clients, until that person should be discovered. As it was late, he would ask leave to defer the examination of his three witnesses until the next morning.

The crowd poured out of the place and went flocking away in excited groups and couples, talking the events of the session over with vivacity and consuming interest, and everybody seemed to have had a satisfactory and enjoyable day except the accused, their counsel, and their old-lady friend. There was no cheer among these, and no substantial hope.

In parting with the twins Aunt Patsy did attempt a good night with a gay pretense of hope and cheer in it, but broke down without finishing.

Absolutely secure as Tom considered himself to be, the opening solemnities of the trial had nevertheless oppressed him with a vague uneasiness, his being a nature sensitive to even the smallest alarms; but from the moment that the poverty and weakness of Wilson's case lay exposed to the court, he was comfortable once more, even jubilant. He left the court-room sarcastically sorry for Wilson. "The Clarksons met an unknown woman in the back lane," he said to himself—"*that* is his case! I'll give him a century to find her in—a couple of them if he likes. A woman who doesn't exist any longer, and the clothes that gave her her sex burnt up and the ashes thrown away—oh, certainly, he'll find *her* easy enough!" This reflection set him to admiring, for the hundredth time, the shrewd ingenuities by which he had insured himself against detection—more, against even suspicion.

"Nearly always in cases like this there is some little detail or other overlooked, some wee little track or trace left behind, and detection follows; but here there's not even the faintest suggestion of a trace left. No more than a bird leaves when it flies through the air—yes, through the night, you may say. The man that can track a bird through the air in the dark and find that bird is the man to track me out and find the Judge's assassin— no other need apply. And that is the job that has been laid out for poor Pudd'nhead Wilson, of all people in the world! Lord, it will be pathetically funny to see him grubbing and groping after that woman that don't exist, and the right person sitting under his very nose all the time!" The more he thought the situation over, the more the humor of it struck him. Finally he said, "I'll never let him hear the last of that woman. Every time I catch him in company, to his dying day, I'll ask him in the guileless affectionate way that used to gravel him so when I inquired how his unborn law business was coming along, 'Got on her track yet—hey, Pudd'nhead?'" He wanted to laugh, but that would not have answered; there were people about, and he was mourning for his uncle. He made up his mind that it would be good entertainment to look in on Wilson that night and watch him worry over his barren law case and goad him with an exasperating word or two of sympathy and commiseration now and then.

Wilson wanted no supper, he had no appetite. He got out all the finger-prints of girls and women in his collection of records and pored gloomily over them an hour or more, trying to convince himself that that troublesome girl's marks were there somewhere and had been overlooked. But it was not so. He drew back his chair, clasped his hands over his head, and gave himself up to dull and arid musings.

Tom Driscoll dropped in, an hour after dark, and said with a pleasant laugh as he took a seat:

"Hello, we've gone back to the amusements of our days of neglect and obscurity for consolation, have we?" and he took up one of the glass strips and held it against the light to inspect it. "Come, cheer up, old man; there's no use in losing your grip and going back to this child's-play merely because this big sunspot is drifting across your shiny new disk. It 'll pass, and you'll be all right again,"—and he laid the glass down. "Did you think you could win always?"

"Oh, no," said Wilson, with a sigh, "I didn't expect that, but I can't believe Luigi killed your uncle, and I feel very sorry for him. It makes me blue. And you would feel as I do, Tom, if you were not prejudiced against those young fellows."

"I don't know about that," and Tom's countenance darkened, for his memory reverted to his kicking; "I owe them no good will, considering the brunette one's treatment of me that night. Prejudice or no prejudice, Pudd'nhead, I don't like them, and when they get their deserts you're not going to find me sitting on the mourner's bench."

He took up another strip of glass, and exclaimed:

"Why, here's old Roxy's label! Are you going to ornament the royal palaces with nigger pawmarks, too? By the date here, I was seven months old when this was done, and she was nursing me and her little nigger cub. There's a line straight across her thumb-print. How comes that?" and Tom held out the piece of glass to Wilson.

"That is common," said the bored man, wearily. "Scar of a cut or a scratch, usually"—and he took the strip of glass indifferently, and raised it toward the lamp.

All the blood sunk suddenly out of his face; his hand quaked, and he gazed at the polished surface before him with the glassy stare of a corpse.

"Great Heavens, what's the matter with you, Wilson? Are you going to faint?"

Tom sprang for a glass of water and offered it, but Wilson shrank shuddering from him and said:

"No, no!—take it away!" His breast was rising and falling, and he moved his head about in a dull and wandering way, like a person who has been stunned. Presently he said, "I shall feel better when I get to bed; I have been overwrought to-day; yes, and overworked for many days."

"Then I'll leave you and let you get to your rest. Good night, old man." But as Tom went out he couldn't deny himself a small parting gibe: "Don't take it so hard; a body can't win every time; you'll hang somebody yet."

Wilson muttered to himself, "It is no lie to say I am sorry I have to begin with you, miserable dog though you are!"

He braced himself up with a glass of cold whisky, and went to work again. He did not compare the new finger-marks unintentionally left by Tom a few minutes before on Roxy's glass with the tracings of the marks left on the knife-handle, there being no need of that (for his trained eye), but busied himself with another matter, muttering from time to time, "Idiot that I was!—nothing but a *girl* would do me—a man in girl's clothes never occurred to me." First, he hunted out the plate containing the finger-prints made by Tom when he was twelve years old, and laid it by itself; then he brought forth the marks made by Tom's baby fingers when he was a suckling of seven months, and placed these two plates with the one containing this subject's newly (and unconsciously) made record.

"Now the series is complete," he said with satisfaction, and sat down to inspect these things and enjoy them.

But his enjoyment was brief. He stared a considerable time at the three strips, and seemed stupefied with astonishment. At last he put them down and said, "I can't make it out at all—hang it, the baby's don't tally with the others!"

He walked the floor for half an hour puzzling over his enigma, then he hunted out two other glass plates.

He sat down and puzzled over these things a good while, but kept muttering, "It's no use; I can't understand it. They don't tally right, and yet I'll swear the names and dates are right, and so of course they *ought* to tally. I never labeled one of these things carelessly in my life. There is a most extraordinary mystery here."

He was tired out, now, and his brains were beginning to clog. He said he would sleep himself fresh, and then see what he could do with this riddle. He slept through a troubled and un-restful hour, then unconsciousness began to shred away, and presently he rose drowsily to a sitting posture. "Now what was that dream?" he said, trying to recall it; "what was that dream? —it seemed to unravel that puz—"

He landed in the middle of the floor at a bound, without finishing the sentence, and ran and turned up his lights and seized his "records." He took a single swift glance at them and cried out:

"It's so! Heavens, what a revelation! And for twenty-three years no man has ever suspected it!"

21

Doom

He is useless on top of the ground; he ought to be under it, inspiring the cabbages.

—*Pudd'nhead Wilson's Calendar.*

April 1. This is the day upon which we are reminded of what we are on the other three hundred and sixty-four.

—*Pudd'nhead Wilson's Calendar.*

WILSON PUT ON enough clothes for business purposes and went to work under a high pressure of steam. He was awake all over. All sense of weariness had been swept away by the invigorating refreshment of the great and hopeful discovery which he had made. He made fine and accurate reproductions of a number of his "records," and then enlarged them on a scale of ten to one with his pantograph. He did these pantograph enlargements on sheets of white cardboard, and made each individual line of the bewildering maze of whorls or curves or loops which constituted the "pattern" of a "record" stand out bold and black by reinforcing it with ink. To the untrained eye the collection of delicate originals made by the human finger on the glass plates looked about alike; but when enlarged ten times they resembled the markings of a block of wood that has been sawed across the grain, and the dullest eye could detect at a glance, and at a distance of many feet, that no two of the patterns were alike. When Wilson had at last finished his tedious and difficult work, he arranged its results according to a plan in which a progressive order and sequence was a principal feature; then he added to the batch several pantograph enlargements which he had made from time to time in bygone years.

The night was spent and the day well advanced, now. By the time he had snatched a trifle of breakfast it was nine o'clock, and the court was ready to begin its sitting. He was in his place twelve minutes later with his "records."

Tom Driscoll caught a slight glimpse of the records, and nudged his nearest friend and said, with a wink, "Pudd'nhead's got a rare eye to business—thinks that as long as he can't win his case it's at least a noble good chance to advertise his palace-window decorations without any expense." Wilson was informed that his witnesses had been delayed, but would arrive presently; but he rose and said he should probably not have occasion to make use of their testimony. [An amused murmur ran through the room—"It's a clean backdown! he gives up without hitting a lick!"] Wilson continued—"I have other testimony—and better. [This compelled interest, and evoked murmurs of surprise that had a detectable ingredient of disappointment in them.] If I seem to be springing this evidence upon the court, I offer as my justification for this, that I did not discover its existence until late last night, and have been engaged in examining and classifying it ever since, until half an hour ago. I shall offer it presently; but first I wish to say a few preliminary words.

"May it please the court, the claim given the front place, the claim most persistently urged, the claim most strenuously and I may even say aggressively and defiantly insisted upon by the prosecution, is this—that the person whose hand left the bloodstained finger-prints upon the handle of the Indian knife is the person who committed the murder." Wilson paused, during several moments, to give impressiveness to what he was about to say, and then added tranquilly, "*We grant that claim.*"

It was an electrical surprise. No one was prepared for such an admission. A buzz of astonishment rose on all sides, and people were heard to intimate that the overworked lawyer had lost his mind. Even the veteran judge, accustomed as he was to legal ambushes and masked batteries in criminal procedure, was not sure that his ears were not deceiving him, and asked counsel what it was he had said. Howard's impassive face betrayed no sign, but his attitude and bearing lost something of their careless confidence for a moment. Wilson resumed:

"We not only grant that claim, but we welcome it and strongly indorse it. Leaving that matter for the present, we will now proceed to consider other points in the case which we propose to establish by evidence, and shall include that one in the chain in its proper place."

He had made up his mind to try a few hardy guesses, in mapping out his theory of the origin and motive of the murder—guesses designed to fill up gaps in it—guesses which could help if they hit, and would probably do no harm if they didn't.

"To my mind, certain circumstances of the case before the court seem to suggest a motive for the homicide quite different from the one insisted on by the State. It is my conviction that the motive was not revenge, but robbery. It has been urged that the presence of the accused brothers in that fatal room, just after notification that one of them must take the life of Judge Driscoll or lose his own the moment the parties should meet, clearly signifies that the natural instinct of self-preservation moved my clients to go there secretly and save Count Luigi by destroying his adversary.

"Then why did they stay there, after the deed was done? Mrs. Pratt had time, although she did not hear the cry for help, but woke up some moments later, to run to that room— and there she found these men standing and making no effort to escape. If they were guilty, they ought to have been running out of the house at the same time that she was running to that room. If they had had such a strong instinct toward self-preservation as to move them to kill that unarmed man, what had become of it now, when it should have been more alert than ever? Would any of us have remained there? Let us not slander our intelligence to that degree.

"Much stress has been laid upon the fact that the accused offered a very large reward for the knife with which this murder was done; that no thief came forward to claim that extraordinary reward; that the latter fact was good circumstantial evidence that the claim that the knife had been stolen was a vanity and a fraud; that these details taken in connection with the memorable and apparently prophetic speech of the deceased concerning that knife, and the final discovery of that very knife in the fatal room where no living person was found present with the slaughtered man but the owner of the knife and his brother, form an indestructible chain of evidence which fixes the crime upon those unfortunate strangers.

"But I shall presently ask to be sworn, and shall testify that there was a large reward offered for the *thief*, also; that it was offered secretly and not advertised; that this fact was indiscreetly mentioned—or at least tacitly admitted—in what was supposed to be safe circumstances, but may *not* have been. The thief may have been present himself. [Tom Driscoll had been looking at the speaker, but dropped his eyes at this point.] In that case he would retain the knife in his possession, not daring to offer it for sale, or for pledge in a pawnshop. [There was a nodding of heads among the audience by way of admission that this was not a bad stroke.] I shall prove to the satisfaction of the jury that there *was* a person in Judge Driscoll's room several minutes before the accused entered it. [This produced a strong sensation; the last drowsy-head in the court-room roused up now, and made preparation to listen.] If it shall seem necessary, I will prove by the Misses Clarkson that they met a veiled person—ostensibly a woman—coming out of the back gate a few minutes after the cry for help was heard. This person was not a woman, but a man dressed in woman's clothes." Another sensation. Wilson had his eye on Tom when he hazarded this guess, to see what effect it would produce. He was satisfied with the result, and said to himself, "It was a success—he's hit!"

"The object of that person in that house was robbery, not murder. It is true that the safe was not open, but there was an ordinary tin cash-box on the table, with three thousand dollars in it. It is easily supposable that the thief was concealed in the house; that he knew of this box, and of its owner's habit of counting its contents and arranging his accounts at night—if he had that habit, which I do not assert, of course; that he tried to take the box while its owner slept, but made a noise and was seized, and had to use the knife to save himself from capture; and that he fled without his booty because he heard help coming.

"I have now done with my theory, and will proceed to the evidences by which I propose to try to prove its soundness." Wilson took up several of his strips of glass. When the audience recognized these familiar mementoes of Pudd'nhead's old-time childish "puttering" and folly, the tense and funereal interest vanished out of their faces, and the house burst into volleys of relieving and refreshing laughter, and Tom chirked and joined in the fun himself; but Wilson was apparently not disturbed. He arranged his records on the table before him, and said:

"I beg the indulgence of the court while I make a few remarks in explanation of some evidence which I am about to introduce, and which I shall presently ask to be allowed to verify under oath on the witness-stand. Every human being carries with him from his cradle to his grave certain physical marks which do not change their character, and by which he can always be identified —and that without shade of doubt or question. These marks are his signature, his physiological autograph, so to speak, and this autograph cannot be counterfeited, nor can he disguise it or hide it away, nor can it become illegible by the wear and mutations of time. This signature is not his face—age can change that beyond recognition; it is not his hair, for that can fall out; it is not his height, for duplicates of that exist; it is not his form, for duplicates of that exist also, whereas this signature is each man's very own—there is no duplicate of it among the swarming populations of the globe! [The audience were interested once more.]

"This autograph consists of the delicate lines or corrugations with which Nature marks the insides of the hands and the soles of the feet. If you will look at the balls of your fingers—you that have very sharp eyesight—you will observe that these dainty curving lines lie close together, like those that indicate the border of oceans in maps, and that they form various clearly defined patterns, such as arches, circles, long curves, whorls, etc., and that these patterns differ on the different fingers. [Every man in the room had his hand up to the light, now, and his head canted to one side, and was minutely scrutinizing the balls of his fingers; there were whispered ejaculations of "Why, it's so— I never noticed that before!"] The patterns on the right hand are not the same as those on the left. [Ejaculations of "Why, that's so, too!"] Taken finger for finger, your patterns differ from your neighbor's. [Comparisons were made all over the house— even the judge and jury were absorbed in this curious work.] The patterns of a twin's right hand are not the same as those on his left. One twin's patterns are never the same as his fellow-twin's patterns—the jury will find that the patterns upon the finger-balls of the accused follow this rule. [An examination of the twins' hands was begun at once.] You have often heard of twins who were so exactly alike that when dressed alike their own parents could not tell them apart. Yet there was never a twin born into this world that did not carry from birth to death a sure identifier in this mysterious and marvelous natal autograph. That once known to you, his fellow-twin could never personate him and deceive you."

Wilson stopped and stood silent. Inattention dies a quick and

sure death when a speaker does that. The stillness gives warning that something is coming. All palms and finger-balls went
down, now, all slouching forms straightened, all heads came up,
all eyes were fastened upon Wilson's face. He waited yet one,
two, three moments, to let his pause complete and perfect its
spell upon the house; then, when through the profound hush he
could hear the ticking of the clock on the wall, he put out his
hand and took the Indian knife by the blade and held it aloft
where all could see the sinister spots upon its ivory handle; then
he said, in a level and passionless voice:

"Upon this haft stands the assassin's natal autograph, written
in the blood of that helpless and unoffending old man who loved
you and whom you all loved. There is but one man in the whole
earth whose hand can duplicate that crimson sign"—he paused
and raised his eyes to the pendulum swinging back and forth—
"and please God we will produce that man in this room before
the clock strikes noon!"

Stunned, distraught, unconscious of its own movement, the
house half rose, as if expecting to see the murderer appear at
the door, and a breeze of muttered ejaculations swept the place.
"Order in the court!—sit down!" This from the sheriff. He was
obeyed, and quiet reigned again. Wilson stole a glance at Tom,
and said to himself, "He is flying signals of distress, now; even
people who despise him are pitying him; they think this is a
hard ordeal for a young fellow who has lost his benefactor by
so cruel a stroke—and they are right." He resumed his speech.

"For more than twenty years I have amused my compulsory
leisure with collecting these curious physical signatures in this
town. At my house I have hundreds upon hundreds of them.
Each and every one is labeled with name and date; not labeled
the next day or even the next hour, but in the very minute that
the impression was taken. When I go upon the witness-stand I
will repeat under oath the things which I am now saying. I have
the finger-prints of the court, the sheriff, and every member of
the jury. There is hardly a person in this room, white or black,
whose natal signature I cannot produce, and not one of them
can so disguise himself that I cannot pick him out from a multi-

tude of his fellow-creatures and unerringly identify him by his hands. And if he and I should live to be a hundred I could still do it. [The interest of the audience was steadily deepening now.]

"I have studied some of these signatures so much that I know them as well as the bank cashier knows the autograph of his oldest customer. While I turn my back now, I beg that several persons will be so good as to pass their fingers through their hair, and then press them upon one of the panes of the window near the jury, and that among them the accused may set *their* finger-marks. Also, I beg that these experimenters, or others, will set their finger-marks upon another pane, and add again the marks of the accused, but not placing them in the same order or relation to the other signatures as before—for, by one chance in a million, a person might happen upon the right marks by pure guesswork *once*, therefore I wish to be tested twice."

He turned his back, and the two panes were quickly covered with delicately lined oval spots, but visible only to such persons as could get a dark background for them—the foliage of a tree, outside, for instance. Then, upon call, Wilson went to the window, made his examination, and said:

"This is Count Luigi's right hand; this one, three signatures below, is his left. Here is Count Angelo's right; down here is his left. Now for the other pane: here and here are Count Luigi's, here and here are his brother's." He faced about. "Am I right?"

A deafening explosion of applause was the answer. The Bench said:

"This certainly approaches the miraculous!"

Wilson turned to the window again and remarked, pointing with his finger:

"This is the signature of Mr. Justice Robinson. [Applause.] This, of Constable Blake. [Applause.] This, of John Mason, juryman. [Applause.] This, of the sheriff. [Applause.] I cannot name the others, but I have them all at home, named and dated, and could identify them all by my finger-print records."

He moved to his place through a storm of applause—which the

sheriff stopped, and also made the people sit down, for they were all standing and struggling to see, of course. Court, jury, sheriff, and everybody had been too absorbed in observing Wilson's performance to attend to the audience earlier.

"Now, then," said Wilson, "I have here the natal autographs of two children—thrown up to ten times the natural size by the pantograph, so that any one who can see at all can tell the markings apart at a glance. We will call the children A and B. Here are A's finger-marks, taken at the age of five months. Here they are again, taken at seven months. [Tom started.] They are alike, you see. Here are B's at five months, and also at seven months. They, too, exactly copy each other, but the patterns are quite different from A's, you observe. I shall refer to these again presently, but we will turn them face down, now.

"Here, thrown up ten sizes, are the natal autographs of the two persons who are here before you accused of murdering Judge Driscoll. I made these pantographic copies last night, and will so swear when I go upon the witness-stand. I ask the jury to compare them with the finger-marks of the accused upon the window-panes, and tell the court if they are the same."

He passed a powerful magnifying-glass to the foreman.

One juryman after another took the cardboard and the glass and made the comparison. Then the foreman said to the judge:

"Your honor, we are all agreed that they are identical."

Wilson said to the foreman:

"Please turn that cardboard face down, and take this one, and compare it searchingly by the magnifier, with the fatal signature upon the knife-handle, and report your finding to the court."

Again the jury made minute examinations, and again reported:

"We find them to be exactly identical, your honor."

Wilson turned toward the counsel for the prosecution, and there was a clearly recognizable note of warning in his voice when he said:

"May it please the court, the State has claimed, strenuously and persistently, that the blood-stained finger-prints upon that knife-handle were left there by the assassin of Judge Driscoll. You have heard us grant that claim, and welcome it." He turned to the jury: "Compare the finger-prints of the accused with the finger-prints left by the assassin—and report."

The comparison began. As it proceeded, all movement and all sound ceased, and the deep silence of an absorbed and waiting suspense settled upon the house; and when at last the words came—

"They do not even resemble," a thunder-crash of applause followed and the house sprang to its feet, but was quickly repressed by official force and brought to order again. Tom was altering his position every few minutes, now, but none of his changes brought repose nor any small trifle of comfort. When the house's attention was become fixed once more, Wilson said gravely, indicating the twins with a gesture:

"These men are innocent—I have no further concern with them. [Another outbreak of applause began, but was promptly checked.] We will now proceed to find the guilty. [Tom's eyes were starting from their sockets—yes, it was a cruel day for the bereaved youth, everybody thought.] We will return to the infant autographs of A and B. I will ask the jury to take these large pantograph facsimiles of A's marked five months and seven months. Do they tally?"

The foreman responded:

"Perfectly."

"Now examine this pantograph, taken at eight months, and also marked A. Does it tally with the other two?"

The surprised response was:

"No—they differ widely!"

"You are quite right. Now take these two pantographs of B's autograph, marked five months and seven months. Do they tally with each other?"

"Yes—perfectly."

"Take this third pantograph marked B, eight months. Does it tally with B's other two?"

"By no means!"

"Do you know how to account for those strange discrepancies?

I will tell you. For a purpose unknown to us, but probably a selfish one, somebody changed those children in the cradle."

This produced a vast sensation, naturally; Roxana was astonished at this admirable guess, but not disturbed by it. To guess the exchange was one thing, to guess who did it quite another. Pudd'nhead Wilson could do wonderful things, no doubt, but he couldn't do impossible ones. Safe? She was perfectly safe. She smiled privately.

"Between the ages of seven months and eight months those children were changed in the cradle"—he made one of his effect-collecting pauses, and added—"and the person who did it is in this house!"

Roxy's pulses stood still! The house was thrilled as with an electric shock, and the people half rose as if to seek a glimpse of the person who had made that exchange. Tom was growing limp; the life seemed oozing out of him. Wilson resumed:

"A was put into B's cradle in the nursery; B was transferred to the kitchen and became a negro and a slave [Sensation—confusion of angry ejaculations]—but within a quarter of an hour he will stand before you white and free! [Burst of applause, checked by the officers.] From seven months onward until now, A has still been a usurper, and in my finger-record he bears B's name. Here is his pantograph at the age of twelve. Compare it with the assassin's signature upon the knife-handle. Do they tally?"

"The foreman answered:

"To the minutest detail!"

Wilson said, solemnly:

"The murderer of your friend and mine—York Driscoll of the generous hand and the kindly spirit—sits in among you. Valet de Chambre, negro and slave—falsely called Thomas à Becket Driscoll—make upon the window the finger-prints that will hang you!"

Tom turned his ashen face imploringly toward the speaker, made some impotent movements with his white lips, then slid limp and lifeless to the floor.

Wilson broke the awed silence with the words:

"There is no need. He has confessed."

Roxy flung herself upon her knees, covered her face with her hands, and out through her sobs the words struggled:

"De Lord have mercy on me, po' misable sinner dat I is!"

The clock struck twelve.

The court rose; the new prisoner, handcuffed, was removed.

CONCLUSION

It is often the case that the man who can't tell a lie thinks
he is the best judge of one.

—Pudd'nhead Wilson's Calendar.

October 12, the Discovery. It was wonderful to find America, but it would have been more wonderful to miss it.

—Pudd'nhead Wilson's Calendar.

THE TOWN sat up all night to discuss the amazing events of the
day and swap guesses as to when Tom's trial would begin. Troop
after troop of citizens came to serenade Wilson, and require a
speech, and shout themselves hoarse over every sentence that
fell from his lips—for all his sentences were golden, now, all
were marvelous. His long fight against hard luck and prejudice
was ended; he was a made man for good.

And as each of these roaring gangs of enthusiasts marched
away, some remorseful member of it was quite sure to raise his
voice and say:

"And this is the man the likes of us have called a pudd'nhead
for more than twenty years. He has resigned from that position,
friends."

"Yes, but it isn't vacant—we're elected."

THE twins were heroes of romance, now, and with rehabilitated
reputations. But they were weary of Western adventure, and
straightway retired to Europe.

Roxy's heart was broken. The young fellow upon whom she

had inflicted twenty-three years of slavery continued the false heir's pension of thirty-five dollars a month to her, but her hurts were too deep for money to heal; the spirit in her eye was quenched, her martial bearing departed with it, and the voice of her laughter ceased in the land. In her church and its affairs she found her only solace.

The real heir suddenly found himself rich and free, but in a most embarrassing situation. He could neither read nor write, and his speech was the basest dialect of the negro quarter. His gait, his attitudes, his gestures, his bearing, his laugh—all were vulgar and uncouth; his manners were the manners of a slave. Money and fine clothes could not mend these defects or cover them up; they only made them the more glaring and the more pathetic. The poor fellow could not endure the terrors of the white man's parlor, and felt at home and at peace nowhere but in the kitchen. The family pew was a misery to him, yet he could nevermore enter into the solacing refuge of the "nigger gallery"—that was closed to him for good and all. But we cannot follow his curious fate further—that would be a long story.

The false heir made a full confession and was sentenced to imprisonment for life. But now a complication came up. The Percy Driscoll estate was in such a crippled shape when its owner died that it could pay only sixty per cent. of its great indebtedness, and was settled at that rate. But the creditors came forward, now, and complained that inasmuch as through an error for which *they* were in no way to blame the false heir was not inventoried at that time with the rest of the property, great wrong and loss had thereby been inflicted upon them. They rightly claimed that "Tom" was lawfully their property and had been so for eight years; that they had already lost sufficiently in being deprived of his services during that long period, and ought not to be required to add anything to that loss; that if he had been delivered up to them in the first place, they would have sold him and he could not have murdered Judge Driscoll; therefore it was not he that had really committed the murder, the guilt lay with the erroneous inventory. Everybody saw that there was reason in this. Everybody granted that if "Tom" were white and free it would be unquestionably right to punish him—it would be no loss to anybody; but to shut up a valuable slave for life—that was quite another matter.

As soon as the Governor understood the case, he pardoned Tom at once, and the creditors sold him down the river.